The Wizards of Magog

N A Preece

The Chronicles of the Sight
From the Golden Tome -
Part Three

AuthorHouse™ UK Ltd.
500 Avebury Boulevard
Central Milton Keynes, MK9 2BE
www.authorhouse.co.uk
Phone: 08001974150

©2011 N A Preece. All rights reserved.

No part of this book may be reproduced, stored in a retrieval system, or transmitted by any means without the written permission of the author.

First published by AuthorHouse 3/18/2011.

ISBN: 978-1-4520-8221-9 (sc)
ISBN: 978-1-4520-8222-6 (dj)

LCCN number: 2010919555

Any people depicted in stock imagery provided by Thinkstock are models, and such images are being used for illustrative purposes only. Certain stock imagery © Thinkstock.

This book is printed on acid-free paper.

Because of the dynamic nature of the Internet, any Web addresses or links contained in this book may have changed since publication and may no longer be valid. The views expressed in this work are solely those of the author and do not necessarily reflect the views of the publisher, and the publisher hereby disclaims any responsibility for them.

WEST SUSSEX LIBRARY SERVICE	
201171799	
Askews & Holts	18-Apr-2013

The Chronicles of the Sight From The Golden Tome

Books in the series:

Time Will Tell
The Ogre Witch-Queen
The Wizards of Magog

    The series is by no means definitive and is merely a selection of events that are recorded in the Golden Tome. It is the history of the Council of the Sight and their struggles to maintain order in a land that is home to many different races. It is a record of the constant challenges that arise to test the resourceful seers. That which is written in book one is but the beginning of a new chapter in the life of one of those seers; Urim, Tome-keeper.

    Book two continues to delve into the adventures of those who aided the seers in their conflict against one who rebelled. A different challenge came in the form of Amethyst, witch-queen of the ogres and of her initial ambition to rule the forests that developed into a desire for dominance over the seers. This difficult time in the history of the land deals with how they faced that challenge.

    Book three records the conflicts our intrepid group of friends faced when they come up against an ancient enemy of the seers; the Wizards of Magog. The battle between two worlds ensued, separated by the energy barrier. It was the darkest challenge to the Council of the Sight that they had faced since Seers Tower was built millennia ago.

Visit: www.thegoldentome.com
Cover design by Milford Arts

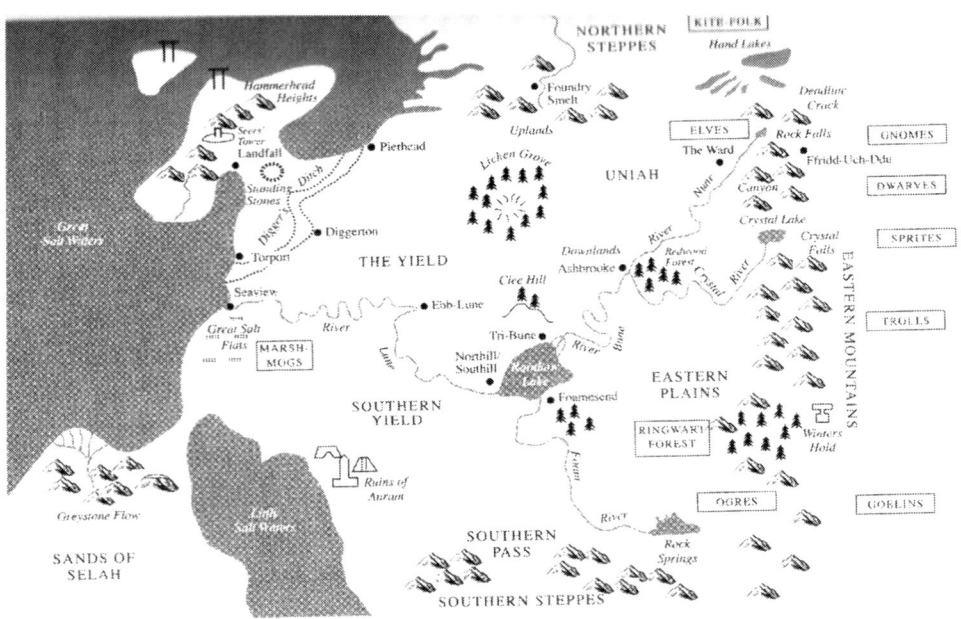

Contents

Map		iv
Prologue		vii
Chapter 1	Auger's Twist	1
Chapter 2	An Unwelcome Visitor	9
Chapter 3	The Power to Control	19
Chapter 4	Lost and Found	29
Chapter 5	Reunited	39
Chapter 6	Night Visitor	49
Chapter 7	Jetta	57
Chapter 8	Foam River	67
Chapter 9	Worlds Apart	79
Chapter 10	Foamsend	89
Chapter 11	Journey to Northill	99
Chapter 12	Northill	109
Chapter 13	A Message of Importance	117
Chapter 14	The Search for Hamill	127
Chapter 15	Wizards' Conclave	135
Chapter 16	The Montage	143
Chapter 17	Taken	153
Chapter 18	Shadows from the Deep	163
Chapter 19	Sea of Sand	173
Chapter 20	The Ruins of Anram	183
Chapter 21	In Search of a Myth	193
Chapter 22	Intervention	201
Chapter 23	Anramites	209
Chapter 24	The passages of Anram	219
Chapter 25	Ghosts	227
Chapter 26	The Keystone	237

Chapter 27	The Great Salt Flats	245
Chapter 28	The Rod of Retribution	255
Chapter 29	The Fountain and the Tower	265
Chapter 30	Marsh-Mogs	275
Chapter 31	Deliverance	283
Chapter 32	Seaview	293
Chapter 33	The Sea Voyage	301
Chapter 34	Landfall	311
Chapter 35	Poles Apart	319
Chapter 36	The Worlds at War	329
Chapter 37	Seers Tower	339
Chapter 38	The Council of the Sight	349
Chapter 39	Induction	359
Chapter 40	The Ninth Seer	369
Chapter 41	Urim, the Seer	381

Prologue

Previously:-

Ebon watched the confrontation taking place in the witch-queen's coven through his vision-window, mounted on a stand in his sanctuary. He had obtained it soon after his entry into his prison world from the previous owner of the fortress that he had made his own. He had managed to capture both by subterfuge and treachery; supplanting the warlord when he had been distracted by Ebon's accomplices. The warlord had paid for his slackness with his life.

Amethyst was supremely confident and spoke to Ebon as if he were nothing but a child. 'I intend to keep the brat of a seer for myself. He adds a special quality to my collection and now that I have his staff, I have decided to keep it. Besides, you are stuck there in your world and I am here with the staff. Now that you no longer hold the staff of the portal I do not see any possibility of your being able to take possession of this one. Therefore I shall have it for my own. Once I have the Forester's staff, my collection will be complete and I shall need a new hobby. I need something to challenge me so I have decided to capture all of the seers, one by one, and make their staves and talismans my own. Now that would be an endeavour worthy of my talents and a suitable undertaking to keep me amused.'

He was furious with what Amethyst had just told him, even more so because of his inability to strike out at her. He was keenly aware of his helplessness to take an active part in the affairs unfolding in the witch-queen's coven.

Ebon had cursed her for her evil trickery and knew that he was powerless to do anything to prevent her from doing exactly as she said. She had become more powerful whilst he had been robbed yet again of his powers by his nemesis, Urim. First the interfering seer had defeated his gnome army at Northill and then at the Tower Urim had pushed him through the energy barrier into the world he was trapped in. Urim stole the staff of the portal from out of his hands leaving him at the mercy of the forces of this world that ruled by fear and oppression. He would have to find another way to control those around him.

From the time of his arrival in this world Ebon had plotted and schemed his way up the ladder of power and authority. It had been easy for him as his mind was sharp and cunning. He knew how to manipulate those around him. He had taken many months to rise above the turmoil and the strife, to create a band of followers and become established as a force to be reckoned with. That had been seriously damaged by Urim's interference but he had a few tricks up his sleeve yet.

Using the vision-window's connection to Amethyst's reflector, Ebon had watched in amazement as Trapper appeared from nowhere and rushed towards his image, the dwarf's face twisted with rage. The embittered seer stood as a witness to what transpired as Amethyst battled against her attackers then cowered in fear himself as the blast from one of her spells was diverted into Amethyst's reflector. The dark charm bridged the gap between their worlds and he found himself being drawn into the inky black tendrils that grabbed him and drained the strength from his body. Warmth leeched away and an icy cold gripped him, forcing him away from his vision-window. The picture clouded and he no longer saw into Amethyst's coven.

He saw nothing; he heard nothing but felt a chill wind blow though his mind. He would have fallen into a dark, bottomless pit had it not been for his determination. Drawing upon an inner resolve he forced his arms out in front of him and brought the black power of the spell into a writhing ball of fury between his hands, spitting sparks of energy. Gathering every ounce of his will he thrust it away from him and it flew into the air, out through the open window of his sanctuary, before it slammed into the fountain in the courtyard. The water in the base of the fountain boiled intensely with great droplets of brackish water being flung into the air. Where these splashes landed on the flagstones around the pool, the stone turned black, fizzing and disintegrating the minerals, leaving shallow depressions in the surface. He went to inspect the inky blackness and looked down into the depths but it would not reflect his image. There was no ripple of disturbance to trouble its surface; it just lay flat and lifeless. Ebon felt the pull of the water and had he been weaker he would have been drawn into its depths never to emerge again. He noted for future use, the effects that the pool had on him and he determined to try it on someone to see what happened.

He returned to the viewing-window in his sanctuary and peered into it but all he saw now was a swirling black mist that would not clear. What became of Amethyst he did not know but he guessed that she had been thwarted in her efforts to subdue the forester to her will. She had probably been overpowered by the combined forces that had united against her. Amethyst would have brought the vision-window in his world in line with her reflector had she survived the challenge against her. She would have wanted to gloat and to show her hour of glory to him.

He tried without success to obtain a view of her coven; punching his fist into the palm of his hand he ground his teeth in frustration. That was another thing that Urim was responsible for ruining. Had he not taken the staff of the portal from him, he would have succeeded at the battle of Winters Hold.

Despite her double-crossing him and cheating him out of the staff she had taken from Hamill, he would still have given her aid when they attacked her in her coven. She could have proven useful in his battle against the seers. Now it was probably too late and he would have to rely upon a different source to help him obtain his purpose in returning to wreak vengeance on the seers.

Whilst he was still a seer at the Tower he had read about a conflict that had taken place between the seers and a group of wizards who had been banished to the world of Magog that he was now in. It had taken place millennia ago when the Tower had been built and the opposing forces had been separated by the energy barrier.

He had laboured long and hard to become acquainted with the details behind the affair and had recently succeeded in making contact with the wizards. He had discovered that there were five of them, each with their own particular ability, but when brought together, they were a force to be reckoned with.

He had recently received a response from them via an envoy in reply to his approach. In his letter to them he had explained his intent to depose the seers and requested the aid of the wizards in doing so. He would have made contact with them before had he been in a position of strength but he had needed to gather his forces and build a reputation before the wizards would see in him a personage of note.

Ebon had not liked being on the receiving end of Urim's interference, especially with him taking the staff of the portal from him. That had been an embarrassment to his pride but Ebon was resilient. He knew that things would turn his way eventually; they had to. With the support that had been promised from the wizards he would break through and wrest from the hands of those who had wronged him, the mantle of power he desired. When he had finally triumphed, he would show no mercy in his retribution against the seers.

The disappointment and frustration that had followed his inability to dominate Amethyst washed from his mind. It was her fault and not his that they had failed. Her cheating him out of his revenge against that brat of a seer, Hamill, not to mention Jon and Urim was the reason he would not be sitting in Seers Tower as its sole ruler. This was not the end of his ambition however; he had survived yet again and would find a way to complete his objective. Even before the fiasco at Amethyst's coven he had been planning and making arrangements for his return to dominance. There were many who had rallied to his cause with the promise of wealth, power or revenge. Ebon was motivated by them all, each one competing within him to be the strongest influence. All three played their part and came into effect when needed the most. He knew well the weaknesses and passions of those who supported him and manipulated their desires to suit his purposes.

Ebon saw this setback as another opportunity and not a defeat, if nothing else he was tenacious and was determined that one day he would succeed. There was a spring in his step as he paced the room; he looked forward to the next encounter with Urim. No longer did he fear his nemesis, he was confident that he held the upper hand now that the wizards were behind him. He dare not consider any thought of failure this time. The wizards would not tolerate any shortcomings that might be displayed. Too many had sought their support before and been brought to task when they had not delivered on their promises.

Ebon had no intention of giving them the opportunity of doing the same to him. He had been busy making other plans as soon as he had become aware that Amethyst had been manipulating him. He had played her game and taken pleasure in allowing her to believe that he was succumbing to her spells but he was immune to them. In his studies when he was at Seers Tower he had delved into the darker magic and practiced becoming resilient to it. His foresight had been justified and he had demonstrated his prowess by casting off the spell that would have overcome any lesser person.

One of his captains entered the room and bowed low before him. 'Sire, three of the lord wizards have arrived.'

'Splendid. Show them in.' Ebon stood before the large stone fireplace with his back to the room and rested his outstretched hands on the mantle. He wore a black hooded robe, similar to that which he had worn as a seer. He had become accustomed to the style and enjoyed the air of mystery it gave him. As he waited for the wizards to come in he steadied his nerve and resolved to face them with a superior manner. It would send a message to them that he was not a man to be trifled with or taken lightly. The burning question on his mind was whether they had brought what he wanted with them. He heard them enter and turned slowly to meet their gaze. What he saw chilled him to the bone.

Three shadows, tall and dark, that appeared to be from another realm stood at the head of the few steps down into the room. Their tattered robes billowed as if blown by an unseen wind that blew between worlds and a chill emanated from them. He saw into their red, blazing eyes that stared unblinking back at him. Their faces were hidden under the darkness of their hoods. The one in the centre carried a thick, white rod. The wizard held it out towards Ebon, inviting him to take it.

Ebon quailed at the sight as he realised that it was not made of wood, it was the thigh bone of a large man. He had not been prepared for this and it took him a few moments to regain his composure. Moving forward on unsteady legs he grasped the proffered rod. He winced as a cold that burned shot up his arm and pierced his heart then was gone. His eyes betrayed the fear that had taken hold of him and the wizard, still holding on to the rod, forced him to his knees.

'Here is the Rod of Dread. It was made from the bone of he who dared to fail us when we first came to this world. With it you will be more powerful than any who raise their hand against you. Succeed in uniting the feuding warlords under one supreme commander and you will be rewarded. Fail and your soul shall be bound to serve us for all time.'

The words cut him to the core and he knew that there would be no second chances if he should fail in his attempts to unite the different factions that fought each other. His overriding ambition still remained the same however; to wreak his revenge on the seers.

'I shall not fail.' He gasped as the wizard released his grip on the rod.

'That you may know we are able to find you in whatever world you may hide should you fail, we will show the extent of our reach.' He said nothing more.

The two wizards that flanked the one who had spoken moved noiselessly past him and stood by the vision-window. They brought it to life and Ebon saw the last stages of what had transpired in Amethyst's coven. He watched as Jon and Hamill joined with Auger and were lifted up and out of the coven in the whirlwind. His suspicions had been correct; Amethyst had been defeated.

The wizards folded their arms into the folds of their sleeves and bowed their heads. Ebon felt rather than heard the stirring in the air that gathered in strength as an almost inaudible hum began to rise in pitch to a steady drone. Ebon, still on his knees before the first wizard, watched in awe as the two at the vision-window created a powerful blast of air and directed it at the whirlwind that Auger Wind-rider was controlling. Like a striking hawk it pounced on the unsuspecting travellers and shook them unmercifully pulling at the fabric of the wind and tearing it apart. Ebon saw the wind fail and Jon, Hamill and Auger fall to the ground. The vision cleared and the two wizards moved away and stood waiting for the one who had spoken to join them.

'We await your report with eagerness. Do not fail to come at the appointed time.' With that the wizards seemed to melt away into the shadows and Ebon was left alone.

Ebon held a hand to his head as a searing pain ripped through his mind. He knew when and where to make his report and was shown what his fate would be if he were not to attend. The wizards had left him with the impression, deeply set into his mind. He raised himself to his feet, dazed and troubled by his meeting with them. He had not been prepared for the intensity of the encounter and for the first time he doubted his ability to control the forces of this world. The sooner he overcame the feuding warlords, the sooner he could return to his world and lay claim to the title of Master Seer. Then, and only then, would he be able to bear down on the wizards; destroying their grip on this world of shadows and become supreme controller of both worlds.

Holding the Rod of Dread aloft in an outstretched arm he shouted out his challenge to the seers. 'You shall not prevent me from returning and wreaking vengeance now, Urim. Not now that I hold this rod. I am more powerful than ever and I shall have my revenge.'

His eyes blazed with fury and a passion that consumed his reason burned in his breast. Ebon would return to be master of the land or he would become a slave to the wizards if he failed. That was something he would not even consider.

A faint red spark flashed in his eyes and was gone.

Chapter 1

Auger's Twist

Things do not always turn out as one would expect and being leagues away from where one intended to be can be a little frustrating.

The flight with Auger Wind-rider and Hamill did not last very long. Soon after they had left the confines of the coven, they were engulfed by a powerful force that wrenched control of the wind from Auger's hands. No matter how he tried to regain dominance over the element they were tossed around like peas in a rattle. Sensing that they could be in danger of being seriously injured, Auger wisely decided to try and set the three of them down on the ground as safely as he could. He battled against the force that was shaking them and managed to draw more power from his staff to obtain a rapid, but safe, descent.

The three of them tumbled to the ground as the wind that Auger had been battling to control lost its momentum and dissipated into thin wisps of air. Fortunately for them, the capable seer had managed to get them close enough to the ground so as not to cause any serious injury when the wind finally evaporated.

They dropped to the earth from about head height and Jon rolled forward as he hit the ground, preventing him from sustaining any injury. His dignity was a little ruffled, but no one saw, so he stood up and dusted himself down. Apart from his pride being bruised, he was unhurt. In fact he was rather pleased with himself; wishing that there had been others there, apart from Hamill and Auger, to witness his dexterity in managing to save himself from harm by the skilful use of his acrobatics.

'Where were they?' That was the question that he wanted answering. He had not travelled the land as extensively as the seers so he did not recognise his surroundings and things had looked so different from the air. They could not have come very far from the coven and the newly re-named Hazelwood forest. Searching the horizon he could just make out the dark band of trees that was the edge of the forest.

What an exhilarating experience the ride had been. It had filled him with wonder until they had been grasped by some other power that had thrown them off their intended course. He had been looking forward to meeting with Urim again and the prospect of going into Seers Tower at last. He wondered if the three of them would be able to get there from wherever they were. The first thing was to determine that very thing.

'Where are we?' Jon asked as he helped Hamill to his feet. His friend had not been as agile as Jon had been and he had ended up entangled in a bush. Fortunately it was the non-prickly type and, with Jon's help, he was able to regain his footing, straighten his cloak and steady himself with his staff.

'Thank you my friend. Are you alright? I saw you fall and was so busy making sure that you landed safely that I forgot about where I was going to end up.'

Hamill's keen concern for others well being had been developed from years of studying at the Ward and in the lands round about, it had almost been his undoing. The two friends checked each other for any sign of injury but apart from a few scratches that Hamill had received, they were in good shape. Auger however had not had as good a landing as them. He had caught his foot in a root that had been exposed by the eroded soil on the top of the hill they had been deposited on. He lay sprawled on the ground, flat on his back, with his face covered by his hood; his cloak had been torn but apart from that he appeared to be unhurt.

Jon and Hamill ran across to where he lay and Hamill immediately administered to him. He carried out a swift but thorough examination of the seer to ensure that he had not sustained any permanent damage. He had received a blow to his head, evidenced by the bruising that was already appearing on his cheekbone. He was going to have a real shiner of a black eye by the next day. Hamill concluded that Auger had concussion as the older seer's vision was blurred and he felt sick. They managed to help him to his feet and he winced with pain as he tried to put weight on his left leg, promptly collapsing to the ground in distress.

'Yes, I wondered if you might have done some damage to your ankle. It looked a little swollen but I couldn't be sure until you tried to stand on it.' Hamill frowned in consternation and worried over Auger as he searched through his pack for a dressing to help restrict the swelling and give support to his ankle. It was giving him some discomfort but what was of more concern to the injured seer was that his staff had been broken in two. That did not bode well for them as without his staff he could not control the wind. Neither would he be able to use his staff to help him as an aide with his walking. The best thing that they could do was to find somewhere nearby that they could rest until Auger was recovered sufficiently to be able to walk again.

Using the talisman to summon the wind would be a risky thing to do without his staff. True he could utilise Hamill's but it would not have the same strength or ability and certainly would not be able to keep the wind under control long enough for them to return to Seers Tower. Each seer held a particular role on the council and using another's talisman was always less efficient or effective. They would have to fend for themselves as best they could until such time as they were able to think of a way out of their predicament.

Looking out over the landscape it was clear that they were nowhere near where they had intended to be. Hamill guessed that they had been diverted far from their intended course and been blown south towards Rock Springs. He could see a river in the distance reflecting the sunlight from its surface and he thought that it might be Foam River. If it was then they were a long way from home with an injured seer and only one staff of power between them, the journey would be a difficult one. Hamill concluded that his staff had served him well up till now so did not believe they would have to face too many difficulties.

Taking stock of the situation Hamill outlined their circumstances to the others. 'I still have the use of my staff and the lodestone talisman. I also have the communication stone that Holdhard gave to me. As soon as we find somewhere to rest I'll make contact with Colonel O'Rourke at

Northill and ask him to send a messenger bird to Terra Standfast. He'll no doubt be concerned about what has happened to us. We're all alive and apart from Auger's tumble we are well so things could be worse.'

A clap of thunder rolled in across from the plains and dark clouds gathered from the east. There would be a storm before too long.

Jon rolled his eyes at the thought of being caught out in the open when the cloudburst came.

'You're right Hamill; things could be worse so let's not tempt fate. I've seen enough rain and mud to last a lifetime. Let's try and find shelter quickly or else we'll be caught out in it. I noticed a small hamlet not far from here. It didn't look much but, as the Great Salt Water mariners say; any port in a storm; and it looks like there is going to be a storm.'

Jon picked up the two pieces of the broken staff and secured them together with some twine from his pouch. He and Hamill then stood either side of Auger and gently supported him between them, helping him along as best they could. They made their way down the gentle slope of the hill towards the hamlet in the hope that they could reach it before the rain started.

They were in sight of the hamlet and had but a half a league to go to the outskirts of the small group of buildings when the first drops of rain fell. Not wanting to cause Auger too much discomfort they continued to support him between them. Hamill was able to place a protective shield above their heads with the power of his staff, keeping the rain off them.

'Now why didn't you do that when we were struggling through all that mud back in Uniah?' Jon asked with a hint of exasperation in his voice.

Hamill looked somewhat abashed and confessed. 'I am afraid to say that I didn't think of it then. Being a seer is still very new to me, but even if I had I could not have maintained it and stayed on my feet for more than a couple of paces. Anyway, it's a bit academic now. Sorry.'

Jon shook his head and then smiled and winked at his friend to show that there was no harm done and that he bore him no unkind thoughts.

They were able to arrive, without a drop of rain on them, at the door of a building that looked like it could serve as lodgings for travellers. There was no sign displayed and Jon thought that they might be out of luck until he noticed a small card in the window that read, 'vacancies'. He sighed with relief and knocked on the door. He crossed his fingers and hoped that there would be enough room for the three of them. Hamill shut off the power from his staff and doused the shield. Immediately the great drops of rain pelted down on them as if it had been waiting for the shield to be removed.

'Thanks, Hamill; you could have waited until we were inside.' Jon complained as his clothes soaked up the water that seemed to drench them as if tipped from a bucket.

'Sorry about that; I didn't want to advertise the fact that Auger and I are seers. At least not until we have to.'

The door opened and a young lad of about twelve let them in, calling out to his mother that they had guests. 'Mom, we have three guests and one of them is in need of some help by the look of it.'

A middle aged woman with greying hair that had been tied back in a bun and was trying desperately to be loosed came rushing into the hallway. She pushed at her hair with wet hands, attempting to put it back in place then dried her hands on her apron and directed them to take Auger into the parlour.

'Welcome gentlemen, set your friend in the chair by the fireplace. Cameron, light the fire and get some hot water from the stove will you pet.'

'Mom, I keep telling you, not to call me that.' Cameron rolled his eyes with embarrassment at being called that in front of visitors.

'Well, alright then my lad.' She ruffled his hair and smiled, looking at him with love in her eyes. 'Look lively now.'

Cameron ducked away from her fussing and lit the fire before dashing off to fetch the water.

Thank you ma'm.' Hamill said, offering their thanks. 'We were not sure whether you were taking in guests until we saw your notice in the window.

'Oh you can call me Judith, and the lad's name is Cameron. Just call for him if you need anything, he's a willing lad, bless him.'

Her son returned with the water and handed it to his mother before she sent him to get the rooms ready. He raced off without a word of complaint, eager to please her.

'He's a good lad. I don't know what I'd have done without him. Ever since his dad passed away, he's had to do a lot of growing up.' She smiled lovingly as she watched him dash away.

'Thank you Judith, I can look after our friend now that we have him settled.'

Hamill had removed his travel cloak and was opening his backpack to get a fresh dressing. Seeing that he was of elfish blood, Judith assumed that he would be trained in medical matters and stepped aside to allow him more room to attend to Auger.

Judith gave the three of them a cursory looking over, just to make sure that she would feel comfortable with them staying in her home. 'Would you like something to drink gentlemen, or some food perhaps? I could put together a quick sandwich to see you through to the evening meal if you like.'

Jon answered for them all as he checked with Hamill and Auger to see if they were hungry. They nodded and Jon thanked Judith, asking for hot chicory for the three of them. 'You are most kind, thank you. My name is Jon. I'm from Ashbrooke, to the north of the eastern plains. This is Hamill from the Ward and this is Auger...from Ffridd-Uch-Ddu...He's a dwarf.'

Judith raised an eyebrow and gave them a curious look before smiling broadly. Her soft features showed her inner warmth as her eyes sparkled with kindness. 'Of course sir, I mean Jon; whatever you say. It doesn't concern me who you are, it's what you are that matters to me and I can see that you are all good folk. You need have no concerns here. Only I would appreciate it if you didn't let on to my lad who you really are. He's likely to get ideas about things if he were to know that we had two seers staying with us it might give him ideas and get himself into mischief.' She turned and left the room to get them something to eat and drink.

The three of them stared at each other wide eyed, speechless at how discerning Judith had been but happy to know that she could be counted on to keep their secret safe.

Jon had not realised just how tired he had been until he awoke to find that he had slumped to the side in the comfortable armchair by the fire. Hamill too had succumbed to fatigue and was sat opposite him with his head back and his mouth open, snoring. Jon thought it was probably that noise which had woken him up. Auger sat on a couch with his leg propped up, puffing away on a long stemmed clay pipe. The bruising around his eye was beginning to develop into a patch of purple and blue. His eye was beginning to close a little. (Fortunately Hamill had applied a cold compress when they had arrived at the boarding house and that had kept the swelling to a minimum.)

'Ah, so you've decided to join the land of the living again have you. I believe that you deserved that rest young Jon. We'll leave Hamill to continue with his. You've both exerted yourselves beyond that which you could deal with any longer without a good rest.'

Jon looked around him sleepily, content to let the aches and pains of his body dictate that he remain where he was. It had grown dark and the fire crackled in the grate, giving a warming glow to the room. Jon remembered the last time he had sat like this, back at his home when Hamill had come to call on him. It was raining, as it had been then, but on that occasion it was driven by the fury of the witch-queen. Listening to it beat against the window pane he could feel that it was simply a rainstorm and nothing else. He smiled to himself contentedly and settled further into the armchair, safe in the knowledge that Amethyst would not raise her hand against them again.

He remembered that they had been caught by something that had forced Auger to lose control of the wind and they had needed to find shelter here. At least they were away from the storm where they could rest until Auger was better able to travel. But what was it that had happened to cause the sudden change in direction and to tear control away from a seer. Whatever it was, they were secure here and neither Hamill nor Auger seemed to be perturbed by it so he decided that if they were content, so should he be. Despite his reasoning he could not settle and asked Auger what he thought of the situation.

'I have to admit that I do not know what happened. I do know, however, that it was not a natural occurrence. What we felt was a deliberate attack upon my powers but, as nothing has materialised to follow on from that attack, I believe that we are safe enough for now. I shall need to consult with my fellow seers back at the Tower before any conclusion can be drawn from it. I think that it would be as well to make contact with Terra as soon as Hamill is awake and let him know of our situation. What is of immediate concern to me is the breaking of my staff. Without it we will not be able to safely use the wind again.'

'Are you not able to call it up again then?' Jon asked, a little perplexed that Auger would not have considered using Hamill's staff to control the wind.

'Oh yes, I can do that alright. It's just that the power within my staff; and mine alone, is sufficient to control the element of air. True the other seers, such as Hamill, can do so but for only a limited time and distance. The talisman will only work for me with my staff. That is, all except for Terra Standfast. As leader of our Council he has the ability to use all and every talisman as he requires by virtue of his own talisman, the Scroll of Mastery. He alone holds the ability to control all of them, whilst we can only use our own, or those of another seer for a short period of time.

'Oh I see.'

Jon was beginning to understand how Urim had been able to do all the things that he had when they had battled against the threat from Ebon. He recalled that Urim had been told the secrets of the scroll by Senior Bridgeman, the dwarf elder back in Ffridd-Uch-Ddu and been sworn to secrecy. Jon could see why that would be necessary. If that information were to get into the wrong hands, someone like Ebon would have been able to withstand everything that the seers could do. The encounter with the rebel seer could have had a totally different outcome. No wonder Urim had been so keen to ensure that Ebon did not gain access to its knowledge and power. His admiration for Urim increased as each little piece of information that became clear to him fell into place.

Cameron appeared at the door and announced that dinner would be ready shortly. 'Mom wants to know whether you would rather eat in here by the fire so as not to disturb your injured friend by getting up and going into the dining area. We can serve it to you on trays if you like.'

'That will be fine thank you. We hope that it will not put you to any inconvenience by doing so.' Auger responded.

'It's no problem at all. I'll let my mom know that you'll be eating in here.' He hurried back to the kitchen to tell her.

Hamill snorted and awoke. Looking around bleary eyed he said. 'What's that? We'll be eating in here. What a good idea.'

Jon stifled a laugh and kicked the sole of Hamill's boot to make sure that he was properly awake. 'Trust you to wake up when dinner is ready.'

Chapter 2

An Unwelcome Visitor

Terra Standfast was worried. He paced the floor of the council chamber deep in thought. Every now and again he would stop and check the hands on the time piece that wound slowly down from midnight of one day to midnight of the next. It then began again with the notches of the wheel recording the passing of the days of the week and the weeks of the month. It was unique in the land and had been kept in working order by the faithful attentions of the folk who served in the Tower. It had never stopped since its installation many years ago. Terra wondered whether it had failed now as the time seemed to drag by.

It seemed as if many turns of the hand had passed, yet only a half of one had gone since he had begun to be concerned for the well being of his friend, and fellow dwarf seer, Auger Wind-rider. His face bore the furrows of concern, deeper than any he had displayed before. Auger, Hamill and Jon should have arrived at the Tower by now. Something had happened. He knew it and hoped that they had not come to any harm.

Frustrated by their delayed arrival, he decided to climb to the top of the tallest spire in Seers Tower so that he could look out across the land in the hope that he might see them. The ascent to the platform at the very top of the Tower was an arduous one and he had to rest half way in order to catch his breath.

Opening the door out onto the platform he held onto the rail that was the only thing preventing him from being dislodged by the wind and falling to the ground. He stood there for a long time searching the horizon for any sign that would signify the return of Auger with Hamill and Jon. The chill wind seemed to blow right through him. Any other being would have quickly returned to the warmth and shelter of the Tower but he was a hardy dwarf and it took more than a little cold air to deter him.

'What could possibly have prevented them from getting back?' Terra thought as he gave a last long look out into the distance before sighing wearily. He went back inside the high spire, closing the door on the wind and the cold. Night was drawing in and whilst he and Liam were secure behind the fortified walls of the Tower, he did not know where Auger and the two young friends were.

He had a bad feeling about it all and he determined to seek Liam out and have him deal the cards. Maybe they could shed some light on what was at the back of all this. His footsteps echoed down the confined stairwell, the light from his lantern flickered in the draught as he descended the time worn steps back to his chambers.

The other thing that troubled him was the whereabouts of Urim. He should have been here to assist him and the other seers in Hamill's confirmation as a seer. Hamill had done well and could now be fully admitted as a seer into the Council of the Sight. The days of his probation following his inauguration would normally have lasted for a year, perhaps more. But he had seen more challenges in the last few weeks than any other would have met with in that time. He had earned the right to sit in full council.

What of Jon? Terra was troubled over him and knew not what to do for the best. Urim had made his viewpoint clear on the matter and despite what he had said; Terra needed to be sure within himself that it was the right time to do what Urim proposed. Was it the right thing to do? As always, when trying to decide on a matter, into his mind would come the saying, "Time will tell". Urim often used it and he was right, but how to know if what he now recommended was indeed the right thing to do.

Sighing wearily again with the decision weighing heavily upon his shoulders, the old dwarf sat at his desk amidst the books and parchments that lay around him. As he studied his room he said in a quiet voice. 'One of these days I'll tidy up in here, but then I'll never be able to find anything.' There was order to the apparent chaos of his private room, despite its resemblance to a dumping ground for unwanted paraphernalia. Terra rallied himself and rose from his chair. He stretched to relieve his aching body and made his way slowly to call on Liam in his chambers.

The seer was engrossed in his charts and they littered the floor as he had discarded them in his efforts to unravel his conundrum. He had dealt the cards after searching through his almanac and found a rift in the threads of the energy in the land. Terra found him pouring over the figures he had been calculating, screwing the paper up and throwing it across the room at the waste basket. He was not a very good shot and balls of crumpled paper lay around the basket as if they had been spewed forth from its depths.

'Should I come back another time my friend? It seems that you are preoccupied.' Terra asked a little surprised at his friend's apparent unease.

Liam looked up, his face filled with consternation. 'No, no, come on in. You are just in time in fact. I have discovered a most disconcerting thing. I am unable to read beyond a certain point in time but what is most worrying is that on each occasion that I have dealt the cards, they have revealed a different outcome. No two readings have been the same. It's as if the future cannot be foretold. I have studied the charts that have served me well up to now but they have ceased to make sense. I am at my wits end and need your counsel. I was about to seek you out and ask for your opinion and guidance. What am I to do?'

Liam was indeed 'at his wits end' as he had put it. Terra had never seen his fellow seer and friend so distracted and knew that his own feelings of impending danger were not imagined. If what Liam had said about his not being able to read the future was true, then their troubles could be about to begin. Things were not adding up in their favour. The worried dwarf smoothed the furrows on his brow with gnarled fingers and found a seat amongst the chaos of Liam's room. It was worse than his. He made a mental note to raise the matter of being organised at the next council meeting.

'Tell me what the matter is Liam and then perhaps we can make sense of it between us.' Terra offered with a patience that had been developed from years of application.

'I'm not so sure that we can, the cards seem to be following a pattern all of their own. The only one that remains constant is the card that represents the energy barrier, as if everything revolves around it like a flipped coin. How it will come down is unknown and, frankly, it has me baffled.'

Terra was also baffled by what his friend had said. 'So Liam, tell me in words that I can understand just what it is that you are saying to me.'

Sitting behind his high desk, Liam looked forlornly at the senior member of the Council of the Sight, pondering how best to frame the words that would describe the situation. 'I am not sure how to explain something that is inexplicable but I shall try. When I set the cards this morning the patterns fell in an orderly fashion and it was plain to read. The pictures were ordered and stable. Gradually, over the day the patterns have shifted from being regular to having random fluctuations until I can make no sense of them. It's as if a change has occurred in the stability of the energy beneath the Tower causing spikes or gaps in the fabric of the barrier. I am concerned that The Montage has had an unsettling effect on it. I don't know how else it could have become so unstable.'

Terra had sat with his hands clasped together and listed intently to what Liam was saying. He was silent for a few moments before leaning back and sharing his thoughts with the frustrated seer. 'It may be that what you have said about The Montage is correct but I doubt it. From what you reported to me of the event here at the Tower, you followed the prescribed steps to the letter and without fault so I believe that we must look elsewhere for our answer.'

Terra blew his cheeks out and leaned forward. 'Liam, I was going to ask you to deal the cards as Auger has not returned with Hamill and Jon. I fear that all is not well and that they may be in great danger. What you have told me raises fresh concerns that there is a problem abroad of which we are unaware. I believe that it is now even more important for us to try the cards again in order to obtain an answer. If we are to have any chance of being prepared for what lies ahead I must know what fate is getting ready to deal us. Excuse the pun my friend.'

Liam smiled at the unintended reference to the cards and agreed to give it another try but he was not confident of having any success. He stood at the card table and shuffled the deck thoroughly before laying them down, one by one. Terra looked on, intrigued with the skill of the seer and held his breath as the pictures were revealed. Card after card was placed on the table surface in a particular, time honoured order. At first the cards seemed to be turning in the proper manner as Liam concentrated on his task but soon a frown appeared on his face and a sharp intake of breath was followed by a sucking on his teeth. He stopped turning the cards and looked at Terra.

'This is the last one and it holds the key to what is here. If it is anything other than the symbol of the energy barrier, then the casting is undone and it makes nonsense out of what has been laid already.' Crossing his fingers to ward off bad luck, Liam turned the final card from the pack. He breathed out heavily and his shoulders sank. Shaking his head he showed Terra the card that he had just turned. It had the picture of a serpent on it. 'It is as I had feared, the casting has been undone and I can not see what lies ahead.'

'Take heart my friend; you have done all that you can. It is not your fault that the cards are as they are. We must find a way to see what lies ahead however; I do not relish facing the coming challenge blindly.'

'You believe then that there is something amiss?' Liam asked the question knowing that Terra was rarely wrong about his feelings.

'I do and it has something to do with Auger and his two charges not returning from the south as we had arranged.'

Liam considered the words of his friend, and leader of the body of the seers, before offering a thought that might bring hope. 'If Emerald were here, she could use her crystal and see what it was that we are missing. There must be an explanation as to why the cards are turning as they are. Can we not make contact with her somehow?'

'I am afraid that all the while she remains in the sprite realm, we are unable to contact her from here. I gave her instructions to stay there as long as she felt her presence was required. The attack on the sprites by the nymphs may mean that she will be there for some time so we can not count on her being able to help. She will probably be unaware of our need unless we can find a way to get a message through. As you know, sending a bird would serve no purpose as it would not know where to go; what with their realm being beyond the boundaries of our world.'

It seemed to the seers that the two of them were on their own in solving the conundrum that faced them. Where or who to turn to for advice was not an option for it was they who the folk of the land came to for help with their problems. The seers were at the top of the ladder when it came to these things, if they had no answer then there was none.

Leaving the frustrations of the situation behind them in Liam's room they made their way to the dining area. It was strangely empty without the other seers even though folk sat at tables nearby, the two seers were a world apart. They ate their evening meal in silence but their minds were churning over the details of what had been discovered in a vain hope of coming up with an answer. None came and Terra decided that he would retire to his rooms to rest.

The rigours of the last few weeks had worn heavily at his energy reserves and he knew that he could not find the answer he was searching for unless he managed to get some sleep; perhaps tomorrow would bring the solution to their predicament. Excusing himself from the table he left the sounds of the dining room behind him and wearily climbed the stairs to his chambers. Before preparing himself for the night he sat at his desk holding his head in his hand, thinking things through.

Several turns of the hand later he awoke, having dropped off to sleep; the room was in semi-darkness as the lantern had burned low. He rubbed his eyes and shook the fatigue from his body. The shadows had deepened and the half-light played tricks on his senses. He could have sworn that the drapes at his window had moved, yet the window was closed. A sudden chill made him shiver and he instinctively jumped with a start when a shadow came at him from across the room. The breath was robbed from his lungs as the blood within his veins turned to ice.

'Remember me, Terra.' The voice was a whisper from the past. A voice he knew only too well; Emrys; Chief of the wizards.

Springing to his feet Terra clutched his staff and brought it to bear before him, ready to use its power against his deadly nemesis. Using his staff, he caused the lantern to burn brightly and the room was filled with a clear, blue light. Searching the darkness where the light could not penetrate he sought the one who had dared to enter the Tower after all these centuries. Terra had not been there when the seers and wizards had fought for mastery in the land and the Tower had been built as a lock between the worlds. He knew of the tales though, and had inherited the knowledge of what had happened between the seers and the wizards in those dark and unhappy days. He had studied those troubled times and was as familiar with them as he was his own.

The seers had been pitched in battle and fought against the wizards who had challenged them for supremacy in the land. The powers of the land had been fragmented and all but destroyed the very existence of the two factions; one for good and the other for evil. For countless ages the two bodies had held the balance in the world; eight seers and eight wizards. The wizards had wanted that which was against all that the seers held true, to subject the folk of the land to their will and have the different races become their slaves. This the seers could not allow and the conflict between them had raged over many years. It had destroyed the civilisation of the Anramites to the south and the desert sands had claimed their war-ravaged city of Anram, covering it with shifting sands.

When the confrontation had ended there were only five of the original eight wizards left. Erin, Megan and Galan had been killed in the fiercest of battles giving the seers a distinct advantage. The seers had eventually prevailed with the loss of one, Emerald Crystal-gazer, a sprite who had served faithfully for many years amongst them. A replacement for her was found quickly and the seers were able to banish the remaining wizards to a different world; that of Magog.

The energy of the worlds had created a barrier between them that had remained intact and not been broken until Ebon had used it against the seers in his attempt to rule in their stead. Terra began to realise that it was this that had been at the root of his concerns these past few turns of the hand.

Terra stood his ground defiantly, his steady gaze searching the dark recesses for the shadow that had been Emrys. He knew his voice as he had encountered him not long after he had been called to serve as a novice to the previous Terra Standfast. His mentor had shown him the other world where the wizards had been banished. It was a world of horror and violence where the wizards ruled with a tyrannical fury. There they had found Emrys the leader of the wizards and had faced him across the barrier. They had not been able to come into contact with each other but Terra had the memory of that time etched into his mind.

'Your powers are not enough to stop me, old dwarf. We are ready to claim that which was ours and you shall feel the agony that we felt when wrenched from our home world. We can not die; you and your kind saw to that after you defeated us. For many generations we have waited for the opportunity to strike back at you. Now that time has come and you shall be the ones to be banished. The folk of your world will gladly see you gone by the time we have finished, and then they shall be our slaves; just as we had determined before.'

His voice was a low, evil whisper that was gone almost before it hit his senses. Terra peered into the darkness of the alcove near the door; two orbs of blazing red stared back at him, unblinking, malevolent and filled with hatred.

'Not whilst I or my fellow seers live. We will use our powers against you as our forebears did and we shall prevent your return.' Terra Standfast lived up to his name and although he was gripped with a cold fear that robbed him of movement, he stared right back at the wizard and defiantly rejected Emrys' threats.

'But it is too late. We are already here. One who was amongst you gave us the key to unlock the door between our worlds. I come to tell you that you will not succeed this time. We shall rule and you shall die.'

The shadow flew at him from the darkness of the alcove, causing Terra to flinch instinctively, and the dark shadow disappeared into the ether. The warmth returned to the room and Terra stumbled towards his chair, his legs robbed of their strength. The power of his staff faltered and the lantern went out leaving the room in a murky gloom. A knock at the door roused him and Liam entered, holding his lantern aloft, spilling light into the room.

'Is all well with you Terra? I thought I heard you talking to someone and I had this strange feeling that all was not well. You look shaken. What has happened?'

Terra recounted his experience and the two seers sat together in silence for a while deep in thought. 'We must send out the birds to call a meeting though how we are going to get together in time without Auger's help I do not know.'

'Perhaps it is better that we are apart. It could be that we can work more effectively that way against these wizards. We have the communication stones, at least Hamill does. If we can reach him we might be able to co-ordinate our defence from around the land. It only needs the two of us to control things from here.'

'You may be right Liam. If only Urim were able to help us, I feel certain that he would be able to tell us what to do.'

The two seers gazed into the light of the lantern. They both wished that the seer, who had defeated Ebon and released them from the imprisonment the malicious seer had inflicted upon them, was here to help them now but he was not. He had gone to deal with other matters that were pertinent to him.

'Do you suppose that he might know of our plight and return to help us again?' Liam asked tentatively.

'We can only hope so Liam, for without him I do not see how we can prevent the wizards from carrying out their threat to return. I fear that we will be lost, yet I cannot believe it will happen. I am certain that we will overcome them somehow. The question is, how?'

Chapter 3

The Power to Control

Ebon stood on the first stage of the great staircase of the main hall at the centre of his fortress. Before him were gathered an innumerable mass of heavily armed soldiers, captains of his army. Each one of them had sworn allegiance to him, seeing their chance to make something of themselves that they would never have the opportunity to do otherwise. These had been the downtrodden and the rejected from amongst the mighty of this world but Ebon had taken them and made them strong. Every single one of them was in his debt for he had seen their potential and taken them to new heights of power.

Greed, avarice, jealousy, lust for power; all of these had been the hallmark of their weaknesses. Ebon had fed their passions and drawn them to his cause, promising them that they would receive, as their reward, revenge on their enemies; retribution against slights and wrongs committed against them as well as wealth, power and the command of his army.

Those who served faithfully were advanced in the hierarchy of his domain where they could exercise their yearnings for whatever it was that drove them on. There was the occasional bickering amongst them and petty jealousies but that was to Ebon's advantage. It kept his leaders sharp and alert. It was the survival of the smartest and Ebon was the smartest of them all. He did not allow any to come close to him, any who did felt the cold sting of death. There was always someone eager and ready to step into their shoes. No, he did not mind their squabbles and intrigues because it meant he always had the very strongest of them to be in command of his forces.

A few weeks ago, one of those closest to him had carried out an abortive attempt to remove him from power. He had met with a sudden and violent end. Ebon had known about the secret plotting and had been making preparations to deal with it when another of his 'loyal' captains took the matter into his own hands. He promptly dealt with the individual, removing the threat to the banished seer. Ebon had rewarded him handsomely and he now stood to the fore of his high captains gathered in the hall below. The man had made another step forward in his search for glory. Ebon would have to watch him closely, he had proved himself to be callous, greedy and without morals. Just the sort Ebon liked to have as his personal guard. They changed on a regular basis being either despatched by Ebon himself before their plans of supplanting him were realised or by another who was eager for their position.

Ebon held the Rod of Dread above his head and the assembled captains of his armies bowed before him. They pounded their fists against their body armour with resounding booms and cheered aloud. He gloried in the power that it had brought him. None dared challenge him or would stand in his way now. They knew from whence the Rod had come and recognised their inability to undermine him whilst he held it. The wizards had demonstrated that they had seen in Ebon a suitable commander and chosen him to wield it. None were keen to incur the wrath of the wizards so there would be no attempts against him now. None would dare.

The massed forces at his command were not intended to be used against the seers. Oh no, they were for his battles in *this* world; the first would be against Weylin, the warlord whose territory bordered his own. Ebon was no fool; he knew that if he were to command respect and keep control of his forces then they had to have a cause. It was not enough that they share in his, that of defeating the seers; they needed something tangible, something here and now, something that they could see and feel. So it was that he had come up with the plan to capture the fortress of his neighbouring warlord, Weylin. It would achieve two things. Firstly it would provide the perfect opportunity to satisfy his forces need for action, and secondly, it would give him his chance to test the power held within the Rod.

Ebon ground his teeth together in anger and frustration knowing that he had been unfortunate in having to contend against Urim in the past. It should not have been possible for the meddling seer to have been free to challenge him. No matter, it was quite possible that Urim had done him a favour in many ways. Ebon realised that if he had not been exiled to this ferocious world, he would not be in the position of power that he was in now.

Ebon was ready to unleash his eager forces against Weylin and crush any resistance he might offer. He did not anticipate the confrontation to last for long, not if what he had heard of the Rod of Dread was correct. Others had wielded it in the past and swept all opposition before them only to fall foul of the wizards when they failed to submit themselves to their will. Ebon was confident that he would succeed where others had failed. Nothing would stand in his way of achieving that which he craved; to wreak vengeance on those who had wronged him and to have all who lived, serve and pay obeisance to him.

He would rule two of the thirteen territories before the end of the day and consolidate his power, increasing his standing as a man to be feared. He had learned, however, not to be too hasty. He would put the Rod to the test before even thinking about facing the seers. With the power of the wizards behind him and his knowledge of the way in which the seers worked, he felt confident he would succeed in defeating them. Then he would turn his attention to the wizards. This endeavour against Weylin would show him how effective the Rod was and enable him to discover its true power.

Ebon rode at the head of his vast army astride a massive lizard-beast that had two heads, saliva dribbled from the corners of their mouths. Whenever the huge beast shook its heads, the vile liquid fell amongst the soldiers on either side. Screams of excruciating pain rang out as the parts of their bodies that were unprotected by armour dissolved at the touch of the slime and they were taken away to be treated or put out of their misery. The ranks of soldiers on either side of the beast quailed in fear and they held back, allowing Ebon to ride ahead. They were fearful of the poison from the great beast that Ebon rode and did not dare to disobey the powerful seer for fear of the Rod. Their dread of it being turned on them kept them in line. It was a powerful deterrent against them turning on the rebel seer who allowed them to satisfy their greed for the spoils of war.

Ebon played a dangerous game but it was one that he knew well and he watched his back with great vigilance. His captains helped to maintain order and he controlled them by virtue of the things he had promised them, when he was eventually established as the supreme ruler. They would participate in the plundering of the two worlds and be his marshals.

Ebon considered the score or more who were closest to him and had pledged their obedience to serve his will. Ebon knew that their loyalty ran only so far as he delivered on his promises. From time to time he had rewarded them with the things that they coveted; power, wealth and the sating of their passions. He knew how to keep a dog at heel and that's all they were to him. They were no more or less than his dog Khan had been to him. The hound had proved to be faithful to Ebon and he felt he owed it to him to avenge his death by bringing the dwarf who killed him to task.

When Ebon had disguised himself as a soldier back in Northill, he had discovered that it was Trapper who had fought with the animal and brought his life to an end. Ebon had made a promise to the dead hound that he would shed the blood of the dwarf that had killed him. Unfortunately he had mistaken him with his twin brother as they stood in the meadow outside Seers Tower and grabbed Tracker instead, so his promise remained unfulfilled.

The great army marched into the valley at the far end of which was the forbidding fortress that was Weylin's stronghold. Had he not had the Rod he would have thought twice about approaching as he did now, at the head of an invading army. The plan was simple, Ebon would destroy the gates to the fortification and his soldiers would charge through and capture the bastion. Weylin was to be taken alive and delivered to him. What the soldiers did once inside was no concern of his but he had given strict instructions not to raze the place. It would serve no useful purpose to destroy something that could be of use to him later. He would establish one of his captains here and install him as a Marshal, dealing out justice where required but acknowledging that Ebon was his master.

The battle against Weylin was swift and decisive, nothing that the warlord and his forces threw at Ebon and his army had any effect. Volleys of arrows were shot from the top of the outer walls in great clouds that arched down on the assembled ranks. They had little effect as the soldiers raised their shields above their heads and the missiles could not penetrate the formation. Time and again the bands of arrows rained down upon them causing only minor casualties.

The bombardment ceased before long as the archers realised that it achieved very little against the effectiveness of the defence. An eerie silence fell on the whole scene as the attacking forces waited impatiently for the signal to charge forward. They were eager for the battle to commence and a gradual murmur grew to a crescendo of yelling as a mighty roar was raised that rebounded off the walls and echoed across the plain where the ranks of eager troops stood.

The army of soldiers shifted from one foot to the other, straining like a dog on a leash to be released; Ebon raised his arm gripping the Rod of Dread and urged his beast forward so that he was alone in front of the gathered troops. A hushed awe stilled the roar of the massed forces as another volley of arrows flew into the air and headed towards the vulnerable seer. It seemed that he was doomed but the deadly missiles simply bounced off an invisible shield of energy like an upturned bowl that covered him and the two headed lizard. All around the seer the arrows stuck in the ground in a perfect circle leaving the inside clear where Ebon sat astride his beast.

With the Rod of Dread held high he rode right up to the gates of the fortress. Arrows, spears and rocks were thrown at him in a desperate attempt to bring him and his beast down, all to no avail, nothing that was thrown at him had any effect. Ebon felt as if he were invulnerable; nothing could deter him from achieving his aims. He pointed the Rod at the gates and he felt the power gather within him as it pulsed forth a mighty blast that shattered the sturdy gates sending great chunks of splintered wood into the courtyard beyond.

The force of the blast rocked him in his seat and he clung

desperately to the reins to steady himself. He marvelled at the strength of the shockwave that had erupted with such force from the Rod. A tingling sensation had flowed through his hand and into his body. It was followed by a surge of euphoria that swept through the jubilant seer as he watched his soldiers charge forward, hungry for the spoils he had promised them.

Within a turn of the hand the battle was over and Ebon had been acknowledged as the new warlord of the territory. As for the unfortunate Weylin, once he had been delivered to Ebon, he was never seen again but now there were two rods. The one Ebon had received from the wizards he kept. The other was held by one of his captains who would remain there as his representative. It had no power within it other than as a symbol of what it represented. But only Ebon and his captain knew this. They wanted to maintain control and it was rumoured about that the Rod had imbued its power into the new, smaller rod that Ebon presented to the newly appointed Marshal of the city, Tredan, one of Ebon's most loyal supporters.

Believing that Tredan held a rod almost as powerful as the one Ebon wielded would keep order in the fortress whilst he was away. Ebon knew those who were close to him well and was confident that his new marshal would be faithful to him. His captains knew that Ebon would cut them down as soon as look at them if they failed him or tried to usurp his authority.

This was the first territory to fall to him by means of the Rod of Dread; it would not be the last. He had proved its effectiveness and had been amazed at the intensity of its power. He now felt certain of the outcome against the seers and gloated at the prospect of seeing Urim; Terra and all the other seers kneel at his feet before he stripped them of their powers. Ebon planned to invoke The Montage and have them exiled to different worlds where they would remain apart from each other and alone. They would be shunned by the folk of those worlds and be outcasts, reduced to begging for scraps. They would not have the power or the opportunity to threaten him again; then his revenge would be complete and he would rule as he should have done before.

'They will yet rue the day that they turned on me, denying me the right to rule in the stead of Terra Standfast.' He revelled in the thoughts of his dominance over them.

The world of the seers would become a mirror image of this one, where terror reigned supreme. Ebon would be master there as well as here in his prison world. He would find the way to escape its boundaries and live in splendour, that is, once he had overcome the wizards.

His meeting with them had shaken his confidence but it had not taken him long to recover his nerve. He had adjusted his plans so that he could be successful against the might of the banished wizards. Having actually been in their presence had taught him a great deal. Before, he had thought of them as nothing more than another band of individuals that had formed a union not unlike that of the seers but now he knew different. He now realized that he must be more prepared and become stronger if he were to have any chance of overcoming their combined resistance. They were no mere mortals and could not be fought as such. They were creatures of power now and it would only be by power that he would be able to defeat them.

Their weakness lay in that they cared not who ruled in the territories, so long as they received the tribute that was demanded of them each month. Before they would be aware, Ebon would be in control of the land and with the might of both worlds behind him he would send them to the abyss they should have entered centuries ago. First he must deal with other matters; the seers.

He knew that without the power of both worlds behind him, he would fail.

Flanked by his brother wizards, Emrys peered into the Pool of Knowing as they studied what it revealed. They had gathered in the gloom beneath the mightiest fortress in the land, Hangman's Heights. Within the five sided chamber that contained the dark pool they witnessed the first step that Ebon took in binding himself to them. Unwittingly he would play right into their hands, bending his mind to their control every time he used the Rod. He would not even know that he was gradually becoming their puppet, their slave. Emrys had told Terra that they had a key to unlock the energy barrier. Well, Ebon was that key for the wizards to be able to return to power in the old world and Emrys would turn it soon.

When Ebon had created the energy shield around Seers Tower, he had caused a weakness to occur in the fabric of the power that separated the worlds. The wizards had felt it and had been desperately seeking a means to utilise that weakness in order to return to the world of the seers. They had succeeded in gaining an advantage in that they could influence some of the things that went on, such as attacking the wind that Auger had been controlling. Emrys had even been able to break through for a few moments of time when he confronted Terra in the Tower. It was only a small victory but with Ebon becoming ever more entangled in their web of intrigue, the wizards would soon have the ability to open the way back.

The seers could have no inkling of what lay ahead; all they knew was that the wizards had found a way to return. They did not know how or when that return would be. One thing was for certain; Ebon would play his part in all of this and believe he was doing it for himself. Only when he had defeated the seers would he realise that he had bound himself forever to the will of the wizards and that far from being their master, they would be his.

Emrys smiled and deep from within the darkness of his hood that covered his face came a low chuckle of delight as he saw the battle unfold and Ebon bring the power of the Rod into play. 'Nothing can prevent you from being mine now seer. You will be the means of us wreaking our revenge upon the Council of the Sight. Our return will be a gloriously dreadful day in the history of their world and you shall see the demise of the seers as a reward for playing your part.'

There was something about the former seer that the wizards liked. He was totally without scruples and would stop at nothing to achieve his aims. Very few of the folk that had come to their attention matched him for cunning, cruelty and deviousness. It would be a shame to have to despatch him at the end of all of this. Perhaps he could prove far more useful to them than they had first envisaged.

Maccus; second in authority to Emrys and the most shrewd of them all demanded their attention and posed an unusual question to his fellows. 'My friends, we have waited far too long for our revenge upon the seers. Now we have that moment within our grasp I wonder if we might be blinding ourselves to the opportunity we have before us. It seems to me that we might be missing a chance to enhance our strength. We were once equal in number to the seers and because of them we lost three valuable associates. I see in this fool the makings of a valuable asset to our essence. He may yet be able to offer us more than we had at first thought.'

He had the attention of the other four wizards and without speaking, one by one they nodded in agreement to what Maccus was suggesting. That Ebon might be the one they had been seeking to join with them and become a wizard. All turned to look at Emrys for his approval of what they were proposing; to add Ebon's unique abilities to their own. Long moments passed and the chief wizard nodded his consent.

'It is a pity that we will not have the pleasure of seeing him suffer as the rest of the seers; however, he does hate them almost as much as we do. Yes, I believe that you are right, my brother. He will make a valuable addition to our number but I fear that his ambition may be too great to be contained. Let us continue with the plan and we can assess his worth at a later time. It will do no harm to let the Rod do its work. If he masters its power then he will indeed prove his worth.'

Riding back in triumph from his easy victory over Weylin, Ebon had time to consider his next move. Now that he had proved the power of the Rod of Dread he needed to put the plan into effect for his attack on the seers. It would not be an all-out frontal assault. That would be logistically impossible as he had no army to command there. This needed to be a more subtle approach.

The concept of his plan had occurred to him quite by chance and had grown from the use of the viewing-window. Months ago he had managed to make contact with Amethyst in the world of the seers and a link had been established. Putting together his knowledge of the dark magic that Amethyst had mastered and his abilities as a seer when he had held the Lodestone, he developed an idea. The witch-queen had been able to look through the eyes of others; why could he not do the same. It would not be magic that brought this about but the unique power that the wizards had infused within the Rod. With it he could control not just the eyes and ears of his subject but also their will. He had already selected the one who would be the recipient of this daring manoeuvre and he was keen to put it to the test.

Chapter 4

Lost and Found

Their dinner was delicious and gratefully received by the weary threesome. Jon and Hamill particularly had been in need of a decent meal and Judith duly obliged them with a hearty roast lamb dinner with minted potatoes, carrots and peas. To follow they were treated to freshly baked apple pie with cream. Sitting back in their chairs with a hot drink, they wallowed in the comforts of home, all but forgetting how they had come to be there.

Occasionally Auger would wince as he tried to move and find a more comfortable sitting position only to return to his original one. In the end he gave up and rested his head against the back of the sofa. Not much was said between them as they were all feeling very tired and agreed that an early night would do them all the world of good.

The two friends tried to help Auger up the stairs and after a few attempts at it, Auger shooed them away. He sat on his bottom, hitching himself up backwards, a step at a time with his leg stretched out before him. Eventually they managed to get him into his room where he assured them that he was able to get himself ready for the night. The feisty dwarf was very determined to see to his own needs and not be a burden to them. Sitting on the chair beside his cot he assured Hamill that he would be able to manage.

Jon and Hamill were sharing the next room and somewhat reluctantly left Auger, feeling certain that he needed their help but again he waved them away. No sooner had they got to their room when they heard a thump and a bump followed by a muffled grimace of pain. They raced back in to Auger's room where they found the hapless dwarf in a heap on the floor with the quilt cover, grasped in his clenched fist completely covering him. As gently as possible they helped the dwarf, embarrassed by his situation, to a sitting position, Hamill insisted on staying to help him. Reluctantly Auger agreed and grumbled about not being able to look after himself.

'I'm as useless as a candle without a wick. Who'd have thought that I would be in need of a nursemaid; no offense meant to you Hamill.'

'None taken, it is my privilege to help. Now, let's get you settled. There's no need for you to stay Jon; I'll see you in a few moments.'

Leaving the injured seer in Hamill's capable hands, Jon went back to their room and prepared for a much needed good night's sleep. Hamill joined him soon after Jon had clambered into his cot. They did not think that there would be a need for them to stand guard, as far as they knew there were no problems in this region and decided that they were being overly cautious. After all they had just put an end to the threat that Amethyst had posed, what else was there to worry about? Gratefully they settled down into the soft feather mattresses, pulled the quilts high over their heads and were asleep within moments.

There was a jangling in Jon's ears that would not go away. It came from a long way away but was getting closer until he opened his eyes and became aware that a brass bell was being rung.

'What on earth is the matter? What's all the fuss about?' He glanced across to see if Hamill was still asleep but his cot was empty. 'Well, I guess it's time I was up and about.' He said sleepily.

The day had dawned and Jon could hear the cheerful chirping of the birds and the lowing of cattle out in the fields. If he hadn't known any better he'd have sworn he was back at his home in Ashbrooke. Climbing lazily out from beneath the covers he sat for a while on the edge of his cot letting the cobwebs in his mind evaporate before stretching away the stiffness in his bones. He had slept well and, if truth be known, was a little reluctant to be raised from his slumber. Managing to wash and put on some clean clothes from his pack he realised that he needed to do some laundry. Looking around for his other garments he discovered that they were missing.

'I've been robbed.' Was his first thought and then he berated himself for being so quick to jump to conclusions. Hamill had more than likely taken them down and arranged for them to be cleaned and pressed. Still half asleep he descended the stairs and poked his head around the doorpost to the parlour. It was empty; then he heard muffled voices coming from the rear of the house. Walking through the dining room and out of the full length widows he came across the others tucking into a cooked breakfast along with toast and marmalade.

'Well now, you decided to get up at last did you? I thought the sound of the bell would do the trick; come and have something to eat.'

Hamill and Auger were eagerly demolishing the bacon, eggs and grilled tomatoes that had been placed before them. Auger managed to sit sideways at the table with his leg resting on a chair. Jon sat opposite Hamill and smiled a welcome to Cameron who was eagerly running to and from the kitchen with supplies of food for the three guests.

'Shouldn't you be at school by now my lad?' Jon asked; surprised that the lad was still at home.

'No it's Saturday, I don't go to school on Saturday.' He gave Jon a despairing look and rushed off to get him his cooked meal.

'I don't need to ask how your eye is Auger; I can see its colouring up nicely. How's the ankle today?' Jon enquired.

'I'm fine thank you but I don't think that I shall be going anywhere in a hurry.' The dwarf replied, carefully adjusting his sitting position.

Hamill nodded in accord; he couldn't say anything as his mouth was too full of toast but he did manage a confirming grunt.'

Jon's food arrived and he duly did it justice by polishing off every last scrap. He took in the beauty of the day, enjoying the warmth of the sun from the clear blue sky. They were further south than at Ashbrooke so the weather would be that much warmer anyway and with the spring season fast passing by, the summer would be upon them before they were aware. As they sat out in the open and breathed in the fresh air. It reminded him so much of home. He heard Judith singing in the kitchen and he recalled how his mother used to do the same. Memories came flooding back and he did not hear Hamill's question. 'I'm sorry, Hamill. What did you say?'

'I asked you if you felt better for your sleep.'

'Oh, yes, thank you I do. I hadn't realised just how tired I was and waking up to find that I hadn't been dreaming and that I *was* snuggled up in a cosy cot was a pleasant feeling. I wish that we could stay here for a while longer, except that we ought to be making our way to Seers Tower.'

'Seers Tower; I've always wanted to go there; I've heard so much about it and the seers. Are you seers?' Cameron stood at Jon's shoulder with a fresh pot of chicory that he placed on the table, looking eagerly at the three of them.

Jon had forgotten about not giving away who they were and had spoken just as Cameron had come out of the kitchen after ferrying dirty dishes to his mother. He was wide eyed with excitement at having seers staying in his home. The singing from the kitchen stopped abruptly and Jon caught the disgruntled look that Judith gave him through the open window. Shaking her head she continued to sing but the lilt had gone from her voice and the song had lost its joy.

'I'm sorry, I hadn't realised that the lad had come out of the kitchen and I forgot about what we had promised.'

'You *are* seers then. I thought you were when I opened the door to you yesterday but I didn't dare believe it. To think that we have three seers staying in our house; just wait until I tell Elliot; he'll be so jealous.'

'Oh, I'm not a seer; it's these two who are seers, not me.' Jon said quickly, not wanting the lad to think he was just in case he did something wrong.

'Better not go telling anyone about us son. Best keep it a secret.' Auger tapped the side of his nose and winked.

'Don't you go getting any ideas young man; you leave these gentlemen alone, do you hear me now?' Judith chastised him.

'But Mom; they're seers and they're here in our house. Don't you see how great this is? Elliot will just burst with envy when I tell him.'

Judith came out from the kitchen drying her hands on a cloth, leaving the dishes until later.

'Now you just settle down young man. You're not going to tell your friend any such thing. In fact I want you to promise me that you will keep the fact of who our guests are to yourself. I mean it.' She added quickly when she saw the response forming on his face.

'Oh Mom; this is the best thing that's happened around here for months, years. Why can't I tell him? I promise I won't tell anybody else.'

'No, and that's final. These gents don't want half the village bothering them and that's what will happen, you mark my words. Tell one person and the whole village will know about it.'

'Perhaps I might make a suggestion Judith.' Auger volunteered. 'Perhaps the lad would like to visit Seers Tower with us, once I am fit to travel that is.'

Cameron's face lit up and his mouth gaped open. 'Do you really mean that? I can go with you. Can Elliot come too?'

'Yes, Elliot can come too.' Auger laughed but Judith's expression was far from pleased.

'Oh, I don't mean now you understand. I am unable to take you there just yet but when I can, I promise you that you shall visit there, with your friend, but you must promise not to tell anyone about us being here now. Do we have a bargain?'

Cameron was overjoyed and readily agreed to the deal, shaking Auger's hand to seal the agreement. Then looking at the seer with suspicion asked. 'You do mean it don't you? You're not just saying it to keep me quiet.'

'I swear by my beard that I will do as I have promised.' The wise dwarf placed a reassuring hand on his shoulder, looking him square in the eyes.

'That's great. I promise not to tell. When do you think you might be better?' He could hardly contain his excitement.

'Cameron, be off with you now and leave us in peace. You'd best get that room of yours tidied or you won't be going anywhere.' Judith swiped her hand across the top of his head, deliberately missing him but he dodged the blow anyway and ran off to do as he was told.

'He's a good lad that one.' Auger complimented her on her son's character.

'Yes; that he is. You needn't worry about him; he'll keep his promise; he's a lad of his word besides, he'd not want to miss out on a visit to Seers Tower. You won't forget him will you? Only I know that sometimes these promises can be easily given but rarely fulfilled.'

'Madam, you have my word of honour; he and his friend shall see our Tower and they shall both ride in the wind with me there and back again.' Turning to Hamill, Auger said. 'Hadn't you better make contact with Colonel O'Rourke and get a message through to the Tower about our situation?'

'Yes, I must do that right away but I think I will do it indoors away from any prying eyes.'

'Quite right and tell them to let Terra know not to worry about us. We'll be fine. We'll be back there soon enough.'

Hamill nodded and went inside, leaving them to enjoy the relaxing peace of the tranquil garden.

Settling himself in a comfortable chair in his room, Hamill put his hand into his pouch to get the stone. He could not find it, nor was his lodestone anywhere to be found. He turned the contents of the bag out onto the mattress but apart from some personal possessions there was no sign of the stones. Panic welled up inside as he tried to think where they could be. Had he put them on the side table? No, they were not there or anywhere else that he could think of to search. They were definitely not in his room. He went into Auger's room and searched there; nothing. He went downstairs into the parlour, delving deep into the sides of the chair he had been sitting in yesterday, still the stones refused to be found. He sat down and covered his face with his hands in exasperation and worry. 'Where are they? They must be here somewhere. I'm sure I had them in my pouch; I know they were there yesterday after we had landed on that hill. Maybe they dropped out of my bag.'

He examined his leather bag thoroughly but there was no sign of a hole or a loose seam. There was no way that they could have fallen out. He reached the conclusion that he had been trying not to reach. Someone had taken them. It would not have been Auger or Jon but he decided to check with them first, just in case they were playing a trick on him. If they were it was not a very funny one and he would certainly let them know what he thought of their practical joke. He hurried out into the garden and approached the other two with determination. A restrained fury was evident in his features. 'Have either of you two hidden my stones?'

They looked at him nonplussed and laughed, thinking he was joking with them.

'I fail to see what's so funny about this. You'd better tell me where they are. I think it in very poor taste to play a trick like this. Tell me what you've done with them.'

Auger and Jon paled as they realised that Hamill was deadly serious and denied any knowledge of them.

'Are you telling us that the stones are missing?' They both asked, afraid in case they had fallen into the wrong hands.

'Yes, that's what I have been saying only I thought, or rather hoped, that you were playing a trick on me. I really can't find them.'

'Then there's only one explanation, someone must have taken them. The question is, who?'

They bowed their heads not daring to look at each other for fear that their expressions would give them away. None of them said anything but they all knew what the others were thinking. Cameron had taken the stones.

They all gathered in the parlour where Judith stood with Cameron held defensively against her apron as she withstood the gaze of her three guests.

'You must be mistaken sirs. He wouldn't do such a thing. He's a good honest boy. He's never done anything like this before. Have you looked everywhere for these stones of yours?'

'We have and it grieves me to suggest that the boy took them but we cannot think of any other explanation for their loss. Unless of course you...' Hamill did not finish his sentence and wished that he had rather not started it but all avenues had to be explored.

Judith was highly indignant at the insinuation that she would have taken them but she bit her tongue and kept control of her anger. The three visitors felt deeply ashamed to level these charges against their host and her son but they all felt they had no choice. They had to be found. To go on without them was inconceivable and to remain here was now quite out of the question. They had insulted both Judith and her son and could not be expected to remain under her roof and be given hospitality unless they withdrew their accusations, which of course they could not. Something had to be done to ease the tension that was building up and resolve the dilemma.

Judith decided that there was only one thing that could be done. Turning Cameron around to face her she rested her hands on his shoulders and bent forward to look him in the eye.

'Now lad, I am not going to be angry with you if you have taken these stones that mean so much to these gentlemen;' she used the word as if it caught in her throat; 'but I need to know if you know where they are.'

The unhappy lad was bravely holding back a flood of tears and Judith also kept her emotions under control as she waited to hear his response.

'I haven't taken them Mom, honest I haven't. I wouldn't dare do anything against the seers; honest. They promised me I'd go to see their Tower; I wouldn't do anything to upset them.'

His face was a picture of misery and his will power dissolved as he burst into tears.

'There you have it gentlemen. I believe my son is innocent of this theft.'

'I too believe him to be innocent Judith, I too.' Hamill meekly said apologetically. The others nodded sombrely in agreement, deeply ashamed at having caused so much distress.

Auger fidgeted in his chair and spoke for the three of them. 'As representatives of the seers, I wish to offer our apologies for the upset we have caused you by this most distasteful episode. Unfortunately it does not resolve our predicament. I wonder Hamill if you should try to locate them by the use of your staff.'

Hamill looked up as if he had received an inspiration. 'Of course, now why didn't I think of that earlier?'

'Perhaps you should have, and then all of this might not have been necessary.' Jon said pointedly and Hamill coloured with embarrassment but went to get his staff. He was gone but a few moments when they heard a cry from the room upstairs.

'I have them, they're here. Jon, Auger, I've found them.' He rushed downstairs and entered the room holding both stones in his hands. 'I don't know how they got there but they were just lying on the mattress as if they had been there all the time, only of course they hadn't.'

They all stood stunned by the reappearance of the stones and Judith gave Hamill a withering look as if to say; 'you fool, they were there all the time, you just hadn't seen them and how dare you suggest that my Cameron would steal them.' (It was a look that Hamill would recall from time to time and wince at the memory.)

Ebon watched the scene unfold with glee as he peered through the vision-window from his other world and he chuckled at the success of the initial testing of his new found powers. Not only did the window into other worlds work again but he was able to influence the minds of those he wished to manipulate. It had been a strange experience to be in control of another's actions.

He had applied his mind to the task and found that it was rather like operating a marionette; pulling the strings of the person's mind through impressions as opposed to physical wires attached to the body. It amounted to the same thing though; the target of his thoughts had been totally unaware of his actions and to all intents and purposes was a puppet in his hands. This was going to be easier than he had hoped and he relished the idea of confronting the seers; finally gaining his revenge upon them for his being banished into this harsh world. Urim would grovel before him at his feet. The interfering seer would not be able to stop himself.

Ebon reflected upon how Amethyst must have felt when she exercised control over others through the means of her magic. It was intoxicating and he resolved to learn more about how he could enhance his powers. He already felt that he was her superior in these methods as each time she used a creature she could only see and hear what it did, then when she was finished with it, it died. He was able to do far more and the object of his attention felt no ill effects afterwards.

Ebon was elated by the success of his endeavour and decided to try it again soon in order that he might develop his ability. He had several subjects that readily came to mind. Some of his captains were acting rather awkwardly when they were around him and he suspected some sort of intrigue between them. If he could access one of their minds then he could determine what they plotted against him and use his new found talent in foiling any attempt on his life.

Chapter 5

Reunited

Jon, Hamill and Auger settled their payment to Judith for her hospitality and again apologised for the slight that they had caused her and her son, Cameron. There was nothing they could do to make amends for the insult to the boy's integrity other than to pledge that Auger would return and fulfil his promise once they had returned to Seers Tower. The dwarf seer gave Hamill a reproving look for having caused all the upset in the first place and Hamill averted his eyes with a look of embarrassment.

Leaving the hamlet behind them they struggled forward towards Rock Springs and the small town of Ferryford. They knew that there was a boat yard at the settlement where they could obtain passage down Foam River to Rainbow Lake. The plan was for them to catch the ferry from there and cross the lake to Northill where they could get a coach to take them to Seers Tower. They might, however, decide to continue by boat instead, down the River Lune to Seaview; the main port on the Great Salt Water coast. They could then obtain passage on one of the great wooden sailing ships that plied the waters along the coast to Landfall where they were only half a day away by coach. It all depended on the weather when they got to Northill as to which route they would take.

Jon rather looked forward to going on one of the ships as he had heard tales of them but never seen one. It would be quite an adventure to make the last leg of their journey in that way. He reflected on what had happened to them since leaving Amethyst's coven and their unexpected detour caused by whatever it was that had made Auger lose control of the wind and having to seek refuge in Judith's small guest house.

The memory of their stay at Judith's left a bitter taste in Jon's mouth as he thought of the hurt that had been inflicted on the young lad, Cameron, and the trust that had been betrayed by Hamill's accusation that the lad had taken the stones. There was nothing they could do to retract that hurt and it pained him to think of it. He determined that when they made it back to Seers Tower and Auger was able to use the wind again, that he would ensure the promise to the lad was kept and he would be able to visit, along with his friend Elliot. At least, he hoped that it would lessen the discomfort he felt about the situation. He had learned a great lesson from this; that is to never make an accusation that could not be substantiated. He brought his thoughts back to the present and bent his mind to the task of helping Auger as he limped along, supported between him and Hamill.

They were stopped in their tracks shortly after leaving the outskirts of the village by someone hailing them.

'Hi there; would you mind if we joined you?'

Jon recognised the voice yet hardly dared to believe his ears. Turning around his eyes confirmed what his ears had told him. Walking towards them at a brisk pace were Braun and six dwarves.

'Mason; what are you doing here? Braun, Javelin, Archer, Digger, you're all here. How did you find us?'

'That was easy we just followed our noses.' Javelin teased.

'But I don't understand how it was that you found us' Jon said, filled with joy at seeing them.

'It's not so difficult; Archer and I were on our way to meet you at Amethyst's coven having discovered that the ogre, Mordecai had sold Leader to a group of ogres who had taken him to be enslaved there. We saw you leave the coven in the wind and watched as you were taken by some invisible force and swept south, away from your intended course to Seers Tower. We thought that we might be able to help and knowing that Trapper would want to come too we went in to the coven to meet with him. We saw what you had accomplished there and, we might add, were very impressed with the result. When we told the others what we'd seen, the seers, Eden and Elise encouraged us to follow after you and said that they would notify the others at the Tower what had happened.

As we had suspected, Trapper was eager to join us and Leader, Digger and Mason also insisted on coming along. As for Braun, when he heard what had happened, nothing would stop him from being left out of the search for you all. Considering your need might be urgent we set off immediately to try and find you, eventually tracking you down to the hamlet where, after making some enquiries, we set out after you and here we are.'

Javelin recounted their story as if it were nothing more than they would do any day of the week but Jon knew that they would have pushed themselves pretty hard to have caught up with them so quickly. His admiration for them grew and he wiped away a tear of gratitude and respect for these hardy dwarves and the resilient metal-master.

'Now then, what seems to be amiss here; can I be of assistance?' Digger asked, seeing them helping the injured seer. The amiable dwarf was limping slightly from his own wound sustained in the fight at Winters Hold but he gave it no thought as he saw that Auger was in need of assistance.

Hamill explained what had befallen them but omitted the bit about Cameron and the stones.

'Well then, it's as well that we found you. We'll make a stretcher for Auger and carry him between us. We can all lend a hand, that way it won't be too difficult a task.' Javelin organised the cutting down of a couple of saplings and had them secure a couple of travel blankets making a comfortable hammock in which Auger could be carried without discomfort.

'Thank you my friends; your aid is most welcome.' Auger said, gratefully easing himself onto the stretcher.

'Now then, where are we headed?' Javelin enquired.

'We're making for Ferryford at Rock Springs to charter a boat and make our way to Foamesend. From there we'll travel back to Seers Tower.' Hamill replied.

'In that case we'd better get going if we want to reach there without spending too much time on the road.'

'You may proceed.' Auger said in an imperious voice gesturing with a royal wave of the hand.'

Digger and Leader winked at each other and shook the stretcher;

Auger had to hold on to avoid being toppled onto the ground causing them all to smile.

'Oh, I'm sorry! Did we nearly drop you?' Digger teased and chuckled.

Jon had to suppress a giggle at the look on Augers face when he thought that he might end up in a heap at the side of the road; the seer soon recovered his senses though and laughed along with the others.

'I say; steady on.' Hamill reproved them for messing around with the injured dwarf seer.

'Sorry, Hamill, we were only kidding.' The two dwarves replied, holding back their mirth.

With a firm hold on his subject and able to connect with him at any time, Ebon was able to know everything that they did as if he were there amongst them himself. He revelled in the feeling of power and control that he had over them. He could be party to their most closely guarded secrets and they would be none the wiser for it. He nodded in satisfaction at what they proposed and readied himself for the next phase of his plan. When the wizards had caused Jon and the two seers to be thrown off their intended course, he formed the germ of an idea that had grown and developed into a daring plan. He would ensure that they followed that plan by manipulating one of them without him even being aware of it.

Ebon had gained a great deal of knowledge in his time at Seers Tower and knew of a way in which to open the link between the two worlds; the one in which he was held prisoner where the wizards held sway, and that of the seers. In order for that to happen he had to have the use of a seer's staff. Seeing as he could not have one himself he would have to use it vicariously and he was in the perfect position to do so. He had not felt this smug since imprisoning the seers at their Tower and he smiled a crooked smile; savouring the sweet taste of victory that would soon belong to him.

Braun offered to take a turn in carrying one end of the stretcher but Archer pointed out that if he did so, Auger would have to cling on for dear life as the tall metal-master stood chest and head above the dwarves. They thanked him for the offer but Auger gratefully declined, preferring to lay horizontal.

'How long before we get to Rock Springs.' Jon asked the injured seer.

'We should get there some time later today, all being well. I have travelled this part of the country only a few times but I recognise the landmarks and by my reckoning we should reach the settlement there in time for the evening meal.'

That was welcome news for them all and they travelled on through the pleasant countryside enjoying the green fields and gently rolling hills along the trail to Rock Springs. As they travelled, Jon listened as Braun related his story of how he had been captured by Amethyst.

He had been keeping watch over the others the night they had camped at the edge of Ringwart forest when he became aware of being watched from the woods. He had seen a set of eyes looking at him and he had not remembered anything else until he had awakened in Amethyst's throne room. She had held him bound by a spell that meant he was unable to move and she kept him there, questioning him about the others but he had refused to say anything. Eventually she had lost her temper and thrown a black cloud over him and the next thing he remembered was being held in stasis in one of her cubicles. He had seen Hamill incarcerated in the same manner but had been unable to say or do anything. He guessed that Hamill was also in the same state as he and was unable to communicate. Then a little while later the chancellor appeared in the cubicle next to the seer. Braun recalled being awed at the powers that the witch-queen possessed and had sunk into a deep melancholy, thinking that if Hamill had succumbed to her spells, then there was little hope for them to succeed. His mood had changed however when Jon and the others had arrived and freed them from their captive state.

Jon and the dwarves listened eagerly to his tale and shook his hand with genuine gratitude for his safe deliverance. Jon noticed that Hamill was looking pensive; he did not join in with the general rejoicing at the outcome of their venture and asked what was wrong.

'It's Ebon; although we saw the spell that Amethyst threw at us hit the reflector and grab hold of him, I am not certain that my task is complete. I was to have ensured that he was dealt with once and for all but I have no means of knowing whether that is the case. The thing that worries me is who was responsible for interfering with Auger's control of the wind. Then there was the incident with the stones; I know that they were missing, yet there they were, on the cot as if they had been there all the time. These things must have been caused by someone with tremendous ability, beyond that which I would give Ebon credit for; yet who else would want to strike at us other than him.'

Jon saw the point that Hamill was making and walked alongside his friend in silence considering his words. He could not come up with any other answer than Ebon. 'You may be right but I can't see any alternative for us than to get back to Seers Tower as quickly as we can and consult with the seers. Urim would know what to do.'

'Yes you're right, of course. There is little to be gained by fretting about it. I have no other suggestions than that which you have offered. Still I feel that he is somehow involved with all of this. I can't shake the feeling that he is watching us and I get the strangest feelings in the pit of my stomach.' Shaking his head and straightening his shoulders, Hamill smiled at his friend and slapped him on the back.

'Let's not worry about him now; there is the matter of deciding what food we are going to eat tonight. I think I might have a big juicy steak. What about you?'

Jon smiled at his friend's sudden change of mood and at his thought of what he was going to eat. It was just like Hamill to be thinking of food, but now he mentioned it, Jon thought how nice a thick steak would be for dinner and he embellished the thought with mushrooms and fried onions. His mouth watered at the prospect and found that he walked just that little bit quicker than before.

Dinner was every bit as good as he had imagined it to be and he patted his stomach contentedly. The inn at Ferryford on the edge of

Rock Springs was small but welcoming and a cosy fire had warmed them all after having bathed and changed their clothes. The local store had proved invaluable in providing for their needs. They had sorely been in need of fresh clothing, even Auger and Hamill had bought clothing more appropriate to their needs and had their seers cloaks laundered. The mood at the inn was friendly and the landlord was able to supply them all with rooms for the night.

Between them, Hamill and Digger had been tending to Auger and they were pleased with how his ankle was responding to the rest and treatment. Hamill had bought some herbs and ointment at the store which he had applied to the sprain to help with the healing process. As for his eye, it had turned purple and yellow. It was a real shiner.

They had just completed their meal when a man wearing a hooded cape entered. He stopped in his tracks when he saw the group of dwarves with Braun and Jon sitting at the tables they had been assigned for their meals.

'Well I never... Jon, Hamill, Braun, dwarves; what a pleasure it is to see you again.'

Mystified as to who it could possibly be who would know them this far away from home they were a little nervous as the stranger approached. Removing the hood and slipping off his cape, he passed the counter area and spat into the bowl provided for that very purpose. Harry, the driver who had taken them to Seers Tower all but pounced on them, pumping their hands with fervour. His blackened teeth showed in a broad grin in response to seeing them.

Jon wondered why it was that he indulged in such a vile practice of chewing that awful weed. It left him smelling stale and musty besides the fact that it was not good for him and discoloured his teeth so badly. Harry was such a nice man when you got to know him. He concluded that it was necessary for him to appear this way so as to identify himself with those with whom he associated. Whatever the reasons, it was not enough to prevent Jon from truly liking him; sure he was a bit rough around the edges, but he had to be in order to survive in his line of work.

'Harry; what brings you here?' Jon asked in amazement.

'I might ask you the same question.' He said, grinning with pleasure. 'I have been on an errand for Captain Perkins but I am on my way back to Northill in the morning with my report. What about you? There's nothing amiss is there? Is there anything I can help with?'

'Well, actually; seeing as you are going back to Northill tomorrow, perhaps we could travel with you.' Jon asked hoping that the answer would be yes.

'With the greatest of pleasure; it will be my privilege. Have you arranged for a boat yet?'

'We did try earlier but were told to come back in the morning. They didn't appear to have any boats spare.' Javelin said.

'Leave that to me, I know a few people who can pull a few strings. If you were to try and hire a boat by yourselves you'd pay twice what you should. I'd better see to it right away before they close for business. Don't wait up for me I'll see you in the morning at breakfast. Be ready to leave at the seventh turn of the hand.'

With that he jumped up from the table and donned his cloak, disappearing out of the door before they realised that they had not given him any tokens for payment.

'That was a bit of luck, meeting him here like that. He has probably saved us a great deal of inconvenience.' Hamill commented before rubbing his hands together with a look of glee in his eyes. 'Right then; how many of you want to join me for a game of sticks before we retire for the night?'

Hamill was disappointed as everyone made their excuses and went off to their allotted rooms. He looked crestfallen and Jon almost agreed to play but could not face the prospect of another game where Hamill cheated. He would deny it of course but this was something that the new seer had not yet managed to curtail in his efforts to conform to the ways of the Council of the Sight.

'Sorry Hamill, I'm too tired to play and we need to be up early in the morning. I'm sure you'd not want to miss breakfast.'

The prospect of starting the day without food in his belly was something that he could not contemplate and so reluctantly accepted that no-one was going to play sticks with him. If it were possible for someone to have a black cloud hanging over them, then Hamill would have one.

Jon smiled to himself, then taking pity on his friend, promised to challenge him to a game when they reached Northill. That helped and

Hamill perked up a little, even managing a grin as Jon tripped him as they went up the stairs to the room they were sharing for the night.

'You realise that I'm only sharing with you on the condition that I be allowed to get to sleep first, otherwise I'll be kept awake all night by your snoring.' Jon teased his friend.

Hamill objected to the remark saying. 'If you think I snore loudly, you should hear yourself.'

They both laughed and upon reaching their room, settled down for the night; within minutes they were both snoring.

Chapter 6

Night Visitor

Jon turned onto his side and blinked; he was wide awake and even though it was still quite dark he could see that Hamill was missing; his cot was empty and the coverings thrown aside. Jon raised his head and searched the room for any sign of his friend; he was nowhere to be found. Perhaps he had gone to the washroom to relieve himself; having consumed rather a lot of drink that evening he may have awakened to find he was in discomfort.

After waiting a while for him to return and still no sign or sound of Hamill; Jon's curiosity got the better of him so he decided to investigate. Dressing quickly, he slipped out of the room and tip-toed down the stairs into the main eating room. Jon was able to easily traverse the open plan area as the moonlight lit the room with its diffused light. He stopped suddenly as he became aware that the door to the outside stood open; a shadow flickered on the veranda. Carefully he crept forward trying to be as quiet as he could but stubbed his toe on a chair which scraped noisily on the wooden floor and made him emit a muffled cry of pain.

'Keep quiet you fool.' The voice came from out of the darkness and was unmistakeable; it was Urim. Jon felt his presence and saw the seer emerge from the shadows behind the door; he held a finger across his lips and fixed Jon with a severe look.

Jon could scarcely contain his excitement at the prospect of being with the seer again and had to put his hand over his mouth to stifle the exclamation of surprise that would have burst from his lips had Urim not signalled for silence.

Jon was motioned aside and Urim stood by the open door, concealed from without but ready to grab anyone who should enter. Soft footsteps padded along the wooden boards on the veranda. Suddenly, catching Jon unawares, Urim leaped from concealment and laid hold on whomever it was that had stopped just short of the entrance, pulling the surprised visitor into the room and spinning him around to fall upon the floor. Urim slammed the door closed behind him and pinned the intruder to the floor with the end of his staff. A pale blue light emitted from the top of the staff illuminating the room now that the door had closed, shutting out the moonlight.

Prostrate on the floor before them and quivering with fright was the strangest being he had seen. He was slight of build with bright red hair and a green ringed, cloth hat pulled down over the top of his ears; he wore a green and brown tunic, on his feet were bright red, felt slippers, his leggings were made from the same green ringed material that his hat was made of.

'Well now Imp; what are you doing here?' Urim's question demanded answering as it was asked in such a commanding way; Jon felt its force and the poor imp must have been shaken to the core. Jon had never seen an imp before but from the descriptions that had been given of them when travellers had visited Ashbrooke, it was plain that this wretched creature was indeed one of them. Apparently they were normally very secretive and would avoid contact with humans and the other races; stories of them, along with their cunning and mischievous ways, had almost become legendary.

'Please don't hurt me seer; I only want to pass on a message that has been entrusted to me for the Seer Hamill. Are you he?'

The imp's voice was shrill and cutting to the ear and Jon discerned an edge of trickery to it; the imp lay prone under the end of the staff, not daring to move a muscle.

Urim glared down at the imp with clear mistrust and leaned a little more upon the staff causing the already uncomfortable imp to wince. 'No, I am not he; but if you will give me the message I will ensure that he receives it.'

The imp was clearly not happy about this and ground his teeth in frustration, his eyes rolling in fear at being pinned to the floor beneath the tip of a seer's staff.

'Forgive me sire; I mean no offence to you but I may only deliver this message to the seer by the name of Hamill.'

Urim paused for a moment, chewing on his lower lip before removing his staff and allowing the grateful imp to get up and brush the dust from off his clothes. He rubbed at the spot beneath his ribs where Urim's staff had held him fast. As he edged away from the seer, a fine line of blue power snaked out from the base of Urim's staff and secured itself around the ankle of the irritated imp who let out a cry of frustration at being treated so disrespectfully.

'Please permit me to introduce myself; my name is Tyrell and I was a friend to the Forrester Cornelius, known to you as the carer of the Cedar forest until his capture by the Ogre Queen, Amethyst.' He bowed before sitting down on a stool nearby and looked from Urim to Jon and back again expectantly. A frown creased his brow as he looked at them again before asking. 'Am I right in assuming that you are a seer?'

Urim waited a little before responding to the unexpected question by the imp. 'Yes; I am Urim of the Council of the Sight; this young man is Jon from Ashbrooke.' Urim offered no other insight to the inquisitive imp's searching look.

The imp simply shrugged as if it did not matter and waited for a further response or question from the seer. When there was none he coughed and straightened himself, clasping his hands in front of him. The three of them waited for the other to speak first, no one offering any further detail to their conversation.

'I really must speak to the seer, Hamill before it is too late. Do you know where he is?'

Urim leaned on his staff and glanced across at Jon, raising a questioning eyebrow as to the whereabouts of the missing seer. Jon shrugged apologetically and shook his head as he raised his hands in a manner that indicated that he had no idea and could not be held accountable for his friend's movements.

Tyrell fidgeted as he wrestled with indecision but finally addressed himself to Urim. 'Well, I suppose that as you're a seer that I could leave the message with you. Can you promise me that you will see to it that he will get the message?' Urim nodded and the imp started to reveal what he had been charged to convey. 'I have been sent by Queen Ella of the sprites to inform you that he, Hamill, is in danger. She has learned that Ebon seeks to use him to open the way back into our world for the wizards.'

Urim frowned and asked in his commanding voice to explain. 'Why should we believe you? You're an imp and imps are renowned for their tricks. Why should Queen Ella send you and not one of her sprites? Why did Emerald not come to warn us instead?'

'You ask a lot of questions seer that I do not know the answers to. I would rather not have come but I owed it to her for her kindness to me in the past. Perhaps she knew that we imps could travel the land without being seen. To know why she sent me, you would need to ask that of her yourself.' The imp shrugged, then smiled and disappeared. The cord of power that had been wound around his ankle fell loosely to the floor and dissolved away.

'I might have known he would do that. You can never hold on to an imp for long. Well, Jon; I guess we had better go and find Hamill to tell him what the imp has related to us.'

Jon did find him, in the wash room, asleep whilst sitting in one of the cubicles. Jon recognised the sound of his snoring and he woke him by calling his name through the locked door.

'Hamill; Hamill, come on, wake up. You need to get back to your room; you can't spend the rest of the night down here.'

'What; who; is that you Jon? I'm sorry, I must have dozed off.'

'Well, you'd better come out; Urim is here.' Jon heard an exclamation of surprise followed by the sound of water flushing away. Hamill emerged bleary eyed carrying a lantern that he had used to light his way.

'Did you say that Urim was here?'

'Yes, I did; now come on, before he does one of his disappearing acts again.' Jon hurried his friend along, afraid that Urim would indeed leave them without another word.

The two of then found Urim sat at a table deep in thought. 'Hello Hamill; are you well?'

'Yes, thank you. What brings you here Urim? Don't misunderstand me, it's good to see you of course; it's just that we had expected to see you before when we were confronting Amethyst.'

'I was there as I had promised I would be; you just didn't see me that was all.' Urim spoke as if they should have known he was there.

'Oh!' Hamill said as if he understood. The two friends looked at each other and shrugged. They knew Urim better than to try and clarify what Urim meant.

'Hamill, I have to relay a message to you that was delivered here tonight by an imp sent by Queen Ella. You must tread carefully on your journey back to Seers Tower. There are many dangers that threaten your safe return; not least of all, Ebon has plans to usurp your position.'

'Ebon, but I thought he had been taken care of by Amethyst's magic. I knew it was too easy. I said, didn't I Jon, that I felt it was not over and done with?'

Jon nodded in confirmation of what Hamill had said.

'It is not, as you have said, over and done with. I now realise that it is up to me to finish what was left undone last time. I shall have to watch for the right moment to tackle him and ensure that he does not escape again. You will not be able to deal with him this time Hamill. Now, I want you to be on your guard. I must leave you now and prepare to play my part in all of this. I can be of no help to you at this time. The two of you will be able to handle things without the need for me to be constantly at your side. Braun and the dwarves will keep you out of too much trouble.'

'You can't go now Urim, you've only just arrived.' Jon said, pleading with him to stay a little longer.

'I'm afraid that I must; my presence here will serve no purpose and I must find a way to enter Ebon's world so that I can deal with him before he grows too strong. You shall see me again before too long and we shall finish this episode at Seers Tower when this is all over.'

'When what is all over Urim; I thought we had completed what we had to do and it only remained for us to return to the Tower?' Hamill asked.

'You have only just begun my friends. There is yet more to be faced and only when Ebon has been dealt with can we ever be sure that he will not be a threat again. The lives of future generations are in your hands my friends. Farewell until we meet again.' Stepping back, Urim vanished into a hole in the air that had opened up when he tapped his staff on the floor, it closed with a popping sound and they were left alone again.

It was some time before they were able to get back to sleep, 'though eventually they did, but the morning came far too quickly for them both and neither of them wanted to be first up. Hamill had seemed to fall back into his old habit and it was not until Jon queried him about it that Hamill conceded that he found it difficult to conquer his desire for sleep.

'I have felt rather strange for the last few days and there are times when I can't remember what I have been doing. It is rather worrying to say the least. Oh well, there's no sense in dwelling on it. We have to get moving or we'll never get to Seers Tower.' Flinging the covers back he leaped out of his cot and proceeded to get ready.

'For someone who likes his sleep you certainly get up with vigour.' Jon said as he rubbed the sleep out of his eyes before stretching and lazily dangling his legs over the side of his cot.

'I found that it is the only way for me. If I don't get up quickly; I lay there and go back to sleep. Besides, I reckon that it's almost seven of the hand and unless we hurry, there will be no time for breakfast so you'd better get a move on if you want to eat.'

Jon did hurry; the last thing he wanted was to miss breakfast. Braun and the dwarves were already eating when they entered the dining room and Jon found that Hamill had been right, they were behind time. It was almost time for Harry to arrive so the two friends quickly helped themselves to what they wanted to eat then sat with Auger and Braun on a table nearby.

The dwarves could not resist a little fun and levelled their sense of humour at Hamill. 'Who was first down for breakfast this morning Archer?' Javelin asked, knowing full well that it was Braun who had led the queue for the morning meal.

'Now that's a difficult question to answer. Ordinarily I would have said that Hamill was first but I don't recall seeing him here when we came in. How about you Trapper? Did you see who was first to get their breakfast?'

'Wasn't it Hamill? Oh just a minute; I seem to remember that it was Leader.' Trapper replied, getting in on the joke.

'No, it wasn't me; I was behind Digger and Mason.' Leader responded.

'That means if it wasn't any of us it must have been Hamill.' Javelin concluded with an innocent expression that lit up his face with amusement.

Hamill was nodding his head and smiling as he realised that the dwarves were teasing him about not being first down for breakfast. It seemed that he couldn't win. He'd be teased for being first every time and on the one occasion when he was late he got teased all the more.

They all continued with their meals but every now and again a snigger or two would be heard from the table that the dwarves were seated at followed by a splutter as they choked on their food or drink. Archer finished his meal and walked over to Hamill placing a comforting hand on his shoulder. In between the odd chuckle he apologised if they had offended him and that they had meant no harm by their comments.

'That's alright, it was rather amusing and I promise that I will always remember your fun at my expense.' Hamill did not mean anything by his remark other than to get his own back on the dwarves. They, looked at each other and the sniggering stopped, spoonfuls of cereal were held half way towards their mouths or toast was suspended mid bite. What did Hamill mean by his comment? It was Hamill's turn to laugh and he did so with mirth, pointing at the worried looks on their faces until they too began to laugh, realising that the seer had got his own back.

They had all finished their meal and were washing it down with a hot drink when Harry arrived. He smiled broadly, showing his blackened teeth, and spat in the bowl; something that always caused Jon unpleasant feelings at the back of his throat. Despite that, having Harry with them as they travelled back to Northill gave Jon a feeling of security because he had obviously travelled this way before. He would know things about what the journey held in store for them that none of them would.

'Good morning all. Are we ready to get started?' Harry greeted them brightly, rubbing his hands together to warm them after being out in the chill morning air.

They all affirmed that they were and hurriedly went to collect their things. Hamill would not allow Auger to return to his room but asked that Digger would collect his bundle of clothing and the broken staff. Auger's ankle was much improved and he could put his weight on it now but Hamill insisted that it still needed rest before he could walk on it properly. The dwarf seer winced as he tried to walk and had to agree with him. Braun had helped the injured dwarf down stairs this morning but Digger and Mason had been assigned to look after him during their journey downstream today.

They all looked to Auger as the senior member of the group and the one to have the final say in things but when it came to anything to do with Auger's ankle then Hamill was most definitely in charge. When they had all gathered again in the dining area with their few belongings they followed Harry out of the inn. It was a beautiful day, the sun shone and the birds chattered in the trees nearby. It cheered their spirits and a feeling of well-being flooded over them as they made their way across the square towards the boatyard staying close to Harry who led the way.

There was quite a lot of activity as the folk of the settlement had been hard at work for several turns of the hand. Folk were intent on their tasks whether it was going about their work or mothers ensuring that their children got to school on time. Jon observed that one little boy appeared not to want to go but his mother would hear nothing of it and ushered him along ignoring his screams of protest.

Harry led them down a series of lanes until they arrived at the river where they gathered on a platform close to the rivers edge whilst Harry made the final arrangements. Soon they would be on their way; Jon was excited about the journey but was most looking forward to reaching Northill and seeing Captain Perkins again.

Hamill was not quite as enthusiastic; he did not feel very happy when it came to travelling on water but this was the quickest way for them to get to Northill. He hoped for an uneventful trip and rubbed his brow with his hand as a headache that had been developing since he got up sent a searing pain through his head.

Chapter 7

Jetta

Meanwhile in the world of Magog, Ebon continued to grow in power and strength. His armies spread fear and dread amongst the many factions across the battered land. City after city and stronghold after stronghold fell to the might of his forces. So great was the fear of him that several of the warlords had surrendered themselves to Ebon in an effort to save themselves and their dominions from destruction. Whilst it had lessened the destruction that had been wrought, it had not saved them from the grisly act of Ebon's creating new Rod's of command from their bones. Each new victory saw the creation of a different rod which was then given to one of his commanders as he appointed them to be marshals over the conquered territories.

The captains of his armies squabbled amongst themselves and fought each other for position and for the opportunity to be the next to hold prominence. Every one of them lusted after the right to stand in a position of power, to be a marshal and to have command of a garrison. They wanted the power to rule, albeit in a subservient way to Ebon. None dared oppose him, though they coveted the Rod and the power that it gave. Fear of the wizards kept them from challenging the one who wielded it.

They were smart enough to know when they were on to a good thing and allying oneself to the former seer was definitely a good thing as far as they could see. The days of the wizards reign over the land was drawing to a close, or so Ebon had convinced them, and the new ways of the deposed seer were about to begin. They wanted to be a part of it and would do anything to latch on to his rise to glory. That meant disposing of any who they thought might stand in their way. A dark and chilling new era had dawned in the world of Magog. If the ways of the wizards were feared, then the days of Ebon were to be filled with dread. He held the future in his hand; by virtue of the Rod of Dread and he was using it to good, or rather, ill effect.

One of his captains in particular held as great a desire as Ebon himself for power. His name was Fergus and he had become one of Ebon's staunchest supporters and fiercest commanders. There was madness in his eyes and those who ever challenged him had either backed down or perished. Ebon had watched him for some time and realised that he was a man with as much longing in his heart for dominance as his own. Ebon realised that he could not allow Fergus to remain as he was; he was too much of a threat to Ebon to be left in place. Sooner or later he would turn against the seer and attempt to supplant him.

Ebon had pondered for a long while as to the best course of action and smiled contentedly when he had hit upon an idea. There was something that he had wanted to do for some time but had not found the right person on whom to try it. Fergus would do perfectly for his purposes. It would be risky; there was no guarantee that it would work but if it did, then Fergus would have his wish realised, although not in a way he could have foreseen, and Ebon would be invincible. That is, so long as Ebon held the Rod; only then would he be totally in command.

Ebon had hatched a plan that should serve them both and summoned Fergus to meet with him in his garden. The former seer was not certain as to the outcome of his plan; it would either advantage them both or prove a disaster. Either way Ebon was confident that he would benefit from it. He knew that he had to act quickly or the power hungry captain would try to depose him and usurp the power that Ebon had managed to wrest in this troubled world.

Standing in his garden near the fountain, he studied the inky blackness into which the spell that Amethyst had cast against him had been contained. He recalled how it had almost enfolded him within its grasp when he had stood looking upon its flat and enticing surface. He stood by the pool's edge now, looking deep into the inky blackness, seeing nothing, not even a reflection, wondering what the end result of his plan would be.

The sound of Fergus approaching brought him out of his reverie; he would soon have the answer to his question. The captain bowed slightly to Ebon. The rebel seer smiled to himself at the lack of respect that his captain had shown by his shallow nod of the head and was comforted to know that he was acting not a moment too soon. Any further delay in dealing with his captain would inevitably mean trouble and that was something he could not afford at this time when his whole purpose was bent on victory.

'Fergus; thank you for coming to see me at such short notice; tell me; how are things proceeding with our preparations in the attack on Ailill's stronghold?'

'Very well, sire. The men are gathered and are ready to follow you. They await your command my lord.'

'Excellent. Fergus; I wanted you to come here to help me in a little experiment I have in mind to do.'

Ebon approached Fergus and put his arm around his shoulder. Fergus stiffened in surprise but dared not pull away. This was something that Ebon had never done before; to allow someone this close to him where a quick thrust of a knife would bring a speedy end to life. There was danger in this that unnerved the ambitious captain but he walked with Ebon as he guided him along the path back towards the fountain. They stood at the edge of the mirror-like pool, black and unnerving, with not a ripple or splash from the water that tumbled into it at the far end.

Ebon talked freely and confidently to Fergus about his plans for the future. 'I would like you to take a bigger role in my plans Fergus. I have watched you for some time and I consider you to be the ideal candidate to be my personal bodyguard and chief amongst my captains. Is that something that you would like to become?'

Fergus was taken aback; instead of, as he had feared, Ebon taking his life; he was to be elevated to a much more responsible role. Relieved that he was not going to be disposed of he answered without thinking, not taking into consideration that Ebon could not be trusted.

'Of course sire; I would be honoured to be of service to you. What is it that you wish me to do?'

'I want you to look into the pool.' Ebon directed Fergus's gaze into the inky black water and removed his hand from the unsuspecting captain's shoulder. Ebon steeled himself to withstand the draw of the fountain, knowing what to expect, but Fergus was unprepared and was quickly captivated by the magic within. Gently at first and then stronger as the power gained a hold on his mind, Fergus was drawn closer to the pool. Mesmerised by the beauty of what played in his thoughts; he leaned forward and as a tree that is felled, he toppled face first through, rather than into, the surface of the still, dark water. It did not stir or move in response to him entering its depths but swallowed him without a sound. Moments later, trails of lightning crackled through the water below the surface and the darkness stirred like a thunder cloud and gathered to a focal point where Fergus had entered the pool.

The water cleared and a shadowy figure appeared in the bottom of the fountain. It opened its eyes; they were black pearls within an ebony face. Slowly the figure raised itself and came up out of the clear water and stood silently in front of Ebon. The dark creature that had once been Fergus was now a being of magic; a magic that crackled over the surface of his oily skin and waited only to be released.

Holding the Rod before him Ebon asked his dark angel. 'Do you know what this is?'

In a gruff voice the creature replied. 'Yes sire; it is the Rod of Dread and I must obey whoever wields it.'

'That is good. Now then, you need a new name; I have decided to call you Jetta; you shall carry out my orders only and stand at the head of my armies as its chief captain. Is that to your liking?'

'I will obey.' Jetta gruffly replied in a voice that grated and he bowed from the waist in homage to Ebon; wielder of the Rod of Dread.

Ebon headed each campaign he waged astride his two-headed lizard at the forefront of his armies. All manner of men and women had gathered to his banner to fight and to die in search of glory, wealth, power and fame. Ebon the Dreadful they called him and quailed at the mention of his name as it was spoken amongst them. None dared to oppose his will.

There were too many stories of how he dealt with his enemies. None were spared, not even those who had been faithful in the past, even Fergus, his most feared captain had disappeared. However a new incentive to obey the rogue seer had emerged from some dark pit; it was said that he had been conjured up by black magic. Ebon's new bodyguard, Jetta, so called because he was a being of jet black power, who was immune to the weapons of any who raised them against him, only Ebon was mightier than he because of the Rod.

This dark demon had appeared as if from nowhere and shadowed Ebon's footsteps which added to the mystery there was around him. They had learned to fear him almost as much as they did Ebon for no-one survived a confrontation with him. This was a new threat presented against anyone who would even as much as look as if they were harbouring plans against Ebon. Wherever he went, his dark angel was at his side ready to unleash bolts of pure black power that sizzled and spat as they flew through the air at their victim. The unfortunate recipient would be covered in a swirling cloud of raw energy that ate at their being until nothing remained but a memory.

Wherever Ebon had obtained him from must have been a place of cold, cruel evil and few wished to suffer the fate that was dealt out by his hand. The first time that he had appeared was when Ebon emerged from his sanctuary and stood at the head of the wide stone stairway that allowed entrance to his stronghold. Ebon said nothing to the gathered captains about his new companion; he knew that Jetta's presence would be announcement enough and it gave him huge satisfaction to see their reaction at his appearance. Shocked faces were quickly masked with expressions of acceptance but their eyes still flickered with fear at what the presence of this dark demon may mean.

Their questions, though unspoken, were quickly answered as the next day they entered into battle against Ailill, the latest warlord to come under the reach of the outcast seer. All who gathered in the field of combat, with the prospect of a fierce clash, were mystified when Ebon commanded them to lay down their weapons. They looked at each other in disbelief as the order to do so was usually directed at those who were defending the strongholds that they besieged. Yet here they were, within a league of the warlord's stronghold, being told to lay down their arms. They hesitated in obeying Ebon's command; something that had brought a swift end to others who had been slow to obey.

Jerking the reins back, Ebon pulled his two-headed mount round to face the massed troops and bellowed out in a rage to obey his order or face the consequences. Most did so instantly but there were some, who were new recruits to his army, who were reluctant to do as he had directed and were slow to follow the order. That was their undoing. Ebon turned and whispered something to Jetta who also sat on the back of the great lizard.

Slipping effortlessly from the beast, Jetta strode casually forward and stood a few paces from the guilty soldiers. Stretching forth his arms towards them, a ball of black fire crackled into life between his outstretched hands. The soldiers stepped back in alarm and raised their shields to fend off their impending doom, one of them threw his spear at Jetta but it simply burst into flames as it touched his body and disappeared in a plume of smoke. Moments later the soldiers ceased to exist. Jetta had thrown the ball of fire at the cowering troops and they had vanished from sight as the fire surrounded them and crackled with vicious intensity. The cold air around them had burned with the heat that had been generated and a shallow clap of thunder witnessed the demise of the soldiers; there was nothing left other than a scorch mark on the ground. Smiling in satisfaction, Ebon announced. 'Let this be a lesson to all who would disobey me.'

Turning the lizard back to face the stronghold he urged the beast forward with the Rod of Dread held aloft and called for Jetta to come with him. The huge army that had travelled to do battle with the warlord of this stronghold held back, not certain as to what they should do. The captains simply watched in bewilderment, waiting for their orders. They had expected to follow Ebon a little further before he went on alone to use the Rod against the defences. It was usual then for them to storm the stronghold as they had in the past. Watching their leader approach the outer walls, they witnessed the typical response of a besieged city as a cloud of arrows arched over the walls towards Ebon. They landed around him in a perfect circle, just as they had done previously in the other attacks but what happened next took them by surprise.

Jetta moved forward and again a hail of missiles arched their way over the wall. Ebon dropped the Rod, removing the power that protected them, and Jetta threw his ball of black fire at the arrows, incinerating them in mid flight. Stretching his arm out towards the main entrance he sent a bolt of red lightning at the gates. The strong wooden gates burst into flames and disappeared leaving the metal hinges dangling uselessly from the gateposts. Striding forward, Jetta marched up the ramp and through the open gateway. He was not unopposed; fierce attacks were launched at him as wave after wave of defenders threw themselves against him but he could not be stopped.

Cries of alarm and screams of terror resounded from within the walls as a terrible vengeance was exacted by this demon of destruction. Some endeavoured to escape from the scene by fleeing the fortress through the open gateway. Turning to nod at his captains, Ebon gave the command for them to round up the escaped soldiers and to force them into his service or face annihilation. Never in the history of the land had so much terror been raised by a single entity. Not even the wizards with all their cunning and power compared to this.

Ebon's army stood dumbfounded and watched the unfolding drama with as much horror as if it were they who were being assailed. Desperate and mean though they were; this was truly something that should not be taking place and they sympathised with those who were fighting and dying in the defence of their city.

Many of Ebon's soldiers turned away and returned to their homes, sickened by what they had witnessed. If this was what was to be unleashed upon the folk of this land, they would rather have no part in it. Apart from that; with such a destructive force at his command, Ebon would have no need of an army. He would have need of no-one other than his creation that had been born of magic.

For all Ebon's success, there were still many warlords to overcome and time was running out. The appointed reckoning drew near when he would have to give account to Emrys in his promise to unite the land under one ruler. He did not believe that he was ready to confront the seers yet and he knew that to face the wizards would be his undoing. He was still far weaker than they and despite his confidence and bravado now that he had Jetta, he realised that he needed to garner more power than he currently had at his disposal. The power that lay beneath Seers Tower would be needed if he were to be successful in his bid to overcome the might of the wizards and have a chance of deposing all five of them. He knew that he would not be able to just walk into Seers Tower and help himself to that power unopposed. What he needed was to find another way to tap into the earth-power.

He had learned through his studies of the old scrolls and parchments when he was still a member of the Council of the Sight, that there was an alternative way into the world of the seers other than the one in the courtyard at the Tower. It was known as the keystone and Ebon intended utilising it in his design to ensnare the seers and defeat the wizards.

The place where this keystone was situated was at the other side of the land from the seers, at the Ruins of Anram, the ancient home of the wizards. The keystone was the mirror image of the shaft in the courtyard at the Tower. Being diametrically opposed to each other in their very nature, where there was a void that plunged into the depths of the earth at Seers Tower, there was none at Anram. A solid stone circle with the keystone at its centre lay in the depths beneath the pyramid at the centre of the ruined city.

That was where he had to challenge the seers from; by utilising the negative power that lay deep in the earth. The keystone was the means by which he would wrest control from out of Terra Standfast's hands and defeat the wizards at the same time.

Ebon realised that this was the means by which he could re-enter his world; without a staff he was powerless there; but if he could use someone else's, he could achieve what he had desired for so long. By using someone else to act for him he would be able to safely ignite the dormant power that lay beneath the stone. Then with the combined powers of both worlds at his command and with the protection of Jetta, his dark creation, he would face the wizards and force them to obey his will.

First he had to strengthen his grip upon the one who would unwittingly open the way for him to return.

Emrys and his fellow wizards watched in interest at this latest outcome from the dark depths of their five sided chamber.

'This poses a problem does it not?' Maccus said with a hint of concern in his hollow voice having witnessed the fall of Ailill's stronghold.

'Perhaps; we shall have to keep a close watch on this dark creature and find its weakness. It could be that Ebon has plans on using him against us but I still believe that the former seer can serve our purposes well. Remember my brothers that without Ebon we are doomed to stay in this world for ever. If he succeeds in opening the way between the worlds we can escape this nightmare and return to our world. There we will be free to contend against the seers and we shall be victorious.' Emrys spoke with a conviction that rallied the others to his cause and dampened the rising fear that Maccus had injected into their thoughts.

'It is a huge gamble that you are taking in order to return to the old world. Are you sure that it is a price worth paying? There is much to be said for our way of life here. After all, are we not masters of all we survey?'

Emrys could feel the argument swaying in the favour of his chief rival and hissed his words back between clenched teeth. 'You call this living? What we have is nothing compared to what we were robbed of all those centuries ago. You may be content to remain here and satisfy yourself with being a master of this world but I am not. I shall not rest until I have driven the life from out of every last seer and swept their world with a destruction they have never seen before. We shall have our revenge for what they did to our fellow wizards.'

The room fell silent as the wizards all bowed their heads and each of them there recalled the battle that they had fought and lost; how their beloved city of Anram had been destroyed and three of their kind killed. They knew why Emrys was so fixed on gaining revenge for their defeat.

'We all of us understand that you still bear the hurt of losing, Erin, your wife; but she was also my sister. We all of us bear the scars of that day. I would only counsel against acting too hastily and blindly where this seer is concerned; he worries me...us.' Maccus was the only one of the wizards who was brave enough to challenge Emrys but the other wizards nodded in agreement and Emrys reluctantly acceded to their counsel.

'You are right of course, Maccus, to raise your concerns and I thank you for your words, all of you. We shall keep a careful watch on what he does. If he continues to wage war on the other warlords then he will depend even more upon the Rod of Dread and that will be his undoing. Each time he uses it, he becomes more dependant upon it and its power binds him to us. Eventually he will become like us and he may join with us in our fight against the seers. It is after all what he wants himself and his knowledge of them would prove useful to us in our move against them.

Chapter 8

Foam River

Jon looked at the river; it was not very deep at this point and the crystal clear water babbled over the rock strewn bed. He wondered how they were going to get in a boat that would be big enough for all of them and yet still be able to float in this shallow stream. Looking down the wooden platform that ran alongside the river, he noticed the array of canoe-type longboats that were tethered to iron rings secured at various points. Obviously, this was going to be their mode of travel down to Rainbow Lake. They were not very deep sided and Jon hoped that they would not be going through any rough water or they would run the risk of capsizing and being swept away.

Harry caught Jon's expression of concern and reassured him that all would be well. 'There's no need to be alarmed Jon; I've travelled this way before and although it looks quite unnerving. It really is fun and we are perfectly safe in the hands of the boat handlers.'

Harry joined them and indicated that they should get into the boat nearest to them. There were several boatmen who stood around waiting for them to be seated. The head boatman gave strict instructions on where they should sit placing Braun, as he was the heaviest, in the middle. The dwarves sat in front of the metal master whilst Jon and Harry got in behind him with Hamill and Auger at the back.

With their bags secured beneath their seats, they set off. Jon was surprised that only two of the boatmen got in with them, one in the front and one at the back. There was plenty of room still for them all but the other four strung a rope between them, secured it to the front of the boat and began to haul them downstream. The shallow draught of the long boat scraped across the rounded pebbles of the river bottom as the four boatmen hauled it along. The two in the boat, back and front, used poles to direct the boat away from the banks of the river and any obstructions in the water.

Jon watched the four men in awe as they hauled the boat along. They were dressed in very simple clothing, just a short sleeved top and three-quarter length trousers. Only one of them had sandals on, the others were all bare footed. He marvelled at the way in which the four men bent their backs into the effort of keeping the momentum of the boat going along the shallow river. It was a slow journey initially as the boat scraped across the bed of the river in places but it promised to be an exciting one further down. Jon heard the dwarves talking excitedly about the rapids further down the river and he began to feel very nervous about the whole thing. He was uncertain that the boats were up to the job of getting them safely through as they navigated the rapids and boulders of the fast flowing current where the river deepened. Jon decided to place his trust in what Harry had said.

He was curious as to what Harry had been doing since they had last seen him after the episode with Ebon at Seers Tower so he asked him about it. Harry explained that he had returned to Northill where he had recovered from the wound that Tom had inflicted upon him during their fight. Captain Perkins had then sent him on a mission to the folk of the Eastern lands to gather information that might alert them of any troubles that could affect the people of Northill. Captain Perkins was a cautious man, especially after the problems of last year, and left nothing to chance. His agents were to be found, or not as the case may be, in all parts of the land. His network of spies had been quickly organised and was now established so as to be able to get word to him of any problems by the quickest means possible, carrier bird.

The agents were totally unaware of who the others were so that they could not give away any information of the network should they be captured and tortured for information by those who they were spying on. Each agent would reveal themselves only as necessity and circumstances required.

'I have been gathering information in these regions for some time and keeping the Captain abreast of any news that I thought would be of interest to him. Recently I have been relaying news of any movement concerning Amethyst and her ogre army, but I believe that you have already dealt with that problem.'

Jon was amazed that Harry should have heard about their clash with the witch-queen and wondered how he had managed to be so well informed. He was filled with admiration for this unlikely paragon of good and for Captain Perkins. The man who had saved Jon and Anna from being swept over the wall at Northill had certainly had a positive influence on the defences of the land and at Northill itself. Harry turned his head to the side and spat; wiping his chin with the back of his hand he continued as if nothing had occurred but Jon's stomach turned at the act and he found it difficult not to gag.

'Some time ago there was a group of unsavoury looking characters who passed through on their way to Winters Hold in search of work; I made some discreet enquiries about them and they seemed to check out alright.'

Jon thought it rather amusing for Harry to refer to them as 'unsavoury characters'; one look at the driver would have made any timid person avoid contact with him. Jon could not help but smile at the way he described them. He surely could not be ignorant of the way he appeared himself; but there again, maybe his appearance was contrived so as to distract folk from thinking him anything other than what he appeared to be, a driver.

Jon turned to have one last look at Ferryford as it nestled at the foot of the valley, amongst the fir trees that covered the lower slopes. Although it was a small settlement that consisted of a few wooden cabins, the tavern and a few shops; there were plenty of folk busy with some kind of work or another. Jon thought that it was obviously a place of greater importance than first sight portrayed. He wondered whether it was always this busy or whether the festivities at Winters Hold had meant an increase of business for the townsfolk.

There was little activity amongst the cabins but nearer the waters edge, where the boat yard was situated; there was a flurry of goings-on where boats had been hauled up onto trestles for repair; the blacksmiths forges were busy and the clang of metal being worked against an anvil echoed along the water.

A league or two downstream, the river began to broaden and the boatmen had to manoeuvre the vessel through channels as the cool, clear water bubbled over the submerged rocks that lay strewn across the bed of the shallow river. There were banks of shale and pebbles at various locations causing occasional little rapids and whirlpools. The air was crisp and clear, chilled by the fresh, clean water flowing into a gorge that opened up like a cut in the high rock face ahead of them. The water, charged with the power of the melting snows and glacier high up in the Eastern Mountain range, frothed with the force of its tumbling over the shallow river bed. A dull roar, as the crashing of waves on the sea shore, drew Jon's attention ahead of them; rapids.

The boatmen on board guided the boat to the bank where the other four slipped the rope from their tethers and jumped in. Taking up hand paddles and sitting at strategic points, they steered the boat into the main channel where the current strengthened and Jon clung on to the handholds in readiness for the turbulent ride over the white water.

'This is where the fun begins.' Archer bellowed over his shoulder to Jon.

Jon's stomach churned, along with the river, and he hung on tightly as he was thrown about by the lurching boat. The dwarves seemed to be treating it as some kind of fun experience, commenting to each other on the pleasure it was giving them as they were tossed up and down off their seats. With each plummet of the boat as it rode every obstacle, they would cheer and laugh, all except Leader. He, like Jon and Hamill, had never been over rapids and they were all more than a little worried that they would end up in the water and be drowned.

Jon could not see Braun's face but he did notice that he was clinging to the handholds very tightly as his knuckles were white with the effort of holding on. The big man did not say anything or make a sound of any sort; he just sat like a rock on his seat, refusing to be moved by the swaying of the boat. Water splashed on board in large quantities and one of the men was busy bailing out with a bucket.

'If this is what the dwarves idea of fun is then I wouldn't like to join them when they get scared.' Jon thought that the dwarves were quite mad. 'Don't they realise how dangerous this is?' He asked himself silently.

Eventually the water calmed and they were able to sit without being thrown around as if they were rag dolls. The dwarves applauded the efforts of the boatmen who grinned with satisfaction. They used their paddles to steer them clear of any obstructions and the sound of the rushing water receded into the background until it was silenced by the turn in the river. Jon loosed his grip but noticed that Braun still held tightly. He leaned forward and touched the metal-master on his arm whereupon, Braun jumped. 'What? Oh! It's over then? We're all safe? I mean everyone is alright?'

'Yes, Braun, we've made it through. That was quite some adventure, don't you think?' Jon asked, concerned for the big man.

'Oh yes, certainly. I wasn't scared. I knew we'd get through safely of course.' He responded loudly so that they all heard, then more tentatively. 'I suppose that there are more cataracts further down that we will need to navigate?'

Javelin turned around to answer him with a huge grin on his face. 'That was just a little one. You wait until we get to Canyon Breach, then you'll see some fun.'

'Oh! Thanks, Javelin.' Braun said with a sense of uncertainty in his voice, then leaned forward and tapped the dwarf on the shoulder. 'How long before we get there?'

'Where do you mean, the rapids or Rainbow Lake?'

'Well, both of them.' Braun replied, hesitantly.

'We should be at the rapids in a couple of hours, just about lunch time and if all goes well we should reach Foamesend, where the river enters the lake, by late afternoon. We will stop there for the night; there's a nice inn where we can get a good meal.'

Braun sat back in his seat and Jon wondered what Canyon Breach was like. Javelin spoke as if the last rapids were not as large or as fast as the ones they would see ahead. Braun tapped Javelin on the shoulder again and asked. 'Will we be going through before or after lunch?'

'Probably before; it isn't recommended that you travel these rapids on a full stomach, it's better to get through and then stop for a bite to eat. I'm looking forward to the pork pie that the boatmen give us to eat; the jelly inside is particularly good.'

Braun thanked the dwarf and sat still for a moment before sitting forward holding his head in both hands between his knees, groaning slightly.

'Are you alright, Braun?' Jon asked, gently touching his arm again.

'I'm fine; or at least I was until Javelin mentioned the jelly in the pie. My stomach feels a little sensitive after those rapids.'

'I know what you mean; though having been through them, I'm sort of looking forward to the next ones. The dwarves were right; it is fun, in a scary sort of way.'

Jon and Hamill had both rather enjoyed the experience after their initial fear had subsided and Auger had grinned mischievously at them when they reached the slower part of the river. Harry had also enjoyed the ride and spat before showing his blackened teeth as he laughed good naturedly at the timidity of the metal master. 'Not to worry Braun, with your long legs you'll be able to walk through the rapids.'

Braun smiled amiably but his lips twitched nervously as he obviously was not looking forward to the experience.

For the rest of the morning they made good progress on the fast flowing river and the boatmen kept the boat moving at a steady rate. The countryside was a joy to behold with trees and meadowland on both sides. On the north bank the land was fertile and extensively farmed. Mason told Jon and Hamill all about the land they were passing through, interspersed with personal experiences of his visits here. Digger occasionally corrected him when he got his facts wrong. It was all in good spirits and the two dwarves exchanged jibes with the older more experienced dwarves. Jon was fascinated to hear their stories and as dwarves like to talk about their adventures, there was no letting up in their tales.

Jon was particularly eager to hear about the deserts to the south. There were two of note; those to the south of Northill that stretched to the Little Salt Waters and on the other side, the Sands of Selah or the singing sands as they were sometimes called.

'Why are they called that?' Jon was curious to know.

Digger leaned closer to him and related the stories he had heard. 'That's because travellers have returned from there with tales of lost companions who have wandered off into the night and never been seen again. Apparently they are lured away by the call of the Vixens, mythical creatures that sing with such pure voices that they captivate all who are able to hear them. Not everyone can but some have spoken of beautiful singing when sitting around the camp fires at night and in the morning their friends awake to find that they have disappeared into the desert. Their fellow travellers followed their tracks until they vanished; wiped away by the desert winds.

Jon sat mesmerised by the tales of the vixens; he had heard tales before of the desert and had always wanted to see it. He tried to imagine a place like that, a vast area of sand like a sea, only without water. The heat was something to be feared, apparently, as it beat unmercifully down on anyone who ventured into its ever shifting sands. Great sandstorms would wipe away any trace of one's existence and it would be impossible to try to follow any maps as the dunes would alter from day to day. There were maps, of course, based on the rock formations and bluffs that rose out from the desert. There were guides who would lead travellers safely through but unless you had one of these guides, there was little chance of getting across alive.

It all seemed so far away and unreal as Jon took in his surroundings as they followed the course of the river and felt the cool breeze that wafted along the waters surface. Jon let his hand dip into the cold, clear water and watched the drips fall from his fingers. He thought of the river Nune that flowed into Ashbrooke and how it had always fascinated him; wondering, as a young boy, where the paper boats that he had set adrift in its current would end up. They probably had not got very far, having become waterlogged they probably never made it further than a league or two out of town. That was years ago now but the thoughts of a happy childhood, playing by the eaters edge, brought a smile to his face and he leaned his head back to bask in the warm sunlight that played on the rivers sparkling surface.

Just after midday, they heard the roar of the rapids before they saw them and realised that they were soon to experience the white waters of Canyon Breach. The water was deep and dark at this point, flowing slowly, giving no warning of what lay ahead. As they rounded the bend in the river they saw that it changed from its calm and leisurely meander, to a raging torrent. Javelin was right, the other one was just a babbling brook compared to that which lay ahead of them. The river narrowed and entered another gorge but this time the cliffs rose high above their heads and there was no way of getting out of the boat and walking around them. They had to go with the flow.

'Get ready for the ride of your life.' Archer shouted over his shoulder above the roar of the white water. Five of the dwarves were laughing with glee at the prospect of 'shooting the rapids.' Harry also seemed to be happy at navigating the treacherous waters but Leader, Braun and the rest of them were not so certain. Jon had clung on to the handholds for dear life when they went through the last one; what this would be like, he could only guess.

The boatmen positioned themselves in readiness for the onslaught; their paddles striking into the water with a fast rhythm that propelled them towards the point of no return. Braun sat bolt upright; his legs braced against his chest and his hands firmly grasping the handholds.

Jon risked a glance back at Hamill, he grinned nervously unsure as to whether he was going to enjoy this experience or not.

They were caught by the rip of the current and were thrown backwards with the force of the water as it swept them headlong towards a large rock that jutted out from the water. The swirling water smashed into them as the boatmen steered clear and avoided hitting the rock by the narrowest of margins. Down the boat went as it rode the first of the cataracts drenching them all. The dwarves in the front got the worst of it but they just cheered with glee; their beards dripping water.

Slam! Another side current hit them and they almost went over, into the roaring water. Harry grabbed hold of Jon by his belt and yanked him back onto his seat. Had he not done so, Jon would have been catapulted out of the boat and lost in the turbulence.

'Try to hold on.' Harry shouted above the roar.

Jon thanked him but his words were lost in the noise and he pitched backwards, almost tumbling out of his seat as they went over another drop in the river bed. This time he held on and did not need Harry to steady him.

'That's better, you've got it now.' The driver shouted into his ear.

There was no time to think what might happen to them if the boat actually capsized or if one of them were thrown out. All his concentration was on staying in the boat and his reactions to the movement as the boat pitched one way and then another. They were all drenched by the endless spray that erupted over them as they ploughed through the water, the boatmen paddling and steering the boat out of danger. They only hit something once; Jon felt it jar the bottom as they rode the last but one cataract before he was drenched again.

A shout went up from the boatman at the back and Jon tried to turn and see what the matter was but another jolt sent him flying into Harry and they both had to hold tightly as they went over the last cataract. The water started to ease and the boat to move more steadily. They had made it through.

Now that it was over Jon wished that they could do it again. Having faced his fear and conquered it he felt invigorated by the experience. He turned to ask if Hamill had also enjoyed it but he was not there, neither was Auger. They had been thrown out of the boat just as they rode the last but one cataract. That was what the boatman had shouted; to tell the others at the front that they had lost two of their passengers.

They steered the boat to the bank of the river and into calmer water where they halted to see if they could find the two seers. The water flowed past, topped with white foam from the torrent that they had just navigated. 'That must be why it is called Foam River.' Jon thought to himself abstractly. He was more concerned for the plight of his friend, Hamill and for Auger, searching desperately for any sign of them so that they could rescue them. Minutes went by and still there was no sign of them. Jon checked to see if their belongings had also been lost but he found Hamill's staff and pack, together with Auger's, still securely tied beneath the rear seats. Without them they would have problems, especially without Hamill's staff and his stones. That is presupposing that they survived to tell the tale. Jon refused to believe that they had gone. He remembered how he felt when Mason had been swept away in the flooded cavern last year. He had survived, Hamill and Auger would too.

Then one of the boatmen shouted and pointed towards something that was floating not far from them. Securing a rope around his waist, one of them dived into the river and swam towards what Jon could now make out to be one of the seers. His cloak was wrapped around his head so Jon could not see who it was and desperately hoped that, whichever one of the seers it was, he was still alive. He crossed his fingers and begged the powers that be that it was Hamill and that they had found him in time.

The boatmen hauled on the rope and dragged the boatman and the limp form of the seer to the river bank where they immediately set about resuscitating the unmoving figure. Straining to see who it was over the gathered boatmen, Jon sighed with relief when it was announced that the seer was breathing. Finally and much to his joy, he saw that it was Hamill, a wet and concussed Hamill it must be said, but it was his friend. He was alive and well, though still very groggy, coughing and spluttering as he lay propped up on his side. He was ashen faced and cold from the effects of his time in the water. The dwarves had stood back to allow the boatmen to administer to Hamill but now that he was recovering, they crowded round and slapped him on the back.

Javelin jested with him and berated him for scaring them. 'Next time you fancy a swim, do it in a pool, not in the middle of a rapids'

The other dwarves all made remarks of the like manner before expressing their appreciation to the boatmen for saving their friend.

'We're certainly glad to see that you are alright.'

'For a minute then I thought that we had lost you.'

'How are you feeling?' Jon asked, concerned that he might suffer some ill effects.

Hamill smiled weakly. 'I'm fine; a bit woozy but I'll recover soon enough. What about Auger? Did you manage to find him? The boat tipped and I saw that he was falling out so I grabbed hold of him but we both ended up in the water. The last thing I remember was hitting my head on something hard, probably a rock.'

'Well, you appear to be in one piece; let's hope that the rock suffered no damage when your hard head hit it.' Javelin, ever the joker, teased.

'I'm afraid that we haven't found Auger.' Jon replied to Hamill's question about the missing seer.

They all went silent and an uncomfortable tension fell on the group of friends. A couple of boatmen kept a watch on the river for any signs of the seer but he was nowhere to be found. They believed that he had drowned. It had been a miracle that they had been able to rescue Hamill. It was not very often that someone fell into the rapids but if they did then that was usually the last time that anyone saw them alive again.

Harry spoke; his voice and manner were both respectful and sad. 'What I suggest is that Hamill changes into some dry clothes and gets some rest. We will help the boatmen look for Auger; perhaps you dwarves could search along the river bank here whilst Braun and I cross to the other side in the boat and search there. Once we've landed, we can search that side and the boatmen can paddle up and down the river and see if they can find him in the water.'

It was agreed by them all to do that and they set about their task in silence. Jon and Hamill waited whilst the search was undertaken, anxious for the welfare on the dwarf-seer. Jon had wanted to join in the search but had been told that Hamill would need his companionship until they had any news. He had agreed to stay with his friend and they both chewed absentmindedly on some food that one of the boatmen had provided for them. Their minds were focused on the possibility that Auger had gone.

Some time later the others returned to report that their searching had been without success. They had not been able to find any trace of the seer and had been forced to conclude that he had drowned.

Harry squatted next to Jon and Hamill. 'I'm afraid that we must accept the inevitable. It is not very likely that we will find him without a prolonged search. His body could be caught at the bottom of the river or be tangled amongst the reed beds that we were unable to access. I am sorry for this; I only wish that I had better news for you but we must move on.'

He was right, of course, but it did not make it any easier to leave and they all felt the loss of the seer keenly, especially Hamill who chastised himself for not holding on to Auger and preventing him from falling out of the boat and drowning. Gathering their shattered feelings together, the group reluctantly got into the boat and they set off for Foamesend in the remote hope that somehow the seer would turn up.

Chapter 9

Worlds Apart

The seers had a problem to solve and the only way that Terra could see to solve it was to invoke The Montage. Whatever way he looked at things the only option he had in order to move things on was the one thing he dreaded to do. The question he had to ask himself was should he do it now or wait and see what transpired. Without Urim to advise him it was very difficult to know what to do for the best, but he was not here. The one person whom he had come to rely on these past few months was away, fulfilling a duty that needed his attention.

Urim was close to apprehending Ebon and they, the seers, had to ensure that the troublesome former-seer could never disturb the equilibrium of their world again. Too much pain and suffering had been inflicted on the folk of the land to allow one of their own, as it were, to be allowed to get away with his crimes without facing the consequences of his actions.

Sitting alone in his room, Terra felt oddly ill at ease. There had been no news about the whereabouts of the missing seers, Auger and Hamill. He had no stone with which to make contact with them, only the birds. Only one message had come in and that was from the seer Eden. She had informed him that Auger and the other two who were with him had run into trouble controlling the wind. Braun and the dwarves had gone in search of them to help them if needed.

He had sent messenger birds out to those others in the land who held the communication stones, asking for their help in making contact with either Auger or Hamill. He asked if they would let him know if they made contact with them. The colossi had said that they would do so as and when they had the time to spare; they were busy with a crucial stage of the redevelopment of their mountain city. The sprites could only communicate with them via Emerald and Terra had not been able to get a message through to the sprite world. He assumed that they too were busy with rebuilding, not just their shattered homes but their way of life.

His hope was that Emerald would use her crystal to see that they had need of her back at the Tower. Then she could return, enabling them to mount a stronger defence against the dark power of the wizards that was inevitably going to be levelled against them all.

Terra had hoped that the dwarves at Ffridd-Uch-Ddu would help in his request but he had been confounded by the reply that 'they would take it under advisement and debate the matter at their next meeting'. He was not told when that meeting would take place and had sent another message asking for a speedy decision. The mayor had replied saying that the next meeting was scheduled for the following week and he would be sure to let the seers know the outcome.

Terra was furious with them. Ever since that new mayor had been elected there was little of any good that had been accomplished. All they seemed intent upon was ensuring their own safety by completing the defensive walls around their city of Ffridd-Uch-Ddu.

'Why I've a mind to go there myself and blast that wall to pieces.' As a dwarf himself, Terra understood only too well how politics and politicians took up a lot of their time. They were a people who loved to debate things. Most of all they loved to be involved in a fight and he could not understand why it was that the Mayor was being so obstructive to his requests. In the past the dwarves had always been ready and willing to give aid where it was required as had been demonstrated by the events of last year. Something had changed and Terra Standfast, the leader of the Council of the Sight, would find out what it was and see that it was put right. It did not feel right; nothing felt right anymore.

His only hope now lay with either the elves at the Ward or Colonel O'Rourke at Northill. He had promised to try and make contact with Hamill but, as yet, Terra had received no word back from him. Every few turns of the hand for the past two days, Terra had climbed to the top of the tower and scanned the horizon for any sign of Auger and

Hamill's return with Jon or of a messenger bird. A few birds had arrived but they only carried routine messages concerning requests for advice from neighbouring communities.

Ever since that night, when he had been confronted by the image of Emrys and Liam had been unable to read the cards, he had felt a pain in the pit of his stomach. It had been gnawing away at his nerves and it was wearing him down. In all his time as leader of the Council of the Sight he had never been as anxious as he was now. The greatest threat that had ever been known to the stability and order of things was when the first seers had been challenged by the wizards. Now many centuries later, it was happening all over again; he needed to know how to act; what to do and when. If only Urim were available to advise him, as keeper of the golden tome, the history of this land, he would know what to do; but he was not here and he could offer no advice at this time.

Terra had done the only thing that he could do, considering the state of affairs; he and Liam had established an energy barrier around the Tower. It was much like the one that Ebon had created, only this one permitted the coming and going of the seers and other folk. The power that fed the defences was designed to protect against any further intrusion by the wizards and their kind. All the time seers were in control of the energy beneath them they stood a chance of protecting the folk of the land from any interference from outside of their world. The wizards must not be allowed to gain a foothold here or the entire land would be subjected to a dreadful warfare, just as it had been when they had fought against the wizards and defeated them all those years ago. Terra could not allow such a thing to happen again; he would use every means at his disposal to avoid such a catastrophe.

Unbeknown to Terra Standfast at this time, Ebon was gaining strength in his prison world of Magog as he conquered territory after territory and defeated warlord after warlord. His ambition of being sole ruler of the world of the wizards was beginning to take shape. There were thirteen warlords in total and he had successfully taken seven of them. He was more than half way towards achieving his goal. He guessed that the wizards would be aware of his activities and that he had created Jetta to be his bodyguard. What he would say to them was that he needed the folk of the land to fear him; only then could he gather the entire resources of the land behind him. Once he had accomplished the task of uniting the land, he could utilise his forces as one when the time came for him to invade the world of the seers. Ebon felt secure and confident in his plan now that he had the power at his command that Jetta represented. He was confident of succeeding in his aim to defeat the wizards and dominate both worlds.

Using the Rod of Dread filled the deposed seer with tremendous energy and he revelled in the new found power. What Ebon did not know, and was totally unaware of, was the unseen effect it was having on his mortality. As he became stronger, so his grip on life was becoming weaker; he would soon become subject to the wizards instead of their master. Had he known the full extent of the price he was paying, he probably would have chosen a different way of claiming his victories. Even by using Jetta to force each warlord into submission bound him ever closer to them as he controlled his dark angel by means of the Rod.

Ebon was working out his own fate and one day he would have to account to his masters. That day would come, and he would have nowhere to run and no-one to turn to for help. It would be far too late for that. There was no escaping the day of accountability, despite him thinking that he could outwit anyone who dared to challenge him. When the time came for him to pay the price there would be no way out and he would have to submit to the terms of his agreement. He should not have been so eager to obtain the power that he thought he needed, for by doing so, he handed over control of his destiny into the hands of those who cared little for him.

Maccus stood alone in the central chamber, staring into the pool through unblinking red eyes, observing each move that the former seer took. The wizard learned more and more about Ebon and how he worked; what it was that drove him on. He was right to have thought that he would make a valuable addition to their conclave. Never before had he come across anyone so driven by the prospect of gaining revenge on his enemies and ruling as a supreme power. Maccus pondered this and decided that he liked the rebel seer; he was dishonest, underhanded, malicious and somewhat insane. All of these qualities not only made him a formidable ally against the seers but also a powerful foe should he turn against them and that is exactly what he was expecting Ebon to do. It is what he himself would do if he was in his position.

He saw what Ebon had achieved thus far with the aid of the Rod of Dread and smiled a crooked smile. Soon Maccus would put his own plan into action but he was not ready yet so he bided his time. He was in no hurry to challenge Emrys for the leadership of the conclave. Had not Emrys become leader by similar means to those that he was employing now? For far too long the body of wizards had followed Emrys, all to no avail. They had striven for centuries to escape from their prison world and had ravaged the resources of the land. It mattered not to them the destruction that it caused or the terrible suffering that they had brought upon the inhabitants. Their only concern and the reason that they had survived for so long was to bring retribution upon the seers and to establish themselves as the only power, not just in this world but in the others as well.

Until Ebon had entered their world and a weakness had been discovered in the energy barrier between their worlds, no progress had been made in wreaking vengeance upon the seers. It was time for a new leader to take control and he would be the one to do it. When the time came, Emrys would see that he had been out manoeuvred by his brother wizard and would back down, allowing him to take control. He would recognise when he had been defeated and would step aside. It was either that or be banished from their society. Somehow Maccus thought that he might choose the latter but hoped that he would chose to stay.

Maccus saw in Ebon the chance that he had been waiting for, someone who would be bold enough to challenge them. Then, when Emrys demanded their joining with him to bend Ebon to their will, he and those who followed him would withhold their support and allow the former seer to prevail. Or so he would be allowed to think. Then Maccus would strike and wrench control of the conclave away from Emrys and enslave the deluded seer into an everlasting servitude. That, or Ebon would be permitted to join with them and become a wizard. Secretly Maccus hoped that Ebon would join with them; his attributes would enhance their collective abilities and make them even more powerful. Besides, if Emrys did leave them, there would be a vacant position in their number. If Ebon chose not to join with them then he would become to them what Jetta was to Ebon, a pet; a very powerful one admittedly but there were ways of controlling him.

The wizards had ruled here by force of will under the leadership of Emrys and all that this world had to offer them they had taken but that was not enough. Their thirst for knowledge and control had driven them to the brink of destruction when they had challenged the seers, thinking that they were the stronger of the two bodies. They had been wrong and had suffered the loss of three of their number; amongst them was Erin, wife to Emrys and bearer of the sword of darkness. She, along with Galan and Megan had fought fiercely but had been overcome by the cunning of the seers.

The seers had utilised the energy beneath their Tower to slip in and out of different worlds, gathering allies to their cause. The three wizards had tried to do the same but had been tricked and suffered a painful end, deep in the underground fortification at Anram. The three of them were there to this day, unable to remove themselves from their enchantment. Their bodies lay sealed in stone tombs and had by now turned to dust but their spirits still roamed those passages. They were forever tied to the burial chamber by the keystone through which they had tried to find others to join their cause. Now they were unable to leave Anram, unable to find rest.

Maccus and others of the wizards did not wish to return there. This was their home now.

The darkness suited them here; why should they want to return to their old world, only Emrys wanted that, so that he could be with his beloved Erin. Well, if that was what he wanted, he could have her. Emrys would be outcast from their society and sent back to their old world where he would become a shadow who stalked the passages of Anram in the company of his dead wife.

He, Maccus, the new ruler of the wizards and of the world of Magog would take control of all who had followed Ebon. There would be anarchy and death between the squabbling hordes that the wizards could glut themselves on for millennia. With Ebon's new protector becoming his to control, none would dare defy him or rise up against him. He would be the most feared wizard that had ever lived. The thought appealed to him and he gave a shallow chuckle of satisfaction.

Life, what was life anyway? Certainly not what he once was or what he saw before him in the mirror now. He, along with the other wizards who had survived the conflict against the seers, no longer lived in a mortal sense. They had passed beyond that, yet they had a physical presence that permitted them to indulge themselves but that body was wretched. Their spirits could roam at will, clothed within their gowns, all that they had been able to bring with them from their former life. The seers needed to be brought down but he had little interest in their world beyond that. Without the seers to watch over them, the folk of the land would descend into warfare and they could feed off of that through the energy that connected their two worlds. No, he was content to let things run their course and when the time was right, he would be ready to strike.

Urim held tightly to the Staff of the Portal, he had been able to use it to enter and leave the worlds of the seers and that of the wizards unobserved. He had been like a shadow, moving amongst them, protected by the power of his talisman. He had found that it was difficult to utilise all three aspects of power at his disposal. The talisman, representing the golden tome; his seers staff and his new ability to travel wherever he wanted by stepping through a door in space by means of the staff of the portal. He had discovered that the staff he had liberated from Ebon allowed him to make use of all his old skills as well as those that were available through the new staff. He had therefore left his own staff in a safe place and would retrieve it when it was time.

By utilising the power of the staff and his talisman, he had been able to bring the shadows of the recent past before him so that he could observe all that Ebon had achieved and he knew what his next move was. Being forewarned of his intent enabled Urim to take whatever action was necessary to foil his plans. He had allowed Ebon to continue unmolested lulling him into a false sense of security but Urim had decided when and where he would face Ebon and bring him to task. He had succeeded before and he would do so again, only this time there would be no escaping the penalty that justice demanded.

The staff of the portal would enable him to do that and it must be kept from ever falling into the wrong hands again. He had determined to give it into Terra's care once he had dealt with Ebon. The mystery was why Ebon had not used the staff to escape out of his prison world? Perhaps it had simply not occurred to him; then Urim reasoned that it was probably because he was no longer a seer and could have only limited use of the staff. Urim, however, with the power of his talisman was able to do far more than Ebon could do now that he was bereft of any power from the world of the seers. Ebon's control over the staff had been limited but even so he had been able to bring about many deaths through its misuse. Urim however had only good intentions in all that he did and he had not been subverted by the power that was at his command.

At last a message came through from Northill by one of the birds. It arrived late one afternoon and was delivered to Terra immediately. It concerned the missing seers, Hamill and Auger. It was not the news that he had been hoping for although he had suspected that all was not well. Colonel O'Rourke reported that he had been unable to make contact with them. At first he had thought that there was a problem with the stone he was using but it had worked perfectly well when he had contacted the elves at the Ward and then the colossi at the mountain city. He had tried getting through to Hamill again and again, at different times of the day and night; all to no avail. Hamill was simply not responding.

Something was preventing the stones making a connection. It was as if a dark curtain had fallen between them stopping any attempt to raise him. Terra sent a message back, thanking the Colonel for his assistance and pondered on what it could mean. He had suspected that there was a problem as he had been feeling a bleak darkness in his mind that could only be because of the influence of the wizards. He did not doubt for a second that they had a hand in this and he became even more concerned than he had been before.

For once Terra was at a loss as to what to do and he retired to his room to contemplate what options lay before him. He knew that by invoking The Montage he would be able to create the opportunity with which to gather strength to him, but the risks were great. He was still there in his room several hours later when Liam knocked at his door.

'I have brought you a tray of food my friend. It will do you no good to starve yourself.'

'Thank you Liam; come on in. Put the tray on the table will you. It is most thoughtful of you but I must continue for a while longer with my fast. It sharpens the mind to go without food for a time.'

'That may be true but I have observed that you have eaten very little these past few days and I am concerned for your wellbeing.' Liam leaned forward and laid a comforting hand on the dwarf's shoulder.

Terra looked up, smiled, and with a twinkle in his eye teased the old elf. 'I might have known that you'd have had your spies watching me.'

Liam stood back and made a face that expressed mock astonishment; 'Who, me? Why perish the thought. It doesn't take a deal of the cards to tell me when you are neglecting yourself. Don't forget that I've known you long enough now that I can read you like a book.'

Terra laughed, the first time that he had done so for a while, and he stroked his beard. 'Thank you Liam, I believe that you are right and I admit defeat. What did you bring me to eat? It smells rather tempting.'

Chapter 10

Foamsend

There had been little or no conversation between them on the last leg of their journey; everyone was still shocked at the loss of the seer, even the boatmen were reticent to speak. The splash of the paddles as they dipped into the water was the only sound that was made for quite some time.

Ferrymen on the quayside at Foamesend saw them coming and guessed that something was amiss as they were behind their scheduled arrival time. Jon saw the lead boatman signal from the boat to those at the wooden landing stage and there was a wave of acknowledgement in reply. Hushed conversations took place as they landed and a messenger was despatched to alert the inn of the arrival of more guests. The day was fading into darkness and the lights of the town began to twinkle into life as they drifted to a halt against the jetty.

Harry helped Jon and Hamill bundle up their belongings, along with Auger's pack and his broken staff, then assisted them out of the boat. The lights along the landing stage helped them see to find their footing so that they were able to traverse the planks without slipping and falling into the river. Still without a word the group of dwarves led them up the gentle slope towards the town where they would find the inn and the promise of a good hot meal.

The town was full of life as folk bustled around them, finding their way home following the activities of the day. They approached the three story inn, the tallest building in the High Street, apart from the church. The spire stood taller than everything else and was a landmark for all who travelled the area.

A coach, pulled by a team of snorting horses, arrived just as they got to the inn. It turned off the road and into the courtyard through the archway where it narrowly missed the corner stone, placed there to protect the main walls of the building. Livery staff attended to the horses as the passengers disembarked, stretching the stiffness from their aching bodies; clearly grateful to have reached their destination. House staff collected their luggage and led them through to the reception where they were allocated accommodation.

The travellers were talking of the events that had transpired at Winters Hold at the time of the festivities and of the battle that had taken place between the defenders of the city and the ogres.

'I was so pleased that Lord Hidel decided to hold the games after all that had happened. It would have been a shame not to have continued with the festivities.' One male passenger said.

'I think it was lacking in respect for those who had died during the invasion of the city.' A female replied.

'I can understand your feelings Christine but I have to agree with Gerald, I think that it was the right thing to do. Besides, what a games it turned out to be with that metal-master winning for the second time. Whoever placed a bet on him doing it again would have won a pretty penny, I can tell you.' One of their companions said.

'Don't tell me that you bet on the dwarf to win, Adam.' Gerald exclaimed.

'I'm afraid I did, much good that it did me. He was robbed of the title, I'm sure of it. Those judges must have been blind not to have seen what happened.'

'Oh come on now Adam. It was all within the rules of the games, besides, the dwarf had an unfair advantage because of his height, or should I say lack of it.'

They all laughed and then seeing the dwarves begged their pardon saying that no insult had been intended. Javelin bowed his head slightly and replied that none had been taken but even so the passengers from the coach hurried away feeling rather uncomfortable.

The desk clerk welcomed them to the inn and informed them that they had already been allotted rooms, a messenger from the waterfront had told him of their arrival.

'Will you be taking the coach to Northill in the morning or continuing on by the ferry at midday?'

No-one seemed to know which option they would take so Harry spoke up for them all. 'We will be boarding the ferry so will not need the early call to breakfast, thank you.'

'Very well gentlemen, the valets will show you to your rooms. Will you be requiring dinner this evening? It is served at the seventh turn of the hand in the food hall. I can reserve places for you if you wish.'

Jon was hungry but did not feel like eating; even Hamill uncharacteristically showed little interest. A black cloud had settled over him and he appeared distracted and distant. When asked about having an evening meal he was somewhat reluctant to commit himself to eating. That was not like Hamill at all but they put it down to his feelings of sadness at Auger's loss.

'Um, well, I suppose I ought to have something to eat. What about you Jon? Are you going to have a meal?' He said with a distant look in his eye.

'To be perfectly honest with you I don't have much of an appetite but I know that I'm hungry, so we should really have something or we'll not be able to sleep later.'

Harry encouraged them with a friendly smile but there was sadness in his eyes. 'Now come on you two; I sympathise with the way you are feeling but the simple matter is that you have to keep up your strength so I strongly recommend that you do have a hearty meal and a hot drink. You'll feel better for it afterwards, believe me.'

Having organised the dining arrangements for them all; they were shown to their rooms by eager young lads who took their packs and bundles. They respectfully accepted their guests need not to be engaged in conversation; having obviously been apprised of the situation regarding Auger beforehand. News concerning the loss of a passenger on the river travelled fast and everyone they saw was polite and gracious. They had been allocated single rooms which were very comfortable and Jon looked forward to getting a good night's sleep having had an interrupted night previously, what with Hamill, Urim and the imp.

Jon wondered, as he got ready for dinner, what it was that Ebon had in mind for them and how he was going to accomplish it from his prison world. Jon thought that this journey back to Seers Tower could actually be as eventful as his previous wanderings, declaring out loud to no one. 'There was me thinking that all our problems were over. No wonder the seers are constantly busy if this is anything to go by.'

Having washed and dressed in fresh clothes Jon felt a lot better; he was actually looking forward to eating now and was glad Harry had persuaded him to join everyone for the evening meal.

They all sat at a large table that had been specially laid out for them in an alcove of the food hall. It afforded them a bit more privacy and they were able to settle down without interruptions. As the evening progressed and the relk and ale was passed around, the tension that they had all felt began to melt away and they were able to laugh a little at things from the past. Javelin proudly showed off the scar from the wound that he had suffered when fighting the gnomes at Northill and set about recounting the tale, with a few embellishments. He was encouraged by his fellow dwarves and the flagons of relk were constantly refilled so that there was never any shortage of it.

They were getting rowdier and more boisterous as their consumption of it increased but Jon knew that, despite their high spirits, they were not being disrespectful to Auger. In fact it was quite the contrary; whenever a dwarf fell in battle or on a quest, they were lauded by their friends and this is what they were doing for Auger; immortalising his name in a saga. The story was far from over so the ending was not yet known but the telling of the tale deserved to be done properly. Javelin raised his beaker and called for a toast. 'Here's to Auger; favoured to become a seer and to keep the ways of the land. May his name never die; Auger.'

Everyone stood and drank the toast but before they could sit down Jon proposed another toast. 'Here's to absent friends, long may they continue to live in our hearts and in our minds.'

'To absent friends.' Cups, beakers and flagons were emptied and Braun called out for more, a look of joy beamed from his face; the drink was having its affect and he slurred his speech. He sat down heavily and belched then giggled before his head went back onto his chair and he started to snore.

Harry stood and proposed one more toast, saying almost reverently. 'Raise a cup to our good friend the metal-master, Braun; noble and dependable; as true and faithful a travelling companion as you could wish to find.'

'To Braun.'

The Wizards of Magog

The big man continued to snore and they all laughed, settling into different conversations around the table, they relaxed and began to let the sorrow of Auger's parting slip away from them. Auger would have approved.

One person who approved, but for a different reason, looked on in satisfaction as the friends sat around the table. Ebon stood in front of his viewing-window, watching the scene out of the eyes of the one he had managed to bring under his power. He would use this 'puppet' to aid him in bringing the powers of both worlds into his hands. He wanted to know what stage his plans were at concerning Jon and Hamill. He saw that Auger was not amongst the group and discovered that the seer had been lost. 'Excellent; I am glad to see that things are going according to plan. That will be one less seer I shall have to worry about. It will take them too long to find a replacement for him. I shall have completed my plans and dealt with them all before they have a chance to even think about it. Things couldn't be going better.'

Darkness enfolded the sanctuary that Ebon called his own; Jetta stood not far from him, ever ready to do his mater's bidding. Dark and silent, never sleeping but constantly alert. Crackles of black magic would explode over his body like tiny fireflies waiting to erupt into life like some dormant volcano. None who opposed Ebon dared move against him now, Ebon doubted that even the wizards would prevail if they were to challenge him in his quest for power and glory. He had succeeded in subjecting the last of the warlords to his will and he was now the commander of all the land's armies. It was almost time for him to show his hand but he must make certain that he could maintain control over his 'puppet'.

Combined with Jetta's abilities, he would soon be in a position to challenge the wizards. First he needed to control the power that separated their worlds. He had been able to bend it to his purposes before when he erected the barrier around Seers Tower. Now that he knew how he could tap into the negative side of the energy beneath the land of his former world he would unleash such forces that both worlds would tremble. Seers and Wizards alike would sue for peace and submit themselves to his will; then he would exact his revenge for all the wrongs that had befallen him; none would be spared. They would act as an example to all who would stand against him and he would reign supreme.

All he needed for him to succeed was to take control of a seer's staff and open up the keystone that lay deep beneath the buried city of Anram. That was something that he would have no difficulty in doing. What he had to do was get his 'puppet' to find the keystone and place his staff in the centre; the rest would be simple.

Jon dreamed he was in the garden where he and Anna would walk hand in hand, talking together and basking in the feelings that they had for each other. This time however it was different; he was sombre and downcast as he related to Anna the loss of Auger on their journey down the river.

'Jon, you must bear these things, for such is our lot. None of us knows when our time has come to depart for the next life. All we can do is to live our lives as well as we can by doing good to those we encounter along the way.'

'You're right of course but it does not take away the sting one feels at the loss of a dear friend. I find solace in the times when we are together and I look forward to our meetings yet it does not wholly satisfy my need to be with you.'

'Nor I you, beloved; we must be content with what we have, then, when our time comes to pass on, as it surely must, we can be together always.' Anna's reassuring presence and calming words soothed the worries and sadness of his heart away and he smiled as he looked into her sparkling eyes. She was right, she always was and he was grateful to have these fleeting moments together. They were becoming few and far between but they always occurred at just the right time for him. When he needed to see her the most, there she would be, resplendent in a flowing dress drenched in sunshine. The peace of the land she was in reminded him of the sprite realm and he loved his visits there almost as much for that as for being with Anna.

Morning came and he lay snuggled in his cot for a few moments savouring the memory of his dream. He knew that it was more than that though and he would recall each time with her in such clarity that it was almost as if she were with him all the time. He prepared himself for the day, packing his belongings and making ready to leave. They had until midday at Foamesend before the ferry would take them across the lake to Northill and his spirits lifted in expectation of meeting Captain Perkins again.

Hamill was already in the food hall and helping himself to the breakfast treats. Jon smiled warmly seeing that his friend had recovered from the melancholy they had all felt weigh heavily upon them. Jon too felt a new lightness about him following his conversations in the night with Anna. 'I see that you have regained your appetite.' He said to his friend.

Hamill nodded as he could not say anything due to a mouthful of cereal he was chewing. Eventually he swallowed and replied stating. 'The dwarves taught me a valuable lesson last night; that it did no good to mourn the loss of a friend for too long. Rather one should celebrate their life with the memory of who they were and to continue to do so. They bade their farewell to a fellow dwarf and although he is gone, he will never be forgotten.'

'Yes, they do have a way of being able to accept whatever happens with great dignity. I admire them for that. Have you seen any of them yet?'

'No, they were up earlier along with Braun and Harry. They left word with the desk clerk that they were going down to the landing stage. Apparently they have gone back up the river to search again for any signs of Auger before we leave.'

The two friends sat together in silence for a while, lost in their own thoughts; then Jon had an idea. 'Hamill, do you think that you could find where Auger is by using your staff?'

'I don't know; I hadn't thought of it. I might be able to, it's certainly worth a try, but I don't know how to.'

'What if you were to use the stone the colossi gave you to communicate with the other stones, maybe by using your staff you could get it to show you where he is.'

'Yes, it might do at that. Jon, you're amazing; let's give it a try.' They hurried up to Hamill's room and locked the door so that they would not be interrupted in the attempt. Hamill held the stone and staff then closed his eyes. The staff let off a green vapour that arched over the seer's head and filled the clear stone where it swirled around before forming into shapes. Hamill opened his eyes and stared into the stone, searching for what he wanted to see. Gradually a picture emerged from the green fog and the still form of the dwarf could be seen lying tangled in a reed bed just below the rapids that had claimed his life and almost cost the life of Hamill as well.

Tears stung in their eyes as both Jon and Hamill saw the picture in the stone before it vanished into the green fog then cleared as the power within Hamill's staff was withdrawn. They now knew for certain that the seer was dead and there was nothing they could do to change that.

'I should forward a message to Seers Tower and let them know of Auger's passing. They will need to start looking for a replacement. They don't have a stone there yet because I have charge of it so I shall have to make contact with Colonel O'Rourke and ask him to send a messenger bird informing the Council.'

Hamill stared into the stone, concentrating on sending the message but nothing happened. He tried again without success and scratched his head in puzzlement. 'That's strange; it doesn't seem to be working. I'll try to contact Janine Tanner at the Ward instead, if I can do that, she can relay the news to Terra Standfast. Again there was no response from the stone; it was almost as if it had lost the ability to work as it should. Hamill was becoming desperate and tried contacting the colossi but again there was no response.

'I can't understand it; the stone obviously works because it showed us where Auger is but it will not act as a means of communication anymore. Something is amiss here and I am at a loss as to what that might be.'

'Do you think that Ebon might have something to do with it?' Jon asked almost fearful of the fact that he might have.

'I guess he might and if he does then we need to be even more careful in what we do. We should not underestimate him; he is determined to wreak his revenge on us all. Come Jon, we must get a message to the others about where to find Auger and break the news about the stone too.'

Hurrying down to the waterfront, the two of them found a boat and its crew ready to paddle up stream. Telling them of their need to find the others the boatmen jumped into action and they were soon making their way back up towards the rapids. The going was slow as they fought against the current and Hamill became impatient so he moved to the back of the long boat and sat next to the steersman. Placing his staff into the water he summoned the power within it to propel them against the flow of the river and they made good headway. Before long they saw two boats ahead of them, searching the waters on either side of the river. The dwarves were in one with Braun and Harry in the other.

They waved a welcome, amazed at how Hamill had been able to propel the boat along at such a speed. When they had drawn close enough Hamill explained what he had been able to see in the stone. The three boats made towards where Hamill had indicated and sure enough, tangled in the reeds and hidden from sight, they found the body of the seer. Hamill stayed in the rear of the boat, not wanting to witness what he had already seen in the stone. Self-recrimination hit him hard for not managing to save the dwarf seer but Braun comforted him; telling him he had done everything that he could, nearly losing his own life in the process. Hamill tried to smile but his eyes were too red and his face frozen in remorse.

The journey back to Foamesend was as silent as it had been the first time. Having located and retrieved Auger's body, they made their way straight back to the town. It was decided that they would wait until tomorrow to take the ferry to Northill. There would not be enough time to make the preparations required for the shipment of Auger's body to Seers Tower. They wanted to ensure that he would receive the burial that befitted him, in the tombs of the seers.

Finding Auger's body finally brought it home that the seer had gone. Jon and Hamill had secretly been hoping that he had simply been lost, washed ashore where they could not find him and that he would eventually turn up safe and sound. It was not to be; Auger had drowned. The faithful and valiant dwarf had been overcome by the torrent of water that flowed through the gorge. It was rather a sad end for the seer; being a dwarf he would have preferred to have given his life in battle. Instead he had become victim to an accident but at least his body would be returned for his burial when they could honour him properly.

Chapter 11

Journey to Northill

Arrangements were made for them to accompany Auger's body and to return to Seers Tower via Northill by taking the noon ferry tomorrow instead of today. It had been decided that they would cross the lake to Northill and stay there for the night then continue down the River Lune to Seaview. From there they would travel by ship up the coast to Landfall and the final leg would be completed by coach. Hamill and Jon had hoped to visit with Captain Perkins for longer but under the circumstances, that visit would have to be curtailed. They looked forward to their overnight stay but they would have to continue their journey the next day.

The rest of the day passed slowly but their mood brightened as time went by and the evening meal was eaten with a little more gusto. One could not help but be cheered by the joviality of the dwarves and their tales of fighting the gnomes. It seemed that the two races were constantly at variance with each other, resulting in skirmishes and sometimes major battles. These were more prevalent in the border regions where the boundary line between dwarf and gnome was constantly being contended.

Hamill had been encouraged by Braun and the dwarves to put behind him any thought of failing Auger. He had not; accidents happen and unfortunately there was nothing anybody could do to change things. Gradually Hamill's melancholy lifted and he even suggested a game of sticks. Jon really did not want to play as he knew how keen Hamill was and he always seemed to win. On the odd occasion he did not, he would sulk and Jon did not want his friend to fall any deeper into depression than he had been these past couple of days. However if no one wanted to play, that would depress him even more so Jon decided, that for the benefit of his friend, he would play a couple of games. Braun and Harry joined them but the dwarves decided that they would visit some of the other taverns in Foamesend; just to get the real flavour of the town, so to speak.

'Don't make too much noise when you come back, there are other folk staying here as well you know.' Jon said, smiling, knowing full well that for a dwarf to be quiet after a few rounds of relk would be almost impossible.

'We'll be quiet as mice, I promise.' Archer replied grinning mischievously.

The six dwarves left them to their game, bidding them goodnight. 'Don't wait up for us; we'll likely be late getting back.' Javelin said over his shoulder as they went out the door.

'We'll be lucky to see them before lunchtime tomorrow if I know anything about dwarves.' Harry remarked good-naturedly then spat into the bowl placed beside his chair by the landlord.

'Why do you chew that awful stuff anyway?' Jon had wanted to ask Harry for some time and could not put aside his curiosity any longer.

'It's a habit I picked up when I was working incognito, shall we say. I haven't been able to give it up since then. Oh, I know it's bad for me and one of these days I'll stop doing it; I just haven't got around to it, that's all.' Harry held his hands up defensively and grinned, showing his blackened teeth.

Jon really liked Harry, despite his chewing habit, or maybe it was partly because of it, he didn't know. Anyway, he would rather be here, sitting in his company along with Braun and Hamill than anywhere else right now; except maybe with Urim.

The games of sticks held their attention for some time as round after round went to Hamill, which pleased him no end. There were a couple of times when Harry looked like he would win but then just at the last he would make a mistake and the game would go to Hamill. Jon was not certain whether the driver was doing it deliberately or not until Harry winked at him when, yet again, he made a mistake in Hamill's favour.

As for Braun, with his large hands he was not very good at the game at all and was always the first to drop out. He would laugh at his own clumsiness each time and a warm feeling of camaraderie pervaded the niche in the corner of the room where their table was situated.

Jon yawned and stretched. 'Well, I don't know about the rest of you, but I'm about done in and am ready for a good night's sleep. I admit defeat and vote that we recognise Hamill as the master player.' He raised his hand as did Braun and Harry. 'Let it be a lesson to us all, never to play sticks with Hamill ever again.'

'Oh, come now, that's not fair. Who else am I supposed to play with?' Hamill pleaded in mock complaint.

'Well, if things don't work out for you as a seer you could always make a living out of playing sticks for money.' Harry whispered, not wanting to broadcast the fact that Hamill was a seer. Most folk accepted that he was a physician from the Ward. It was what Hamill had intended for folk to think, which was not that difficult seeing as that is what he used to be.

Braun and Jon laughed at the thought of Hamill being a professional gambler and the metal-master gave him a playful slap on the back. It made him choke on the mouthful of ale he had just taken and he spluttered to get a gasp of air.

'Braun, if that was a friendly pat on the back, I would hate to be on the receiving end of one that you meant seriously.' Hamill choked as he spoke, still trying to get a proper breath of air into his lungs.

The three friends went to their rooms but Harry decided to stay up a little longer and take a walk. He was accustomed to doing so just before retiring. 'It's amazing what you can learn from folk at this time of the day. I have been able to gather very interesting facts in the past. I shall not be long though; I'm feeling a little tired; good-night my friends, sleep well.'

'Good-night, Harry.' The three of them replied and stumbled off to their rooms, yawning and stretching as they climbed the stairs to the second floor where their rooms were located.

Hamill felt in much better spirits than he had earlier and was quite talkative. He even spoke of Sylvia, something that he had not done for quite some time. Unfortunately for Hamill, Jon was too tired to listen and fell asleep almost as soon as his head hit the pillow, leaving Hamill alone to his thoughts.

The young seer rested with his hands behind his head, staring at the ceiling, thinking about Sylvia and wondering how she was doing as the new physician at Winters Hold. He fancied that she would do an even better job than he would have done. Reflecting on things, Hamill realised that he would not have been happy there as the court physician. He preferred to be out and about and not stuck in one place. He had come to appreciate the open road during his time learning the arts of a physician, right up until the time he had met Jon and Anna.

Turning to look at Jon as he slept, Hamill was grateful for their friendship and wondered how Jon coped with knowing that Anna was no longer with him. Then he remembered that Jon had told him that she was not dead and was still able to communicate with him. Hamill envied him that; no matter where Jon went, she would always be able to speak with him and Jon with her. Sylvia on the other hand was in Winters Hold and for all Hamill knew he would never visit there again. He decided not to think on it anymore and turned over to give in to whatever dreams came to him. As he closed his eyes a single tear dropped onto his pillow and he was asleep.

Morning came and Hamill awoke with a renewed feeling of energy. The melancholy that had pressed down on him lately had gone and he felt that he could face anything that was asked of him, only let it not be sailing in rough waters. If there was anything he had not been able to deal with, it was the feeling of being sea-sick and he was not looking forward to the sea trip from Seaview to Landfall. If he could have done, he would have travelled by coach but it would have taken too long compared with the sea voyage. He put the thought behind him as there was a long way to go before he had to worry about that.

He tried to use the communication stone in an attempt to contact Colonel O'Rourke but still nothing came through; it remained clouded and opaque. Hamill could not understand why it had ceased to work and hoped that there was nothing wrong with those he had tried to contact. He had supposed that it was the stone that was at fault, but what if it was the other stones that were not functioning because of some calamity that had occurred. He reasoned that it was far more likely to be his stone that was experiencing the problem than for all the others to cease working.

Jon and Hamill met with Braun and Harry for breakfast but there was no sign of the dwarves.

Harry said to them as they ate. 'I didn't think we'd see them. They would have been rather late getting back to the inn; it was after midnight when I got back and there had been no sign of them. The desk clerk told me that they would have to ring for the night porter to let them in.'

'It's rather unusual for them to have gone off and left us on our own but then we have always had to guard against any surprises before. I suppose they thought that there was no danger to guard against and decided to make the most of it.' Jon offered by way of explanation.

'Well, they're missing a really good breakfast, that's all I can say.' Hamill was back to his normal self and had piled up a large tray with a variety of foodstuffs.

Harry looked on in amazement at the quantity of food that Hamill proposed to consume; he had not eaten with them before when Hamill was hungry.

'Don't worry Harry; we've all become used to him now. I must say that it's good to see the old Hamill back with us.' Braun smiled broadly and went to give him a slap on the back but remembered the effect of the last one and settled for a gentle pat on the shoulder which Hamill appreciated.

Just as they were finishing their breakfast the main door opened and the six dwarves walked in, bright and breezy. 'Good morning all.' Trapper greeted them cordially. They were still wearing the same clothes they had on when they left last night.

'Have you been out all night?' Jon asked amazed at how alert they all were if they had been.

'Yes, we caught up with some old friends who told us that since Amethyst had been dealt with, trade between our two nations have begun again. What's more the marauders in the hills are being rounded up by the ogre army patrols. The roads between us will be a lot safer than they were before.' Javelin fairly brimmed with excitement at the prospect of being able to move freely again in that region of the land.

'That is good news indeed.' Harry replied with a thoughtful nodding of his head. 'We shall be able to open all roads throughout the south east beyond the Eastern Mountains because of that.'

'To think that we are at last able to live in peace with the ogres after all this time; Jericho is obviously being true to his word.' Mason added.

He had always wanted to be able to travel those areas and delve into the ancient past of their races by excavating certain sites. Digger too was keen to return home and make preparations for an expedition. The two of them chatted animatedly about where they would go and what to do first.

'Of course Jon, Hamill, we will want to accompany you to Seers Tower first, before we even consider going home.'

'Thank you.' Jon replied. 'We would be glad of your company.'

There was a lot of commotion as the dwarves settled themselves down for a hearty breakfast and if Harry thought that Hamill had a good appetite, he was even more taken aback by the amount the dwarves consumed.

A man from the landing stage at the river approached whilst they were still eating and asked Harry if they still intended taking the noon ferry to Northill.

'Yes we shall all be going.' Then, taking him aside, Harry whispered so as not to distract the others. 'Have the arrangements been taken care of for the transportation of our friend's casket. We would not want there to be any mishaps.'

'Everything has been arranged just as you asked Harry. I saw to it myself.'

'Thank you Luke, I appreciate your help.' Harry gripped the man's arm with a firm grip of gratitude.

'Not at all, there's nothing that's too much trouble for a good friend. When do you think you'll be passing this way again?'

'Not for a while, there is something I must do before I can set out on any more errands.'

Intrigued by Harry's comment but knowing him well enough not to ask, Luke shook hands with him. 'I'll see you off at the ferry then. See you later.'

Returning to the others Harry suggested that they get packed as soon as possible so that their belongings could be transported to the docking point for the ferry. That would give them enough time for one last look around Foamesend before the ferry arrived. They would need to be ready to board a half-turn of the hand before noon. They should take care not to be late as the ferry would not wait for any latecomers.

They were all present at the appointed time and started to go on board; there was no need for any cabins as they should be in Northill by late afternoon, all being well. The journey across Rainbow Lake was never a bad one but on occasions a strong wind had blown up and delayed the ferry's arrival. The weather looked clear and so Hamill particularly was grateful for what promised to be an uneventful crossing. The passengers were all instructed to stay in the saloon area until they had got underway as the crew needed to raise the sail and would need free access to the decks whilst they did that.

Watching the men go about their tasks was fascinating to Jon as he had never been on the ferry before and he marvelled at the dexterity of the men as they clambered aloft by means of the rigging and set the sail. It billowed into life in the moderate breeze and soon they had cast off from the staging and manoeuvred out into the deeper water, headed towards Northill.

Jon looked forward to a happy reunion with the friends they had made there last year. In particular he was keen to meet up with Captain Perkins and Colonel O'Rourke who had fought with him against Ebon and his gnome army.

The word came that they could leave the saloon if they wanted to go on deck and take some air. Not needing a second bidding Jon made his way along the corridor to the observation deck with Hamill wobbling along behind him hanging on to the rail for support.

'Come on Hamill, what's the matter? You're acting as if there was a storm outside.' Jon encouraged his friend.

'Don't joke about it please it makes me queasy just thinking about it.' Hamill replied gripping the rail tightly and holding his stomach with the other.

'Ha, ha; don't tell me you're feeling sea-sick; we've only just left the landing stage and it's as smooth as the duck pond back in Ashbrooke.' Jon laughed at Hamill's comical attempts to steady himself when the ferry hardly rolled at all.

'I think I'd rather wait inside if it's alright with you; I don't think the air would do me any good.'

'Alright, Hamill, if you'd be happier; I want to have a look outside but I'll come back in a little while. Are you sure you'll be alright?' Jon asked his friend, a little concerned when he saw how the movement of the ferry affected the seer.

Hamill didn't answer him he just nodded then turned around and made his way gingerly back to the saloon where he hoped he could sit the journey out. The dwarves were also in the saloon playing cards; they had made this journey several times before and made use of the time to relax. Harry stretched out in a comfy chair with his wide brimmed hat pulled down over his face and his feet up on a stool; clearly not wanting to be disturbed. Braun sat watching the dwarves play their game but looked up when Hamill came back in, wobbling uncertainly on his feet. The seer steadied himself on the furniture as he found a deeply upholstered chair and sank gratefully into it. He closed his eyes and covered his face with his hands before sighing and settling down to try and sleep. Braun got up and walked across to him and asked how he was feeling.

With one eye remaining firmly closed Hamill looked up at the large man and just groaned, holding his stomach as if it were to be parted from him somehow.

'Oh, I see; feeling a little queasy are you? I'll let you alone then. Jon outside is he? I think I'll join him, we don't want him falling overboard now do we?' He grinned then realised what he had said. 'I'm sorry Hamill; I forgot about what happened to Auger.' Not knowing what else to say, Braun shuffled out of the saloon feeling a little uncomfortable because of his inappropriate remark.

Braun found Jon at the bow of the ferry enjoying the feel of the wind on his face. 'Hello Jon, I thought that I'd join you, Hamill isn't feeling very well and I inadvertently joked about you falling overboard without thinking about what happened to Auger.'

'Oh, well, try not to worry about it, he's probably feeling too ill to have noticed.' Jon replied, trying to reassure the gentle metal-master.

The slight wind drove the ferry smoothly through the clear waters of Rainbow Lake. Jon could see why they called it that as the colours were vibrant on the tiny drops of water from the bow as it cut through the ripples on the surface. The lake spread out ahead of them with no sign of the other side; all Jon could see was a thin dark line with two small lumps on it. Jon asked one of the sailors, who passed by, what they were; he explained that they were the two high spots near the lakeside, the old city fort of Northill and Clee Hill. Fascinated with the news Jon could not wait until they drew nearer and he could make out the features of Northill. He wondered whether he would be able to see the funicular railway from the lake.

Looking down into the water he was amazed to see shoals of brightly coloured fish swimming just below the surface. They were obviously the rainbow trout that the lake was named after; this type of fish normally swam in rivers but this was the only place that they congregated in large numbers. That is probably another reason why the lake was named Rainbow Lake, after them. He watched them for ages, fascinated by the flashing to and fro as they followed alongside the ferry. He supposed that all it would take to catch one would be to throw a line over the side; one could not fail to catch a fish they were so numerous.

Jon and Braun went back into the saloon to check on Hamill and found him asleep; Harry was also asleep snoring gently under his hat. The dwarves were still engaged in their game of cards, puffing away on their pipes producing a cloud of smoke above them. Some of the other passengers were sitting at the other end of the room so as not to be too close to the obnoxious smelling weed the dwarves were smoking.

Dwarves loved it but it did nothing to enhance relations with other folk from around the land. Jon and Braun were invited to join in a game or two and Braun decided that he would but Jon preferred to go outside again rather than sit in a smoky room. He scanned the horizons in front and behind them and saw that they were about half way across; the two rises in the landscape that were Northill and Clee Hill could be seen much clearer now and the fortification atop the old hill fort was easily discernable.

The crossing took four turns of the hand to complete and they reached the staging not far from Southill as the light was starting to fade. Standing on the jetty, waiting for them to arrive was one of the officers from Northill. It was Captain Perkins and Jon waved a greeting which was returned

Chapter 12

Northill

Jon was delighted to see his old friend Captain Perkins again and wondered why he was waiting for the ferry to arrive. Then he remembered that Harry was one of his agents and supposed that he was waiting for him there with new orders. The passengers all had to go back into the saloon again whilst the ferry was secured to the landing stage and they were asked not to smoke; this brought a welcome smile to those who did not appreciate the smell of the dwarves' weed.

The group of friends disembarked and Captain Perkins greeted them all with a hearty shake of the hand and a pleasant smile.

'Jon, I am so pleased to see you; when I was told that you were arriving today I cancelled all my duties so that I could make suitable provision for you all.'

'You knew we were coming?' Jon asked in amazement then looked at Harry who was grinning and nodding his head. 'Yes, I included a message about you in the report I sent by bird to the captain. He is aware of all that has happened since we met the other day.' Harry explained before seeing to the unloading of their belongings; in particular, Auger's casket.

Hamill was grateful to have his feet firmly planted on solid ground again and was as pleased to see Captain Perkins as Jon but he was still feeling a little unsettled by the crossing and held his hand on his stomach as he walked. He really did not look very well, grimacing as if he were in pain.

'Are you alright Hamill? You seem to be in discomfort.' Perkins asked, concerned that Hamill might be displaying signs of the sickness that had been prevalent in Northill.

'I'm fine thank you; really I am. It is just that I don't travel well on water. I shall be well enough in a moment or two.' Hamill reassured him.

Jon smiled in a caring way and nodded to the captain that what Hamill had said was true. Perkins turned his attention to their needs and told them that he had arranged accommodation for them all. 'I have not forgotten that some of you have the freedom of the city so special arrangements have been made to celebrate your return. All are included of course.' He said looking at the other dwarves who had not been party to the battle against Ebon and his forces last year. 'Follow me; I expect that you will be surprised at how much we have accomplished in rebuilding the two cities since you were here last. Let me show you the earthworks that we started recently. Our first priority had to be the buildings that were damaged in the siege and the restructuring of the walls in Southill.'

Captain Perkins proudly escorted them through a series of turns that wound between banks of earth that labourers were busy constructing on the meadows below the huge walls that surrounded the city. He led them into the lower city of Southill where many of the houses were still being repaired but there had been a lot of progress made. These buildings had been virtually demolished when the gnome army ransacked it; smashing windows and setting fire to some due to their frustration at not being able to get to the service tunnel. Jon wondered what had been done to protect it, now that it was known abroad where the entrance was located.

As the group passed through the narrow streets towards the lower gate of the funicular, they were able to see how quickly the repairs had been completed to the damaged buildings inside the walls. It was an astonishing accomplishment in such a short time. Captain Perkins watched their response then had to admit it had not been all down to them.

'The colossi helped us considerably with the major work; we were hard pressed to keep up with them at times. They worked wonders with getting things back to normal and with helping design the new defences. What do you think of it?'

'I have to say that I'm impressed.' Jon said amazed by what he had seen.

'If you think you're impressed with what you've seen so far, wait until you see the funicular and gatehouse.'

The group progressed through the streets that were starting to get busy with folk returning to their homes from their places of work. Many did not give the group a second glance but there were others who remembered them from when they had been here with Urim and nodded politely giving them a friendly smile. The dwarves chatted excitedly about their time here and explained to Leader, Digger and Mason what had happened as they progressed through the streets. They pointed out various buildings that featured in their story, namely the house where they had sheltered before going, in disguise, amongst the gnomes.

They entered the small square where they had battled with the troll and gnomes before entering the lower tower to the funicular. The gatehouse had been completely rebuilt following its near total destruction when the gnomes employed the trolls to demolish it in search of the service tunnel. Looking above the tower, Jon saw the higher end of the funicular as it reached the upper gateway built into the great tower. He remembered being on the top of the tower when Captain Perkins had rescued him and Anna from being blown off during the storm that had swept over the fortress and surrounding area.

'Do you notice anything different here Jon?' Perkins asked with a glint in his eye, waiting for his response.

Jon searched the railway track and gatehouse but could not see that anything had altered from before.

'Look at the entrance at the top, can you see that there is now a fortified door where the cars enter the tower. That means that when the car is not at the top, no-one can get in. As the car approaches it triggers a cantilever that opens the door allowing it to dock at the station.'

'That's amazing; you promised that you'd make a few changes and I can see that you've been true to your word. This place is even more secure than it was before.'

'There's a lot more than this, believe me; when we've finished no-one will ever want to besiege us again. Look at the top of the walls up there in Northill; can you see that they have been extended out? Well that allows us to drop all kinds of things on any attackers below; anyone trying to scale the walls would not stand a chance. It is not completed yet but eventually it will be added to the walls right the way around Northill. Let's go in to the lower gate; I want to show you more.' He led the way in; everything had been rebuilt following the destruction at the time of the siege.

Jon noticed straight away that there was no lower stairway to the service tunnel. 'Oh! I see that you've blocked the way to the lower entrance. How do you get in from here now?'

'That, I am afraid is restricted information, for obvious reasons I cannot tell you. You understand I hope?'

'Yes, of course. I had wondered what measures had been taken to protect the entrance. Sealing it off like this is a wise thing to do.'

'Come on, let's board the car that will take us up to Northill, we'll get you all settled into your rooms then see about having something to eat.'

'Great, I'm famished.' Hamill said; eager to eat now that he was starting to feel better.

'I see that your appetite is as good as ever. Congratulations, by the way Hamill, on becoming a seer. We were all pleasantly surprised at the news.'

Hamill nodded. 'I bet you were not half as surprised as I was?' He chuckled.

Captain Perkins knocked on the door to Jon's room, after a few moments Jon opened it. 'Are you feeling up to a quick guided tour of the battlements? The view has changed somewhat from when you last saw it.'

'Yes, I'd love to; we have an hour to spare before our meal. Let's call for Hamill; I'm sure he'd like to come as well.'

'Oh, he's with Colonel O'Rourke at the moment; I don't think that he'll be free for a while yet.'

Jon was a little surprised but then thought that it was probably the sensible thing for Hamill to do; he was a seer after all. He would want to apprise the colonel of their situation and try to get a message through to Terra Standfast at Seers Tower that they were on their way back and also inform him of Auger's demise. That was something Jon did not envy his friend. It would bring back painful memories for him. Jon had noticed how Auger's death had troubled Hamill and despite the seer's apparent good humour of late, Jon knew his friend well enough to know that he still blamed himself for the seer's death. An air of despondency hung on his shoulders like a lead weight that dragged him down.

Others had noticed it too and had tried to cheer him up and Hamill had rallied his senses but Jon saw deeper. There was something not right about him; something that Jon could not see or comprehend, a shadow had fallen over Hamill that clouded his features and furrowed his brow. To anyone else the seer appeared to be perfectly alright but Jon knew differently. He made a conscious decision to keep an eye on his friend; to be at hand should Hamill need any help.

He made a mental note to talk to Braun about his concerns; he knew that the big metal-master had grown to like Hamill, despite his earlier annoyance with him when they first travelled together. Perhaps, between the two of them, they could watch for any sign of the dark mood getting any worse. The last thing they all needed was for Hamill to suffer a breakdown of some sort.

Captain Perkins led Jon along the corridors; they were quiet now compared to when he was last here with the hustle and bustle of soldiers rushing from place to place. Now they passed only a few as they made their way up to the top of the great tower. He remembered it well and walked out onto the top stage with a little trepidation, holding onto the side walls, steadying himself from dropping to the floor as his knees were shaking. He was surprised to be feeling this way, he was not usually scared of heights, but the memory of nearly being blown off the battlements that night of the storm unsettled him. Gulping down his fear he stepped forward determined not to let it get at him and he grew calmer.

'Are you alright Jon?' Perkins asked, seeing how Jon was reacting.

'Yes, I'm fine now, thank you; just for a moment I felt a bit giddy, it must have been all those stairs.' He didn't want to admit to his misgivings, feeling that it was silly.

Jon saw that the enhancements to the top of the ramparts had indeed made it possible to better defend against assault and was suitably impressed with what the folk of Northill had achieved so far. What amazed him even more was the view that greeted him across the lower Yield.

It was beautiful now; trees and grass had been planted and grown as far as the eye could see. Even in the fading light Jon could see that it must have been a huge effort to have done this. The trees must have been brought in from other places and replanted as they could not have grown to this size in less than a year. There were orchards full of fruit trees and clusters of bee hives; the land further round to the east, along the banks of the River Lune had been ploughed and planted. It was a real transformation from the muddy battlefield it had been turned into when he was here during the confrontation with Ebon.

'It's a pity that you can't stay for longer; there is still a lot more to see and I'm excited at the progress we are making.'

'You certainly have achieved a great deal; you must be very pleased with the results.' Jon complimented his friend.

'Thank you Jon, I am. It's just a shame that we have to go to these lengths in order to have safety in the land. Still, it is because of these defences that we can have that peace so I suppose it achieves what is intended. You must be hungry by now, shall we go and get our dinner. We might even get there before Hamill.'

'Oh I doubt that.' Jon laughed.

They did get there before Hamill, but only just; they stood ready to choose their meals from the hot buffet that had been prepared when the seer hurried into the dining hall. 'Huh, you beat me to it. I had trouble getting away from Colonel O'Rourke, he would insist on asking me questions about what had happened at Winters Hold. Never mind, at least I didn't miss dinner. It smells lovely; what have we got?'

They looked at the menu displayed over the serving counter and made their choices then took the food and sat together at a large table, leaving enough room for Braun and the dwarves. The three of them had almost finished their main course when the others arrived amid the clatter of trays as the place became busier. No sooner had they all sat at the table when Hamill jumped up and excused himself saying that he had some things to do.

'I'll see you at breakfast. I checked with Harry and apparently the boat to Ebb-Lune leaves mid morning from the jetty. That means we can have a lay-in if we want. See you in the morning.'

'That's strange.' Jon half whispered to himself.

'What's strange?' Braun asked, catching the comment and the bemused look on Jon's face.

'Oh, nothing; I guess we all deserve a good rest after what we've gone through these past weeks.' Jon's comments went largely unnoticed and they continued with their meal.

Colonel O'Rourke came into the dining hall and Jon motioned for him to join them, which he did. 'Hello Jon, it's good to see you again. I see that Perkins is looking after you, is everything to your liking?'

'Yes, thank you. You know your meeting with Hamill earlier caused him to miss being first in the queue for the meal, we beat him to it, which must be a first.'

'I'm sorry, I don't understand, I haven't seen Hamill yet; I've arranged to meet with him afterwards; he sent me a message saying that he had important things to arrange. Having dealt with Urim in the past I've learned never to question a seer so I agreed.'

Jon and Captain Perkins exchanged glances and the captain shrugged his shoulders with a look of 'but that's what I was told' on his face.

'Oh! Well, perhaps Hamill meant that he was seeing you afterwards; but why did he leave so quickly? It's very unlike him.'

'Who can fathom the mind of a seer; they have a way all of their own from what I've seen. Colonel O'Rourke suggested and continued with his meal.

Jon was confused and a little concerned about Hamill. He had been behaving strangely of late, ever since they were at the village after being dropped to the ground when Auger lost control of the wind. He decided that the colonel was probably right. It was almost impossible to understand the thoughts of a seer and yet Jon thought that he knew Hamill better than anyone else. He let the matter drop from his mind and continued his conversation with Captain Perkins.

'I have to admit that I'm looking forward to going inside Seers Tower at last. It's just a shame that we can not stay here a little longer because we have to continue on our journey tomorrow.'

'I'm sorry to appear a little confused Jon; did you say that you were going to Seers Tower? I thought you are going to Anram?'

Jon looked at Perkins nonplussed. 'Did you say, Anram?' Jon exclaimed and the others in the company stopped eating and talking to listen to their conversation. 'Why would we want to go to Anram? I thought it was an ancient ruined city, buried by the sands of the desert?'

'Yes it is; well, I could be wrong; perhaps Hamill is planning on going there on his own. All I know is that he has arranged to go there tomorrow. I was going to talk to him about it after dinner.'

Jon could not understand why they should be going to Anram and not back to Seers Tower as arranged. Surely Hamill did not intend leaving them all to travel back without him and what had happened to cause this change of plan? Hamill was becoming more and more like Urim in that he kept things close to himself and did not share any information. It was so annoying; Jon had hoped that the friendship between Hamill and him meant that they were able to relate to each other. This demonstrated that he had been wrong about that.

Jon had been right about Hamill's mood change and this latest revelation was giving him cause for concern. Why would Hamill lie to them about his meting with Colonel O'Rourke and then tell them that he was retiring for the night only for the colonel to say that he was having a meeting with the seer afterwards. Another thing that troubled Jon was Hamill's reference to having a lay-in tomorrow when Jon knew that Hamill got up early now, as part of his regime in being a seer. These inconsistencies worried him because this was totally out of character for his friend but he decided not to say anything to the others, not yet anyway.

Chapter 13

A Message of Importance

Following the evening meal, Jon could not settle; his mind was filled with worries about Hamill and he was confused about what the colonel had told him. He had been pacing his room for some time trying to understand what was going on. He had even gone up to the battlements and sat looking out over the darkened fields and the lights of Southill below that twinkled and fluttered as draughts caught the flames of the lanterns. He recalled the time that he had been here with Anna when Ebon was encamped against the city with his gnome army.

They were hazardous times and he had mixed memories; the joy of having Anna with him and the friendships that had been forged through adversity. That was all mixed with the sadness of losing some of those friends both here and at Seers Tower. He let out a time weary sigh, shaking his head slowly as if to remove the painful memories from his mind.

After some thought on the matter in hand he decided that he needed to talk with Hamill about his concerns and find out why Colonel O'Rourke and Perkins were under the impression that they were going to Anram.

Making his way to his friend's room, he knocked on the door; there was no answer and when he tried the handle he found that it was locked. Either Hamill was inside and did not want to be disturbed or the seer was somewhere else. Jon did not know what to do so he went to Colonel O'Rourke's office in the hope of finding out more about Hamill's plans. Jon could not understand why Hamill was acting the way he was; he had obviously taken Auger's death harder than they had all thought.

Reaching the colonel's office he knocked on the door, there was the sound of movement from within so Jon opened the door and poked his head into the room where he found the colonel going through some papers. 'Oh, hello Jon; I was expecting Hamill to arrive, he's a bit late; have you seen him?'

'No I haven't; I was hoping that you had seen him. I've been looking for him but he doesn't seem to be anywhere. I came to see you in the hope that you would be able to enlighten me on what Hamill had said about going to Anram.'

The colonel looked at him with just a hint of surprise for a moment before replying. 'I'm afraid that I have told you all I know and that information came to me via one of the sentries who reported that he had been approached by the seer. Apparently he had wanted to know if there was anyone that knew their way across the desert.'

Jon chewed his lower lip, bemused by what the colonel had told him. 'Colonel, I am more than a little concerned about Hamill. He has been behaving strangely of late and has been more secretive than he ever was before. I went to his room to talk to him about it but he wasn't there and I don't know where he is.'

'You don't have to worry about me Jon.' Colonel O'Rourke said but it was Hamill's voice Jon heard. The colonel seemed to wobble and Jon thought he was having trouble with focusing his eyes when Hamill appeared where the colonel had been sitting.

'Hamill; what are you up to? I've been worried sick about you; why couldn't you tell me that we were going to Anram?'

'That's because we are not; I am but I shall be taking some soldiers with me as an escort. You and the others will be continuing your journey to the Tower and I shall join you there after I have completed my mission.'

'What mission?' Jon asked; surprised at what Hamill had said.

Hamill looked through glassy eyes and spoke though his mind was elsewhere. 'I am to close the opening through which the wizards could return.'

Jon sat down in surprise at what Hamill had said. 'Wizards; what wizards? When did you know that you were to go there?'

'I received a message through the stone that I should meet with another of the seers there.' Hamill said, still with the same dazed look in his eyes.

'Is it working again then?' Jon asked, surprised that Hamill had not said anything to him about it before.

'Yes.' Hamill was no more responsive than that and he continued to look into space with a vacant expression on his face. Then he came to himself and looked surprised to see Jon there.

'What did you say Jon? I think I must have had my mind elsewhere.' Hamill's expression returned to one more natural to him.

'Oh, nothing; I was just wondering whether you wanted to play a game of sticks?' Jon thought quickly so as not to make Hamill think he was unsure of his friends actions. The point about playing sticks was a test that Jon had put to him almost without thinking.

'Not just now thank you; I have some things to attend to. I'll see you in the morning; goodnight.'

Hamill walked from behind the desk and left the room, Jon was left standing there shocked and bewildered. This was very unlike his friend; he had never known Hamill to pass up an opportunity to play a game of sticks and his vagueness was so uncharacteristic. Jon decided that he should find the others and tell them about it so he made his way to the rest area that they had been shown earlier, hoping to find them there. He smelled the smoke from up the corridor before he even reached the room. The dwarves were relaxing and smoking their pipes; Braun was nowhere to be seen; obviously he had wisely decided to be elsewhere.

Jon approached the dwarves who considerately extinguished their pipes. 'Javelin, my friends; there is something that I must talk about with you, it concerns Hamill.'

Jon shared his concerns with them and his fears about how Hamill had been behaving including the meeting he had just had with Colonel O'Rourke, who had turned out to be Hamill in disguise.

'You are right to be concerned, Jon; we too had noticed a change in his behaviour but had not wanted to worry you. Now that you have shared your feelings with us we can all be vigilant for any oddities we observe. As for him going to Anram without us; it shows just how little he knows us. We would not dream of letting him leave us behind. We shall be ready to travel with him just as soon as he is ready to leave. Leader, I suggest that you organise a watch so that we will be alerted as to when Hamill tries to sneak out of Northill. Now then Jon, let's you and I find the real Colonel O'Rourke and notify him of our plans.'

As the two of them approached the colonel's office, the sergeant of the guard stepped forward and asked what their purpose was. 'Oh, it's you sir; my apologies but I have to protect the colonel from unnecessary intrusions.'

'That's quite alright sergeant. May we speak with the colonel on a matter of some urgency?'

'Of course, sir; if you would wait here for a moment, I will let him know that you want to speak with him.' The sergeant went in and muffled voices could be heard from the office; then the door opened and they were ushered in. The sergeant left them alone and closed the door behind him.

'Colonel O'Rourke sat back in his chair clasping his hands. 'Well now Jon, Javelin; what can I do for you?'

'This may sound rather strange colonel but is there any way we can verify that you are indeed the colonel?' Jon asked, trying not to sound impolite.

Colonel O'Rourke was stunned, taken by surprise by the unusual request but he smiled and nodded his head. He had learned from his experiences before when they fought Ebon together to trust Jon and the dwarves. Lifting his voice he called for the sergeant and within moments the door opened and the sergeant entered, ready to handle any given situation, except the one that he encountered. 'Sergeant, would you verify that I am who I am?'

'I beg your pardon sir?' The sergeant asked nonplussed by the order.'

'It's alright sergeant; it is just that a situation has developed that requires you to confirm my identity.'

'Well, yes sir, I can confirm that you are Colonel O'Rourke.' The sergeant clearly showed that he was totally bemused by the request.

'How long have you been in attendance with the colonel this evening sergeant?' Javelin asked, raising his eyebrow inquisitively.

The sergeant looked at the colonel and was given the nod by him to answer the question.

'Apart from when he had something to eat, all day sir; I or one of my men have him constantly in our sight, for security reasons you understand.'

'Does that satisfy you both?' The colonel asked calmly.

Jon and Javelin nodded.

'Thank you sergeant, you may leave us now.'

The sergeant did so wondering if what he had just experienced was real or a dream.

'Our apologies sir but we had to be certain' Jon said sheepishly.

'Not at all; it was rather amusing actually' I've never before had to have my identity confirmed in such a way and to see the expression on the sergeant's face was worth it. Now, as I said, what can I do for you?'

Jon explained his concerns over Hamill and recounted his experience earlier when Jon had thought he was speaking to the colonel but in fact it had been Hamill.

'Of course, if what you have told me is correct, and I have no reason to suppose otherwise, then you would naturally want to know if it were really me you were talking to.'

Jon went on to tell the colonel all that had happened to them since leaving Amethyst's coven, being as brief as he could. 'So you can see why we are concerned.'

'Indeed and your plan is to go with Hamill when he leaves in the morning?'

They both nodded.

'In that case there is no time to lose, I shall see to it that you are properly provisioned and will have you alerted when Hamill is ready to leave. No-one can do so without my authorisation. We are still trying to recover from the effects of that sickness. You needn't be alarmed, we are all in good health now; it is merely a precaution on my part. I am sending a report to Terra Standfast about your safe arrival and to tell him about Auger. Do you wish me to inform the seers at the Tower about your plans?'

'If you would please colonel; I think it may be as well to do so. Hamill told me that he received a message through the stone but it had not been working properly for some time and I am worried that he may be mistaken.' Jon explained and thanked the colonel for his assistance.

'Not at all; I am only too pleased to be of assistance. I wish you well.' he stretched forth his hand and shook Jon and Javelin's hands.

Making their way to their rooms Javelin decided that as the colonel was going to tell them when Hamill was leaving he would let Leader know that a watch tonight would not be needed. It would be better for them all to get a good night's rest.

'I shall see you in the morning then Jon, sleep well.'

'Thank you Javelin; I hope you sleep well too, good-night.' Jon made ready for the night and had his belongings packed ready for a quick start tomorrow. He was tired but found that he could not sleep. He tossed and turned trying to get more comfortable but it was his mind that felt uncomfortable, not his body. Eventually he did drift off to sleep but it was to troubled dreams of Hamill but instead of it being his friend it was Ebon and he was behaving just like the rogue seer.

A thick darkness fell over Jon in his dream and he found that he could not control his body; it was as if someone were pulling the strings of his mind. A maddened laughter echoed throughout the large hall he was in and he was being forced to walk forward towards what looked like a circular stone. The dream ended and he finally fell into a deep and restful slumber, imagining himself in the realm of the sprites where the soft strains of music soothed his troubled mind.

'Jon, wake up quickly, Hamill has gone. He left a message with the guards not to disturb us and he left at first light.' Archer was rushing around in an animated frenzy, urging Jon to get ready as quickly as possible. Jon found it difficult to take in what Archer was telling him but eventually it sunk in that Hamill had deliberately left them behind. Rushing to get dressed, he hurried to join the others who were already gathering at the funicular. Captain Perkins was there making sure that all was in order for their journey. He had organised four soldiers who had experience in the desert to travel with them.

'I have packed provisions enough for a week but you will need to refresh your water supply at the several oasis marked on the map that my men have with them. You would be hard pressed to find them without their knowledge. Hamill has a couple of turns of the hand head start on you but you should catch up with him before he gets to Anram. Take care and don't listen to the vixens, if you should happen to hear them, they will lead you astray and that would be the last we ever saw of you. Good luck my friends.'

Captain Perkins closed the door of the car and the sound of water rushing through pipes and tanks signalled the commencement of their descent to Southill. The view from the car was breathtaking. The sun bathed the plains before them and they saw the River Lune cutting through the lower Yield. Beyond that there was a lush green landscape that stretched to the horizon. Somewhere beyond the vegetation lay the desert wastes, endless dunes of sand with no shelter from the heat of the sun. It was there that they hoped to catch up with Hamill and find out what it was that was driving him to Anram.

Hamill pressed forward without a guide or the safety of any soldiers to accompany him. He would have preferred to have had some company but he knew that what he had to do would carry some element of danger and he did not want to be distracted by having others around him. He knew that he had to achieve his task before the wizards could arrange to invade the world of the seers. The message from Terra had been short and confusing. It was as if he had been talking through syrup; he hardly heard what the leader of the seers had said and no image came into the stone. All Hamill knew was that he had to be at Anram in a few days in order to prevent the biggest calamity of all time.

It was because of the urgency and the risk that was involved in this errand that he had decided to leave the others behind. He had not wished to place them in danger and so had withheld his plans from them. With any luck, Hamill thought, he would have completed what he had to do before the others caught up with him. He knew that they would follow him; there was little he could do about that but at least by having such a good head start he hoped to have spared them from what might lay ahead. To ensure that he got away without them noticing he had told the guards to leave his friends to sleep as what he was about to do was something he had to do on his own. Because he was the seer and the one they assumed was in charge of the party, they had followed his instructions and not woken them.

It was not until Colonel O'Rourke went to his office in the morning that he found a message that had come in by bird at break of day from Seers Tower. It was in response to the colonel's message that Hamill had received his instructions and was proceeding to Anram as requested. In it Terra had written with haste and great concern, telling him that he had not sent a message to Hamill. Being troubled by the news, especially after what Jon and Javelin had told him, he asked the guards about Hamill and they reported what had happened. He immediately ordered the others to be woken and to have Captain Perkins report to him at once. He had placed the captain in charge of the outfitting of the group last night and he turned to him to ensure that everything had been arranged and would be in place in time for them to go after the seer. The captain was as good as his word and they started out soon after the colonel had learned what had happened.

Jon, Braun and the dwarves were now in a desperate race against time to catch up with Hamill. Whoever had sent him that message it was not Terra and fears were growing for Hamill's safety. Terra did not know the content of the message that Hamill had received but had guessed its importance and despatched a messenger bird as soon as he could, warning Colonel O'Rourke of the danger they were all in. Hamill must be prevented from getting there alone; Jon was instructed to find his friend at all costs.

Pushed on by the urgency contained within the message from Seers Tower, they set a fast pace, being aided by travelling on horseback until they reached the desert. The dwarves particularly enjoyed the ride and behaved as if they were on a fairground attraction. They were used to walking everywhere so to be able to ride was a great pleasure for them. Braun's mount was of a different breed to the others and was more used to hauling cargo freight but due to Braun's build he needed a stronger horse.

They reached the edge of the desert after some hard riding and stopped at an inn to have something to eat. They were all hungry as they had not stopped to eat breakfast so tucked into their meal with relish.

'Take care not to eat too much, we have a long way to go and we need to be able to push ourselves beyond our best efforts. You will not get far on a full stomach.' Javelin advised.

Sparing little time to prepare, they set off out into the desert, following the four soldiers who were to lead them through the treacherous sands in safety.

Chapter 14

The Search For Hamill

Hamill had been given a horse to use on the first step of his journey with instructions to leave the animal at the inn he would find at the edge of the desert. From there it would be returned to Northill with the next group of soldiers that came through. There were regular patrols so there was no need to worry.

He had made good progress, despite being unused to riding and after seeing that his mount was properly stabled he set off into the desert heading into the south. He forged ahead whilst the terrain was easier to travel as he knew from his studies of the maps that the journey would become much harder. He would have to call upon all of his resources to overcome what he knew lay ahead.

Several hours later he had made good progress; he had come to the dunes and the change in terrain had just started to slow his pace. The sun's heat was starting to make its presence felt as it climbed higher into the cloudless sky. Looking back the way he had come he thought that it would be safe enough to try using Auger's talisman and call the wind. He wanted to traverse the remainder of the desert to Anram without having to slog his way through the sand.

Taking the whistle from his pouch he put it to his lips and blew; no sound was emitted but he knew from when Auger had used it that it was a sound not audible to the ear. Using the power within his staff to control his calling of the wind, he waited a few moments before feeling a stirring on the hot air. Looking out into the desert wastes he saw a faint twist of sand spiralling its way towards him. He smiled with satisfaction;

he had not been too confident of being able to control it so the sight of it coming his way filled him with relief.

As the funnel of wind came closer, a bright blue flash sparked within its swirling mass and Hamill thought that he saw a figure appear inside it. Within moments the spinning column of sand wavered in its course and it veered off back into the desert. No matter how Hamill tried to recall it, by repeatedly blowing on the talisman and raising his staff, it steadfastly refused to return. He was left standing there astonished and frustrated at what had happened.

He was certain that he had seen someone appear in the wind but could not understand why his control had been wrenched away from him. Who but another seer could have the power to take the wind away from him? What he did not understand was who would do it and why? Perhaps the power in his staff was insufficient to overcome whatever or whoever it was he had seen. He tried to call it up several more times but eventually put the talisman away and sighed wearily. It appeared that he would have to travel through the desert on foot after all.

For him to have been able to call up the wind successfully only for it to be snatched away from him was disconcerting. Turning over the possibilities of who it could have been in his mind he ruled out Auger, who would have been the first one he would have suspected. He also discounted Eden and Elise as they would still be with the ogres helping them to establish the forest again. As far as he knew, Emerald was still in the sprite realm, Terra and Liam would still be at the Tower and would not leave it unattended.

Surely Ebon could not be responsible; he was banished from the world of the seers and imprisoned in the other world. Besides, Ebon had been overcome by Amethyst's magic when it had caught him through the reflector. Then he remembered what Jon and Urim had told him about the imp and his message from Queen Ella. Ebon was still very much a threat to them and if what the imp had relayed were true, then Hamill needed to be on his guard. He concluded that it must have been Ebon somehow, but how? The only other possibility was that it had been Urim; but why would he do it? He did not understand and put the matter to the back of his mind, concentrating on the task in hand.

His immediate need was to get to Anram. He thought about using his own talisman to become something more suited for travelling through this dry wasteland and tried becoming the colossus, Holdhard. He made the transition without any problem but the weight of the stone man made it very difficult to walk in the dunes. He then tried being a grist but as he flew up into the air the currents that blew above the desert surface were so strong that he was driven back as opposed to going forward. He could not catch a thermal that would lift him above the disturbance so he had to abandon that idea. It was with some reluctance that he had to admit that the only way he was going to get to Anram was on his own two feet. He groaned inwardly at the prospect of doing so but pressed forward, determined to complete the task that he believed Terra Standfast had placed upon him.

Jon and the others found the going was fairly easy at first; the sand was compacted and flat, meaning that they could travel without becoming too exhausted. There were tracks in the sand that were confirmed to be that of the seer and they followed the trail south towards Anram. When night came there was a discussion as to whether they should continue on, navigating by the stars with the light of the moon to illuminate the way. They decided that as long as it was safe to do so they would continue to follow the tracks and rest later. Any ground they made up on Hamill would be welcome.

Eventually the soldiers called a halt and they rested for the night with the resolve to start again before it got light. The dwarves volunteered to take turns in standing watch, leaving the others to sleep. In six turns of the hand they would need to be up and moving again. A stick was placed in the ground and markings laid out so that they could tell what time it was by the shadow it cast from the light of the moon.

Dark images filled Jon's mind again and he had a restless night, dreams of being chased by Ebon who stared at him through maddened eyes across the gulf that separated them.

Morning broke and it was time to start after Hamill again. The day arrived too quickly for Jon but he was more concerned about his friend than he was about any loss of sleep. At least he did not have to stand a turn at guard duty and had managed to get a full night's sleep, despite feeling as if he needed at least another few turns of the hand. Pushing forward again at a blistering pace, they made good headway before the heat of the sun started to sap the energy from them. Their water was rationed so that they would have enough until they arrived at the first of the water holes. Jon was desperate for a drink but resisted draining his flask; he knew the soldiers were right to restrict how much they drank.

The lead soldier halted their march forward and studied the tracks left by Hamill. 'It would appear that he has gone off at a tangent to the course he should be following. If we stick to our route we may catch up to him before too long as this way is shorter. If you are unaware of these things you can be travelling for leagues out of your way. It would appear that is what has happened to Hamill. We can follow after him if you like or we can take the shorter route, the decision is yours; what do you want to do?'

Javelin turned to Jon who nodded towards the south, the shorter way. 'I agree; we will follow your advice and go the other way. Hopefully we will be able to catch up to him before too long.'

They were allowed to take a sip of water before continuing. The dunes were becoming harder to climb now and a lot of effort was required but fortunately, before they had travelled very far, the terrain flattened out and they were able to make good headway again. Had they chosen the other trail that Hamill had taken they would have had to traverse a vast area of shifting sand dunes

The heat was making their journey uncomfortable now and Jon missed his footing several times as he stumbled across the desert surface. He fell on to one knee and Braun, who was staying close to him, hauled him back to his feet, dusting him down. 'Are you alright young Jon?' The kindly metal-master asked him.

Jon nodded breathlessly and plodded on through the sand, the sweat stood out in beads on his forehead and his throat was sore with the want of water. He supposed that the others were in much the same condition so he did not complain. Looking at Braun, Jon marvelled at how he managed the heat. Whether it was cold or hot, the metal-master seemed to be able to cope with whatever they faced.

A breeze wafted across the floor of the desert sands cooling the air by its movement. It was still hot air but because it moved it felt cooler and brought a welcome relief to the travellers as they struggled to keep the pace set by the soldiers who led the way. Whilst the breeze had been greeted with thanks it also meant that it could be the precursor for a sand storm. That was something they would rather do without as it would hold them up and time was of the essence. The only consolation was that Hamill would also have to deal with it.

They were travelling along a dry river bed that ran through the canyon that had been carved out of the soft sandstone hills that surrounded them. Hamill would have had to climb the gradient where the rock started to rise out of the sands, making the going heavy. The soldiers told them that there were more dunes the way Hamill had gone which would mean that he would be making slower progress. They, on the other hand, could make better speed by following the course of the river bed where it was far less arduous a journey.

The wind began to increase and soon they were battling against it as it stirred up the loose particles of sand around them. The leading soldier signalled for them to make for the base of the cliff some way off to their right so they all turned aside and headed for the cover that it provided. No sooner had they made it to the cliff than the sky darkened and the wind began to blow harder.

'A sandstorm is headed our way; you'd all better cover yourselves to protect against the sand or you will be blasted by it.' One of the soldiers shouted against the rising howl of the wind and the sand started to sting as it blew into their faces. They managed to cover themselves with their cloaks and blankets, in fact, anything that would shield them from the sting of the sand particles. Jon was somewhat relieved to be able to stop and rest and the heat had dropped to a more manageable temperature. As he sat curled up in his makeshift shelter he could feel the wind clawing at the edges of his blanket like fingers, trying to rip it away from him and expose him to the full blast of the storm.

He did not know how long they had been sheltering as he had fallen asleep but it must have been some time because, when he was awakened by the silence that followed the howling of the wind, he was buried up to his waist in sand. Pulling the cover aside, he looked around and saw that they had all been similarly covered by the wind-blown sand at the base of the cliff. A few of them were standing up and shaking their clothing free of any loose particles that had managed to work their way underneath. Jon stood up, dragging his legs out of the bank of sand that had been blown up around him. The desert storm had blown itself out, leaving behind it an altered landscape. Naturally the cliffs were still there but the floor of the canyon had been changed by the shifting of the sand. Several dunes had formed nearby where there must have been an eddy caused by an outcropping of cliff face that trapped the swirling sand.

Shaking off the last few grains from their clothes, Jon and the others followed the soldiers away from the shelter of the cliffs and continued to head south. The soldiers told them that they would soon come to a steep escarpment that they would need to ascend. It would be quite a struggle as it was made up of loose shale and for every step forward they ran the risk of slipping back two or three. This shorter route, that they had taken in order to catch up with Hamill, had its challenge and this was it. Before long the great slope came into sight and Jon gasped as he took in the height of it.

They stood at the foot of the loose shale and Jon wondered whether they had made the right decision in coming this way after all. The soldiers, guessing what they were thinking, assured them that, despite the difficulty it presented, it was by far the quickest route. Once they had made it to the top, there was a clear run to Anram, albeit across the desert. Hamill had taken the longer course and they would catch up with him in a little while.

The soldiers organised them into a line with the dwarves following the corporal and another soldier who would take the lead. A rope was secured between them to prevent anyone falling and hurting themselves, or others. Jon and Braun were to come after the dwarves with the other two soldiers at the rear. Checking that everyone was ready, the corporal started up the slope, dislodging several loose stones. What they had been warned about was true, for every step forward they would struggle to make progress. There were several large boulders lodged in the slope and corporal made towards the first and nearest one, walking carefully across the loose stones rather than straight up.

As he progressed, with the others following in his footsteps, they hardly seemed to make any headway at all but slowly and carefully they ascended the slope. Jon held on to the rope to help give him some stability but he slipped several times, as did others. Gradually they edged their way up to the top from boulder to boulder across the face of the shale, first one way and then another.

There were several moments that gave them some concern especially when Braun slipped; he fell onto his face and slid quite a way down the slope. Jon had thought that he was going to be dragged down with him but he dug his heels in and managed to stand on his feet, trying to hold the big metal-master from sliding too far down. Jon nearly fell down himself as Braun's weight tugged on the rope in his hands. Fortunately the soldiers were able to hold them and Braun gingerly got to his feet again. It took them longer to scale the slope than Jon had thought but at last they managed it without anyone being injured.

They stopped to rest and recuperate from the arduous climb but could only do so for a short time as they needed to find the first oasis before dark.

'We must get going if you want to find that seer of yours; he will not be too far ahead of us now.' The corporal said as he wound the ropes up and secured them in the packs.

Wearily Jon got to his feet and readied himself for the chase; shielding his eyes against the sun he established that it was early in the afternoon. The heat of the day had not arrived yet but they would be out in the midst of the sand when it did.

The dwarves marched on without complaining whilst Jon, although not outwardly doing so, wished that they were somewhere cooler. They trudged through the sand desperate to find the oasis. At one point Jon thought he saw the trees that indicated that they were near until they vanished in the heat haze. It was a vision and not the real thing; it lay perhaps many leagues away and only appeared to be on the horizon. It tantalized them with false hope and made their thirst more acute.

The corporal stopped and inspected the ground, signalling for Javelin to join him. They squatted down and searched the sand ahead of them then looked to the side, pointing away across the sands. Javelin nodded and returned to tell the others what they had found. He was quite excited and told them that they had found Hamill's tracks. They had come in from the east and now they were following the same course as them, going south. It was impossible to tell how far ahead he was but it was more than possible that they would meet up with him at the oasis. He would be foolish to go any further than that today, as would they.

They followed in Hamill's footsteps for some time before they crested a dune and sighted the trees that surrounded the life giving pool of water. Jon thought that it was another vision but this time it did not vanish and his heart soared within him. Soon they would be able to quench their thirst and Hamill would have to explain why he had left them back at Northill.

As they made their way across the sand towards the trees they could see no sign of the seer but they were some way off yet. As they drew nearer Hamill stood and stared at them in disbelief. His shoulders sagged and he sat down holding his head in his hands. 'I knew you would come after me but I had hoped to complete my task before you found me.'

'Why, Hamill? Why did you leave us?' Jon asked; wanting to know.

Hamill looked up at his friend with a faint smile. 'I wanted to spare you all the danger that I must face. The message I received from Terra Standfast warned me to make haste and I believed that I would make better time on my own.'

'Hamill, the message wasn't from Terra, Colonel O'Rourke was sent a message by bird telling him so and that we were to find you at all costs.'

'But if he didn't send me that message, who did?' Hamill asked, astonished at what he had been told.

'I don't know but Terra said something about wizards from Magog; do you know anything about them?'

'Yes, a little and that is more than I want to know. If we are being faced with a conflict with the wizards then we had better be more vigilant than ever before.'

'Well, I believe that if we are to find out if it was the wizards, we must continue on as though you were still following the instructions you were given in that message.' Jon tried to encourage his friend and placed a consoling hand on his shoulder. 'Tomorrow we will all travel together and find the city of Anram where I am certain that this mystery will be solved.'

'You are right Jon; I don't know why I ever thought that I could do it all on my own. Thank you for being such a good friend; you, Braun and the dwarves. Without you all I would have failed long ago.

Chapter 15

Wizards' Conclave

Emrys and the other wizards had not been idle in the time that Ebon had been gathering strength to himself. The rebel seer may have control over the warlords, he may even have that dark angel, Jetta constantly by his side but there was one thing he did not have; the ability to see ahead. Just as the seers utilised components of the earth to reveal future events to them through Emerald's crystal and Liam's cards; the wizards also had their means of discerning what was to come.

They had built their fortress around The Pool of Possibilities that they had discovered shortly after gaining power over the ruling body of Magog. True it did not always show them what would happen, only what might be; yet it had served them well in defending against others who had thought themselves invincible. Every one of them who had thought to outwit the wizards had perished and been forgotten to history; only the wizards remembered them and had grown wise as to the ways of men.

It mattered not to them that Ebon had control of the armies of men in this world. It held no threat to them that a creature of magic, Jetta, had appeared in the land. True it had given them some cause for alarm when he first appeared but quickly realised that Jetta was controlled by means of the Rod and although Ebon wielded it, they controlled it. Once that fact had been established he had ceased to be of any concern to them. All that mattered was that they held the key to the future of this world and nothing that Ebon would do or could do altered that fact.

They had exercised dominance ever since their arrival in this once pleasant land and they held its future in their hands still and would not be moved out of their place. Ebon would be confounded in his attempt to overthrow them. He would come to realise that although he thought he was serving his own ends, ultimately he would discover that he had been acting for them all along.

The conclave of wizards had become aware of his entrance into their sphere of existence when he had been snatched from the world of the seers. They had, at first, wanted to capture and torture him by every means at their disposal. He was a seer and that was all they needed to know for him to be the object of their attentions. Deposited here amongst the hostile and inhospitable factions that ruled the land under the watchful glare of the wizards he had soon made a name for himself. They had seen him rise to the challenges of this world and had taken a keen interest in his progress. They began to realise that through Ebon they had found an opportunity to return to the world of the seers and to inflict upon them all the full weight of their hatred.

Ebon, unaware of the interest he was attracting from the wizards, recruited others to his cause, flattering them with promises of wealth and power. The fact that Ebon had none to give them at that time did not prove an obstacle in his rise to power. He promised them much in return for their loyalty to him and rewarded those who were faithful to him with the spoils of war.

His following had grown in number and ferocity, in cunning and in treachery. Often Ebon had narrowly escaped the assassins' blade as first one and then another of his chief captains had risen against him, vying for control. Each time he had discovered their plans Ebon had arranged for another of his captains to despatch them with the promise of a rich reward. Others, eager to prove their loyalty to him, warned him of potential danger from those around him and had eliminated the offender to impress the scheming seer. They too had received their reward but not all had lived for long afterwards as there were always others who waited in line to replace them. It was a bitter struggle of kill or be killed in the lucrative but dangerous rise to glory in Ebon's domain.

Maccus had been the first of the wizards to see the potential in Ebon and of the longed for hope of gaining a foothold back in their old world; the one that the seers had banished them from. He had studied Ebon's movements and got to know his moods and how he thought. 'Yes,' Maccus had thought; 'here is the one we have been waiting for all these years.' The wizard was not so much interested in returning to the old world as he was in gaining his revenge on the seers; in that he was in complete accord with Emrys. Where they differed was in where they would continue their existence after their victory against their arch enemies.

Emrys wished to return, to find the place where his dead wife's soul lingered in the passageways of Anram. Whereas; Maccus was content with what they had been able to carve out for themselves here in the world that was called Magog by its inhabitants.

Maccus had long held the opinion that Emrys was blinded by his grief to the potential that still remained here in this world. They had fought a long and difficult battle with those who had used to rule here. At first the wizards were welcomed and treated with sympathy when they had recounted the wrongs committed against them by the seers to the Junta that governed the land. Great pains were taken to relay the stories of injustice and despotism that the wizards had sought to overturn in their own world, only to have lost three of their kind and to be banished by the power that the seers unjustly exercised against them.

The seven leaders of Magog were completely taken in by their stories and, truth be told, were a little afraid of these five beings from another world. The Junta was merely a joint council with no power other than that which they had through force of will and the backing of their armies. The wizards saw the opportunity to wrest control of this world from their hands and replace these dictators with themselves as the ruling body. That would enable them to harness the resources of the land and begin the process by which they could return to the world of the seers and wreak their revenge.

Their first task had been to locate the source of this world's power. Somewhere beneath the land lay a vast source of energy that connected the two worlds. It would also have the ability to open up something like The Montage that the seers had control over in the other world. The first step in their plan was to seize control of this world from the Junta so that they could be in command and unite the many tribes in a common purpose. It would be the wizards' purpose but the folk they ruled would be led to believe that they were searching for a source of power that would bring prosperity to all.

One by one, over a period of time so as not to arouse suspicion, the leaders of the Junta disappeared and were replaced by others whom the wizards had corrupted with promises of wealth, power and position. Within a year of their arrival in Magog, the Junta was completely controlled by the wizards and where there had been counsel and debate that would decide the affairs of the land, there was anarchy and greed. Warlords established territories and exacted harsh justice upon the inhabitants who suffered greatly under the new regime. An age of despair weighed heavily on all the land as its resources were stripped by the needs of the wizards. The lust for wealth and power by the men who governed under the watchful glare of their new masters, the wizards of Magog, ensured that the folk of the land remained subdued and enslaved.

Emrys and his fellow wizards laboured for many years, sending their scouts out to search for the most likely places from which they could tap into this world's energy source. Always the same report came back; the scouts had been unable to discover where the energy could be found. At first the wizards dealt harshly with them but realised that it served no effective purpose other than to cause the scouts to come back with false claims. When these places were investigated, they turned out to be nothing but geological oddities or some such thing. Eventually they had found a channel through which they could access the energy but it provided only limited power so that they were unable to invoke a Montage as the seers had done. That meant they were restricted in their abilities but it was enough to set them above the folk of the land and to maintain control by means of force and fear.

The one thing that they discovered quite early on was that it did provide them with enough power to use in prolonging their lives to the extent that they were all but immortal. It did have a side effect though and they discovered it too late to stop it. Their bodies began to dry and shrivel; the years demanded that something should be given in return for their longevity. That price was to forego the pleasures that a mortal body could provide. They no longer could create another being or enjoy the savour of food; their bodies were no longer capable of digesting it.

Their sustenance, instead, now came from the energy beneath the land; it was the energy that existed throughout the universe. That is why Maccus did not want to leave this world; he feared that when they were separated from it for any great length of time, they would die.

They had finally managed to tap into the energies that had lain beneath the surface for ages past without it being disturbed; now they were able to harness the negative side of that power. As they were no longer mortal beings of flesh and blood but withered, dried out carcasses, their bodies offered little other than to house their embittered spirits.

Thus they had traversed the line between life and death and were somewhere in-between. Capable of utilising heightened powers without the means of physical aids such as the seers' staves and talismans; they were able to create for themselves a new existence. It was one that sustained them indefinitely and so they had remained from that point in time onwards, unable to die but not capable of living an ordinary life. There was a price to be paid for everything it seems and this was the price that they had to pay for their immortality.

They had searched for many hundreds of years for those who could be considered as replacements for the three wizards who had been killed in their battle against the seers. They had found none who had passed the test, though many had tried. One thing that Ebon had done that had impressed the wizards was his attack upon the sprites by sending the nymphs and Grists of Geddon against them. It showed just the right amount of cold-hearted malice that the wizards appreciated in their protégés.

There had been a number of them in the past who had been groomed to join them as additional wizards but none had come up to expectation. Somewhere along the line they had fallen foul with their own mistaken sense of invulnerability. Basking in the protective powers of the wizards they had risen to positions of great influence only to fail when it came to recognising the wizards as the true power in the land. They had believed that they had outgrown their need for the wizards, being drunk with power and their own self importance.

The most notable had been the giant, Custennin, from whom the wizards had created the Rod of Dread. He had passed into folk lore and mythology but the wizards remembered him well. They had inflicted a special penalty upon him for his duplicity and marked him as the one who would live forever in the minds of the folk of this world. They had torn him asunder and sent his body parts to the four quarters of the land, all except his right thigh, from which they had created the Rod.

It was rumoured abroad that his family had tracked down the different pieces of his mutilated body and brought them together again then buried them in a secret place. All that was left in order for Custennin to be at peace was for the thigh bone to be restored to him. It seemed that it would never happen because it served another purpose, that of the Rod of Dread and none who wielded it would surrender it up.

Now, gathered together in conclave, the five wizards met to discuss Ebon's plans to invade the old world with his massed armies. It fell neatly into line with their desires to face their antagonists, the seers, and the overall plan of conquest was drawing to a head. Ebon continued to grow in strength with the warlords coming under his control through the marshals he had established in each stronghold. What was even more pleasing to them was the steady progress the ex-seer was making towards being brought totally under their influence by means of the Rod.

Ebon still did not realise the effect it was having on him and the need to use it was growing stronger each time he exercised its power. Soon he would have to make the choice; either to join with them as a member of their conclave or to face complete annihilation. Given the choice, they were confident that Ebon's lust for power and control would sway him in their favour. He, above all who had tried, had shown more promise than any and Emrys, along with the other wizards anticipated a surge of renewal with the inclusion of the rebel seer in their midst.

The creature Ebon called Jetta had been a surprise development that they had not foreseen but they were confident that he posed no threat to them, after all, he was controlled by Ebon and Ebon was controlled by the Rod and the Rod was controlled by them. Therefore there was no need to be concerned about what Jetta might or might not do; he held no significance to their overall plans. Should Ebon join with them, he would be permitted to retain the creature; if he did not, then they would probably be able to find a use for his dark angel.

If Ebon did not meet their expectations, it would prove a

disappointment to them but they had faced such situations before and carried on with their search. Sooner or later someone would arise who would be worthy of the invitation to join with the five wizards and increase their number to six. Then their ability and power as individuals, as well as a conclave, would also increase. Ebon showed much promise in the fulfilling of that dream but then so had all the others and they had failed.

Somehow Emrys thought that Ebon too would fail and prepared himself for that moment. When the time came for Ebon to face them and deliver the Rod back into their hands there would be no mercy for the rogue seer. He was either going to be one with them or he was not, it was a simple choice to make; life everlasting or death.

Chapter 16

The Montage

Terra Standfast had sent out a warning to all who were confederate to their cause, via the birds, telling them of his plan. He had been overwhelmed by the response. No-one had questioned his decision and all stood firmly behind him, offering their support and asking if there were anything they could do to help. In truth, there was very little that could be done by anyone else but the seers. They had stood as guardians and protectors of the land ever since their epic confrontation with the wizards and their triumph over them. It was now down to them to engage the wizards in battle again in an attempt to retain peace in the land.

The wise old dwarf knew that it was a difficult task, one that may cost him his life in the process but he reasoned that he had been fortunate enough to have led a happy life. It mattered not if it were required of him to lay it down now, just so long as the wizards led by Emrys did not gain a foothold in their world. That is why Terra had decided to invoke The Montage. It was the only way that they could defend against them. The energy beneath The Tower had held firm for all these centuries, it was now up to him to ensure that it would continue to do so.

He sat in his room pondering how best to act and realised that in order to be certain that they held sway over The Montage, they required at least one more seer to be present with them. He and Liam would be unable to induce and control it properly without the steadying sight of a third seer.

'If only Urim were able to stand with us I would feel much better about this.' His thoughts were dark and filled with sorrow that his dear friend was unable to do so. They were indebted to him for so much already; they all owed their release to Urim from being imprisoned by the energy barrier that Ebon had created. History would write a double chapter in the Golden Tome about his exploits in his honour. It was because of Ebon that all of this had come about and Terra determined that they would bring a final end to his interference from the other world.

Ebon had shown such promise in his early years of being a member of the Council of the Sight but had been subverted by his quest for power. He had escaped justice for his misdeeds up until now but this time he must be brought to task.

Terra knew that one of his hopes lay in what Urim could do in his mission to find and detain the troublesome former seer. If he could prevent him from opening the doorway between the worlds, then Terra was confident that they could keep the wizards from coming through but in order to do that they had to offer them the bait of The Montage. Once they had entered into it, then the seers could determine where the wizards would end up. He had made a study of Emrys, the lead wizard, ever since he had been inducted as a novice to the dwarf who had held the title of Terra Standfast before him. He believed that he knew Emrys better than the wizard did himself and counted on his contempt of the seers to lead him through the door of the trap the dwarf was to lay. He knew that if he were to stand at the door, Emrys would not be able to resist coming for him. He was to be the lure that would bring about an end to this matter, one way or another. The wizard's hatred for them was too strong to be governed by reason and Terra pinned his hopes on that hatred to overpower reason and force the wizard's hand.

The first stage of the plan required that another seer join them at the Tower. Hamill and Jon could not come, besides; they were an integral part of Urim's preparations in apprehending Ebon. They could not be taken away from that, no matter what the cost. Eden and Elise had invoked The Montage last time, under the guidance of the more experienced Liam, and were eminently qualified for the task yet they were unable to be at the Tower as they were still with the ogres. Without Auger here to help them by invoking the wind to transport the two seers, they could not get to the Tower in time.

Colonel O'Rourke's message that Auger had been lost was a severe blow to him and now that the redoubtable dwarf was no longer with them he had to be replaced. Unfortunately there was no time to do so. The seeking for and inauguration of a replacement would take too long which meant they were one seer short on their council. That left Emerald; she was still in the sprite realm, helping them recover from the devastation wreaked upon them when the nymphs and the Grists of Geddon attacked.

By using The Montage she could make the transition between the worlds and be brought through to help them but it would be a close run thing. He and Liam would have to commence the act of invocation and there was a risk that it would open up the door between here and Magog before it did that of the sprite realm. Like a throw of the dice determined who would win or lose a game of chance; opening up the doors between worlds would be down to chance whether the right one opened first. There was no way of telling. Last time, Liam had been able to give the signal to Eden and Elise as to when to commence but now the cards were erratic and unreliable; they could not be relied upon to tell them when to act.

Terra hoped fervently that Emerald was using her crystal to foresee their need and would be ready to join with them when the time was right. Maybe she, from her position in the sprite realm, could influence the timing of the invocation so that her journey through would occur before the wizards were aware of it. It was a faint hope but one that Terra took comfort in otherwise he would lack the courage to undertake the task. The future welfare of hundreds of thousands of folk from all over the land depended on him holding true to his duty. He must not let them down. He will not let them down.

The tremors of uncertainty rumbled across the sprite realm like distant thunder that promised of storms to come, only these were no ordinary rumbles of thunder. Emerald felt the trembling of the forces that kept order between worlds as did all of the sprites. Their existence lay on the boundaries of the world that was home to the seers and was bound to it only by the thinnest of veils. Consequently any disturbance in the energy fields that held the worlds in their proper order was felt as minor shock waves across their realm.

Queen Ella still lay confined to her room, such were the extent of her wounds inflicted by the Grist that she had been near death several times and it was only the skill and dedication of the elf orderlies that kept her from slipping away. Weak though she was, she still held council every day to oversee the affairs of her sovereignty. Emerald had been a strong support to her and Queen Ella had called her 'my rock'.

'Without your help and support, Emerald, I believe I would not have been able to shoulder the burdens I have had to carry since the attack. Had you not been assigned to become a seer, you would have been queen and not I. However I too feel the impending turmoil and realise that you have a responsibility to their world as well as to ours. It is not without reason that we chose to be represented on the Council of the Sight and I know that you bear the mantle of a seer with honour, I also know that you must leave us.'

Emerald stood at her side as her queen lay recovering on the soft mattress that cushioned her wounded and weakened body. The 'magic' that the sprites spun over her helped to ease the pain and discomfort but it was not sufficient to heal her completely. The elves arrival had proven to have been just in time to prevent her from losing her grip on life and gradually, over the days and weeks, she had been regaining her strength.

'I am sorry to have to leave for I believe that there is much that I can do to be of assistance to you, my lady. However, your instinct serves you well and I must return to the world of the seers. I fear that all is not well. However something bids me to forbear returning in my usual fashion, almost as if I were not meant to pass through the veil between our worlds. I have decided to use the power within my staff and the crystal talisman to see what I must do. May I have your permission to withdraw from our realm?'

'Of course dear sister; go with my blessing and travel carefully. I too feel that all is not well and advise that caution should be taken on your part.'

'Thank you my lady. I hope that when I return you will be well again. Farewell.'

Ella smiled and took her hand in a loving clasp, pressing something into her palm. 'This may aid you should you fall into difficulty. Come back to us soon.'

As Emerald walked away and headed towards her room, she opened her hand and saw what her queen had given her. It was a tiny, silver bell; engraved around the edges were the words, written in the language of the sprites, 'Ring and I will come.' She wondered what it could mean, 'who, or what, would come. How would she know when to ring and what would happen when she did? There was no way of knowing until the time came for her to use it. Confident that the gift would not be idly given, she placed it within her cloak in a secret pocket so that it would be accessible should the time ever come that she had need of it.

As she walked back to her room, she pondered on the feelings that she had felt of late and why it was that she was impressed not to pass through to Crystal Falls in order to return to the world of the seers. The only way she would know is by searching the crystal talisman. It had never failed her before and she was confident that it would reveal to her what she should do.

What she saw worried her, the images were indistinct and shadows played over the crystal making it difficult to tell what was being displayed. What she did manage to glean from the little that did make sense to her was that she was needed back at Seers Tower and that her arrival there was of the utmost importance. 'So that's why I am not supposed to return via Crystal Falls. I am to wait for the right moment and step into The Montage which will enable me to go straight to Terra and Liam.'

Returning her attention to focus on the crystal she stared deeply into its mesmerising light and made ready to make the transition through the doorway when it appeared. If only she could let Terra and Liam know that she was ready. She concentrated on sending her thoughts through the crystal in the hope that it would be felt by them. She stood nervously waiting for the sign to come that would indicate it was time for her to leave.

The Montage reached through the fabric of all creation, affecting worlds that could only be imagined. The energy that pervaded the galaxy and kept all matter aligned as it should be had been used to hold the wizards at bay. Now it was being used to seal the doorway between their worlds forever. If Terra and Liam could maintain control over which world held dominance, then they had a chance to hold back the tide of evil that was waiting to engulf the folk of this land. If not, then they would die and the wizards would stake their claim to their world.

Not just this one however would fall prey to their lust for power and control. Countless others would be at the mercy of their dark and dreadful desires. Terra knew the price to pay would be high and he was willing to pay it. He was willing to sacrifice himself, as leader of the Council of the Sight, to the energy force in order to keep the folk of this land safe; not just for now but for all time. This would be the greatest battle that he had ever fought and it would determine who would rule at Seers Tower; whether it would be the seers or the wizards.

There was nothing else that he could do; all that could be done had been done. All that remained was to invoke The Montage, hopefully for the last time; it held hidden dangers as well as those he was aware of. It could rend time out of place and realign the worlds in such a way as to make them unstable. They had been fortunate last time in not doing so and needed that same good fortune to smile upon them again. Whatever the outcome, there was no other option left open to them, he had to go through with it or face the fact that the wizards would return; that was something he could not bear to consider.

Standing either side of the shaft, the two old seers faced each other. The Tower was silent, not a sound could be heard. The attendants that saw to the day to day affairs had been sent back to their villages for their own safety. The powers that were about to be unleashed would harm any normal being that happened to be within reach of its energies. The Tower had been emptied of all who could not withstand its effects. Now that everyone had gone, they began the dreadful task of unlocking the barrier between the worlds. Terra hoped that the timing was right and that Emerald would be standing ready. He had a reassuring feeling within him that she was and they commenced the procedure.

Placing their respective staves in the notches at the edge of the shaft they chanted in unison;

'Fire and Water, Earth and Sky, make this binding ours to wield, 'till the damage has been healed.'

A deeper silence fell over the courtyard than there had been before and the ground trembled beneath their feet. A spark of light caught their attention deep in the shaft that gradually built in intensity until it burst forth from the shaft and flooded the courtyard with a brilliance that was blinding. A mighty rushing filled their ears as if they were in the midst of a herd of mighty stallions that were stampeding across the ground. It all but deafened them, then the light fell back into the shaft with a clap of thunder and darkness fell upon them as of deepest night, even though there were several turns of the hand to go before sun set.

The Montage had been invoked for the second time within a few months of the last; it was unheard of in the history of the land. Since its inception, there had been several times when The Montage had been brought into play. That was because they had been faced with no other choice; to have re-activated it so soon after the last time was testament to the desperate measures that were needed to combat the threat posed by that of the wizards.

Terra and Liam were knocked backwards by the force of the blast that had erupted from the shaft. It was a more powerful event than was created by Eden Yield-keeper and Elise Saranya yet it was the same. Terra could not discover what had caused it to be so strong this time; perhaps it was due to the nature of the forces at work. Emrys and the other wizards would be using every means at their disposal to pry the doorway open that connected their worlds in an effort to break through. The two seers stood in awe, watching the dark forces that lay between the worlds tear at the bindings that held it fast between the world of the seers and that of Magog, the world of the wizards.

Whisperings of many voices could be heard ascending from the depths of the shaft. Shouts and screams of dismay echoed up into the courtyard from disembodied spirits seeking to be reunited with their mortal bodies. They had opened the doorway to Geddon. The sound of leathery wings beating against the rancid air grew loud in their ears as the approach of grist heralded its entrance into their world from the shadows of its own. The dreadful creature's appearance was imminent as the sound of its wing beats drew ever nearer. It sent fear through the hearts of the two seers as they stood helpless to prevent the creature from gaining the top of the shaft. Terra considered ending the invocation in an effort to stop it but knew that they had to continue if they were to have any chance against the wizards. Without his staff he would have no defence against the powerful beast but if he tried to use it, The Montage would end. Crossing his fingers he hoped for a miracle.

It came in an unexpected form. The Grist heaved itself clear of the rim of the shaft and roared in triumph as it saw the defenceless seers standing alone, easy prey to the razor sharp talons that it stretched towards them. They would be torn to shreds in moments and it would be free to run amok amongst the local villages causing mayhem and destruction everywhere it went. Bearing down on the old dwarf it eagerly anticipated tasting his blood.

BOOM! A clap of thunder echoed out across the still waters of the lake surrounding the Tower and into the hills of the Hammerhead Heights. The deathly whisperings and desperate groaning of the disembodied spirits were silenced. Terra wondered whether he had gone deaf, the quiet that followed the screams was so intense.

Out of the midst of the darkness that hung over the shaft, Emerald stepped forward and entered the courtyard from the sprite world holding the crystal and her staff before her. The doorway had changed and the entrance to the underworld of Geddon had been slammed shut on the Grist. It must have been halfway through when the scene had changed and it had been cut in half as if by a mighty scythe. Half of its body lay lifeless in its gore on the courtyard floor; the other half must have fallen back into its own world of Geddon.

Terra almost collapsed in relief at the appearance of the one seer he had hoped would make it through. With her help he felt confident that they could prevail over the wizards, despite them being outnumbered.

'What is it that requires such drastic action, Terra?' Emerald knew little of what was happening in the world of the seers other than what she had seen in her crystal. All she knew was that The Montage had been invoked and she was needed at Seers Tower. Seeing the remains of the grist it brought back memories of the conflict in the sprite realm and she shuddered at the thought of more of theses creatures being let loose. 'Have the grists escaped their world?'

'No, we are safe from them. It is worse than that my dear Emerald; far worse than that. The wizards are on the verge of breaking through and we are but few to control The Montage. We need your help to maintain the balance of power. Urim is close to apprehending Ebon and when he does; the gods willing that he does so in time; we will be able to prevent them from coming through.'

A different part of his plan was unfolding across the other side of the land even as they stood at the door of another world as it opened upon them.

Laying their hands on the tops of the staves they gently twisted them in a clockwise direction and removed them from the sockets in the flagstones around the shaft. A burst of light exploded from the shaft before it fell back into the void allowing the natural light of day to return to the Tower. Their heads seemed to spin with a mad sensation of giddiness and a clap of thunder rumbled its way across the Hammerhead Heights. The binding that kept the worlds in place had been completed but the question remained. Had the worlds returned to their former state?

Chapter 17

Taken

Ebon had waited for this moment for a long time, ever since he had witnessed The Montage first hand at Greystone Flow when the seers had invoked it. It had not been used by the Sight in all the time he had been with them but he recognised what it was and realised that it held the possibility of his return to his own world. In calling it up they had foiled his plans to destroy the sprites by sending the nymphs to attack them by means of the portal. He had tried then to capture Anna but had mistimed his jump into her world and ended up tumbling down the side of the mountain in his own, prison-world.

Now he had a better plan and the tool with which to carry it out. It would give him the perfect opportunity to have Urim in his control. When he finally held Anna hostage, Urim, his meddling nemesis, would not dare to move against him. With the Rod of Dread in his hand and Jetta to command, the interfering seer would be forced to stand idly by and watch as Ebon set about taking his revenge. He would unleash the power of the Rod against the seers; there would be no defence against it; not in their world.

The moment came that he had been waiting for and he watched keenly as the entrance to each world passed before him. The viewing-window gave him the perfect way to enter their world as he could draw the energies of The Montage through it waiting for the right door to open before him. There were few who would have the opportunity to enter it. The seers at the Tower, where it had been invoked, could obviously control it to a degree. But others, like him, who had the means at their disposal, could affect a transition and make use of it to go to any world they wanted. All that was needed was the nerve to carry it through.

He rather suspected that the wizards would also be alerted to this chance to return to their home world and would endeavour to face the seers in an epic contest of wills. Whilst they were busy fighting each other, he would be re-establishing himself and transporting his armies through the doorway. He knew now how it could be held open and he would be there to do it, or rather through his instrument in their world.

Ebon would not chance a direct assault on Seers Tower. He would use the keystone, deep beneath the ruins of Anram, to be the catalyst for his triumphant arrival. From there he would gather many to his cause and then march at the head of his forces through the land. All who opposed him would fall before him; the fear of him would spread throughout the land and the Rod would bring him the victory he so desperately sought.

There was one particular doorway he was keeping a lookout for and he readied himself to strike as soon as it appeared. It was the doorway to the world into which Anna had been taken when they both fell into the energy barrier. Why they had been deposited in different worlds he had no idea but he would rectify that. Then he would have a bargaining tool so powerful it made him tingle with delight. Urim would not dare oppose him, not with Anna in his grasp.

The scenes passed before his gaze then Ebon saw his opportunity and grasped at it before it could disappear for good. Using the Rod he held the doorway steady and sent Jetta through to capture his prize. He watched as the fleet footed demon ran through the 'doorway' into the garden world in search of his quarry, Anna.

The dark angel sped from one place to another, seeking the unsuspecting girl who would be the means by which Ebon would nullify the effect of the seer's influence. With her secured in his sanctuary, he could begin his conquest of the world of the seers unopposed. With Ebon urging his armies on, directing them from the safety of his fortress, sending hordes of battle hardened warriors against an unprepared world; there would be little resistance and he would finally be the ruler in Seers Tower.

Jetta ran swiftly, searching high and low, trampling through the pleasant garden, disrupting the peace and tranquillity of the place. Startled citizens screamed in fear and surprise at the appearance of the dark angel that had suddenly entered their existence. Many confronted him trying to evict this maniac from another realm but without success.

'Depart from us and leave us in peace.' Demanded one of Anna's friends; a slightly built man of about thirty years of age.

'I am come to do my master's bidding and I will not go until I have that which I have been charged to obtain.'

More of the inhabitants of this peaceful land gathered to insist that Jetta leave but to no avail. He was once a man of greed and selfish ambition but had changed when he had been encompassed by the dark waters of the fountain in Ebon's garden. He now knew for himself what it was like to be dominated and treated with contempt. No longer did he feel the way he had before, selfish and cruel; he was the captive spirit of a magic so dark it revolted him. It had altered his perception of life and he longed to be free. If he could have his way he would use his power to prevent the atrocities being brought about by the rogue seer.

He could see like no other could how Ebon was changing, becoming more and more dependant upon the Rod and the power that the wizards had granted him. Ebon did not realise that he was losing his humanity, he was becoming a creature of his world and no longer belonged to his original one, that of the seers. The wizards knew how to bend anyone to their will and they had acted with cunning to have Ebon believe that he could defeat the wizards, when all the time he was becoming more like them each day.

Jetta saw all this as if detached from it but he knew that he was very much involved and could not prevent any of this happening; at least not all the time Ebon held the Rod. He was now a creature of dark magic and was tied to the will of Ebon by the power of the Rod. He had no choice but to fulfil all that Ebon commanded him to do; whether he wanted to or not and there were times when he did not. This was one of those times. He was not insensitive to the pleadings of the folk of this wonderful land. He had no desire to harm them or to disrupt their harmonious existence but the power of the Rod of Dread, and the magic that had enfolded him within its grasp, meant that he was helpless to resist. He had to obey the will of the seer and he detested him for it.

Jetta did not harm any of those who opposed him here in Anna's world; in that at least he was able to exercise his own will. He had been charged with the capture of the girl, Anna and nothing else, therefore he would not kill them; he did not need to, he simply brushed them aside with a gentleness that belied his strength. He searched the faces that thronged about him, trying to find the one whom he had been sent for. A huddle of folk near a pergola covered with sweet smelling climbers attracted his attention and he made his way towards it.

Scores of folk were gathering to witness this intrusion into their world, desperate to prevent the creature from completing his task, whatever it was, yet powerless to stop him. There, in the middle of the group of folk was Anna.

Walking boldly up to her he bowed from the waist and addressed her in a gruff but reverent manner. 'Forgive me my lady but I must take you with me. There can be no resistance to me for I have the means at my disposal with which to make you. I would prefer it if you would follow me to the 'doorway' from this world that my master is holding open for us until we go through. Failure to obey me will result in such terrible misfortune for those around you that you would find it too distressing to consider. Will you come with me peacefully or must I demonstrate my power?'

She did not quail before him; instead she faced him with a determined attitude, as if daring him to take her captive. She stepped back and drew back her sling letting fly a small rounded pebble that struck Jetta full on the forehead. If it had been any lesser creature, he would have gone down and never got up again but he was not any ordinary creature. The stone hit his head amidst a flash of black sparks and fell to the floor leaving no mark upon him. All Jetta did was to smile then casually walk towards her and grasp her by the arm; pulling her out into the open. She was shocked that her slingshot had not so much as dazed him; he had simply shaken his head and grinned.

She could offer little resistance and despite her feisty nature; she could not free herself from the firm grasp of Ebon's dark angel. Those nearest her tried vainly to come to her rescue but they were prevented from doing so by some field of force that protected Jetta from harm. Kicking and clawing desperately at the creature in an attempt to be free, she was dragged from her world of peace and safety, through the doorway created by The Montage and held in place by Ebon to stand before him in his sanctuary. Secure within Jetta's grasp and knowing that he had succeeded in his aim, Ebon let the doorway close as soon as they had stepped through and the viewing-window dimmed.

'Hello again Anna; it's so nice of you to accept my invitation. I don't believe that you know my emissary. Allow me to introduce him to you. Anna, may I present Fergus; at least that was his name. Now he is known simply as Jetta and he obeys my every command. Is that not so, Jetta?'

The dark angel bowed before him and growled out in a gruff voice that it was. A ripple of power crossed his face making him appear to contort his lips in a snarl of disdain.

Anna went to speak and deliver a rebuke to Ebon but although her lips moved, no sound escaped them; she was mute again. Only in her new world, it seemed, was she able to talk.

'What a pity, has the cat got your tongue? That is a shame, and I was so looking forward to hearing you scream for me; nice and loud so that Urim would hear. Never mind, I shall have to ensure that he finds out some other way.'

Ebon gloated at the success of his audacious move; it had gone much smoother than he had hoped it would. The next step would be to allow Urim a glimpse into his sanctuary and more especially to see that he had Anna. With her in his power the meddlesome seer would give in to his demands and Ebon would once again wield the staff of the portal that Urim had taken from him. Urim would be helpless to prevent him from returning to his home world and exacting his revenge on the seers.

All his woes seemed to start and end with that troublesome seer. It was as if Urim held a personal grudge against him. Why did he constantly interfere in his affairs? He had no right to; it was none of his business what he, Ebon, did. It mattered not in any case as Ebon had achieved his task. The next step was to ensure that Urim knew that he held Anna and that any interference on Urim's part would result in unpleasant repercussions for Ebon's guest.

Anna was safely secured in a seat behind him with Jetta standing alongside her chair. Planting himself squarely in front of his viewing screen so that his image filled it, he started the search for the seer. He knew that he would be in the world of the seers so using the Rod he exercised his control over it and began the search. The screen flickered into life and he concentrated his mind on the one person he wished to see. Seers Tower came into view as if he were riding on the back of a great bird, its keen, piercing eyes easily able to discern the folk in the courtyard and in the fields round about. Somehow he was able to see right into the Tower itself but there was no sign of the one he sought. The vision changed to that of Northill where there was much activity as folk went about their daily business; all of it meaningless to Ebon. He had no time for the drudgery of ordinary folks' lives and his vision went to Ffridd-Uch-Ddu, the capital city of the dwarves where they were busy completing the defensive walls.

Ebon smiled a crooked smile and sneered in contempt. 'Fools; do you think that such a thing as a wall will stop me from razing your city to the ground? You who have given me so much trouble in the past will learn to call me lord. I have a score to settle with some of your kind and I will revel in their cries for mercy when the time comes for me to call on you. Make haste with your preparations to complete your wall for I will come to you soon and will take pleasure in levelling your puny city; for now, I seek another.'

Passing his hand over the Rod, another scene came into view; it was Foundry Smelt, home of the metal-masters. The thick, black smoke still ascended into the air to form the huge cloud that hovered above the town. It was fed by the soot laden smoke from the many forges that burned constantly below. Urim could not be found. Frustrated at not being able to locate his quarry, Ebon lifted the Rod and brought its tip crashing down on the floor. A spark of power erupted from it and a huge crack split the stone floor, travelling the length of the room. Desperate to find the seer, Ebon stroked his furrowed brow with his hand then relaxed the tension in his shoulders and sighed. 'Where are you Urim? Why can't I find you?'

Suddenly a thought occurred to him and he changed his search from the world of the seers to the sprite realm. No sooner had he done so than he located the seer in the great hall of the sprite queen's palace. He was conversing with Queen Ella who sat bolstered up by plump cushions on a couch that had been placed before her throne. She was still recovering from the dreadful attack upon her and her subjects by the grists that

Ebon had unleashed upon them. Together with the magic of her sprites and the skills of the elf physicians from the Ward, she was making a slow but steady recovery from wounds that would have killed a lesser person.

The fact that Urim was in the great hall of the sprites made it easier for Ebon to relay his message as the walls were hung with mirrors. It was through one of theses mirrors that Ebon could deliver his challenge to Urim. A challenge that would be witnessed by the sprites and therefore one that Urim dare not refuse or else the honour of the seers would be brought under condemnation.

With a wicked glint in his eye, Ebon proceeded to make the connection between the two worlds by concentrating his mind on Urim. He knew that he had succeeded in making the connection because Urim turned and looked him in the eye.

'Ebon; what foul purpose brings your attention to this place? Do you wish to gloat over the harm that you are responsible for causing here amongst these gentle folk, or does some other matter occupy your thoughts at this time?' Urim was in no mood to bandy words with Ebon.

'I must say that it is good to see you too my friend.' Ebon responded sarcastically as he raised himself up onto the balls of his feet and rocked to and fro. He was supremely confident and took pleasure in goading his nemesis.

Urim did not want to waste any time with exchanging 'pleasantries' with Ebon. 'As I have said before, I am no friend of yours. What is your purpose; state it and leave us in peace.'

'Very well, seeing as you do not wish to be civil I shall deliver the message I have to give; or rather there is someone here who can speak far better than I even though she is dumb.'

Ebon stepped aside to reveal Anna, tied to the chair so that she could not signal to him and with Jetta standing menacingly behind her. Anna saw Urim through the screen and shook her head miming that he should not listen to Ebon. She desperately wanted to scream words of warning but she had no voice; it had never bothered her before, but now she was frustrated at the lack of one.

Ebon stepped back in front of the screen, obscuring Urim's view of the distraught girl. 'So there you have it; I appear to hold an ace up my sleeve so to speak and I wish it to be known that I will play it if I have to. Of course you will try to rescue her but let me convince you to do otherwise because I can not be held accountable for what might become of her. What happens to Anna is solely upon your head Urim. Do as I request and she will remain unharmed, try to go against me in any way and she will die; you know that I am a man of my word in this.' This last statement was delivered with a cold conviction.

Urim knew only too well that Ebon was quite capable of doing exactly as he said; chewing at his lower lip he thought of sending a blast of power through the connection between them. The gods knew how much he wanted to do so but he risked Anna's life in so doing and had no guarantee that his action would be successful. He had to admit that Ebon held the advantage. 'What is it that you wish of me?'

'That's better; I knew you would come to see reason. I simply ask that you do nothing, that's all, nothing. You do not interfere in anything that I do otherwise you will never see Anna alive again. Do I have your word, as a seer, that you accept my terms?' Ebon awaited Urim's reply, confident that he would submit to his demands.

Urim knew that he could not do anything that might imperil Anna's safety. His mind raced, trying to find a way out of this predicament. There was none.

'I do.' The words were simply spoken and came from a man who looked crushed and broken.

Ebon thrilled at the impact his plan was having upon his adversary and he gloried in the control he had over the seer. 'Very well, I accept your word and I promise that Anna will be returned to her world after I have succeeded in my task in gaining control over the world of the seers. Urim, you will yet kneel before me and accept me as your rightful lord and master; remember, Anna will always be accessible to me should you decide to go against your word.'

'I will not forget.' Urim sounded as if he were beaten and held his head low on drooping shoulders.

'That is good. I will hold you to your promise. You will have to excuse me now for I have some pressing business to attend to elsewhere. We shall meet again, Urim.'

Ebon closed the connection between the two worlds and stood before the blank viewing-window with satisfaction. A broad grin spread across his face as he savoured the taste of victory over the seer who had so far managed to thwart him in his efforts to gain that which he coveted most, to rule in Seers Tower.

Urim stood in silent contemplation, watched by Queen Ella who waited until the seer had thought things through. When Urim finally raised his gaze, she asked the question that he had been asking himself.

'Are you really going to let Ebon continue unchallenged? I realise of course that you have given your word as a seer that you will not interfere but surely you can not stand by and watch whilst he re-enters your world and takes control.'

Urim shifted his weight from one foot to the other uncomfortable with what had just transpired. He had to keep his word or all that he and the Sight stood for would be placed in jeopardy. There was, however a way that he could act without breaking his word; in fact, Ebon had, in a round-a-bout way, given his consent.

'Ebon said that I would try to rescue her and that is exactly what I shall do. Once I have achieved that, the way will be clear for me to act again as I shall be free from my bond. My promise was dependant upon him holding Anna and was exacted from me because of her being held captive. Once she is out of his clutches, the covenant will be of no effect. Then I will pursue him and bring his plans tumbling about him. He believes that he has won already and that will be his undoing.'

'I see the logic and approve of your plan. Is there anything that I or my sprites can do to assist you?'

'Yes, there is one thing that I would like you to do for me, if you are agreeable?' Urim chewed his lower lip, hesitant to ask for that which he needed.

Queen Ella replied quickly and with a defiant toss of her head in the light of Ebon's challenge. 'You have only to ask it of me and it shall be done.'

'I require some information that I believe you may be able to supply. It concerns the history of the world of Magog and its mythology. Once I have that and I have found what I am looking for, I shall be able to contend with Ebon without fear of recrimination.

Chapter 18

Shadows From the Deep

Having closed The Montage now that Emerald was safely through, the seers turned away from the shaft to meet in the central chamber and consider their next move. They had not reached the doorway that led from the courtyard before a great boom of thunder erupted from the depths of the shaft accompanied by a cold blast of wind that almost knocked them off their feet. Looking back towards the shaft they saw to their horror that a dark shadowy cloud as deep as the night was climbing high into the air above the courtyard. The mass of darkness began to swirl and hiss as three shapes emerged from the maelstrom and took form; wizards.

Terra's deepest fear was being realised before his eyes. The wizards had found a way to bridge the gulf that existed between their worlds and were about to descend upon them with a fury that had been nurtured for thousands of years. They were maddened by their enforced imprisonment in the world of Magog and eager to deal out retribution upon their adversaries. Emrys and two companion wizards appeared amidst the cloud that loomed above the shaft gathering their powers to strike at the startled seers.

Despite their weariness from the energies they had exerted to invoke The Montage, the three seers held their ground with their staves held in front of them to defend against the attack that the wizards were to unleash upon them.

They did not have to wait long for the confrontation to begin. As soon as the three wizards had emerged from the shaft and taken their form, a bolt of energy leaped from their midst and flashed across the courtyard at the three seers as they stood alone. Emerald and Liam were thrown to the ground as the force of the blast hurled by the wizards made contact with the defences put out by their staves. Terra alone stood his ground and thrust the dark power back at the wizards. Emrys had to react quickly to avoid the strike by the surge of power and tried to deflect the blast of their own making away from them. It rebounded angrily against the walls of the Tower, crackling and spitting until it finally lost its potency and fizzled out of existence with a last subdued crackle.

Without flinching Terra formed a lightning strike of his own in response to the wizards attack and hurled it at the three forms. It struck one of them who had been to slow to respond and a shriek of agony reverberated around the confines of the courtyard. Terra knew that he would have to defend himself again and quickly erected a shield around him to prevent any harm coming to himself from their retaliation.

Seeing what Terra had done the other two seers clambered back to their feet and formed similar shield defences of their own. The defensive shields protected them whilst they gathered their composure and sent bolts of raw energy at the three shadows that hung suspended above the shaft in a cloud of darkness. The blazing red eyes of the wizards glared back at the seers with a malevolence that burned from within their embittered souls. Again the wizards defended against the separate attacks launched at them from the desperate seers. They managed to evade any harm as the barbs of the seers lightning sought a target on which to ground. The raw power of the energy invoked against them sliced through the cloud as it boiled and billowed around the wizards.

'You thought that you could control the Montage without any interference from the other side but as you can see, we too have the ability to take advantage of it. There is no act that you do that we cannot duplicate now that you have opened the rift between us. We shall have our revenge upon you and take that which has been denied us for so long.' Emrys spat the words with venom and glee as he saw the fear in the eyes of the seers. Rising up and drawing upon the power that was his to command, Emrys threw his arms down towards Terra Standfast releasing a surge of dark energy that pulsed towards the determined dwarf.

Standing his ground as was typical of his nature the redoubtable leader of the Council of the Sight met the challenge with fortitude. Bracing for the impact, he was surprised when there was no blow to be felt; instead the energy from the leader of the wizards enfolded the shield that protected him, clinging to it and wrapping around it as treacle would around a ball.

Darkness fell around the desperate seer as the power of the wizards sought to cut him off from the others. Terra could feel and see the shield weakening as the dark energy ate away at the skin of his defensive bubble. Soon he would be at the mercy of the negative forces that were intent on crushing him. Seeing the danger that Terra was in; Liam unleashed a flash of brilliant amber power to aid his friend.

His efforts were unrewarded as the flash of energy clashed with that of the wizards as it sought to eat into Terra's shield and simply vanished as if the darkness had swallowed it up. Liam feared that he was powerless to prevent the wizards from destroying the valiant dwarf and glanced at Emerald in dismay; hoping against hope that she would be able to succeed where he had failed. She too saw what had happened and sent her own blast of power at the clawing darkness around Terra, all to no avail. The darkness closed in around their leader relentlessly as the two desperate wizards concentrated their energies on pressing their attack.

Liam and Emerald decided to change their approach and levelled their staves at the wizards sending blast after blast into their midst. Several hits were scored against the wizards but still the wizards poured their energies into tightening the grip around their prey. Working together in unison gave the wizards a greater power and Emrys concentrated that power into the attack on Terra, leaving his two fellow wizards to see to their defence from the other seers' attacks. His eyes glowed with a deeper red as Emrys sensed victory.

It was Terra Standfast that had caused him to lose his wife Erin in the battle fought long ago for control and brought about their final banishment. True this was not the same Terra Standfast he was striving to destroy now; the original Terra had died long ago but that mattered not to him. The fact that this dwarf wore the mantle of that seer and carried the name of his nemesis was sufficient reason for Emrys to hate him as much as he had Terra's predecessors. The wizard bent to his task, ignoring any attempt put up by Liam and Emerald. They were not a threat to him so long as the other two wizards maintained their defence. Drawing deeper upon the combined power of the negative energy that sustained them, Emrys leaned forward as if to force the dark power to crush his adversary.

Inside the bubble of power that Terra had around him, he fought as he had never done before, exerting all his will against the pressure that mounted against him. He knew, however, that he would eventually lose this battle unless the others were able to come to his aid. He could feel his strength weakening and he knelt on one knee bracing himself against his staff; drawing upon hidden resources that he never knew he had. He would not pass on without a fight.

Liam and Emerald, seeing the success that joining together gave the wizards, ran to each other and touched staves. Concentrating all their will into a single blast of power at one of the wizards they unleashed a single beam of raw energy that crackled in the air with its intensity. It smashed into a wizard who shrieked in agony and fell against Emrys, distracting him for a split second. It was enough of a lapse in the wizard's attack for Terra to push the cloud that surrounded him and ate at his defences, away from him. He did not succeed in removing it completely, but it gave him hope and he stood with his feet firmly planted on the ground and he dug his heels in. Slowly the swirling mass of darkness began to retreat and break down. Light appeared as the gloom was dispelled and Terra sent renewed energy through his staff.

Fear began to form in the red eyes of the wizard as he saw his advantage being eroded by the determination of the dwarf and the searing blasts that Liam and Emerald directed at them. He began to think that he would not succeed and that his efforts to regain dominance in this world would be thwarted. His fear turned to dismay as a fresh blast of blue power ripped into his defences and the control he held over the cloud around Terra was torn out of his grasp. The dark cloud that surrounded the battling dwarf dissolved and he was released from the pressure being exerted by Emrys. The negative energies could not be sustained against the red energy from Terra's staff and he was freed.

The resulting backlash from the release of power caused Emrys to fall backwards, gasping at the forces that had been unleashed. Now it was his turn to feel the sting of the seers attack. He had failed when he had thought he was so close to victory. He had nothing else to give except to defend against whatever the seers chose to unleash against him. There were no second chances when confronting a seer; he knew that from past experience and quailed at the memory of the battle when his beloved Erin had fallen along with Galan and Megan. He had to escape this turn of events or face the same fate as they had done. He was not ready for that just yet and determined to survive to fight another day. He had not succeeded in making the breakthrough that he had wanted to this time but there would be other chances and he would be better prepared for them.

Searching for the cause of his failure in destroying the one seer he had wanted to overcome, he saw that a fourth seer had appeared. Urim, he might have known that it was he. In every confrontation that had ever been waged against the seers; it was Urim that had proven to be the thorn in his side. 'Perhaps I should have disposed of him first.' Emrys considered with belated wisdom.

'Gather to me.' Terra shouted the command to the other seers above the howling of the shattered wind. 'Blend with me my friends; allow me to control the united power of the staves.' Terra spoke in barely a whisper but Liam, Emerald and Urim heard his voice in their heads as clearly as if he had shouted into their ears. They closed their eyes and bowed their heads, surrendering their wills to that of their leader. Terra felt the connection between them and formed the power within their staves into a formidable ball of positive energy, drawn up from beneath their feet from the shaft. He threw the energy at the wizards and exerted all of his will into sending the wizards back from whence they came. The forces of two worlds collided and shattered the air with a booming crash that reverberated out across the still waters that surrounded the Tower.

When the seers opened their eyes the wizards had gone and a scene of calm prevailed in the courtyard of the Tower. Emrys and his brother wizards had been thrown back into their prison world leaving the seers free of the threat that the wizards had represented to their world.

Terra leaned against his staff for support and spoke in a whisper as he gathered his strength. 'We must be more careful in using The Montage in the future; we can not afford to allow the wizards to gain a foothold in this world, the resulting horror would be unimaginable. Urim, we are grateful for your timely assistance but how did you know that we were in need and how did you get here?'

'You forget, Terra, that I am the keeper of the Golden Tome; as for my arrival, I used the staff of the portal that I confiscated from Ebon. I must use it again if we are to succeed in our plan to prevent what we have just witnessed from ever happening again.'

'Yes, of course. Thank you again for your service to our cause, we would be in dire straights if it were not for you.'

'I seek only to serve the Sight as I am called to do. You will, by now, have heard the news that Auger wind-rider shall not be returning to you. Hamill and Jon continue on their way with Braun and the dwarves. You must consider who would be best suited to replace him and to become the new Auger Wind-rider on the Council. Obviously it must be a dwarf; I would suggest that you look no further than those who accompany Hamill and Jon; they have proved themselves to be valiant and true to the cause. Now I must ready myself for the next phase of our plan. I shall return when I have completed that which I have been charged with. I will see you soon my friends, farewell.' Using the power of the staff of the portal, Urim stepped into a hole in the air that had appeared behind him and he vanished as it closed around him leaving the others to attend to their tasks.

'Come Liam and Emerald, we have much to do; I am saddened by the loss of our dear friend, Auger; he was a worthy member of the Council and he will be hard to replace. I believe that Urim is right concerning his successor; the dwarves have indeed shown themselves to be noble and courageous. Our greatest difficulty will be in knowing which one to choose. That is a matter that will have to await their arrival; I feel sure that we will know who it is to be when we see them and must put that aside for now. We have delayed long enough from setting matters straight between us and the wizards. Now that Emrys has failed to break through and establish himself here there will be a reckoning back at his conclave. He will have to withstand serious accusations from his fellow wizards and much as I dislike what he stands for, I cannot help but feel for him.'

'You are a true seer, Terra Standfast and I would like to say what a privilege it is to serve with you.' Liam proudly said of his friend.

'I too honour you, noble dwarf. You have led this Council for many years and you have done so with great wisdom and strength. It is my hope that you continue to do so for many years to come.' Emerald bowed her head in recognition of his stature and, along with Liam, saluted their leader.

'I thank you my friends but as Urim has stated, I too, do only that which I am charged to do. Nevertheless I am grateful for your kindness; without your support I could not succeed. The Council, it should be remembered, is greater than one person; it takes all eight of us to act as one for the benefit of the land.'

Emerald shook her head and slapped her side, berating herself for not thinking earlier. 'Queen Ella gave me a token, a little silver bell that she said would aid me in times of difficulty; I forgot about it until now. I wonder what would have happened if I had used it in our battle with the wizards?'

'You may well get the opportunity to try it again, Emerald. I believe that the wizards will be back to renew their fight. Emrys will not be so easily put off; he will be back to try and establish himself here again and next time they will all come.'

The three seers stood for a moment in silence, not wanting to consider the outcome of the next battle against the conclave of wizards. The seers had been hard pressed to withstand this last attack and Terra knew that in order to defeat them and to maintain their stance as protectors of the land they required help from every quarter.

They stood solemnly in remembrance of Auger and considered the challenge they now had in preparing a novice to stand in his stead. As with Hamill, he would have to be tutored by them all and inaugurated as soon as possible. He would have to take up the mantle of the departed seer immediately in order for there to be eight who sat at council. It would be a difficult task for whoever was chosen but one that could be achieved. At such a moment in the history of the land it would prove testing to have two new members of the council who had yet to grow into their respective roles. Hamill was proving to be adept and was learning quickly following his inauguration to replace Ebon. Terra believed that the former physician would yet prove to be a valuable asset to their number. Yet the fact remained that he was still young as to the ways of the seers.

Terra broke the silence. 'My friends, I fear that we can spare no time as yet in mourning the loss of our dear companion, we must continue with the final preparations of our plan. Now that we know what has become of Auger, there is much that needs to be considered.

With the staff of the portal his to command, Urim had found a new and valuable resource to the Council in their battle against evil. Ebon had inadvertently provided him with the means of foiling the rebel seer's plans. Urim was able to travel through the dimensions, to other worlds that before had only been accessible via The Montage. Truly now he could counter that which Ebon strove to do. Urim pondered the significance of this staff and knew that it contained more power than one person had the right to command. After he had dealt with Ebon, he would place it in the hands of the Council of the Sight, for them to consider its use in other events. It would not be right for Urim to claim it as his own, denying its abilities to others of the Council who could benefit from it. That is one area where he differed from Ebon who would have held it for himself. Urim would not be swayed from placing the needs of others above those of himself; he sought only to assist in maintaining the proper balance in the land and between the worlds. In that way, order would continue and the folk of the world they had sworn to protect would remain safe.

He knew what he had to do now and realised that any error of judgement on his part could have devastating consequences. Ebon was a cunning and powerful adversary; his motives were foreign to Urim and diametrically opposed to his own and those of the Council. As he considered what he might do to thwart Ebon's plans Urim thought through several options, discarding each one when he came upon a flaw in its execution. Finally he hit upon the only way he could achieve what needed to be done without causing harm to come to others.

He had been observing things for some time now, hidden from view as he watched matters unfold in retrospect with the use of his talisman. He, as keeper of the Golden Tome, could view the recent past as if he were watching a play being performed on the stage of history. It enabled him to know more about what a person thought and did than any amount of ordinary observation could achieve. His only problem was in what to do with that knowledge and how to influence what he did so that he might be able to complete his task with the least possible disruption to others.

Urim had seen what Ebon had done in sending Jetta to capture Anna and it had taken a great deal of will power to stop from immediately rushing to her aid. He had to remind himself that he was merely observing what had already taken place. Being forewarned, however, of that which Ebon proposed to do once he had Anna, gave Urim the advantage. He would allow Ebon to believe that he was succeeding; that way he could lead the unsuspecting rebel seer into the trap that he and Terra had devised. It was not without risk of course and Urim had to bide his time but ultimately, Ebon would deliver himself into Urim's hands and that would bring an end to the evil that he had brought upon the land.

It had been decided by the Council of the Sight what would become of Ebon once Urim had the rogue seer, but Urim thought that it would be better to let Ebon's own choices determine what should become of him. There is a law that states that one must accept the consequences of one's own actions. It would only be just if Urim were to utilise that law.

Chapter 19

Sea of Sand

The blistering heat dragged at their senses as Jon and the others laboured against the shifting sands. The effort they exerted in trudging through the soft terrain sapped the energy from their aching limbs. Time and again one or another of them would fall to the ground and have to be helped to stand again. Braun laboured more than anyone else because of his weight; he would sink ankle deep in the loose surface that dragged at his feet with invisible hands; clawing at the soles of his boots like wet clay.

Again they were forced to endure the full glare and heat of the sun; travelling by night would have been preferable as the colder air was more suited to walking in the open. However, with no moon now to light the way and only the one glow stone between them; it had been considered too dangerous to attempt it. The heat had been far greater than any of them had expected; with no shade and a limited supply of water between them they were desperate to locate the next oasis where they could rest briefly and refresh their flasks.

Searching for an easier route through the unforgiving terrain kept the soldiers busy, conscious that they needed to keep heading in a south-westerly direction. If they were out in their reckoning by just a few degrees, they would miss their objective and wander for another day or more in this soul destroying desert.

The soldiers from Northill all wished that they had stayed at home and Jon didn't blame them; he wished that he had stayed at home too. The torturous conditions played at his resolve and he would gladly have swapped his present circumstances for those of the Redwood forest back in Ashbrooke. The memory of the cooling breeze as it stirred the branches of the trees and rustled the leaves made him long for the shade. He took a long draught of water from his canteen. It was almost empty and there was little chance of it being refilled before tonight and only then if they located the oasis that the soldiers had told them lay somewhere ahead of them. The thought made Jon's legs feel even heavier and he stumbled blindly on, following in the tracks of the one in front.

Evening drew rapidly upon them and still they had not found the promised water. As the sun set they reluctantly made camp, not daring to travel any further for fear of someone falling and injuring themselves, or perhaps becoming separated from the main group. Jon's throat felt like he had been gargling glass, it was so sore and he was desperately in need of a drink. He emptied the last few drops of precious liquid from his canteen and prayed that they would find water in the morning. He crossed his fingers for good luck.

As he looked around him at the others, he saw that they were all likewise suffering from the rigours of the journey and the incessant heat that sapped their energy. Hamill sat hugging his knees. Jon was even more concerned about him now; he was not his usual self and was deliberately being secretive. He was distant in his manner and when Jon looked into his eyes he had a far-away look in them. There was something troubling the seer; something that he did not want to share with the others. Jon knew better than to pester his friend about it as he knew from being with Urim that whatever it was that was on his mind he would share it when the time was right. Never-the-less, Jon intended keeping a close eye on his friend. Pulling his travel cloak around him he drifted off into a deep sleep, exhausted from the trek through the merciless desert sands.

Jon was mesmerised by the beautiful singing and found that he could not resist the lure of the promise of cool water. He was aware that he was walking, stumbling forward as if he were being manipulated by another force. The last thing he remembered was lying down to sleep, then he heard the most beautiful singing and felt compelled to seek from whence it came. He crept past his sleeping friends, not wanting to share this amazingly wonderful sound. Then he noticed that the four soldiers had also heard the voices and were making their way towards the promise of cool, thirst-quenching water. He followed in their tracks, in the cold of the desert night searching for the life giving liquid.

The leader of the group yelled out and ran forward, dropping to his knees and cupped his hands to scoop the precious liquid and quench his thirst. Jon sank gratefully to his knees beside the pool of water; suddenly Hamill appeared beside him, only he spoke with Ebon's voice, encouraging him to drink. Jon tried not to listen, knowing that Ebon was not to be trusted; he felt the water in his hand and yearned to swallow great gulps of it. As he looked at it he saw the water turn to sand. Letting the sand spill through his fingers he forced himself to his feet.

'I will not listen to you, Ebon; you shall not deceive me into believing that what you have to say would be of benefit to me or any of my friends.'

'Friends? You have no friends; they all despise you and have only suffered you because of Urim and Hamill. They are the seers; you are nothing of any consequence. It matters not to them whether you live or die.'

'That's not true; you are a liar and I will not listen to you any more.' With that he turned around and walked away from the taunts that Ebon levelled at him whilst still in the personification of Hamill. The wailing that had been swirling around him grew in intensity and dragged at his senses, clawing at his will power, enticing him to return and drink the cool fresh water. Jon could see the pool of life giving water in his mind but somehow he knew it was only an illusion. He struggled against it with determination and a resolve that kept his feet plodding on; putting more and more distance between him and the temptation of the water and the taunts that were thrown after him.

Hamill was awakened by a shove from Javelin. 'The soldiers are missing and Jon has gone with them. They left during the night and their tracks lead off in the direction of Anram. Trapper believes that they went in search of the oasis and we are going to go after them. You'd better get ready.'

Hamill groaned with disbelief that they would be so foolhardy as to try to find the waterhole in the dark by themselves and was surprised that Jon would go with them without telling him. He clambered to his feet and they commenced what promised to be an arduous day's hiking. The sun had just risen but already the heat was fierce and beginning to make him sweat. He needed a drink and lifted his canteen to his lips and drank the last drops. He felt like throwing the flask away but realised that it would be foolhardy to do so as he would need it when they did find water.

The dwarves led the way, following the tracks across the desert wasteland, up one side of the mountainous dunes and down the other. It was arduous work to say the least and the day dragged on. Suddenly Leader shouted hoarsely and started to run; the others could not see what he was running for but they stumbled on after him.

Jon regained consciousness to the soothing feeling of water trickling down his throat; it made him choke and he fought to stop swallowing believing that he was being misled into thinking that it was water but really it was sand.

'Jon; Jon, stop fighting; wake up. It's me Hamill.'

Jon was delirious from exposure to the sun and struggled to free himself from his tormentors. 'No it's Ebon; you can't make me drink; it's sand.'

'He's delirious poor chap.' Braun said, concerned for him.

Javelin took Jon by the shoulders and shook him, shouting into his ear. 'Jon, Jon, it's Javelin, you are safe now, we found you; you must drink.'

'Javelin; is that really you?' He whimpered weakly, opening his eyes and squinting against the glare to try and see the trusty dwarf.

'Yes, it's me and Hamill and the others; we're all here; now take a sip of water and you'll feel better.'

Jon recognised the dwarf as he stooped over him. Grasping the proffered flask he drank greedily from it until Hamill took it from him. 'Not too quickly my friend; it will make you ill.'

'Hamill, thank goodness; I feared that Ebon had come back.' Jon spluttered as he drank from the proffered canteen.

They all looked at each other believing that Jon was still hallucinating.

'It's alright Jon, Ebon's not here; where did you go? What happened to the soldiers?' Hamill asked his friend, helping him to sit up.

'I thought I was dreaming; the sound was so alluring and I seemed to float along the ground. I wanted to wake you but I was too intent on listening to the singing. I couldn't stop myself. The soldiers and I found the oasis and they were drinking but then you appeared, only it wasn't you; it was Ebon and something inside stopped me from swallowing. I looked at the water in my hand and knew it was sand. He tried to get me to drink but I turned away and I left them there; I don't remember anything after that.'

'We'll rest here for a while until Jon can walk and then we'll go in search of the soldiers.' Javelin announced to the others.

They all appreciated the chance to take a sip of water and gather their reserves for the trek onwards. They needed to find the oasis soon as the water supply was drastically low. Having been sufficiently rested, the group carried on. Some time later, Jon did not know how long they had been walking; Leader stopped, shielded his eyes against the glare of the reflected sunlight from the white sand and pointed. The others all drew abreast of him and followed where he was pointing. There on the ground a little way ahead lay the four soldiers, face down in the sand. They looked rather odd, stretched out as if they were surrounding a central point like spokes in a wheel.

A few minutes later they reached them, turning them over one by one; Archer announced that they were all dead; choked on sand.

'Poor fellows, they must have been driven mad by thirst. In their deranged minds they probably thought that they had found the oasis and were drinking from the pool.'

'Yes, I've heard of this sort of thing happening. We must watch one another in case it happens to us. You were fortunate to have escaped the same fate, Jon' Digger said.

'Well, we ought to bury them but there would be little point to it. The first sand storm that comes along will only uncover them again. Better to leave them and let the desert take care of them.' Javelin said sombrely.

They all felt bad just leaving their bodies laying in the sand but realised that Javelin was probably right and so they continued on. Jon looked back one last time before losing sight of them as they crested another dune and slid down the other side. He took up his position behind Mason and counted himself fortunate not to have suffered the same fate. He fixed his thoughts on reaching Anram alive and in one piece.

It must have been about two turns of the hand later that Leader called a halt to rest and they sank wearily to the ground. Jon tried to swallow but his mouth had no spit, it felt as dry as the desert itself.

He looked at the others and saw how exhausted they appeared and thought that he probably looked as bad as they did. He was filled with a weariness he had never felt in his life before. He decided that when the others got up to move on, he would stay here. He had no energy left to stand up, let alone to move on. He sat dejectedly and thought of Anna. He missed her and longed to see her, to hear her voice again. He sank to the ground to rest and closed his eyes; he was so weary from trudging through the sand that he lost consciousness.

'Jon...Jon...You must get up and carry on.' Anna's voice came to him through a fog and a brightness like the noonday sun filtered through his closed eyelids. Shielding his eyes from the light he mumbled her name.

'What's the matter Jon? Are you alright?' Hamill asked; his voice cracked as he spoke hoarsely from a rasping throat as he shook Jon. 'We must carry on; we can't be far from the next oasis.'

Hamill helped him get to his feet and they climbed up the slope of the dune of loose sand. It was hard work just placing one foot in front of another without the effort of having to climb these dunes. Gaining the top of the rise, Jon had to blink several times before he could believe his eyes. Passing not a league away from them was a caravan of dromedaries loaded up with bundles and staves. Desert folk; they were traders of beasts and the only inhabitants of this inhospitable region. They survived by moving from one area to another, never staying too long in any one place in order to preserve the precious water reserves of the few water holes that dotted the vast stretches of sand. Hamill tried to shout but he had no voice then pulling his cloak free he began waving it in the hope that someone would see. They did and several of the traders peeled away from the main column and headed towards them. They were saved.

The traders spoke a language peculiar to this region and none of the dwarves or anyone else could speak it so Jon tried the sign language that Anna had taught him. It was not wholly successful but they did manage to communicate with the traders by some of the gestures. What was clear to the traders, without the need for words, was the desperate need of the group for water and dutifully supplied them with it. Sitting in the shade of a hastily erected canopy, they soon felt their strength returning. The traders were keen to move on however and signalled for them to come with them, indicating with their gestures that they were headed for the oasis the group of friends had been seeking.

Some time later, when the sun was at its hottest, they saw the oasis ahead. Jon felt the tension that had built up in his body relax and he went limp, just about staying on the back of the beast he had been propped up on. Seeing the palms and the green vegetation that surrounded the life-saving pool of water was the most amazing feeling and he smiled in relief through cracked lips at the scene that greeted him. It was not a large pool but it was more than sufficient for their needs. Jon understood why these traders moved around; not just because of their business but if they were to stay here then the water would be in risk of being depleted.

They made camp for the night; the traders erecting their canvas shelters that were big enough to hold a company of soldiers. Brightly coloured carpets were laid out on the ground and soft bundles enabled them to sit in comfort. The whole thing was rather exotic and strangely surreal considering where they were, out in the desert wastes. Their sore and blistered skin was treated with a salve that soothed and moistened bringing welcome relief. The best thing of all for Jon was the taste of the sweet water from the pool. He sipped it carefully so that it would quench his thirst better.

The sun began to sink towards the horizon and darkness rapidly descended upon them. One moment it was daylight and the next it was dark but the camp fires had been lit and the light from them and the oil lamps within the shelters gave them enough light to see.

Jon did not know what he was in need of most, food or sleep, now that he had enough water and his skin was recovering from exposure to the sun. The smell of hot food being prepared in a large blackened pot on the main fire convinced him that it was food; he could sleep afterwards but for now, he needed feeding.

Tantalising wafts of spice drifted into the shelter where he sat at the entrance and his mouth watered at the prospect of the meal. He had not realised just how hungry he had been; thirst had been his main problem to contend with but now that he had been given water, he needed to eat. Hamill too was keen to taste the delicious smelling contents of the cauldron and he sat hugging his knees not far from Jon, gazing longingly at the pot, waiting for the moment when the food would be served.

They did not have to wait too long. Plates of steaming food were passed to them all. Jon lifted the plate to his face and he took a long sniff of the steaming contents; it was highly spiced and he could not wait to taste it. Digging in, the flavours swamped his taste buds and he started to sweat but it was delicious. The texture was a little strange, the lumps of meat were a bit chewy but he enjoyed it none-the-less. He certainly had not had anything like it before but it tasted wonderful and he finished the lot.

Braun was not so keen on it and he pushed his food around his plate before laying it aside without eating anything.

'Aren't you going to eat that?' Trapper asked him.

'No, it is not to my liking. You can have it if you want it.'

The dwarf did not need telling twice and helped himself to seconds of the spiced meat stew.

The two traders who had served the meal returned to collect the empty plates and brought them several platters of fruit and sweet things which Braun particularly was grateful for. After having been offered a strong, dark and sickly hot drink, which they all refused apart from Braun who drank it with satisfaction; they retired for the night; grateful for the comfort of the shelter and the hospitality of their rescuers.

During the night, Jon had a vivid dream; a picture came into his mind of a subterranean chamber, on the floor was marked a circle of stones. In the centre was a different coloured stone, a keystone. Standing by the stone was Urim. He reached out to Jon and clenched his hand into a fist.

'You must open the way. One touch of a seers' staff and you will be able to return to Seers Tower instantly.'

Jon awoke with a start, a cold sweat bathed his face and his heart thumped in his chest. Staring wide eyed into the gloom of the section of the shelter that he had been assigned as a sleeping place, he gulped at the air and tried to calm his mind. Breathing heavily he went over the dream again in his mind and burned the picture of the keystone into his memory. When they got there, he would know what to do.

Chapter 20

The Ruins of Anram

The traders were staying at the oasis for a further day or two but Hamill had urged the others to start out as soon as possible and to resume their journey to Anram. They had tried to purchase a beast from the traders but they had none to sell at the moment so they set out across the desert sands on foot taking extra water with them.

Jon considered that the arid wastes surrounding the ruins of Anram deserved their reputation. He asked himself, how long it had been since he had taken a drink of water. There was only so much that they could carry with them and the traders had been kind enough to sell them additional flasks but even with this extra water, they were beginning to run low. The thought of it made him thirsty and he fumbled at the stop to his canister, eager to taste the life giving fluid. It was like drinking from a kettle. The sun had all but boiled it in his flask, yet it was satisfying to his dry, parched throat. His lips had cracked again and he had stopped sweating; a sure sign of being dehydrated.

They should have avoided travelling in the daytime but there had been no choice but to continue on in their efforts to reach the ruins of Anram. Jon felt instinctively that time was running out before the wizards found the way through the void to exact an awful revenge upon the seers for their banishment. The energy of the barrier had to be channelled in the right way if they were to ensure that Ebon would not be able to return from the other world.

Whatever happened now, there was no going back. All that lay behind them was the desert expanse and certain death if they should try to return that way. It was not over yet. They had to reach the buried city that had once been the home of the wizards if they failed to get through then the history of the land would be written by others than they.

What was it that Urim had said? 'The lives of future generations lay in their hands.' Not that it helped them to know that; if anything it only added to the pressure he had felt upon him. Knowing that if any one of them failed it would bring turmoil and destruction upon the folk of the land; the like of which they had never known since the Council of the Sight came into being.

Stumbling across the unforgiving terrain tested their resolve. The muscles in Jon's legs ached from the effort of trudging across leagues of shifting sand. It was reminiscent of his march with Hamill and Gemon through the mud from Ashbrooke to the Ward. He did not know which was worse, the cold and the rain or the heat and the thirst. Each was as wearing on him as the other yet what he wouldn't give for it to rain now.

Hamill had taken to wearing his cloak again which Jon thought rather a strange thing to do in this heat. Then his friend explained that the cloak actually helped him to keep cool as the hot, arid air was kept off his body. The air within the cloak was not as hot as that on the outside. Jon did not really understand but he took his word for it.

A shout from Trapper at the head of the group brought his mind into focus. Looking up and shielding his eyes from the glare of the sun, he saw the dwarf standing at the top of a dune, beckoning them forward. Rallying his reserves of energy, he and the others made their way up the incline, sliding back one step for every two they made forward in the loose sand. Reaching the top he looked out over a barren landscape that stretched out before them; in the distance the sun sparkled on the body of water known as The Little Salt Waters. He did not notice straight away the thing that Trapper had seen and asked what all the fuss was about. Then Archer pointed out the outlines of the ruined city not two leagues away. More importantly, there were trees and a patch of greenery that bordered the city. Water; there had to be water. With renewed energy the fatigued travellers ran, stumbling and sliding down the face of the dune towards the promise of the cool, fresh, life-preserving fluid.

Reaching the pool they all sank gratefully to quench their thirst. Jon was careful not to drink too deeply however as he knew that it would not be wise to do so. Scooping a second handful of water to his lips he closed his eyes in pure bliss, letting the water trickle down his face then scooping into the pool again and splashing the precious liquid over his head. It was wonderful to feel the cooling effect on his skin as it soothed his reddened face. They all likewise appreciated the relief that finding this oasis brought to them, without it they would have been sorely in need.

Looking around him Jon saw that the pool was not a natural one but it had been contained in a purpose built reservoir. Steps that were partially covered with waves of sand led up to where a carved statue of a large cat sat on a plinth. It regarded them imperiously through sightless eyes, guarding the way into the city. His curiosity aroused, he clambered up the steps and rested against the plinth looking out over the expanse of what was once a mighty city. Much of it had been covered by the desert sands, drifted in on the winds that blew out of the south. Broken towers pierced the undulating surface between mounds of sand that presumably covered the buildings of this forsaken city. It had lain in ruins for thousands of years, ever since the battle between the seers and the wizards had resulted in the banishment of the wizards and the formation of the Council of the Sight.

Something caught his attention, stark against the golden hue of the sand; Jon could see an opening at the base of a mound that must have been an entrance to what lay beneath.

'Javelin, I think I might have found our way into the city.'

Climbing up the steps, Javelin shielded his eyes and looked in the direction Jon was pointing. 'You may well be right, young Jon. We shall have to investigate.' Turning back to the others who were filling their flasks with fresh water, he called them to join him. 'Archer, Trapper, it looks like we have our entrance. Let's go take a look.'

The entrance that Jon had seen from the elevated position of the steps was hidden amongst the rocks at ground level. Clambering through the fallen blocks that lay in front of the opening gave them access to the passage that sloped away down into the darkness. Jon had never felt the noonday sun to be this hot before as it beat down on him from above. He had not ventured this far south until now.

The heat that had been so oppressive to them out in the open desert lifted from their shoulders as the shade in the passageway offered them welcome relief from the intensity of the sun's glare. Just being out of the sun gave them respite from the scorching rays and it was with gratitude that they entered into the shelter of the tunnel.

If they had not found the shelter of these passages, they would surely have died from exposure to the sun. It was a marvel that anything could live in this heat. He had noticed a small lizard that morning as it skittered across the dunes, trying not to step on the surface of the golden sand. Whenever it stopped it hopped from one leg to another so as to alleviate the effects from the scolding heat that came from the sand. He had smiled at its comical movements but admired its tenacity and skill in handling the adverse conditions. He had lost sight of it when it burrowed into the sand to escape the hellish conditions in search of the cool that lay beneath the surface.

They rested for a while at the mouth of the tunnel, enjoying the respite from the merciless sun. Trapper let out a cry of astonishment and called the others to see what he had discovered. They all likewise demonstrated surprise at what he had found. Piled in a reed basket Digger had uncovered from the sands that had blown in from the desert, were eight smooth stones. 'You don't suppose that they are glow stones do you?'

'Well, there's only one way to find out. Here, give one to me.' Archer took hold of one from Trapper and stepped further into the tunnel. As he went deeper and the darkness increased, the stone began to shine. It *was* a glow stone.

'How on earth do you suppose they got here?' Javelin asked.

Jon was equally puzzled but slowly an idea formed and he became convinced that Urim had something to do with it. He did not share his thoughts with the others however and left them to their speculations. Javelin put an end to it by saying, 'We will probably never know the truth of how they got here so I suggest we just accept the fact that they are here and we can use them.'

They all agreed and Javelin ensured that everyone was recovered enough from the heat to continue before leading off down the tunnel.

Jon had a deep respect for these hardy dwarves who had never failed to assist them in their endeavours. Javelin, Archer and Trapper had been their companions through all of their struggles, first against Ebon and then, when Amethyst had threatened the land, there they were; loyal to the last. Digger had proven no less a stalwart in his devotion to helping Jon and the seers. Mason and Leader had also shown their loyalty when the time came to give an account of themselves.

Then of course there was Tracker and Gemon, both of them had given their lives in the stand for freedom. Jon did not know what they would have done without them and a lump came to his throat as he thought about them. He marvelled at how willing they were to go wherever they were needed, no matter what the cost. Looking at the dwarves now he saw how uncomfortable they were with the heat. These hardy folk were more suited to the mountains of the Divide; the range Jon knew as the Eastern Mountains. The rigours of their travels were taking a toll on their bodies as they struggled to breathe in the hot, dry air. Still they forged their way forwards, determined to see it through.

Braun was the only one amongst them who was able to bear the heat, being used to the forges at Foundry Smelt. It had obviously toughened his skin and meant that he could withstand the extreme temperature better than they. He had been a stalwart friend to Jon and safeguarded him and the others when danger threatened. If it were not for the friendly giant of a man, Jon supposed that he would be dead long ago.

The glow stones were able to give them more than enough light by which to navigate the pitch black of the passage and the six dwarves led them bravely on into the welcoming cool beneath the baking sands.

It was a marvel to see the extent to which the ancients had gone to ensure that these passages remained open for accessing the inner caverns. Most miners would dig out a square passage, supporting the rock above with wooden beams and tresses. These tunnels were oval in shape, as if a giant egg had been used as a template. Digger was particularly impressed with the skill and workmanship that had been put to use in the excavation of these tunnels. He remarked at how advanced the workers must have been to have bored into the solid bedrock beneath the sand in such a way. Every twenty lengths there were recesses where anyone who met with another going in the opposite direction could pass without hindrance.

Jon followed in the footsteps of the dwarves, the echoes of their footfalls reverberating down the passageway. They came to a junction before they had gone sixty paces where the shape of the passages took on a more conventional look; being square edged.

'I think that the rock must be more solid here and the minors were able to dig it out without fear of it collapsing.' Digger remarked.

'No; look closer; you can see that the walls and ceiling have been lined with large slabs of granite. This place was meant to last for ever.' Mason said touching the wall with what appeared to the others to be an awed reverence.

They decided to split up and search down the tunnels to find out which would be the better way to go. Hamill, Leader and Archer went one way whilst Trapper and Mason went the other. The rest of them waited for them to return and report on what they had found. They waited in the light of the glow stones listening to the footsteps of the seer and dwarves echo into silence.

The stillness of the place wrapped around them like a cocoon. Jon felt nervous about standing around but knew it was the right thing to do in order to determine their best route forward. A shout from Trapper sounded up the passageway and made Jon jump. 'Javelin; this way, we've discovered a room that has a model layout of the city.'

Braun volunteered to go and find Hamill and the two dwarves, then return with them, so he set off after them whilst they all made their way to join with Digger. They found him a little way further along the passage where he was waiting at an opening into a side room. There laid out on a raised platform was indeed a model of Anram. It was covered in a fine dust and as Trapper bent near and blew, it puffed into the air; that set several of them sneezing.

'Careful, Trapper; there's enough dust down here without you circulating it around.' Javelin chided his friend.

'I'm sorry about that; it was a natural reaction; I didn't think.' Trapper apologised to them for having created the dust-cloud but it soon settled.

'Wait a minute; I think Trapper has just found our route through these passages.' Javelin peered closer at the place that had cleared of dust. Drawing his finger along a faint red line on the model, he traced out a series of lines that connected up and formed a pattern. 'I believe that these lines represent the tunnels that we are in and if this is the map room here,' Trapper pointed to a tiny representation of the city in a room marked on the model; 'then this is a model of the model. This is where we are now and by following theses lines we can find our way to the great pyramid where the keystone is located.'

'Well done Trapper; can you make a copy of it and lead us through these tunnels?' Javelin praised the ingenuity of the dwarf.

'Yes, I think so; all I need is something to trace it out on.'

'What about this?' Mason passed his notepad to Trapper who took it eagerly and started copying the route through the city's tunnels.

When he had finished copying the most likely route for them to follow, Trapper announced that he was ready to go. Just in case they got separated he gave a second copy he had drawn to Javelin who memorised the layout before placing it in his pocket.

'Where have the others gone and where's Braun? He should have found them and brought them back by now.' Javelin fidgeted, eager to get going.

'Perhaps they got lost.' Jon said; worried in case something had happened to them.

'Well we can't risk sending anyone else after them and we can't wait around all day. There's nothing else for it but to carry on.'

'Javelin, can you leave your copy of the map here on the model, just in case they make it back. They can catch up with us by following it and go the same way we do.' Jon suggested.

Pressing on into the gloom, Hamill and the two dwarves searched for any sign that would tell them which way they should go in order that they might find the keystone that lay beneath the great pyramid. They stopped occasionally to listen, as a gentle thud could be heard now and again from somewhere behind them. Listening intently for any sound of the others they decided after a few minutes fruitless searching that it would be wiser to return to them and try the other way. In hindsight it had probably not been a good idea to have separated, the last thing they wanted was for them to worry about any lost souls. As they made their way back, Hamill came up against a dead end.

'That's funny. I could have sworn that we came down this way.'

'What's the matter, seer? Have you forgotten our way back?' Archer quizzed, teasing him with a soft chuckle in his voice.

Holding the glow stone closer to the floor Hamill saw their footprints in the dust, cut in two by the solid rock in front of them.

'I knew I was right. We did come this way but the rock has sealed off the way back. I think we can only try another way and hope for the best. The others will have to carry on without us; let's hope that we are able to meet up in the chamber at the pyramid.'

'What chamber? Have you been here before?' Leader asked, confused at what Hamill had said.

'No, I've never set foot in the place until now. I just know somehow that there is a chamber beneath the large pyramid that holds the answer to our search.'

Retracing their footsteps, they continued deeper into the labyrinth. As they turned the corner a soft thud sounded from behind them as another stone slid into place barring the way back. Ahead of them, Hamill thought he caught the sound of bare feet padding along the corridor. Whispering back to the dwarves to keep as quiet as they could, they stole forward searching the ground for signs of the footprints that would be left in the dust by whoever it was he had heard. Sure enough, a couple of turns later, there in the dust were the tell tale marks left by a single person. The prints were not large; Hamill guessed that it was either a small male or a female. Whoever it was, at least they were human.

Braun could not understand why he had not found Hamill and the other dwarves. He should have caught up with them by now; then the tracks he had been following stopped suddenly at a solid rock face. To all intents and purposes it appeared as if they had walked straight through but Braun knew that to be impossible. However Hamill was a seer; maybe they had. If that were the case, he had no way of following them so turned back to tell the others of his discovery.

Keeping his head down so that he could traverse the tunnels without banging his head on the ceiling, he followed his tracks back the way he had come. He was astonished to find that his way was barred by a rock wall. Looking at the ground he saw his footprints and those of the seer and the dwarves cut off by the stone. Then it dawned on him that the place was a huge labyrinth and the way forward kept changing. This was not going to be easy; he was separated from both the dwarves and the seers. He was alone in a maze that could have him going around in circles for ever. Puffing out his cheeks in frustration he shrugged his shoulders and muttered.

'Well, if I'm going to get out of here I have to keep going and hope I find the way out. The others will have to carry on without me.'

Turning on his heels he set off down the corridor following the passageway, the light from his glow stone fading into the darkness as he turned the corner.

Chapter 21

In Search of a Myth

Ebon gloried in his triumph over Urim; at last he had been able to achieve a position of advantage that rendered his adversary powerless to interfere. Ebon marvelled to think it all came because of one inconsequential girl. Urim was a fool to be so sentimental; the girl was of no value other than to be a pawn in this game that Ebon played with him. All the time he held her captive, Urim was powerless to act and the seer had given his word that he would not interfere. Unlike Ebon, who gave his word then broke it at his convenience; Urim would be bound by his code of honour. The rogue seer wallowed in the feeling of control that he had in the matter and smiled with satisfaction.

Turning around, he stood in front of Anna and arrogantly strode up and down gazing at the Rod of Dread, holding it out and inspecting it as if it were a prized possession, which in fact it was; more so than Ebon realised. At every turn of events, when he utilised its power, he became more dependant upon it. It gave Ebon a thrill that swept through him each time he invoked the energy with which it was imbued. He was hooked. His eyes shone with a hint of red that was accentuated by the paleness of his skin which looked thin and emaciated. He was the shadow of what he had once been but the change had been so gradual that he had not noticed. If he had recognised the change he would have shrugged it off and put it down to fatigue.

'Well, Anna; I count myself fortunate to have you stay with me for a while, it has been far too long since we were last together. I do hope that you will be comfortable here. I can assure you that you will not be disturbed, I have seen to that. Oh, I must apologise that the window in your apartment is so high up from the ground but I have placed some bars there, for your protection you understand. I wouldn't want you to fall out and injure yourself. Still, I expect you are tired and would like to sleep. Please forgive me for having kept you; have a nice rest.' Ebon could not help his sarcasm; it was a part of him now, developed from years of bitterness and disappointment. 'Jetta; escort our guest to her room and see that she is made comfortable then bring me the key to the door. This is for your safety again of course Anna.' Ebon said, bowing slightly.

He watched as Jetta took Anna by the arm and escorted her out of the room, she had no choice but to go with him but shrugged herself free of his grasp. Despite his awesome appearance, Jetta handled her with gentleness and respect, allowing her some freedom of movement.

Ebon stepped back to his viewing-window and began the process that he had applied before. He needed to perfect his use of his latest ability, which was to delve into the mind of another when they were asleep. His first attempt had gone well enough when he had chosen one of his marshals in a neighbouring fortress. Following the experiment his subject had reported back to Ebon personally about the experience. It had all gone well and he had proceeded to enter the minds of others, manipulating their thoughts and placing commands deep within their minds that would be obeyed at a later date. He was now ready to continue with the next part of his plan that would take him one step closer in achieving his ultimate goal; dominance over both the seers and the wizards.

Gathered around the pool of possibilities at their inner sanctuary, four wizards debated the outcome of the incursion into Seers Tower. Missing from the meeting was the leader of their conclave, Emrys, who had not been notified of this gathering of wizards. Maccus said nothing to the other three that had joined him in this secret meeting, he did not have to; the report from Wyman and Tredan, the two wizards who had accompanied Emrys when they confronted the seers, was enough.

Maccus had warned them all of Emrys' misguided notion of returning to the world they had been banished from centuries ago. He knew that the others would think twice about it now that the first round of the battle had been lost. He had argued against this intrusion into the old world and now that the seers had been alerted to the fact that the wizards were close to opening the way back into their world, it would be all the more difficult when the time came for the final breakthrough. It was not that Maccus was against obtaining revenge for their misfortunes, he would be the first to strike against the seers; it was just that he saw no sense in returning to a world they were no longer suited for. This world was now their home and it provided all that they could ever require.

The wizards argued about what they should do; should they support Maccus' claim to rule in Emrys' stead or should they let things take their course. They decided to let events unfold without hindrance from them, only then could they decide what to do once the outcome had been established. Watching the way the argument swayed one way then the other, Maccus accepted the outcome with calm dignity; he was in no hurry and could wait a little longer. The tide was turning in his favour and he supposed that it was inevitable that Emrys would go too far in his efforts to return to their old world.

Maccus held no personal grudge against the leader of their conclave, Emrys had led them well and was still a powerful wizard, but what Emrys had overlooked was the lack of desire the rest of them had about returning to the old world. Following the recent incursion into the world of the seers and the defeat that was inflicted upon them at the hands of Terra Standfast and the others; the argument for biding their time until they were confident of victory grew ever stronger.

His fellow wizards felt loyalty towards Emrys and Maccus respected that; he would expect no less were it he who was in the same position. What mattered most, he had said to the others, was that they were united in their cause and that the odds were in their favour. At the present time he did not think that they were.

The one thing that could tip the balance was the arrival of the seer, Ebon, in their dark and terrible wasteland. He could be the key they had been searching for that would unlock the way back for them to exact their revenge. He could also be just the right kind that would enhance their number with the strength of will that he had been exhibiting. With the Rod of Dread in Ebon's hands, he would soon qualify as a contender for a place in their conclave.

Maccus felt sure that Ebon would succumb to the enticements of power within the rod. It was what drove him in his search for more control; becoming a wizard would satisfy his need not only to take revenge on the seers but to have the authority he sought for.

'Yes, he will do nicely and I shall take pleasure in tutoring him in our ways.'

'I hope that you will be able to find what you are looking for Urim. Our knowledge of the matter comes from very obscure records.' Queen Ella bade Urim farewell and good fortune in obtaining that which he sought.

'I am indebted to your majesty; without your help I fear that I would fail to accomplish the deed. I am confident now that all will be well. I am ready to leave your realm now and would be grateful for my being aided in making the return to my world.'

'Of course, Urim; but are you sure that you wouldn't rather wait until night when your transition would be easier on you?'

'No; I have no time to spare. Ebon must be prevented from opening the doorway between the worlds and only I can do that. I must free Anna first and then he will face his reckoning. Besides, when I came here before with the metal-master, Braun, we were both transported into your realm whilst awake. It will do me no harm to return in the same fashion. Farewell my lady.' Urim bowed and held his fist over his heart in the ritual acknowledgement of her position as queen of the sprites.

'Come and see us again soon seer; may your past always guide you in the right way. Our course will always run with yours and that of the other seers' Queen Ella bowed her head in recognition of his status and smiled in friendship. She nodded to her companions who wove their arms in an intricate pattern in the air before Urim. The scene changed before him as a gossamer like web descended over his vision and he felt himself float. He lost consciousness momentarily and found that he was back in his own world, standing by the banks of Crystal Lake. Crystal falls continued to flow without a ripple into the water and he saw the vestiges of the link between the realm of the sprites and his own world disappear, somewhat like a snowflake as it melts in the warmth of the sun.

He had no time to lose, he must get to Seers Tower immediately;

only from there could he obtain that which he sought. His staff of the portal would not transport him to his required destination unobserved. He needed to ride the power of the energy beneath the courtyard to Ebon's world. Once there he would obtain that which he needed to combat the power that Ebon wielded. Without it he would not be strong enough to face him.

Ebon had grown strong in the dark power of his new world; stronger even than when he had faced him back at Northill and Urim would have to tread carefully in order that he not be detected entering the realm of Magog. This must be accomplished without the knowledge of the other seers. If they knew what he was planning to do they would surely try to stop him.

He thought the matter through again, step by step and still reached the same conclusion. Without his intervention Ebon would invoke the negative power beneath the ruined city of Anram and the wizards would return to wreak a cold and deadly retribution upon them all.

Standing firm and with a determined frown on his face, he concentrated on the courtyard. Bringing the power of his talisman and the staff into play, he prepared for the leap through the portal he would create between here and the Tower. A bright light opened up before him and a doorway appeared through which he could see the courtyard at the Tower, shrouded in the shadow of the outer walls. He stepped through as if he were merely entering another room and the door shut behind him with a popping sound. One moment he had been standing on the pleasant green meadow at Crystal Lake, the next he was at Seers Tower.

Checking around him to ensure that his arrival had not been observed he set about creating a link between the staff and the power that lay deep below him in the shaft. He used some of the power from the shaft to erect a dome of energy around him. This was so that he could continue with what he needed to do undisturbed. No amount of interference from the other seers could prevent him now from obtaining his goal. There was one thing that he had to do before that and he concentrated his thoughts on the information that the sprites had given him prior to leaving their realm. The energy surged beneath the flagstones upon which he stood and the ever present hum of power from beneath Seers Tower rose in pitch.

Soon now his presence would be known to the occupants of the Tower and they would try to prevent him from utilising the energy. It was too late now for that and there was no going back. The build up of power was too strong to be stopped. Focusing his thoughts on his destination he threw his arms wide, still holding the talisman and staff, and with a cry of pain, disappeared from sight. The courtyard subsided into quiet again and darkness descended with the fading light of day.

Looking out from his open window, Terra stared into the emptiness where moments before Urim had stood. He shook his head slowly before quietly closing the window and returning to his cot to rest. He had anticipated this action on the part of Urim and had instructed the others not to interfere; they would not have been successful even if they had tried. It was a huge risk that Urim was undertaking but one that Terra had foreseen the seer would make. Whatever the risk it represented, Terra trusted the wisdom of this seer known as Urim; without him, they would all still be held captive behind the energy barrier that Ebon had placed around the Tower. For that reason alone Urim deserved to be given the flexibility to do what he thought was best.

'Good fortune follow you my friend; we are all in your hands.' Terra lay down and closed his eyes, the weariness that he felt drained him of any desire to think any further than getting a good night's sleep. He would discuss their options with Liam and Emerald in the morning.

A bitter cold sent chills through his body and darkness covered his sight like a heavy blanket. Urim had made the transition to Magog. He had felt searing pain as if he were being torn apart atom by atom when the energy beneath the courtyard had been released. Now that agony had gone only to be replaced by the icy cold that seemed to burn into his skin. He called upon the powers that he had command of and caused his staff to emit a light so that he could see, as well as generating warmth that spread through his body from his grasp on the staff.

He was in an old and neglected crypt; dust laden cobwebs dangled from the arches of the stone ceiling and water dripped through a crack in an alcove, forming a pool on the floor. There were no windows or even a door. It was as if the entire structure had been sealed so as not to be disturbed. Stone blocks had been cemented in place where a door should have been; there was no way in or out other than for someone, like Urim, who held a way to 'walk through walls'.

In the centre of the room was a large stone tomb. It was the biggest he had ever seen and must have been at least fifteen measures long. If the information given him by the sprites was correct then this was the final resting place of Custennin, he who had dared to defy the wizards when they first entered this world. There was only one way to find out if the legends about him were true so Urim released his hold on the staff but it did not fall, instead it stood suspended in the air, allowing him to move freely.

He approached the tomb and tested all around the lip of the cover. There was no sign of a catch that might act as a trigger to release it. He tried to move the lid and exerted all his strength against it but it did not budge. What he needed was a lever of some kind' looking around he could find nothing that would be of any use. There were some stone containers in a corner of the room with various items in them, some coins and the remains of some clothing. There was also a wooden chest which Urim opened carefully. Inside it, laid on a velvet cushion was a silver rod with a depiction of a long bone attached to one end. Perhaps this was the means by which he could open the tomb. Alongside the item was a scroll with symbols written on it. He studied the figures and shapes trying to interpret their meaning but they were obscure and revealed no insight into solving his conundrum.

'The answer has to be here somewhere.' He spoke his thoughts. 'Think Urim, think. What was it that the sprites had said about this place that could help me now?' He frowned in concentration, trying to unravel the mystery of the tomb. He puzzled over the inscription on the scroll and slowly the meaning of them came into his mind. He read them as if he were the giant Custennin. Urim had read the legend of the giant and what had befallen him, that he had been sawn asunder by the wizards and parts of him were distributed around Magog. Urim believed that everyone deserved a decent burial no matter who they were and Custennin had only acted to prevent the wizards from enslaving his world. He thought the retribution handed out on the giant by the wizards was totally unjustified.

Following Custennin's death his relatives had scoured the lands searching for his various body parts. The story that had been related to him told that they were successful and had reunited the giant in death. All but one thing was recovered; his right thigh bone and they had no way of retrieving it as the wizards held it. No one who had ever gone up against the wizards had been successful against them; they had been defeated and returned the wiser for it, or had never been seen again. Custennin's family buried him in a place that was to be kept secret from all but one who would know the whereabouts of the giant's last resting place; passing that knowledge on, down through the ages from one generation to another. The events had been turned into folklore and the giant, Custennin, had become a figure of mythology.

Slowly the images made sense to him; it was as if a voice whispered in his mind, explaining what they meant. He understood now and replaced the scroll in the chest; taking what he now knew to be a key, he moved to the head of the tomb and knelt at the base. Searching the carved stonework he came across what he was looking for. It was a figure that represented the giant; he stood on one leg. Where his missing leg should have been attached to his body there was a slot, Urim looked at the key; it was shaped like that slot; in the form of a thigh bone. Inserting the key it turned and he heard the sound of whirring from within the stone casket. Urim stepped back waiting to see what was revealed.

Chapter 22

Intervention

The whirring stopped and the sound of stone grinding on stone echoed through the crypt. Slowly at first and then more noticeably, the great stone lid began to move; little by little the heavy lid began to raise from the base, being lifted on two rows of metal pillars on each side of the tomb; to reveal the remains of the mythical giant, Custennin. The skeleton was huge and well preserved; Urim had never met anyone the likes of this before. Even Braun would have been dwarfed beside the giant and any of the tallest colossi would have had to look up to him when he was alive. The myth was no longer a story, it was fact, and Urim had discovered him but he had not come here to discover lost treasures or to prove the existence of the giant. He had come here for one purpose only, to enable him to withstand the power of the Rod of Dread. It was from the bones of this being that the Rod had been made and it was by the bones of this giant that he could receive protection. Carefully and with respect for the remains, Urim gently removed a small bone from the hand of the giant in the stone casket and placed it in a small leather bag which he put into his pouch.

'I hereby vow to reunite you with the bones that are taken from you, one by force against your will; the other as a means of reunification. I shall return soon to fulfil my promise or I will die in the attempt. I ask that your spirit may help me in achieving that which you desire; to be whole again and at peace.' Urim stood back from the tomb, bowed his head and waited in silence paying his respects to the butchered giant before turning the key again. The lid lowered slowly back into place, sealing the skeleton from the outside world with a slight rushing sound as the air was pushed out from beneath the lid.

The time had come for him to find Anna and to set her free; then the plan that Terra and the rest of the seers had formulated would continue to unfold. Grasping the still lighted staff, Urim concentrated his mind on Anna; he saw her face before him as clearly as if she were standing in front of him. Summoning the power of the staff of the portal, enhanced by the energy beneath Seers Tower, he opened the way for the transition from where he was to the place that Ebon had incarcerated her. The light from the staff extinguished and a door in the air opened in front of him. Daylight spilled through the door that the portal had created and Urim had to blink to adjust his vision. He saw Anna lying on a couch in a small but comfortable room; she was alone and apparently asleep. He stepped through the portal and the transition from the darkness of the crypt to the fortress where Anna was being kept in confinement had been completed. Anna stirred at the sound of the portal as it closed behind the seer and upon seeing him standing in her room was afraid that she was seeing a ghost but then realised that it was indeed Urim and he had come to save her.

'Anna, I have come for you, do not be afraid; you will soon be free of Ebon's grasp and back in the world you have come to know as home; the one where you have a voice.'

Anna sat up and cried with relief at seeing Urim and hearing his voice, she rushed to him and hugged him tightly. Urim returned the embrace and gulped back the emotion that he felt at seeing her again.

She pushed herself away and in a panic began to sign to him her fears that Ebon or Jetta would come and find him here. Urim calmed her anxiety and gently stroked her hair. Smiling he put a finger to his lips and shook his head. 'Have no fear of that; if we were to be discovered they could do nothing to prevent us from leaving, I have taken care of that and we shall shortly have you back in your world. Is there anything here that you need to take with you?'

Anna shook her head.

'Very well then, we shall have you home in an instant.'

Before he could say anything more, the sound of a key being turned in the lock made Anna gasp with a sharp intake of breath, they were about to be discovered. The door opened and Jetta stepped across the threshold into the room; he held a tray of food that he had brought for Anna. Upon seeing Urim he was taken aback momentarily, not expecting anyone other than Anna to be in the room. He calmly placed the tray on a table near the door before turning to face the seer. Jetta grinned and rubbed his hands together to summon up the dark magic that filled his being. Nothing happened and a look of astonishment spread across his face. He tried again but still no power emerged and was at a loss as to why he could not bring the magic to bear upon the seer.

'Why am I unable to raise the dark magic within me?' He asked the seer in surprise.

'Your magic can not harm me; the power that your master wields has no effect on me. Will you stand aside and allow us to leave or must I deal with you as befits a creature of magic?'

Jetta dropped to his knees and pleaded with the surprised seer. 'I ask that you spare my life seer. I have lived in hope that such a one as you would appear; I believe that you are the one I have been waiting for. I wish to be free from the compulsion to obey my master. He has wronged me and tricked me into becoming this creature you see before you now. I realise that there may be no way to return me to my former self but I want to be free to follow my own course. I do not want to carry out the deeds he forces me to do but I cannot disobey all the time he has the Rod and exercises its power. You are the one who can deliver me from bondage; tell me what I must do to help you in your cause and I will do all that I can to aid you but be aware that I am bound to obey my masters will.'

Urim was surprised at this unexpected turn by the dark angel of Ebon's; new ideas formed in his mind and he relaxed his guard, believing that Jetta was telling him the truth. Urim felt the conviction in his words and the look of hope in his dark eyes.

'I shall do all that I can to help you; I understand that you are bound to your master and I promise you that I shall return for you once Ebon has been dealt with.'

Jetta bowed his head in acknowledgement of Urim's words. 'I thank you seer and I assure you that I will try not to kill you should my master order me to do so. Now you must go; I assume that you have the means to escape or I would not have found you here in a locked room.'

'You assume correctly; you may return to your master and inform him that the girl has disappeared. He will no doubt ask you how it was accomplished and you may answer him truthfully that I, Urim, have taken her.'

'Very good; I wish you well, Urim.' Jetta stood and backed away from them watching to see how Urim would accomplish the task of removing himself and Anna from the room.

Concentrating on his destination and utilising the energy he still held open from the shaft in the courtyard at Seers Tower, Urim opened the portal and stepped into it with Anna at his side. One moment they were standing in the open doorway to another world, the next, Jetta was alone.

He smiled with satisfaction, believing that, unlike Ebon, Urim would keep his promise. Jetta knew that some time in the near future he would be free of the compulsion to serve his master and it pleased him. He rubbed his hands together; a ball of black fire erupted into life between the palms of his hands. Nodding with approval he doused the flames and went to report the events to Ebon. As he walked back to the great hall, he could not help but smile at the thought of how Ebon would react to the news.

The pleasant gardens of Anna's world were a welcome tonic to her, she hugged Urim again and tears of joy fell onto her cheeks. 'Oh! Urim; how am I ever going to be able to thank you for coming to rescue me? I don't know how I would have coped if you had not come for me.'

'I could never leave you in danger Anna and it gave me considerable pleasure in being able to thwart Ebon's plans. He believed that he had made it impossible for me to act but he misunderstood my vow. I promised that I would not interfere but I said nothing about not intervening. There is a difference you see; if I had got in the way of Ebon that would have been interference or obstruction which I did neither of. I did overrule his actions however which was intervention, something entirely different. Granted it is a very fine line between the two distinctions, but in this case it was a justifiable difference. I have remained true to my seers vow and kept my promise to Ebon but in a way that has allowed me to act in a very different way to that which he expected.'

'Where will you go now Urim; will I ever see you again?' Anna asked, her eyes brimming with tears of gratitude.

'Most assuredly you shall see me again, now that I have the use of the staff of the portal I shall be a regular visitor. It saddens me however to acknowledge that I am unable to return you to the world of the seers, to be with Jon. I am able to intervene on occasion but I can never interfere with what is meant to be; do you understand? You will never be able to be with Jon in a way that you might possibly desire. The energy barrier can not act against itself; it brought you here and nothing I can do will enable me to override that.'

'I understand, Urim. I know that if it were possible to do so that you would restore me to him but I am content. We are able to be together sometimes; we are still linked somehow, I don't understand how but we are.'

'I know you are Anna and I also know that Jon cherishes those moments with you. Now, although I would wish to tarry with you a while longer, I must deal with the situation in the world of the seers and apprehend Ebon before he can do any more damage. Take care, Anna. We shall speak to one another again soon.' Calling the power of the staff into effect one more time, Urim stepped into the opening created by the portal and disappeared from view.

Anna looked for a few moments at the place where Urim had stood before turning to rejoin her friends who had gathered to her when she and Urim had made their sudden appearance. She was grateful to the seer, feeling a deep affection for him. It was strange how, when she had first met him, she had disliked and mistrusted him but now she felt as if he were her protector. She knew that he would be true to his word and that she would see him again.

Ebon was feeling very pleased with the way things were going; he had just finished speaking with one of his vassal warlords, the one whom he had chosen to help him in his experiment. Ebon had made contact with him through a dream and instilled a message that, if successful, the warlord would relay back to Ebon. It had worked better than he had hoped it would and he was ready now to take his plan to the next phase on the one he held control over in the old world of the seers. Ebon's influence would soon be felt again in those lands and his 'puppet' would unwittingly help him to reinstate himself.

For once Ebon was in a good mood and he allowed a smile to play on his lips. His mind worked constantly, considering every outcome and every action. He had left nothing to chance and with Urim out of the equation now that he held Anna captive, Ebon believed that it was only a matter of time before he would walk the floors of Seers Tower again. This time however he would be master and the seers would be his slaves. He would control both worlds through dominance of the seers and the wizards. He chuckled with delight, savouring the taste of victory over his enemies. At last he would achieve that which he had set out to do many years ago, to rule; he believed that it was his destiny, his right.

Jetta approached Ebon amidst his musing and knelt before him as he sat idly on his throne. 'Master I bring bad tidings, the girl, Anna has been taken.'

'What did you say?' Ebon paled at the news and asked incredulously, his voice rising in pitch as he framed each syllable. 'Who has done this, fetch me the person responsible and I shall have his head.'

'It was the seer, Urim.' Jetta replied, watching Ebon closely and witnessing his incredulity at what he had heard..

Ebon stared wide eyed at the news and shook his head in disbelief. Standing up he shook with rage and ranted in his fury at being deceived by the seer yet again. 'Impossible; I had his word that he would not interfere. He lied to me and broke his oath, well that will be his undoing. I shall not spare him the next time we meet. How did he get her out?'

'He used a staff to create a portal into another world and I was unable to prevent him from doing so.'

'What did you say? You were there and did nothing. Why did you allow this to happen?' Ebon was feeling as if he were about to explode, such was the anger and frustration that he felt.

'I was unable to use my power against him master. I could not raise the magic within me. There was nothing I could do to prevent him carrying out his rescue of the girl.' Jetta sounded contrite but if Ebon could have looked into his heart and seen the pleasure it gave his dark angel, he would have reacted differently.

Woe poured upon the truculent seer as he contemplated all that he had been told. Urim had used the very staff that Ebon had purloined and used it against him. Even Jetta's dark power was useless against him. At every turn this seer, Urim, plagued him with his meddling. He thought furiously on this news and concluded that he must have used a greater force than just the staff because Ebon had placed a shield around the room to prevent such a thing from happening. From the time he had exacted the promise from Urim Ebon had wondered whether he would break his word. Ebon had, he believed, taken all necessary precautions against the seer entering his fortress. He must have used another source of energy to be able to enter and leave without even the least difficulty.

Jetta watched as Ebon boiled with anger and resentment, behaving like a spoiled child who had broken his favourite toy. Ebon stalked out of the hall and rampaged through the fortress in a foul temper; anyone unfortunate enough to get in his way regretted it instantly. Fortunately for most, they heard him coming and stayed out of his path, keeping a low profile until his rage had subsided.

Jetta, meanwhile, waited patiently in his customary place, at the arm of the throne in the great hall. He knew that Ebon would calm down and collect his thoughts. At this very moment Ebon would be working out another of his plans and he, Jetta, would probably be needed to carry out some task or another. The dark angel stood silently contemplating these events. He believed and trusted the word of the mysterious seer Ebon had named as Urim. Soon he would be free to think his own thoughts and to do his own deeds. 'I may even approach the seers and offer my services to them; they must surely have a need for someone like me or at least know where my talents can be best used.' He stood in the emptiness of the great hall contemplating his freedom and smiled.

There remained only one thing left to do now and that was to wait for Ebon to show his hand. Urim knew the trials that the others were passing through and felt assured that they would come through them to assist in the capture of the rebel seer once again. This time however, there would be a proper accounting. Ebon could not be trusted to mend his ways; he was too far gone in his madness. Urim felt sorrow for his state of mind knowing that if only Ebon had been content with the ways of the Council of the Sight, he would have been a tremendous asset to their world. He could have been a force for good that would have helped all who lived in the land. Instead he had become captivated by the idea of being the one to lead; to be the one who held the power of the Sight in his hands. He wanted the glory for himself and held little or no regard for the lives of others.

Urim pondered on what might have been had Ebon made better choices in life and how the future is determined by our actions. He wondered just how far Ebon had taken them off course from a future that held peace and prosperity. Would Urim's own actions here and now have a negative or a positive influence on the future. He would have to wait and see. It was not of any use for him to think on how his actions would affect the future. What did matter was what he did now to assist the Sight in establishing order again. That at least held the promise of a better future for them all.

Chapter 23

Anramites

The maze of passages twisted and turned endlessly through the underground city. The air was surprisingly clean and fresh and a slight breeze blew through the tunnels keeping the air circulated. It was a refreshing change to be out of the heat of the desert but the darkness encroached upon their senses and the walls seemed to press in on them. If any of them suffered from a fear of confined spaces, or of the dark, then this was not the place to be.

Strange sounds whispered along the corridors as if softly spoken conversations were being held in distant rooms and snatches of their words drifted on the moving air. Jon felt unnerved and felt the skin on his head tighten with concern; he consciously had to relax the tension every now and again. He had not liked going on without Hamill, feeling vulnerable without his comforting presence, Braun too had failed to return making him think that this place was alive somehow and conspiring against them. They had waited for some time and called after them hoping for a response but none came. They heard their own voices echo into the darkness and thick silence that held the place bound but there was no reply from their missing friends.

Javelin had appointed Trapper to lead the way and he led them through the passageways following the direction indicated on the map. Soft thuds could be heard every now and again from behind them. Mason, who was bringing up the rear of the group, turned around and peered back into the darkness thinking that he might see what was causing the sound but the thick darkness beyond the reach of the glow stones was impenetrable. He hurried to catch up with the others but could not shake the shivers that ran up and down his spine; he was feeling very uncomfortable, as if he were being watched by mysterious eyes.

Trapper stopped abruptly at a solid wall and scratched his head, mystified at the dead end that had stopped them in their tracks.

'What's the matter, Trapper; have you led us up a blind alley?' Javelin teased the perplexed dwarf.

'Well, according to the map this should be a longer corridor than it actually is and there should be another turning to the left about ten feet further on but it stops right here.'

'We've obviously taken a wrong turn somewhere along the way. All we need to do is retrace our steps a little way and find where we went wrong.' Javelin said; believing that Trapper had missed the turn.

Trapper was not convinced but had to admit that they could not go forward and he began to retrace his steps. Jon and the four dwarves made their way back along the corridor in an endeavour to find the right way through. Trapper had passed them all and taken the lead again following their footsteps until he met with a solid wall that cut across their path. Looking down at the floor, Trapper could clearly see their footprints and they went beyond the wall of rock but the way had been blocked. The dwarf shook his head and turning to Javelin delivered his verdict.

'I am afraid that we must be in an ever changing labyrinth; the map I made is virtually useless because the way ahead keeps changing. Unless we are able to find our way through, we could be wandering around down here for a very long time.' Trapper informed them, tugging at his beard.

'So that must be what I heard earlier, the way being changed by these stone blocks; it has bothered me for some time as I couldn't understand what it was that made the noise.' Mason offered as an explanation, satisfying his earlier unease.

'How long would you say 'a very long time' would be Trapper?' Jon asked; afraid of the answer he would receive.

The dwarf did not reply but gave him a sombre look that spoke more than words could ever do.

'Oh!' Jon did not have to ask for clarification; the look was enough.

'So what do you suggest we do Javelin?' Trapper asked; trying to sound positive.

'I don't see that there is anything else for us to do other than to continue on and try to work our way out. What do you say, Jon?'

They all turned to look at him waiting for his opinion. 'Well, I think that Javelin is right, we won't get out of here by staying where we are and even though the way changes it should eventually allow us to find a way out. With the amount of dust there is on the ground we should be able to tell if we are going in circles.'

'Quite right, Jon; you heard him, Trapper; let's get out of here.' Javelin directed his friend to lead them on, confident that a way out would be found.

Going back the way they had come and hoping that they would strike it lucky, the group followed silently, hiding their concerns from each other but secretly feeling very nervous about the prospect of not being able to get out.

They all looked to Javelin for guidance and the dwarf suggested that they remain alert for any traps, especially when they came to any junctions. 'Watch your step; I've known places like this to have trapdoors that drop into oubliettes. I would recommend that you let us take the lead, Jon. You stay close to Digger and Mason; Trapper and I will lead the way.'

Carefully they made their way along the dark corridors with only the dull light from the glow stones to illuminate the way ahead.

'What was that?' Mason suddenly spun around testing the air with the point of his knife.

'What's the matter?' Javelin asked back down the line, instantly alert and ready for any need for action.

'I'm not sure but I could have sworn that I heard someone walking behind me.'

'Yes, I heard it too.' Jon whispered.

Carefully retracing their footsteps Jon and Mason edged forwards to the last junction a few strides away. Nervously they both looked around the corner, holding their glow stones in front of them. The light did not penetrate too far along the passageway but it was far enough for them to make out shadows in human form shuffling along the corridor in the darkness. They both let out a shout of alarm, more from surprise than from fear; at least that is what they said later. Javelin rushed back to them, eager to know what the panic was about. 'What is it, what did you see?' Javelin demanded.

'I don't know; it looked like there were some folk back there along the passage in the dark beyond the light of the stones.' Mason replied; more than a little apprehensive but excited too. 'Do you suppose that the ruins are inhabited?'

'If it is then they don't appear to need lights for them to get around. I suggest that we follow their tracks and see if we can learn any more about them. Perhaps they could show us the way to the central chamber.' Trapper offered with a hint of relief that he may no longer have to rely on the makeshift map he had drawn.

Javelin thought for a moment, stroking his beard before making his decision. 'I believe that it may be a wise precaution if we were to try to make contact with these folk, whoever they are. It may well be that they are too shy to approach us; I don't suppose that they get too many visitors down here.' He nodded to Mason who took up the lead, following the barefoot tracks in the dust.

They had walked for some time without any further sight or sound of the shadowy figures. Jon was thinking that they were never going to make contact with them when, as they were pressing forward, from out of the gloom ahead of them loomed the ghostly outline of someone standing in the passageway. As they drew closer the figure took on a defined shape; it was more like a tall ape with white hair covering its thin but muscular body. As they drew closer it shielded its eyes from the brightness of the light emitted from the glow stones. Mason stopped short of where the figure stood and the others tried to get a peek over his shoulder at the strange creature.

'What do we do now?' Mason whispered back to Javelin. He did not have time to get an answer as the floor beneath them gave way and they fell into a void beneath the floor of the passage. They did not fall far but the landing was rather heavy and they tumbled into each other ending up in a heap. Fortunately there were no injuries sustained by anyone and they were able to see that they were in a small cell, just large enough for them all to stand and walk a few paces in either direction before reaching the walls. A wooden door with a small barred window was the only means of them having air to breathe.

'Why is it that we always seem to end up in a cell?' Trapper asked with an exasperated shake of his head.

'The good news is that we've always managed to get out of them before so there's no reason why we can't get out of this one.' Javelin said with conviction.

'Is anyone hurt?' Digger asked; his first instinct being to ensure that they had not been injured.

'There are no broken bones but by butt hurts where I landed on something.' Trapper said.

'That was my knee.' Mason said; rubbing the joint as if it hurt.

'Is there any other way out of here other than the door?' Javelin asked; searching for some other means of escape.

'No, it all looks pretty secure to me; unless we can get out the same way we got in here.' Jon replied; hoping that they could. After a quick inspection, they determined that the only way out was through the door and it was locked. The glow stones illuminated the small room revealing two cots against opposite walls and a rough wooden table and chair in-between them. Other than that, the room was devoid of furniture. Straw lay scattered sparsely on the floor and it was thick with dust. It appeared that the room had not been used for some time.

'I have to admit that I don't like the look of things.' Javelin announced; nervously tugging at his beard. 'Trapper, try to get that door open will you; I don't fancy waiting around any longer than necessary. We will either be left in here to rot or they will come for us. Whatever the outcome, I want to be master of my own destiny.'

Trapper pushed at the door with his shoulder before realising that it opened inwards. The only way they could get it open was to hack their way through.

'Stand aside everyone; I'm going to smash this door into tinder.' Taking careful aim at where the lock was situated, Trapper began to cut away the lock with precise blows from his hatchet. Splinters of wood showered them as he steadily chopped away at the frame and door; before long he had it swinging open. Taking a careful look outside with a glow stone held aloft, he reported that there was no-one to stop them from leaving.

Javelin and Trapper led the way out followed by Jon then Digger and Mason. Edging forward and searching the stone floor for any signs of traps, they crept silently through the dark passages. Mason noticed that there was no sound of soft thudding in theses lower passages as there had been in the upper ones.

'Do you suppose that these tunnels stay the same? That there are no sliding stones to alter the way ahead?'

'That's a good point, Mason; you may be right but I don't see what advantage that would be to us.' Digger responded.

'Well, it's just that I thought that theses passages would eventually lead us somewhere as opposed to taking us around in circles.'

'What are you two whispering about back there?' Javelin asked in a low tone.

'It's the passages; they don't seem to be changing anymore. Mason thinks that we will find something ahead of us instead of going around in circles.' Digger explained.

'That's very observant of you Mason, well done; we'll keep alert for signs.'

A little further on, the passage made a left turn and opened up into a large room. The light cast by the stones was just enough to reach to the walls and they could see some sort of altar on a raised dais to one side. This room was clean and had a carpet that ran from the altar to a set of double doors at the far end. Padded chairs were placed at certain points around the room and faded tapestries hung on the walls. Jon looked more closely at one of them and saw what represented eight cloaked figures surrounding the altar. Jon's blood ran cold; it was a scene of a sacrifice.

'Does anybody know who used to live here?' Jon asked nervously.

'Yes this is where the wizards used to live. They had a battle with the seers who expelled them from our world many centuries ago. I remember studying it at the Institute of History back in Ffridd-Uch-Ddu.' Mason informed him.

'Thank goodness for that; for a moment there I thought that these tapestries represented the seers.'

'Oh no; they would never do anything as dreadful as that but it seemed that the wizards did.'

'I think we'd better get out of here as quickly as we can. I don't believe that we would be welcomed if we were to be found here.' Jon whispered urgently to Javelin.

The dwarf joined him and after looking at the tapestry agreed that they should try and find their way to the central place immediately. Nodding at Trapper to lead the way; the dwarf put his hand to the door handle and opened it gently, peering around the edge of the door. It all appeared to be clear and they filed out into another passageway, taking care to close the door behind them.

A few moments later, after they had travelled a little distance down the passage, they stopped suddenly; all of them had heard it; a whisper on the draught that circulated through the complex. It came again only this time from behind them. Listening intently they heard the sound of bare feet padding along the floor.

'What do we do now, Javelin?' Jon asked nervously.

'The only thing we can do; keep going forward and be ready to defend ourselves.'

Javelin now led the way and held his spear ready to throw or thrust at any opposition they might encounter. They passed several doors and tried to open them without success. It seemed that they had to follow the course of this passage, wherever it led them. The sound of bare feet padding along somewhere ahead, faded in and out. There were times when they feared that they would meet the creatures, which they named the Anramites, head on but each time the sound retreated into the distance.

Without sound or warning they found that their way ahead was blocked by several of the Anramites who had appeared as if from out of the walls. Backing away to try and evade them Mason discovered that the Anramites were behind them as well.

'It seems that they have us trapped. I am reluctant to fight them at this point in time because we don't know whether they mean us any harm.'

'They let us fall into that cell didn't they?' Trapper reminded Javelin.

'True but other than that they have not shown any aggression towards us. They don't appear to have any weapons of any kind. I wonder if we are not being a bit too hasty in our judgement here. Remember that it is we who are the intruders, not them. This is their home and we have arrived uninvited.' Javelin's logic seemed sound enough and they followed Javelin's lead by lowering their weapons.

The Anramites ahead of them blinked against the light of the stones and beckoned them to follow them. Javelin nodded and looking back at the others jerked his head in the direction of the creatures. They followed them for some time, eventually stopping at a set of double doors much like the others they had seen back at the altar room. Two of the white ape-like creatures opened the doors and the other three went inside beckoning them to join them but Javelin and the others were reticent to do so, thinking that it might be another cell of some sort. They stood outside for a few moments before concluding that, as there was no other option for them, they should go in, keeping alert for any tricks.

The three creatures encouraged them to make themselves comfortable, all the time shielding their eyes from the glare of the stones. The light must have been blinding to them as it appeared that they went around quite happily in the pitch dark of the underground complex. Inspecting the room they were greeted by pleasant surroundings in what appeared to be a lounge area with a large dining table to the side.

The room was airy and clean, unlike the cell that they had been in. It seemed that the Anramites were trying to make amends for their earlier encounter because food and drink had been supplied for them on the table, ready for them to eat. Still protecting their sensitive eyes from the light, the three creatures left them and the doors closed. There was no sound of a lock being thrown and after a few moments of listening for any other sound, Trapper tried the door; it opened and there was no one outside.

'Well now, it would appear that we were unjustified in being cautious of these folk; we are free to stay or go and there is even food to eat. I don't know about the rest of you but I'm hungry.' Jon sat at the table and selected a few items of food. There were fruits of various kinds, bread, salads and water.

'Wait Jon, it may be drugged or even poisoned.' Javelin warned.

'You may be right Javelin and I suggest you let me try it first. If I fall asleep then you know it's drugged. There's only one way to find out so here goes. Jon stopped with some food half way to his mouth then smelled it; it smelled alright. He licked it, it tasted fine. Satisfied that it was good to eat he popped it into his mouth and chewed. He took bites of all the food that was on the table without any sign of it being drugged. He took a bite of one piece of fruit but within moments he had wrinkled up his face and spat it out.

'What's the matter Jon? Does it taste bad or did you just not like it?' Javelin asked; concerned lest he had eaten something that would harm him.

'Oh I think it's alright; it just tastes foul. Try some, you may like it but I don't.'

Carefully Javelin did the same that Jon had done; he smelled it, licked it then tasted a small amount; he too spat it out. 'You're right Jon, it tastes disgusting. I don't know what manner of fruit it is but I would recommend that we leave it alone. What's the rest of it like?'

'Great; it's lovely; I recommend that you help yourselves to a plateful.'

They did not need telling twice as they were all quite hungry and the food was welcome.

'I wonder where they got it from; there doesn't seem to be any light in the place and they don't like it anyway. If they tried to grow it outside it would need tending and they would have to go outside which is something that they couldn't do; not in the heat and sun.'

'Perhaps they go out at night when it's cooler and darker.' Mason offered by way of explanation.

'You're probably right; anyway it tastes good, that's all that matters.'

One by one they became drowsy and fell asleep; their heads resting on the table in front of them. The doors opened silently and several of the Anramites came in; they quickly covered the glow stones, so as not to be blinded by them, and put them into the packs that the dwarves had with them. Several more Anramites came into the room now that it was darkened and together they carried the sleeping friends out of the room. As they left, others came in with fresh supplies of food and silently restocked the table, leaving the place as if it had not been used.

Chapter 24

The passages of Anram

Jon awoke to find that he could not see. He waved his hands in front of his eyes but saw nothing. 'I've gone blind.' He thought but then remembered that he was in the underground complex at Anram and there was no light in the rooms. The Anramites must have put some sort of sleeping agent in the food, then, when they had fallen under its influence, they had been put in these cells. Javelin had been right to have been cautious about them.

Jon stretched out his hands as he lay on a cot trying to find his way by touch and banged his knuckles on a side table. Feeling around he felt for his satchel and opened it, hoping that his glow stone would be in there. It was and he removed it, the light grew slowly in brightness, almost hurting his eyes after the dark but his eyes quickly adjusted. He was in a small room very much like the one they had all fallen into before only this one was a lot cleaner. He tried the door; it was locked. He was here until someone came to let him out; he hoped that it would not be long.

There was nothing for him to do except sit and wait. Whilst he sat there he contemplated on the circumstances of their position. Since entering this dark underground world, inhabited by these strange beings, they had been wandering around in an effort to locate the central place under the pyramid. He had no idea how near or far they all were from it but it seemed that, unless they could escape from their captors, they would not be getting there in a hurry.

Jon began to wonder why they had been imprisoned and a sobering thought entered his mind that scared him. He remembered seeing the tapestries in the room that had the altar in it and a chill of fear crept over him, causing him to shiver.

He recalled seeing one scene of a group of cloaked figures offering a sacrifice; was that what they were all being kept for; to be offered up as a sacrifice? He imagined the horror of it and he began to fret about the fate of the others. Were they alright? Where were they and why had they been separated? These were questions that he did not have the answers to and no amount of worrying would change that. He checked his belt, he still had the knife and he drew a grateful breath of air as he patted it to reassure himself. 'Thank goodness for that; at least I can defend myself if it comes to it.'

Braun was becoming increasingly irritated with wandering around in these never ending passages and seemingly getting nowhere. He did not know how the others were getting on and hoped that they were having better luck than he was. It was particularly frustrating knowing that the way kept changing and it was impossible to know if he was going around in circles or not. He did check the floor from time to time to see if he was treading in his own footsteps or for signs that he was close to catching up with Hamill and the two dwarves, Archer and Leader.

The dust had always been thick and undisturbed, then he checked again and stopped short in his tracks. The dust was not so thick here and only a slight covering lay on the floor, more to his surprise, there were footprints headed off away in front of him. He held his glow stone behind him and searched the floor to see where they had come from and he noticed that they emerged from under a section of the stone wall. The maze had obviously changed, allowing whoever or whatever it was to walk, seemingly, through a solid wall.

Braun followed the tracks in the hope that they would lead him out of the tunnels and into the central place or at least to make contact with the owner of the feet whose tracks he was following. He held the hilt of his sword just in case he came across any trouble. Thinking about it made him realise that he would not be able to use it in these confined passages anyway. As it was he was having to hunch forward to avoid banging his head on the ceiling.

Nevertheless, there was no other option than to follow the tracks until they either disappeared or they led him to make contact with another living being. He crossed his fingers and hoped that it would be Hamill and the dwarves but it was not their tracks he was following.

Soft thuds could be heard every now and again from back down the way he had come and he assumed that the passages had changed. If he were to go back, he doubted that he would be able to go the same way as he had come. What lay ahead he could only guess at but he had no choice other than to press forward. He was grateful for the glow stone because without it he would not have been able to find his way along these corridors.

'Maybe I should not have started out in the first place; then I wouldn't be in this predicament.' He thought but shrugged the notion off as the last thing he wanted was to get into a fit of temper. For good or bad he was where he was and he had to deal with it.

Leader and Archer led the way along the narrow passages following the prints left in the dust by whoever it was that had left them. They were wary of any possible surprises and held themselves ready to act at a moment's notice. Hamill peered into the darkness ahead of them, looking over the heads of the two dwarves, trying to see through the dark but he was unable to do so. He wondered whether his staff could guide them along the way they should go but decided to hold back on using it for the present. Only if they ran into trouble would he bring up its power. He hoped that Mason was caring for Auger's staff properly; they might need to use it, if they could. Even though it had been broken in two, it may yet have a vestige of power left in it that, used properly, might aid them if they were to fall into trouble; not that the dwarf would know how to use it but Jon might. Hamill had a lot of confidence in his friend and recognised his worth, even though Jon did not. Urim obviously had a plan for Jon and had selected him to help him in the fight against Ebon.

Thinking of the two of them, Urim and Jon, Hamill wondered what the true relationship between them was. First they were led to believe that he was Jon's uncle and then Jon surprised him with letting it slip out that Urim was his father. Incredible if it were true but seers weren't supposed to have any family. The distraction to their role as a seer was too great and it would have been wrong to have separated the husband and father from his responsibilities. When the two of them had talked about it, Jon had said that he believed that Urim was his father' Hamill believed that Jon was mistaken but Hamill did not want to take away his dreams. Whatever their bond it was a strong one and Hamill hoped that one day the truth would be known. He only hoped that it would not be too great a disappointment to his friend who had grown strong in his belief.

These thoughts distracted him as they made their way through the various twists and turns of the passageways, still following the imprints of the footmarks in the dust. As they came to a junction they saw that other footprints joined the ones they had been following. Leader carefully examined the marks and said that there were about six or seven of them. It was difficult to tell exactly how many as they merged into each other at times.

Leader looked up at Hamill as he squatted to get a closer look at the prints. 'What do you propose we do seer? Should we continue to follow these prints down the way they have gone or do you think we would be wiser to go the opposite way?'

'That is a good question Leader and I'm afraid that I don't have a good answer for you. I think that whichever way we go we shall have to deal with the changing maze anyway. However, I think that it would be as well for us to continue following the tracks and see where they lead us.'

Some time passed as they followed the footprints through the unending maze but then they were confronted by the group of the creatures they must have been following. The light obviously hurt their eyes so Hamill and Archer put their stones away whilst Leader held his so that the light was at a very low level. Hardly being able to see anything but shadows, the ape-like beings uttered some strange sounds and beckoned them to follow. Not having much choice, other than to ignore them, the three of them did as they were invited to do. They soon came to a set of double doors which were opened and they all went inside. The inhabitants of the underground complex left them there and closed the door. Wanting to discover where they were, the stones were brought out again and illuminated the room so that they saw a comfortable lounge area with a dining table laden with food.

Braun was beginning to suffer from backache as he continued to hunch forward in order that he might avoid hitting his head on the ceiling. He decided that he needed to have a stretch so he knelt on the floor and eased the stiffness by holding his waist and arching his back. He heard cartilage and bones crack into place and he gave a sigh of relief. Whilst kneeling on the floor he heard the sound of shuffling feet from up ahead. He stopped stretching and listened more intently. Sure enough the noise was faint but unmistakeable; several creatures, individuals, folk, he did not know which, were moving along the corridor.

He put his glow stone in his pocket to douse the light temporarily. He did not want to give his presence away just yet and the light from the stone would certainly do that. Then he realised that whoever these creatures were could probably see in the dark anyway, otherwise they would be carrying lamps of some sort.

The sound grew closer and he became tense until finally, believing them to be almost upon him, he drew out the glow stone. The light flooded the immediate area and Braun gasped with surprise. Not five paces away were three white haired, ape-like creatures. The sudden light caught them unawares and they let out a shriek, covering their eyes and backing away from him. Braun placed his hand over the stone allowing only a trickle of light to escape so that he could make out shadows moving and it allowed the creatures to come forward without hurting their eyes too badly.

Braun spoke hoping that they might understand him. 'Hello my friends; I am Braun of Foundry Smelt and I have been separated from my friends. Have you seen them?'

The creatures tilted their heads to one side and issued a series of sounds that might have been a language of some kind but Braun could not understand it. He ensured that the glow stone was kept from emitting too much light and leaned forward to draw in the dust with his finger, representations of the dwarves, Jon, and Hamill with the seer's staff. The creatures bounced up and down with excitement and nodded their heads, signalling that he should follow them.

With a sigh of relief, Braun went after them, stumbling forward in the near black of the passageway; at last he hoped that he would be reunited with the others.

Jon began to wonder why they had not taken the knife away from him; surely they knew about it and if he was to be harmed then they would have taken it. None of this made any sense. An idea came to him as he sat pondering his situation; if the knife had been able to cut through the display window in Amethyst's collection hall; perhaps it would cut through the door and he could escape to find the others and set them free also. There was only one way to find out so he went to the door and began to trace the edge of the blade around the lock. It sliced through the thick wood with ease, like a hot knife through butter. Soon he was free; grabbing his things he proceeded cautiously along the corridor outside.

Although it was dark, as he had expected, he could see light coming from somewhere down the passageway; that must be where the others are being kept. He hurried forward trying to be as quiet as he could; making towards the light ahead. When he got there he discovered that it was coming from a small barred window and glancing through, saw Digger and Mason, sitting on the cots looking rather depressed. He whispered through the bars; 'Hello you two; are you alright?'

They both started at the sound of Jon's voice but were glad to see him and asked how he had managed to escape.

'Easy; stand back from the door and I'll let you out.' Jon again used his knife and within moments he had the door open and they went off in search of the other two. Again Jon saw a glimmer of light and headed towards it. It was another cell with Javelin and Trapper inside; Javelin, never happy when not in control of a situation, was pacing up and down worriedly tugging at his beard. He looked through the bars of the little window and went to turn away when he did a double take at seeing Jon peering in from the other side. He almost burst out in a shout with surprise but managed to control his voice and whispered. 'Jon, you're free; have you seen the others? Can you get us out of here? We tried to cut our way out as before but the door is lined with metal sheeting. They must have known how we got out of the last one.'

'Yes, Digger and Mason are with me. I let them out of their cell just a moment ago; stand away from the door and I'll get it open so that we can make good our escape.'

Cutting through both wood and metal with his knife, he soon had the door swinging open and they quickly made their way along the dark passage in search of a way out. They were hoping to find Hamill and the others in the central chamber and complete their mission before the Anramites discovered that they had gone. The last thing they wanted was to be discovered now and they prayed for good luck to run their way. Jon crossed his fingers and the dwarves all followed suit.

They had to get out of this place and soon. Time was running out for them to find the keystone and they only hoped that somehow Hamill had not yet managed to get there. Terra's message to them had indicated that something terrible would happen if he did. The floor began to slope upwards for some distance before they met a junction.

'I guess that we're back in the upper level again. Which way should we go?' Jon asked of no one in particular.

'Your guess is as good as any.' Javelin replied.

Hamill and the two dwarves were ready for a meal and sat down to sate their hunger.

'Are we happy that this food is good to eat and not been poisoned in some way.' Leader queried of the other two.

'I think that if we were to be killed we would have known by now. But if it will make you feel better and as a precaution, I think it might be an idea if I use my staff to indicate if there is anything here that should not be eaten.' Hamill was rather keen to have something but recognised the wisdom of the dwarf's words so he held his staff over the food and concentrated his mind on it. The staff jerked away from the food as he tried to hold it steady and a green glow emanated from the piles of fruit and other foodstuffs.

'It would appear that you were justified in being cautious Leader. We owe you our thanks; the food is indeed contaminated and would be unfit for us to eat. I don't know whether it is poison or potions but whatever it is we should not eat it.

Just at that moment the doors opened again and Braun walked in; the doors were quickly closed again; keeping the light from spilling out into the passage. He was as pleased to see them as they were him and they quickly gave their accounts of what had befallen them since they separated. None of them had met with Jon or the other dwarves and were concerned for their wellbeing. Braun was rather disappointed that the food was unfit to eat as he had not eaten for some time and his stomach was beginning to complain.

'I'm sorry about that; I can't help it; when I'm hungry, it rumbles and it will not stop until I've eaten.'

'In that case we'd better get out of here as soon as we can and allow you to eat. Can you wait until then? We don't have a great deal left in our packs and we could give it to you now but I'd rather make our way out if possible. We need to find the others and then locate that keystone. I'll use my staff to try and locate both. Let's keep our stones bright so that these creatures don't come too close to us.'

Opening the doors they quietly left the room closing the doors behind them and crept silently, apart from the occasional rumble from Braun's stomach, along the passages. They followed the green thread of power that Hamill's staff sent ahead of them into the darkness, trusting to its light to guide them.

Jon and the dwarves established that they were not being followed by any of the Anramites, much to their relief, and trudged through the seemingly endless passages. They had been redirected several times by great stone slabs that slid across their path forcing them to go along passageways that led them in directions that could have been taking them in circles for all they knew. The last thing they wanted was to end up back where they had encountered the inhabitants of this warren of tunnels.

Having come up against several blank walls they eventually found themselves in a large vaulted room like a crypt which was big enough to accommodate them all with ease. Two other passages, one on the far side of the room and the other on the left, provided a choice as to which way to leave; the question was; which one led them towards their goal. At the centre of the room were three large stone tombs with effigies of two females and a male laying in state on the top. They obviously represented the likenesses of those who were placed within.

At the heads of the tombs, carved into the stone were their names, Megan, Galan and Erin.

Chapter 25

Ghosts

The old vaulted room was a change from the passages but one could still feel a little claustrophobic in a place like this, especially as it appeared to be a burial chamber. The fact that it was a large room, almost cavernous, made it less threatening. The three tombs in the room added to the spooky atmosphere as they cast eerie shadows from the glow stones.

Digger and Mason, being rather enthusiastic about anything archaic, examined the well preserved stone tombs; they breathed out excitedly and started to carefully brush away the years of dust and grime that had gathered over them.

'Come on you two, we don't have time for any of that. We need to keep moving.' Javelin chided them kindly.

'But they might be of tremendous significance; we can't just walk away from them without at least allowing us to carry out a brief inspection.' Digger pleaded to Javelin, wanting to be given some time to study them.

'Well, I don't have a problem with us taking a short break. We could all do with a drink anyway. You have a quarter turn of the hand to do whatever it is that you want to do, so you'd better make the most of it.' Javelin acceded to their request.

The two dwarves did not need a second telling and soon they were busy taking notes and making sketches. The occasional exclamation of wonder was heard as they discovered different aspects of the tombs. Mason discovered carvings along the edges of the heavy lids of the stone coffins. On close examination the carvings appeared to be writing of some kind but it was in an ancient language that was unknown to them, despite their studies at the academy in Ffridd-Uch-Ddu.

Jon looked around the room with a perplexed expression. 'Javelin, when we came into the room I could have sworn that there were two other passages out of here.'

'That's right Jon, there were, and there still are, one at the head of the tombs and one on the left...oh! Where is it? I could have sworn it was on that side but it's on the right. We must have got it wrong.'

Jon was not so sure and he had an uneasy feeling about this place. If the passageways were subject to change because of the sliding stone slabs that kept altering the way forward; perhaps the exits from the room were also liable to change. He could not be certain but he felt sure that the doorways had been on different walls when they came in.

'Come on you two, you've had time enough to get what you want from those tombs; we need to be on our way.' Trapper studied his makeshift map and led them towards the opposite door to which they had entered the room.

Before they reached it, the room went cold. Not just a chill as with the passing of a breeze but with a deep, penetrating, icy cold that leeched the warmth from their bodies. The breath from their lungs condensed into tiny droplets of water as they exhaled. They all stood like statues, frozen with fear; a stirring of the air stirred the dust making them cough and they shielded their faces with their hands. A low moaning echoed down the passageway they had intended using and Jon heard a whisper in his ear that sent a chill through his entire body. Everyone stood rooted to the ground and they looked at each other, ashen faced.

'Did you all hear what I just heard?' Mason asked, not really wanting to know if they had.

Jon nodded and he swallowed nervously; when he spoke, his voice trembled. 'I have never heard anything as chilling as that voice.'

The dwarves had all drawn their swords or knives; Jon eased his own knife out of its sheath and held it in readiness for whatever it was that he felt was approaching. He did not suppose that he would be much use in a pitched battle but having the knife gave him comfort. He knew that its blade had been enhanced by Queen Ella when he and Hamill had been in the sprite world, so perhaps it would offer a good protection to him now. Swallowing hard he saw that they were all listening nervously for any indication that they were about to receive unwelcome visitors.

They all stood closer together with the dwarves forming a protective shield around Jon, not daring to move. Jon felt that they had been standing still for an eternity. His heart thudded in his chest and he could see that the others were all likewise alarmed by the sound of the voice and the cold that had suddenly descended upon them.

A long low moan echoed down the passage they had used to enter the vaulted room and they could just make out, in the darkness beyond the reach of the light, a shadowy figure like some dark angel that stood sentinel in a graveyard.

A movement up another of the entrances to one of the passages caught his eye; approaching silently through and out of the darkness was a spectral figure dressed in a flowing, ragged black robe. On first catching sight of the figure his heart leaped, he began to relax and smiled with relief, thinking that it was Hamill who had managed to find them; but there was something not right and he stopped short of shouting the welcome that had formed on his lips.

The figure advanced down the passage as if it floated across the floor and came slowly towards the crypt. Jon's skin went cold and his eyes were like saucers. He felt the hairs on the back of his neck stand on end and he froze, transfixed by sheer terror; a ghost.

The figure was female and she carried a long bladed sword that she held in both hands before her, point up. The cowl of her hood shielded her face but he could see her eyes or rather what should have been her eyes. They blazed red and pierced him to the very centre of his being.

He began to back away into the centre of the room and bumped into one of the tombs. He looked over his shoulder and saw that the others were all facing away from him towards the other entrances. There, framed in each one of the passages were two more beings. They also had a ghostly appearance but carried no weapons. Their eyes burned with the same intense red. They were trapped; there was no other way out and they had no idea of how to react to these spectres, or how to deal with them.

The same cold, menacing voice rasped across their senses, demanding to be answered. 'Who are you and what is your purpose here? Why do you disturb our resting place?'

Javelin nodded towards Digger who nervously replied. 'We ask your pardon, spirit; we knew not that this was your place of rest. We are dwarves from the north in company with Jon of Ashbrooke; we are searching for the keystone.'

The sound of a man's voice echoed with a chilling, hollow laugh down the corridor beyond the tombs. 'What would you do with it once you have found it? Tell me if you dare?'

Javelin retorted boldly. 'That is our affair. We mean you no harm and ask that we be allowed to proceed unmolested. We will in turn leave you in peace and disturb you no more.'

The third spectre hissed like a cat and shook her head. 'But you already have disturbed us and we cannot allow you to interfere with the power that lies beneath us; it sustains our existence. Sister, they must not be allowed to pass.'

'You are right Megan; they must not meddle with things that are beyond their comprehension.' Then turning her attention to Jon and the dwarves she said. 'You may try to find it and you may wander where you will but you can never be permitted to have access to the keystone. You shall die here, along with all the others who have tried and failed to find it. Besides, even if you did, you have no means to control it.'

'That may be true of them but not of me.' A familiar voice challenged the spectres.

Jon turned around at the sound and heaved a sigh of relief; Hamill stood in the opening of another entrance to the room that had appeared in the wall. There were now four passages that radiated away from the tombs. He had appeared as silently as anyone ever could; well he was part elf after all. Jon and the dwarves were visibly relieved at Hamill's timely arrival.

A screech reverberated around the room as all three of the ghosts recognised the staff of a seer. The ghosts of the three wizards that the seers had overpowered millennia ago and imprisoned deep beneath the city of Anram, their former capital, shrieked in pure hatred of the newcomer.

Erin, the long dead wife of Emrys, launched herself at the seer and flew at him across the room in an attempt to slice him in two with her sword. The other two remained where they were but reached out towards Hamill with ghostly hands. It was as if they wanted to wrench his soul from out of his body but they dared not approach.

Summoning the power of his staff and the control of his talisman, Hamill changed in the blink of an eye into a Grist of Geddon. The unearthly metal of the sword glanced off the scales of the grist's body with no effect upon it. The grist/Hamill spread its wings and leaped into the air where it caught Erin in its powerful claws and the razor sharp talons ripped into the very fabric of Erin's being. She wailed with pain and tried to escape the grip of the fearsome beast as it continued to claw at her spirit.

Surges of dark power slammed into Hamill whilst he held the form of the grist; the other two had rallied to Erin's aid. The bursts of negative energy knocked Erin out of his grasp and he was thrown against the far wall where the grist crumpled to the floor but quickly shook off the effects of the attack. Erin had no physical body with which she might be killed because she had died long ago but she was badly shaken by the duel with the only creature that could cause her harm; a grist.

Any lesser beings would have passed on to the world of the dead but these were no ordinary beings; they were wizards. She and the other two existed only by the sheer power of their wills and the energy that lay beneath Anram. That energy was regulated by the keystone and they could not allow anyone, particularly not a seer, to interfere with it or they may cease to exist.

Hamill knew that his guise as a grist would not deter the ghosts, only by unlocking the keystone could they be defeated. He had to get to the central chamber beneath the great pyramid and end the flow of power that sustained them. Reverting to his normal self, he sent a bolt of green power blasting at the three ghosts. They shrieked in an agony of torment as the positive energy of the power beneath Seers Tower clashed with the negative energy that sustained them from far beneath the city of Anram. Howling with frustration they threw their arms up in an effort to defend themselves against Hamill's attack.

Reeling from the effects of the energy charge that had been unleashed against them, the three ghosts rallied and sent a dark surge of energy back at Hamill. Jon and the dwarves had to drop to the floor of the chamber in order to avoid being encompassed by the force that they threw at the seer. The ghosts totally ignored the others now; they were intent on being rid of their antagonist. Although Hamill was not one of the original seers whom they had fought against all those centuries ago; he represented the body of seers today and that was enough for them to react with hatred towards him.

The room filled with the smell of burned dust as the conflicting powers of seer and ghost-wizards clashed. Sizzling flashes of green and black crashed against the stone tombs and the walls of the crypt. Jon tried to see what was happening but all he could do was to keep his hands over his ears to protect them against the reverberating blasts of energy.

Curling up against the end of one of the tombs he poked his head around the corner to see Hamill standing behind a shield of green energy that flashed as black bolts of power sought to penetrate it and destroy him. Jon was amazed at what he was witnessing and watched in awe of his friend as he wielded his staff, sending powerful bursts of energy at the three ghost-wizards.

It appeared to Jon that this could go on for some time as neither side was succeeding against the other. Then Hamill ceased sending his attacks against the three spectres and concentrated on his defensive shield. Erin saw his hesitation and pressed her attack on him with renewed vigour, crying out with a shout of encouragement to the other two.

'The seer falters in his attack; now is our time to finish him.'

Jon panicked and wanted to rush forward to aid his friend but knew that he could do nothing against such forces that the ghosts had at their command. He looked on in desperation at Javelin who was also looking worried, tugging at his beard nervously. He crouched alongside one of the other tombs and made ready to throw his spear at Erin, she being the one who seemed to be the senior of the three ghosts. Jumping up he launched the deadly missile at her but all it did was distract her for a moment. The spear went straight through her and Jon heard it clatter onto the floor further down the corridor behind the spectral being. Hissing with rage, she turned her red eyes upon the group of dwarves and blinked. A powerful force hit them and they were all sent reeling across the floor. Jon banged his head against a stone pillar which made him see stars but he was not seriously hurt, just stunned by the force of the pulse of energy that Erin had sent against them.

It proved to them that they were indeed outclassed by these three ghost-wizards. Their only hope was in Hamill but he appeared to be floundering under the intense pressure being brought to bear against him. Hamill still stood entrenched in his cocoon of energy at the doorway. Despite the increased efforts of Erin, Gallon and Megan, they could not penetrate his defences and howled in frustration. Erin grasped her sword in both hands and rushed at him as he stood, head bowed, seemingly open to the blow that she levelled at him. She swung the blade around her head several times emitting a ringing sound from it as it slashed through the air then down in a sweeping arc on the seer.

Hamill never flinched, it was as though he did not care that he was about to be sliced in two. He obviously held immense confidence in his defensive shield; that or he was unaware of what Erin was doing and of the danger he was in. Jon watched with breathless anticipation as the sword descended. The entire room had taken on a surreal time of its own; everything was moving as if it was in slow motion and Jon held his breath as the sword sliced into Hamill's shield. A flash of white light erupted from the contact point and Jon saw the blade continue down and through, it penetrated the shield and with another white flash, Hamill disappeared.

Jon slowly stood up shouting out in dismay. 'No, it can't be.' He froze in horror as Erin raised the sword high above her head in triumph; her red eyes glaring at the ceiling as she shouted out her victory over the seer. Galan and Megan applauded her success and floated forward to congratulate her. The dwarves had sunk to the floor in disbelief that Hamill had gone and Jon stood in the midst of the crypt. Shock drained the blood from his head and he felt giddy so he had to grip the edge of one of the tombs to steady his buckling knees. Hamill had been defeated by the combined efforts of the ghost-wizards with the Sword of Darkness claiming the life of a seer for the first time in many millennia. Sorrow flooded his numbed senses and he still could not believe that his friend had been killed. First Auger and now Hamill, both seers had met an untimely end whilst travelling on this errand. It left the brave little band defenceless and alone to face the vengeful spectres.

Turning their attention to Jon and the dwarves, Erin and her two companions stood close together in order to maximise the effectiveness of their power. Gloating at their success against the seer, they moved in on Jon and the dwarves who backed away knowing that they had no defence against the forces at the command of the spectres.

As the three of them approached, a warm mist wafted across the floor, covering the lower parts of their legs, billowing in between them and the ghosts. The surface of the mist undulated like the waves of the sea and erupted into a fountain of smoke that encircled the startled wizards, rising up around their ankles and holding them fast. Jon could see the three figures as they endeavoured to break free from the confining tendrils of green mist. They tried repeatedly to break free without success and howled in despair. The fog gathered in from all around them and a plume of swirling mist shot up from the ground as it condensed into a form that resembled a figure. It continued to solidify and moments later took on the form of Hamill; he was not dead. The cunning seer had fooled the ghosts into believing they had killed him when in reality he had simply changed his form and escaped the fatal blow that Erin had levelled at him.

Hamill faced the spectres and raised his arms, bringing them together so that he gripped the staff before him and brought it down with a sharp rap on the stone slabs of the floor. The entire room shook with the force of the powerful blow and cracks appeared in the arched ceiling sending dust and debris falling onto their heads. Screaming with frustration at Hamill's appearance after believing that they had killed him, Erin, Galan and Megan threw their united powers against the misty fetters that held them bound. They threw blasts of black energy that cut through the tendrils of power that Hamill had caused to bind the three spectres.

They realised that they were no match for the ingenuity that had been displayed by their unexpected intruder. Hamill pushed his advantage home by holding them within a curtain of shimmering, translucent green energy. No matter how hard they tried they could not escape the encircling bands of power. Hamill was determined to protect his friends and brought his right hand up and focused his power on the three ghost-wizards. Spreading his fingers he caused the energy to separate them and draw them towards him. Slowly they floated across the room towards the three tombs, cocooned in Hamill's power. They made futile attempts to resist but were unable to defy him.

Jon watched awestruck as the scene unfolded before him. Never would he have believed Hamill capable of exercising such control and authority; true he was a seer and he was doing what was required of him but to actually witness it was truly astounding.

One by one the ghost-wizards were drawn towards their separate tombs and were lowered through the stone lids; their shrieks of protest echoed into silence as they disappeared from view. The room had been charged with heat by the unleashing of the power from Hamill's staff and it brought a welcome relief to all who had been subjected to the cold that the three spectres had brought with them.

Hamill stood in silence as he gathered his thoughts and lifted his head; with a weary smile he wiped his forehead with the back of his hand. 'Well, that was rather a challenge I have to admit.'

Jon rushed forward and slapped Hamill on the shoulder then stood back and berated him for what he had done. 'You gave us the scare of our lives. We thought you had been killed. Promise that you will never do that again.'

'I'm sorry; I suppose it was rather theatrical but it was the only way that I could see of being able to overcome them. I had to stop their attacks on me somehow so that I could bring my full power to bear on them and that seemed to be the only way, for them to believe they had defeated me.

'Well, we're certainly glad that you're alright and mightily pleased to see you, Hamill. You couldn't have appeared at a more opportune moment.' Javelin greeted him with joy.

'I'm as glad of it as you are, Javelin. I have been wandering around these passageways trying to find you ever since we were separated.'

'Where are Archer and Leader? Did Braun find you?' Trapper asked, concerned that they were not with the seer.

Braun's deep resonant voice echoed out of the passage that Hamill had used. 'We are here. Hamill instructed us to remain hidden until all was well. For once I am glad that we did as he told us. We heard what was going on.' Braun and the two dwarves stepped from out of the darkness of the passageway into the crypt.

'It has not been easy to find you but with the means of my staff I was able to find a way through this labyrinth. It has taken me a while but I finally managed to track you down to this room. You realise of course that the way keeps changing. We had to double back several times before I was able to take the correct turns.'

'Yes we came to the same conclusion not long after starting out along the passages; then we came up against the Anramites but managed to get away from them eventually, thanks to Jon. After having made our escape we found ourselves here and were confronted by those terrible apparitions. Thank goodness you arrived when you did.' Javelin said, much relieved at the seer's presence.

'Well, let's not dilly-dally around. Follow me and I shall lead you out of here but you must stay close. I don't want anyone to become separated from the group.'

They all nodded, Javelin retrieved his spear then, along with the others, followed Hamill along the passage with the four dwarves keeping as close as they could without tripping over each other. They left the crypt in the quiet that they had found it in, leaving it in the darkness as it closed in like a thick blanket over the tombs.

The dreadful silence of the grave returned and the ghost-wizards were left to rue the day they clashed with the newest of the seers. Hamill Lodestone had come of age.

Chapter 26

The Keystone

The land was still quite young when Seers Tower was in the early stages of being built and it had become necessary for the few who had banded together as the first seers to confront the wizards. They had done so in order to prevent total subjugation of the folk in the land. After they had defeated the wizards, the energy barrier had been established between their worlds; and the seers had established the Council of the Sight.

They had built the place so that the positive energy that lay beneath the great rock that stood like an island in the midst of the cold, dark lake would be protected They also used it as a fortress to defend themselves from any future attack upon them and as a place of sanctuary. It was vital to the peace of the land that no one else arose seeking to use the power over others. It was a place where they could protect the barrier from a world that perhaps would tamper with powers they did not understand.

There had been a price to pay for the first seers; their very beings had been infused with the powers that created worlds and had changed their bodies forever. They were no longer as normal folk; they found that they could not live amongst the races as they once had for they did not seem to age. Their cycle of life had been altered and they were able to live for far longer than others. They would die eventually, from natural causes or even by accident, but to all intents and purposes they were immortal. This condition would pass from one seer to the next as others were sought out to take their place when the time eventually came for them to pass on to the next existence.

With The Montage in danger of being activated by Ebon through the negative power beneath the keystone at Anram, there would be little time in which to accomplish what Urim knew he needed to do. The Montage had never been invoked outside of Seers Tower and the process had always been conducted by means of the positive energy that lay beneath the Tower. However here in Anram, where the wizards had held sway millennia ago, lying beneath the Keystone, was the negative energy of the world of the seers. It was the cap above the vast resource of power that could undo all that had been established by the first seers.

Urim knew that he must act now before it was too late or the future would be a very different place to that which it should be. Ebon must not be allowed to succeed; if he were to unlock the door between the opposing worlds of the seers and the wizards then it would be the end of everything the seers held dear. The races of man, dwarf, elf and all others who held the love of freedom in their hearts would disappear and a cold, dark reign of terror would descend upon them to last for thousands of years. That is why he had to succeed and prevent Ebon from undoing what the seers had sacrificed so much in achieving as the Council of the Sight.

Ebon was blinded by his own desire for power and could not see that he was being manipulated by the forces that were growing in strength within him. The wizards needed someone here, in the land of their origin, to carry out what they were unable to do for themselves. Ebon was the means by which they could succeed and he was using another to fulfil what he thought were his own desires. Urim knew who that person was but he dare not intervene until the very last moment, when the union between Ebon and his puppet was at its strongest; only then could he be stopped.

Waiting now in the vast chamber beneath the main pyramid at the centre of the ruins of Anram, Urim wondered whether what he was about to do was the right thing. He knew that Ebon could not be trusted and that as long as he had freedom to do so, he would seek to dominate others. His lust for power was insatiable and could only be quenched by his complete and utter defeat. Terra was right; Ebon had to be removed from their plane of existence if they were to have peace and security in the lands that made up their world. It pained him to be the one to administer judgement but he would not need to do it if Ebon would only forsake his ambition to rule.

Ebon had been a promising addition to the ranks of the seers when he had joined the Council of the Sight as a novice. He had learned well and grown quickly under the supervision of his kindly tutor and predecessor. His capacity to learn had been astounding and he had developed his knowledge and ability at an incredible rate. It had been that very aptitude to learn that had been his undoing. His quest for knowledge was replaced by the desire for power.

Ebon had been plucked from the world of men almost by chance, happening along the former Ebon Lodestone as the seer journeyed through the land. They had struck up a friendship and the incumbent seer had proposed that his new friend join him at Seers Tower. The chance to really make something of himself decided him to accept and he had developed from there. Had he known what would become of his new novice, the wise and gentle old man would not have been so quick in choosing him to be the one to succeed him.

All that was many years ago now; Ebon had been a young man in his early twenties and was now about the same age as Urim, though Ebon looked younger. He had a youthful zeal about him and the curls of blonde hair had given him the look of a much younger man but all that had gone as Ebon slipped deeper under the control of the wizards.

Urim's thoughts were interrupted by a noise that drifted down through the tunnels that led up to the desert surface. Someone was coming and he knew who it was.

Following the seer and hoping to avoid running into the Anramites they made their way along the narrow passages that honeycombed the lower levels of the ruined city. Hamill led Jon and the others along the tunnel they hoped would lead them to the chamber that lay beneath the central plaza where the pyramid rose above the other buildings. They were guided at every turn by the thread of green light from Hamill's staff that led them through the labyrinth.

From his hiding place, Urim watched as they emerged from the passageway and into the cavernous underground amphitheatre. The light cast from the glow stones that he had left for them at the entrance announced their arrival. They did not need them here; the whole place was a giant glow stone shedding diffused light in every direction. The Anramites did not come here very often as it was still too bright for them; they preferred the darker sections of the ruins.

Urim stayed concealed waiting for the right moment; he knew that it would not be far away. Soon he would show himself and capture Ebon as the outcast seer tried to influence his puppet and open the keystone that would supply the way for the return of the wizards. Their conduit back into the world of the seers must be locked and remain so for the rest of time. They must never again pose a threat to the peace of the land.

'Wow; this is an incredible place.' Jon stood open mouthed as he saw the immensity of the chamber, echoing the shape of the pyramid above them and being set out like an ancient theatre.

'I truly admire the workmanship of these folk in getting the whole structure to support itself like this and stay undisturbed even after all these centuries.' Mason held a particular regard for the ingenuity of the ancient race that had built this structure. Digger too admired the talent evidenced by the building of such a place.

'What was that?' Javelin hushed everyone to silence. Unfortunately Braun's stomach decided to rumble and it made some of them suppress a laugh easing the tension. 'Well, it seems that what I heard may have been your stomach. We'd better finish what we need to do and leave so that we can all get something to eat.'

'Well, now that we are here, let's get on with it. If we're to prevent Ebon in his attempt to open the way through for the wizards we'd better find that keystone.' Hamill was very much for 'getting on with it' so that they could return to the Tower and continue with their separate tasks. He was keen to finish this latest escapade and bring an end to Ebon's interference once and for all.

'I agree with Hamill; we should hurry before anything else happens to prevent us from carrying out our task. We'd better find this keystone as quickly as we can before any of those Anramites appear.' Jon said anxiously.

He seemed agitated and keen to find the stone and he ambled off towards the dais to look there. The dwarves decided to split up and search the periphery of the chamber whilst Braun stayed with Jon. Before the dwarves had reached the sides of the amphitheatre Jon shouted out to them that he had found it. Amazed that it should have been so easy to locate, the others quickly gathered to where Jon and Braun stood. Jon seemed to glory in the fact that he had discovered the keystone and slouched with his arms folded across his chest; he had a smug look of; 'didn't I do well' on his face, which was rather uncharacteristic of him.

They all had to agree, however, that he had every right to look pleased with himself. There indeed was the keystone at the centre of the dais. The pattern of the flagstones radiated away from the circular stone in the centre and the ones immediately around the keystone were of a slightly different hue. They emphasised the fact that the one in the middle was different.

Looking at the pattern in the slabs, Hamill noticed that it looked very much like the courtyard in Seers Tower; only here there was no shaft, just the stones. 'I suppose it makes sense for there to be no shaft here, being as it is opposed to what the seers stand for. The wizards would have things in opposition to us; hence the pattern of the shaft is here, yet it is without the void.' Hamill said.

'Are we sure that this is the right thing to do? I mean what if we actually help Ebon to break free by doing this as opposed to stopping him. How do we know that placing your staff on the keystone will have the desired effect and not what we have come here to prevent?' Archer asked the question that had worried them all ever since they had been made aware of the keystone. No one answered as none of them really knew; they hoped that they were doing the right thing but there was really no way of telling until it had been done.

'Don't anybody move.' Javelin whispered with an edge of caution to his voice.

They all froze and followed his gaze. Unnoticed by them all until now, scores of the Anramites had gathered around the edges of the chamber and more were arriving by the moment. Gradually they pressed forward, seemingly unaffected by the warm light given off by the walls. They came slowly towards the band of intruders, with what intent was uncertain but it did not bode well for the little group if their last meeting with them was anything to go by.

'I suggest that we decide quickly whether we do this or not. We may not have the chance to do anything if we delay any longer.' Javelin's counsel was wise as always.

Jon caught them by surprise as he pushed forward, a glazed look in his eyes. He almost stumbled along as if his feet seemed unwilling to move; he reached out and took Auger's broken staff from Mason's pack, holding the two parts together. He moved forward with a jerking action as if he were a puppet with strings.

'Ebon; remove yourself from him.' Urim stepped out from behind one of the theatre stands at the side and through an archway, onto the dais. He held a strange looking staff which he planted before him and he raised a hand, signalling for Jon to stop.

He did, although he tried not to. Jon pushed with his might against the invisible force that Urim was exerting against him. The Anramites stopped their move towards them and started to retreat away from the presence of the seer who had suddenly appeared as if from nowhere and was using powers that they knew were too strong for them.

'No one is to touch the keystone; the slightest touch by a seer's staff will open the floodgates of Magog and release the wizards from their prison world.'

'Urim; what are you doing here? What do you mean; surely just touching it will not be enough?' Braun stated, amazed at the seer's sudden appearance.

'I assure you that it will be more than enough for one who holds the Rod of Dread.'

They all stood open mouthed at what Urim had said and looked at each other nonplussed unable to understand what he meant. They stood in a loose semi-circle around the place where Jon was still in a dazed state, caught in mid motion. The power Urim was exerting held him in stasis, unable to move.

Urim stepped forward and the others dropped back, making way for him as he faced Jon across the keystone. With a flourish he pulled his hand into a fist and jerked backwards as if hooking a fish on a line. Jon gasped and fell backwards onto the stone slabs of the dais, Auger's broken staff falling with a clatter. The band of dwarves, along with Braun and Hamill let out an exclamation of surprise. The dwarves drew their swords and knives but held back from attacking the shadowy seer who had appeared from nowhere.

Ebon now stood where Jon had done seconds ago; in his hand was the Rod of Dread. He glared back at Urim with hatred in his eyes. The dark form was almost unrecognisable from the rogue seer that Jon had first met only last year. The black robe he wore was in tatters and his pale, thin body struggled against the force that held him bound. The power of the Rod had been draining him of his essence, turning him into a shadow, just as the wizards had become. It would not be much longer before he too would be as they, living yet not alive. There was determination in Ebon still as he strained against Urim's power but he was not strong enough to break free.

'He has been using you, Jon, to further his own ends but he will do so no longer. I am here to deal with him once and for all. I am taking him back to answer to the wizards for his treachery. They shall pass judgement upon him, not us.'

'Curse you Urim, I shall have my revenge upon you some day; you mark my words.'

'That may be so, Ebon; but that day is not today.' Urim took hold of the slight yet strong rebel seer. Ebon felt the power behind Urim's grasp. It was more than a physical strength because the power of the Rod was swept aside as if it did not exist. Ebon could do nothing to resist his pull and stumbled along like a naughty schoolboy at his side.

'Blast you Urim; why must you appear each time just when I am about to complete my last step to victory? I should have finished you when I had the chance; more is the pity that I didn't because I would be master of this world by now.'

'You can not be allowed to succeed, Ebon. Too many lives have been lost and countless others have suffered because of your selfish ambitions. I am here to prevent you from causing more misery. You shall give account to the ones to whom you have sold yourself; they shall determine what becomes of you for I cannot.'

Turning to Hamill, Urim said. 'When we have gone, place Auger's broken staff in the centre of the keystone, there is a dreg of power in it yet but it will not be there for long so you need to act quickly. With Ebon's influence removed and the link to the wizards broken it will be safe for you to use the keystone. You will be able to obtain sufficient power from it to meld the staff into one again and enable the use of the staff to control the wind; I shall meet with you at Seers Tower.'

Holding tightly onto Ebon's arm, Urim held him bound by the power he used and stepped into the open portal that he had created. They disappeared from view; Urim taking Ebon out of the world he would have dominated by fear.

Urim admired the tenacity of the rebel seer and of his ability to have hidden himself within the form of another. The staff of the portal had served Urim well in his endeavours to apprehend Ebon. Urim used it now to relocate them both into the world of Magog where Ebon had been snatched away by the energy barrier outside Seers Tower. Ebon had an appointment with destiny and Urim would ensure that the rebel seer did not miss it.

Chapter 27

The Great Salt Flats

Jon wanted to say something to Urim but he had gone before he could recover from his experience and did not form the words in time. Urim and Ebon had disappeared into the portal that closed with a swish of air and a rippling image that vanished before their eyes.

'He just doesn't stay still for a moment.' Jon bemoaned the absence of the seer as he leaned on one arm whilst lying on the floor; he lacked the strength to stand right now.

Hamill knelt by his side looking into the empty space where Urim had been and answered Jon's forlorn statement. 'No Jon, he doesn't. That is his nature I'm afraid. Here one moment and gone the next but we shall meet with him again, I'm certain of it and we must make our way back to Seers Tower. We have been delayed from doing so for too long and Terra will be expecting us, now that Ebon has been apprehended. Talking of which, how are you feeling now that he has been taken from you?' Hamill asked, concerned that Jon might be suffering from any side effects of his 'exorcism' of Ebon's influence.

'I feel very well thanks; I am a little tired but other than that I would not have known that there was anything amiss.' Jon answered, mentally examining how he felt and clambered to his feet.

'I was rather surprised; to say the least, to see Ebon here and for Urim to have extracted him from you was even more amazing. I wonder how he was able to do it.' Hamill posed the question that all of them thought.

'Which one are you referring to; Urim or Ebon?' Jon asked.

'Well, both really; I suppose it's just another one of those questions that will never be answered.' Hamill looked at the ground and frowned.

Javelin interrupted their conversation. 'I suggest that we do as Urim instructed; then we can get out of here.'

'Yes, you're quite right Javelin; we'd better leave before we have any more trouble from the Anramites.'

Placing Auger's broken staff in the centre of the keystone as Urim had directed him; Hamill took a gasp of air as he felt the power running into the staff. The others saw a pulsing of light that slowly crept up the stem of the staff, joining the two pieces together, until it reached the seers' hand. Letting go of the staff it remained upright, supported by the power from beneath. Hamill kept his hand nearby, ready to grasp it when it had received sufficient energy. When the pulsing light stopped, the staff fell into his hand; it was ready to use.

'Well, he never ceases to amaze me with the things that he knows.' Hamill referred to Urim. 'Now if everyone is ready, we'll make our way out of here. Without Auger I will not be able to control the wind for long or for very far but I should be able to get us across the desert to Seaview. All being well we can charter a ship and before you know it, we'll be back at the Tower.'

Jon and the others all looked relieved at not having to cross the desert sands again and they were eager to get going.

'What about these Anramites, won't they try to stop us and will we be able to find our way out of the labyrinth?' Mason queried.

'I don't think that we'll have any more trouble from those creatures; they seem to have given up on us.' Braun noted.

Indeed it appeared so because all of the Anramites had disappeared, no longer being influenced by Ebon's mind control. He had spread his influence wide in coercing the descendants of the original inhabitants of Anram to try and separate Jon from the dwarves. He had almost succeeded and had it not been for Hamill's intervention, they would have achieved Ebon's aim in that the keystone would already have been opened.

The group's purpose here in locating the keystone had been fulfilled and Ebon had been apprehended, the creatures had no desire to stop them anymore; they were free to leave.

Hamill used his staff to send out a tendril of green light again which they followed as it guided them through the maze. Taking the glow stones with them to light the way they saw no sign of the inhabitants as they moved quickly through the passages unmolested. It appeared that they had lost all interest in them. The journey out from beneath the ancient pyramid did not take long and they managed to avoid any further traps. It seemed that the inhabitants were happy to see them go; leaving them to their dark world beneath the ruins of Anram.

They emerged from the darkness into the sunlight and shielded their eyes; the heat hit them as if an oven door had been opened in front of them. The dwarves thought it would be better to wait until dusk when the cool of the evening would be more suitable for travelling. Jon and Hamill decided that there was no need for them to wait; travelling in the vortex of the wind the heat would not have any effect upon them.

Hamill blew delicately on the small pipe whistle and called up the wind. There was no movement for some time as the heat of the day rested heavily upon the sand that lay around them for many leagues in all directions. Then a gentle whisper of cool air against Jon's cheek announced the coming of a breeze. The wind gathered apace and a funnel of sand approached from the East, swirling around and around but getting closer by the moment. As it neared, Hamill held up Auger's staff to bring the fury of the circling wind under control.

A gap appeared at the base of the vortex and he stepped into the centre, urging Jon and the others to join him quickly. They leaped forward into the gap just in time to see the desert floor fall away beneath them. Jon felt his stomach drop as if it had a lead weight in it and he felt giddy. It was probably because of the sensation of being lifted off the ground as they sped away up into the air, north and westwards towards Seaview and eventually, Seers Tower.

'I'm sorry about the rough lift off just then. It takes a bit of getting used to, controlling the wind, but I will try to get us safely back to the ground again.' Hamill apologised.

None of them answered him. They were all too intent on what was happening around them and trying to come to terms with the peculiar feeling of standing on solid ground, yet there was nothing but swirling air beneath their feet.

When they entered the vortex, it was a swirling blast of sand and air then, some time later, it thinned as they climbed higher and the air cleared. Looking down, Jon saw that the desert had given way to green fields and the thin ribbon that was the River Lune could be seen far away to the north. More fields and tiny dots that he thought were cattle and sheep could be seen grazing on the hillsides.

Flashing by, the wind ate up the distance towards Seaview; the Great Salt Waters loomed before them on the horizon; below, the marshes spread out beneath them where the marsh-mogs dwelt. That was one place that Jon definitely did not want to go.

Hamill seemed to struggle with his control over the wind and he grimaced with concentration. 'I'm sorry about this my friends but I will not be able to hold this together for much longer; we will came down a little short of where I wanted us to be. You'd better brace yourself for a bit of a bump.'

Jon looked down with trepidation, realising that they would indeed be short of where they wanted to be. In fact they were headed for the edges of the salt marsh; the very place he had not wanted to go. He closed his eyes and crossed his fingers, trusting in his friend for their safe landing.

Squelch! They all spilled out of the confines of the spinning vortex as it gave way and dissipated into a few wisps of air.

The group of travellers were scattered over an area of soggy grasses and stagnant ponds. Jon was fortunate enough to have a soft landing in a patch of sodden grass but Braun ended up displacing a large quantity of green algae as he dropped into the middle of pond. The others all managed to avoid the ponds and fortunately there were no injuries other than for a few bruises that would no doubt appear in a day or two. Braun clambered out of the stinking water and tried to brush the algae from his clothing with some course grasses that he tore from the ground. He did not mind the water so much; it was the unpleasant aroma that came from the algae that he objected to.

'Phew, Braun; you could at least stand down wind so that we don't have to suffer it with you.' Archer teased the gentle giant.

'You could give me a hand to get this stuff off me then I wouldn't need to.' Braun grinned back at the dwarf.

'I would if you were not such a mountain.' The dwarf laughed.

Trying to get their bearings, Javelin climbed a small hillock nearby and searched for a path of some sort that they could use to escape from the marshes. He thought that he could see a way forward and signalled to Trapper to join him. The two dwarves consulted for a few moments, gesturing with their hands in the air in front of them as they mapped out the way ahead. The two dwarves joined the rest of the group and Javelin outlined what they needed to do.

'Trapper and I believe that we have seen a way out of the marsh but it will not be easy as the route winds its way past areas that look solid enough but may actually be sink-holes full of liquid mud. One step out of place and that person will disappear, sucked under within moments and we would not be able to rescue them.'

The others all looked apprehensively at each other but nodded their understanding of what Javelin had told them; no one wanted to end up at the bottom of a muddy pit. Hamill apologised again for dropping them into this predicament. 'I really am sorry that I was unable to control the wind for longer; Urim did warn me that I may not be able to hold it together for too long, especially with so many of us needing to be transported. I should have gone directly to Northill, maybe then we would have been able to arrive there safely. I thought it would save time if we went to Seaview instead.'

Javelin spoke on behalf of them all. 'We don't blame you Hamill; we appreciate what you were trying to do and to get us this far so quickly is no mean feat in itself. What we need to do now is try to avoid getting lost in the marsh or falling foul of any sink-holes. At all costs we need to stay out of the way of the marsh-mogs.'

They all agreed with that, none of them wanted to stumble across the dangerous creatures. Jon recalled his encounter with them in the forest near his home at Ashbrooke and remembered the feelings he had at their close proximity. If he never came across another one he would be very happy. He looked around him nervously hoping that they would be out of the marsh before too long.

'How long do you think it will take us to find our way out of here, Javelin?' Archer asked the question that was burning in Jon's mind.

'I am afraid that we might have to spend the night here so I suggest that we find somewhere a bit more suited for a camp site.' Javelin stood waiting for any comments before getting underway but none were offered so he nodded to Trapper to lead the way forward. Archer followed in his footsteps, literally so as to avoid stepping into a sink-hole. Digger and Mason were next, then Jon and Hamill. Braun, still trying to brush the offending algae from his clothing joined the line with Leader and Javelin bringing up the rear. Within a few steps of starting out the two dwarves asked if Braun would mind if they walked in front of him.

'Phew, Braun; we suggest that the first thing you do when we get to Seaview is to have a bath.'

They wrinkled their noses up with the effects of the pungent smell as they passed him but were happier after they had made the change. Braun swung a playful sweep of his arm in their direction that went over their heads but they felt the wind it caused as it passed them. Had it connected they would have felt the sting of it for several days. They gave the metal-master a sideways glance wondering if he had actually meant it but Braun responded with a wry smile that assured them that he missed them deliberately.

Snaking their way through the marsh, the troupe of friends made their way carefully along a track of sorts. They had to constantly change direction in order to avoid ground that looked as if it were unsafe. Each one of them concentrating on their footing and snatching nervous glances around them for any sign of marsh-mogs. They walked for a long time without speaking, making only an occasional slip here and there. Gradually the light began to fade and the way forward became treacherous as dusk started to settle around them. Trapper was leading the way, as best he could before stopping. He turned and waited for Javelin to catch up.

'We need to find somewhere for the night; I think there might be a good spot over to our right. Do you see the rise about a league away with the dead tree on it? We should be able to reach it before we lose the light completely.'

Javelin nodded and signalled for Trapper to make the detour. They reached it a little while later and gratefully sat on the bank of solid earth. It promised to be a very bleak and cold night. The glow stones were brought out of their packs and they gave sufficient light for Leader and Digger to use their hatchets to cut some branches from the old tree and build a fire. The warmth of the flames was most welcome, especially for Braun whose clothes were still damp from the soaking he received from landing in the pool. The steam was soon rising from his clothing as he sat close to the fire and hugged his knees but the others kept their distance due to the pungent smell of the drying algae. The flames from the camp fire made his dark eyes sparkle.

A thick darkness descended all around them on the swamp and the night creatures started to emerge. They could see their eyes shining brightly as they looked at the place where the group were resting. It was decided that a watch should be kept throughout the night and that it would be better for two of them to be awake at any one time. They did not want to run the risk of being caught unawares by any of the creatures of the marsh, especially not a marsh-mog. Hamill and Jon opted to stand first watch; they would wake Digger and Mason for the second watch. The wood that the dwarves had chopped from the tree was running low so more was prepared so that the fire would last though the night. With any luck it would help keep any unwanted visitors away.

The two friends sat together watching the flames of the fire that danced brightly in front of them. Occasionally they would peer out into the dark and listen to the sounds of the night. Hamill had particularly good hearing so they were confident that they would hear anything that tried to approach.

They sat talking in hushed voices so as not to disturb the others, speculating on who would be chosen to replace Auger. Would it be one of the dwarves they knew or did Terra know of another that would be inaugurated in the seer's stead. They were unable to come to any conclusion as there were too many possibilities but they both agreed that Javelin displayed all of the qualities that would be needed to take on such a role. The pale light from the moon casting a dim shadow from the stick that Javelin had placed in the ground signalled their time standing watch had ended and they woke the two dwarves before settling down to get what sleep they could before dawn broke.

When Jon stirred to wakefulness he groaned with the discomfort of having slept on the ground in the open air. He looked forward to the prospects of a nice soft mattress when they got to Seers Tower and all of this trudging around the countryside was over. If only Hamill could somehow use the wind again and get them out of the marsh, that would be something at least.

The fire still burned and Mason was busy boiling some water. Seeing Jon wake up, the sociable dwarf smiled and greeted him cheerfully. The high bank of earth they were on was surrounded by a blanket of mist that ebbed and flowed with a motion that was not too dissimilar to that of the ocean. The fog was quite deep and would easily have hidden any marsh-mogs that decided to approach.

'Good morning Jon; I trust you slept well, I think we had the best room in the house judging by the mist that is on the marsh today.' Mason was always cheerful and his comments made Jon smile. He was the last to stir but no-one minded; they would not be going anywhere all the time the mist covered the ground. It would be too dangerous to attempt leaving the safety of the hill as they would not be able to see where they should walk. They would just have to sit and wait for it to clear.

Breakfast consisted of whatever they had in their packs, which proved to be very little; a few biscuits and some dried fruit. At least they had plenty of water; they had replenished their flasks before leaving Anram. There would be no decent water to be had here in the Flats; most of it was stagnant and probably unfit to wash with, let alone drink any of it. Although no-one said anything the mood in the camp was dampened by the appearance of the mist as it virtually had them trapped on their little place of refuge. The good thing about it was the fact that they were reasonably comfortable; it would have been a whole lot worse for them if they had not found this higher ground for the night.

Braun had managed to clean the foul smelling swamp weed from his clothing now that it had dried and he was not avoided as much by the others. The stink of the Flats was ever present but it was not as thick as it had been. Braun even made a joke out of it, relieving the dark mood that hung over them, as he saw the funny side of it now that he was dry and reasonably clean.

'At least you all knew where I was, particularly if you were down wind of me.' His face creased into a huge grin and he smelled under his arm before letting out a sigh of contentment as if he now smelled as fresh as a flower. He coughed when the lingering aroma caught in his throat which caused them all to laugh. The dwarves all settled down to smoke their pipes and soon a thick cloud of the pungent smoke filled the air.

'You light up those foul smelling pipes of yours and you had the nerve to ask me to walk behind you last night. What a stink! What is it anyway?' Braun toyed with the dwarves.

'It's the best weed you can get east of the Great Divide.' Archer countered; pointing the end of his pipe in Braun's direction as if to emphasize his comment.

Jon thought that they made a strange sight, sitting together, puffing the obnoxious weed as if they did not have a care in the world. They might just as well have been relaxing on a summer evening sitting on the porch of their homes back at Ffridd-Uch-Ddu. Hamill decided to move to the other side of the rise in order to escape the smoke that had been drifting in his direction. It was not long before Jon joined him and they sat together thinking their own thoughts. They did not sit there for long before a low guttural growl drifted out of the mist from the other side of the mound. They were just turning to see what it was when another growl filtered through the mist from somewhere in front of them. Several more blood curdling sounds like coughs reached their ears from other parts of the marsh not far from where they were seated. The dwarves all extinguished their pipes and made ready for action, ever at the alert for danger.

'What was that?' Braun asked with a hint of fear in his whispered question.

Jon knew what it was, he had heard it before. It was the sound of a marsh-mog and there was more than one; they were surrounded by them.

Chapter 28

The Rod of Retribution

Urim held Ebon fast with the power of his staff and despite Ebon's attempts to break free, he found that his command of the Rod had failed him. It was as if it had ceased to work and Ebon felt weak, no longer sustained by the power of the Rod, he had regained his mortal weaknesses with no energy from the earth with which to call upon. The rebel seer could do nothing; only accept that he was powerless to prevent Urim doing what he will with him. Ebon was not in control, something that he had not known for many years and he fell into despair.

Travelling at velocities that could only be imagined, the two of them were transported via the portal from the depths of the underground city of Anram through the ether of space and within time itself. In a flash, Urim and Ebon were taken through the fabric of several dimensions until they reached the destination that Urim had selected. They stood in a darkened room that smelled of damp and decay; at its centre was a large stone feature that held a pool of still water. Ebon lifted his head to see where Urim had brought him and gasped in dismay; they stood in a five sided chamber. Ebon recognised it at once as the place that had been shown to him in his mind by the wizards and where he was to report on his success, or failure, in his attempt to conquer the seers.

They were deep within the wizards' fortification, at the central place where the wizards would gather in their conclave. It was with the aid of the staff of the portal, backed by the energy beneath Seers Tower that enabled Urim to produce a partial Montage and bridge the gap between the worlds. Only with that combination of forces could Urim have managed to penetrate the powers that surrounded the edifice that served as the wizards' sanctuary and enter into their domain.

It was not a place that Urim wanted to remain in longer than was necessary. He let go of Ebon's arm, releasing the hold he had on him through his staff; the frustration that had been bubbling up inside of the hapless seer exploded from him. Ebon fell to his knees, so weak that he could not stand; he ranted and raved at Urim, cursing him for his interference in his affairs.

'Blast you, you deceiver; I'll dispose of you yet and rid myself of you once and for all. You have no right to treat me this way. What makes you think that you have the right to tell me what to do? You don't even belong here; go back to where you came from.'

Ebon raised the Rod before him threateningly in his clenched fist as if to strike out at his nemesis. Urim smiled gently and made no move to either retreat or to confront him. It was as if he had no fear of what Ebon might or might not do. This further infuriated Ebon and he cursed, furious to know that Urim was unafraid of him. What was even more infuriating was that Ebon knew he could do nothing against his adversary. He struggled to find the strength within and stood to face the one being that had been a thorn in his side. He brought the Rod in front of him with a swift jerk as if to protect himself, concentrating his thoughts on summoning the power the Rod represented.

He may not have been able to combat the power that Urim had used against him at Anram, but here in the very heart of the wizards' sanctuary he believed that he would easily turn the tables on the interfering seer. Flashing the rod before him in an arc across his chest, he made to blast Urim from existence. This was the time when he would wreak his revenge on the meddlesome seer.

His face darkened with anger, his lips curled into a snarl of rage and hatred; his eyes blazed red. For too long Urim had held the upper hand but now Ebon was more powerful than he. Backed by the wizards and standing in the very centre of their domain he could not fail to rid himself of Urim, once and for all. His grip tightened on the Rod and his knuckles whitened as he prepared to send a blast of raw energy at Urim.

With all the fury of his mind he determined to draw out enough power so that it would be strong enough to destroy all of the seers, let alone one. Nothing happened and he tried again and again but the Rod would not give of its power. Something prevented it from doing so. Urim saw Ebon's disbelief and decided to tell him why the blast did not come; why Urim could not be affected by the Rod of Dread.

'Ebon; you have no power over me because you would use the source of your power against the one who has discovered the burial place of he from whom the Rod was made. I have covenanted that I would reunite him with that which was taken by force. Custennin, the giant, wishes to be whole again and I have his protection until I make good my promise.'

He held forth a small leather pouch and opened it; from it he produced a small object for Ebon to see. It was a small bone from the finger of a hand but not just any hand; it was from that of Custennin the giant.

'I have the token that negates the power of the Rod; it will do you no good any more. Its powers are gone and no matter how you try, you will not be able to harm me, or anyone else.'

Ebon stood before Urim, grinding his teeth in pure frustration and glared back in defiance and hatred at the one who had been the cause of all his troubles. His chest heaved with the exertion of his emotions until he sank to the ground in utter despair. He let go of the Rod and it tumbled to the floor where it lay lifeless; nothing more than that which it had first been, the thigh bone of a giant.

Ebon clutched at his chest and struggled for breath, his eyes widened in fear as he looked to Urim for help against what was happening to him. Urim was powerless to give any aid; what the Rod had exacted from Ebon whilst it held sway over him was now being reversed. Ebon began to alter in appearance. Where he had been stooped and withered by the demands of the powers he had thought he had controlled; he was now being restored to the condition and health he had enjoyed before becoming subject to the Rod.

His face took on a more youthful look and his eyes cleared; the redness disappeared and the whites of his eyes shone brightly. He was free of the curse he had thought was a blessing and realised now that he had been deceiving himself. In his quest for power he had subjected himself to the will of the wizards until he had become almost as they were. Before too long there would have been no going back; he would have been entirely at their mercy.

What amazed him more than anything else was that rather than trying to destroy Urim, he should be thanking him for saving him from his fate. Reflecting on the past he realised that what he had been trying to achieve was wrong; he looked at the old thigh bone that had been the Rod of Dread. It was true what Urim had said; it had lost its power.

Urim respectfully picked up the old thigh bone that had been the instrument of such dread amongst the folk of this world. The Rod ceased to be anything other than that which it had been; the butchered remains of a mythical giant who had fallen foul of the wizards when they had first arrived in the world of Magog.

Urim looked down on the crumpled form of the once faithful seer He saw how hatred and greed had eaten away at his very soul and transformed Ebon into the shadow of a man he once had been. His physical form may have been restored to him but his mind and his reason had been irreparably damaged.

He felt sorry for Ebon and faltered in his design at leaving him to the mercies of the wizards for he knew they would show him none. Despite his pity for him, Urim realised that he could not be trusted to change his ways. It had been decided by Terra and the other seers that Ebon should remain in the world which had imprisoned him. It was only fitting that Ebon should give account of himself to the wizards, as he had promised to do. It was time to live up to the consequences of his actions.

'Good bye Ebon. I am truly sorry that I could not help you.' Urim considered what else he could have done for Ebon and felt a deep sadness within him that he could not explain. He knew that the decision of the Council to return Ebon to face his fate was the correct one but there was something within him that called out for mercy. It was almost as if they were connected in some way. Urim considered the feeling and decided that it was the brotherhood of the Sight that formed that bond, a bond that was soon to be severed for ever. Not knowing what else he could do or say, Urim stepped back into the portal and it closed upon the world of the wizards with a gentle rush of air that stirred the dust of the ground.

Once again Urim entered the crypt where Custennin's remains were entombed, only this time he knew what to do. Obtaining the key, he inserted it into the latch and turned it. A soft click was followed by the whirring of gears and cogs; the lid opened as it had done before and Urim replaced the finger bone that he had taken the last time he had been there. Carefully, and respectfully, he placed the thigh bone that had been the Rod of Dread, but was now devoid of its power, and laid it inside the stone coffin. Custennin was whole again. Urim looked around as if he were expecting something to happen but there was only silence. What he felt, however, moved him and he had to swallow hard as he was encompassed by a deep and satisfying peace. He whispered into the silence of the tomb. 'Sleep well, my friend and may your rest be undisturbed.'

Not knowing what else to do or say he removed the key and the great stone slab slid back down onto the coffin, sealing it as before. Returning the key to its box, Urim stood in silent reverie for a few moments before he summoned the portal that would transport him to the place he needed to be.

Ebon was left alone, a beaten man. No longer did he have the air of superiority that had accompanied him throughout his campaign of terror. He was bereft of the self assuredness and the haughty curl of the lip. He sat on the cold stone floor, staring out into nothing, a glazed expression in his eyes, a half mad smile played at the corners of his mouth.

He saw nothing and felt nothing; he was numb with the realisation that, once again Urim had robbed him of his attempt to rule. Now, however, he knew that Urim had been right. All that the seers had stood for was right and that he, Ebon, had been the cause of so much suffering. It was almost too much for him to bear. He knew that he was finally beaten; He had lost battles before but this felt different. It was almost as if the walls around him were closing in on him, pressing the breath out of his lungs.

He became aware of a sudden chill in the air and he could see his breath as the tiny droplets of water vapour condensed in the cold. Emrys appeared, bringing the crushed seer out of his reverie. The wizard had flowed from out of the gloomy recesses of the walls as if he had been a part of them and had suddenly become detached. Maccus and the other wizards also appeared to emanate from the walls and converged on the vulnerable former-seer until they formed a circle of darkness around him. They seemed to float above the floor as if they were not really a part of the world.

There was nowhere for Ebon to go and he knew it. Nothing he could do or say now would save him from the fate that awaited him. He had tried to deceive them and to cheat them out of the bargain he had made; more than that, he had tried to usurp their powers and to cast them aside so that he could rule in their stead. It had all come to nothing.

He thought that it was a sad ending to his life, a life that had held so much promise but his greed had got the better of him. His selfish ambitions had brought him nothing but misery and resentment. His lust for power had been shattered by the combined efforts of a simple boy from Ashgrove and the seer, Urim. 'I should have disposed of him when I had the chance to do so instead of playing with possibilities that never materialised. Too late; it's all too late.' He moaned silently.

'We are pleased to see that you have kept your promise to give an account of your actions. We see that you no longer have the Rod of Dread that we allowed you to wield so that you might accomplish your aims of dominion on our behalf. We know that you have failed, just as we failed all those years ago, because of the intervention of the seer known as Urim but this cannot save you from the fact that you failed. You can not escape us now Ebon and we demand payment for our services. It is a pity that you did not tread a different path because you could have received a reward from us instead of our wrath. Had you been more faithful to your promise you could have been one with us and joined us as a wizard in your own right.'

Emrys paused to let the significance of what he had said register in Ebon's mind. The dejected seer looked up into the blazing red eyes of the leading wizard and then at the others in the circle; they all bore down on him with a weight that was almost oppressive. A momentary flicker of hope passed across his face but it fell away as quickly as it had come as he searched the shadowed faces of the wizards, trying to see beyond the glare of their ever staring eyes.

He recognised that it had only been a taunt to deepen his misery. The chance to be one with them had passed. It cut deeply into his soul as he realised that he could have obtained greater power than he had ever had before if only he had not tried to deceive them. If only he had not been so ambitious; if only he had settled for his role as a seer and not lusted after the position held by Terra Standfast as the leader of the Council of the Sight.

If only; they were the words that had followed him throughout this past year, ever since Urim had appeared and tried to release the seers from their imprisonment within the Tower. He had failed at first, beaten by the combined efforts of Ebon's army and the rebel seer's use of the stolen talismans. That was when he had discovered Urim's secret and had tried to prevent him from meddling in his affairs.

Now Urim was the victor and he the vanquished; there was nowhere else to turn; nowhere else to go. He had made his choices and now he must face the consequences of those choices. He considered what Emrys had said about him joining them and becoming a wizard. Would he have wanted to become like them? To be a shadow of the man he was and to live forever as an outcast from the world he really wanted to be a part of? No; he decided without hesitation that despite all the power that he would have had at his command, he would not wish to give up his mortality and become as they were. He decided that he would accept his fate with dignity.

He slowly rose to his feet and stood in calm serenity with a smile on his face. He held his head high and submitted himself to his fate, spreading his arms wide to receive the blow that would bring an end to the man who had been known as Ebon the seer.

His past flashed through his mind. His real name had been David and once, many years ago, he had known happiness and love with a young woman, a girl really, in her late teens. He saw her face in his minds eye before him and a tear formed at the corner of his eye, sorrowful now for the life he could have had but lost because of his greed. He had once held the promise of a simple life, a happy life but he had forsaken it for the opportunity to become a seer.

How he wished now that he had remained with the girl he had left back in Ashbrooke. He thought it ironic that Jon came from the same town that he had lived in all those years ago. He wondered what had become of the young woman with whom he had shared those few months with. He smiled sardonically with the thought that she was probably married now with a family of her own. Too late he realised that that was what he would have been most happy to have had himself; to have raised a family, to have had a son to nurture into manhood. To have been a husband and father would have been the greatest achievement he could have wished for but ambition had got the better of him. His greed had robbed him of reason and his appetite for power had blinded him to the real joy of this life; the love of another. Instead all he had known from the time he became a seer was an empty yearning to control others and to be feared.

Well, he had obtained power and he had been feared but it left him with nothing but frustration and disappointment. Now it was all to be for nothing, all he had achieved was the death and destruction of countless folk in both worlds. His death would pass as just another man who thought he could rise above the rest. He would not be missed; there would be no-one to mourn his loss; no-one would visit his grave. He lived alone and he would die alone. The horrors that had followed him as he bludgeoned his way through life came back to haunt him and he knew that his final destiny would not be a peaceful one.

He had never really believed that there was a god or a great creator but now that he was faced with death, he feared lest there was indeed such a one as a supreme being. He would have to give an account of what he had done not just to the wizards, who would surely demand payment by taking his mortal life from him, but also account to that being who could take his spirit's life.

The thought filled him with a foreboding that chilled the blood in his veins. But it was far too late for him to make amends for what he had done. He had been aware of his choices and he had taken the wrong course throughout his life. No amount of regret could compensate now for the lives he had taken; either by his hand or the hands of others. There was no escape from the consequences of his actions and he knew that he must give an account to those he had sought to betray, both here and now and to the creator of all life. He would find out for himself if there really was a God but there would be no way back for him to take advantage of that knowledge.

He didn't feel the blade as it was thrust through his heart, just the force of the blow against his body, then a chill that made him shiver. He coughed once and darkness embraced him, he collapsed and lay crumpled in a lifeless heap on the floor. The wizards all stood around the body of the one they had hoped would be the means by which they would be able to exact their revenge upon the seers in the other world. It was not to be and he had lost the Rod of Dread, a crime for which he must make recompense.

They gathered closer and the air sizzled with the power that they brought to bear upon the still form. When they moved away all that remained on the floor was a tattered cloak in a dark pool of steaming liquid. Emrys raised his arm above his head, clenched in his fist was a new rod which he named the Rod of Retribution.

Chapter 29

The Fountain and the Tower

Jetta stood gazing into the clear water of the pool at the base of the fountain from which he had sprung. It had been filled with the dark magic that had transformed him into the creature he was now. He hated being what he was and longed for the life he once had as Fergus, up and coming captain of the guard. His life had been simple and uncomplicated compared to what it was now. True he had obtained that which he thought he most wanted; power to control others and to demand respect but it was a respect that was driven by fear not esteem.

He looked at his hands, turning them over and inspecting them as if seeing them for the first time. He watched as the power that had lain dormant in the pool that was now part of him spark with flashes of the power that lay just below the surface of his jet black skin. It was exactly as it had been when contained within the pool of the fountain.

He loathed Ebon for tricking him into his garden and having him succumb to the draw of the magic that now possessed him. It was a cruel, calculated act that Jetta resented more than anything else that he had experienced in his life. True, it was a life that had been filled with intrigue, double dealing and even on occasion, murder. He had not been squeamish about having to shed blood if it advanced him and his ambition but he did not advocate it just for the sake of it.

What he had been forced to do whilst under the influence of the Rod that Ebon wielded was against his will and seared his mind with guilt. His only comfort was that he was powerless to act for himself; the compulsion to carry out Ebon's will had been irresistible. He had tried to resist by using the power that was within him but it was connected somehow to forces that were compelling him to obey and he had found that he could do nothing to oppose it. A deep melancholy settled upon him as he stood by the pool lost in his sadness and despair.

Some time ago he had tried to rid himself of what he saw as a curse by stepping into the pool. He had done it in the hope that it would drain from him and return to the water that had contained it before being absorbed by his body. Nothing happened; he had stood there for a while before stepping out, disappointed that he was still held captive by the dark magic. He had not expected it to work but he had needed to try because he was so desperate to be free.

His hatred towards Ebon grew with each event that Jetta was forced to participate in. Soon the whole of the land would come under the former seer's control; tales of the dark angel had preceded them at each battle and only token resistance had been encountered at the last couple of sieges. Jetta wondered what use Ebon would put him to afterwards; he detested the role he had now and the loneliness he felt. He had no friends, after all who would want to have him as a friend? No, he was feared too greatly by everyone for someone to even think of him as anything but a creature of magic. The solitude within his mind was almost too much to bear and it broke his heart to think that he would live out the rest of his life as this loathsome thing that had sprung up from some dark world.

He did not know how long he would live. Would it be for his natural life span or had the magic altered him so dramatically that he would live forever. He was certainly indestructible, impossible to destroy by any means that anyone could employ against him. At first he had relished the power that his new form had given him and had marvelled that he could face anything knowing that he was immune to any form of attack against him. The novelty had worn off quickly afterwards as he began to realise that he would stand alone, shunned by the society of men that he had so much enjoyed before. He hated the unnecessary killing of simple soldiers who were only trying to do their duty in defending their way of life and their freedom with their lives.

This amount of power, coveted by wicked men, was not worth sacrificing the very thing that made them what they were; their humanity. Jetta counted himself amongst those wicked ones because he realised now that he had been so. He regretted his past and would gladly have died in order to make amends for his crimes but even that was denied him. There was no hope of a future other than to remain a creature of magic; to be used as a weapon against lesser beings by the likes of Ebon who had no compassion and no heart.

A thought occurred to him; it was only a flicker of an idea but it grew into a bright ray of hope that caused his spirits to soar. 'Maybe *he* could help me. He seemed capable enough and he certainly showed no fear of Ebon.' Jetta recalled his brief meeting with the other seer, the one who had appeared in Anna's room and delivered her out of Ebon's clutches.

Jetta had been amazed that his dark magic could not be summoned against this man and he had stood powerless to prevent the seer from freeing Anna from her confinement. With such an ability, to make his own not unsubstantial powers of non-effect, he surely must be able to rescue him from this imposed servitude. Maybe the seer could reverse the process that had transformed him into this vile creature.

How to make contact with him remained a problem that he would have to solve if his wish was to be realised. He felt certain that Ebon would meet with this seer before long and that there would be a confrontation between them; that was when Jetta needed to be on hand to seek the seer's help to be rid of the magic.

Nodding slowly and filled with a new optimism, he turned away from the fountain and left the garden, returning to the main hall where Ebon would be expecting to see him when he wanted him. Ebon was unaware that Jetta had any feelings; he assumed that he was just some mindless slave who was there to do his bidding. Jetta hoped that one day his master would come up against another who was more powerful than he but who was more kindly disposed towards others. Perhaps this other seer was that very person; Urim, that was the name he had given when they had met, Jetta now recalled. If he was and Ebon commanded Jetta to strike him, then he knew that his power would be ineffective against him and Urim would be free to act in whatever way he wished. If it was possible, Jetta would even help the seer to defeat Ebon. The thought gave him deep satisfaction and an inner peace settled upon his troubled mind. He would bide his time until that moment came; then they would see who was master; he firmly believed that it would be the other seer, Urim.

The moment that Ebon lost the power within the Rod, Jetta felt a change occur within him. Something snapped deep in his chest; it felt as if a stretch-band had broken but there had been no pain attached to the sensation.

Ebon had instructed Jetta to guard the way into his private rooms; he knew that Ebon kept the viewing-window there and had witnessed him use it on occasion. Standing with his arms crossed and his back to the entrance door, he felt a prompting to go inside. The urge to do so was pulling at him with a strength that could not be resisted so he turned and tried the door. It should have been locked but it opened easily at the touch of his hand and he entered the quiet suite of rooms. He had been in there before but that had been with Ebon. He felt like an intruder but something drove him on and he wandered through the reception rooms until he came to the one that held the viewing-window.

Again the door opened to his touch and he carefully pushed it wide so that he could see the whole room. It was bare other than for the viewing-window; movement on the surface attracted his attention and he was drawn towards it; he could hardly believe his eyes. What he saw within the mirror-like surface amazed him.

The seer, Urim, who had taken Anna from right under his nose and from out of the midst of Ebon's fortress, had hold of Ebon and delivered him into the five sided room of the wizards' conclave. Jetta witnessed how Ebon tried to resist but was unable to do so. He saw Urim take the Rod and disappear through the portal. He saw the wizards materialise as if from nowhere and he witnessed the dignity with which Ebon finally met his end. The Rod of Dread had lost its power and been taken away; with Ebon gone that meant that his control over him had been brought to an end. That must have been what he had felt; it took a while for it to register but when it eventually did, a grin of elation spread across his face.

He was free of the control with which Ebon had held him bound. A shout of jubilation resounded around the room as he savoured the feeling. 'He was free;' he kept saying it over and over hardly believing the sound of his voice. 'What do I do now?' He asked out loud. He had dreamed of the time that he would be free of restraint but now that it had come he was lost as to what he should do. One thing he did know was that he was not going to stay here; he saw what the wizards had done and he feared that they might try to enslave him to their will. The Rod of Dread may have gone to be reunited with the remains of the giant, Custennin but now they had created the Rod of Retribution. There was nowhere he could hide from them and they would bind him to an eternity of servitude, uncaring for any feelings he may have.

He knew what he must do; he would find the seer, Urim and offer his services in the hope that he might be able to help him be rid of the magic that filled him. How could he make contact with him? How would it be possible for him to transport to where the seer could be found? Where was Urim?

'Seers Tower, of course, that was where Urim would go.' Jetta had heard Ebon talk of it before and he would endeavour to go there but it was in the other world and he had no means at his disposal to get there. His initial joy at realising he was free was crushed; soon the wizards would arrive and there would be no escape from their grasp. He was lost and realised that wherever he went on this world they would find him and turn him to their purpose, controlling him by the new Rod. There was no escaping them and his fate would be worse than before when he had been in Ebon's control.

At that moment of deepest despair he was distracted by a flash of light that blinked with brightness beyond that of the sun. It had come from behind him and then was gone; he jumped with surprise when he turned and saw a hooded figure standing there grasping a strange staff.

'I thought that you might appreciate a change of scenery.'

Urim had come for him. A tear trickled down the face of the dark angel and he smiled with overwhelming joy.

Urim had felt a deep sadness within his bosom at leaving Ebon to face the wizards; he knew that they would show him no mercy. They would treat him somewhat like a cat that has caught a mouse that watches as it tries to escape, toying with the wounded creature until it finally dies. Ebon had brought this upon himself and had been given opportunities in the past to avoid this. He had been a member of the Council of the Sight and promised to be one of the greatest to bear his name before embarking on this mission of madness. He had been consumed by the thirst for control and power and now it had brought him to oblivion.

Still he could not help but feel sorry for what he was to face, he certainly did not wish to experience what Ebon was facing at this moment in time. The image of the former seer sitting crumpled on the floor utterly devastated at what had befallen him had brought Urim no joy, no satisfaction. He felt only sadness and pity but he knew that there was nothing he could do. Urim had to put these thoughts behind him now as he faced the next part of putting Terra Standfast's plan into effect.

Standing at his side now was the dark angel, Jetta, no longer bound to Ebon by the Rod; he was free to do as he wished. Urim knew that the wizards would come for Ebon's creation and bend him to their will so he had made the decision to take Jetta with him, back to Seers Tower.

The portal opened up into the place he had desired to be and he found himself in the throne room, deep inside Amethyst's coven. His arrival caused quite a stir when he appeared out of nowhere accompanied by the dark demon. Eden and Elise were able to calm the troubled ogres who reacted instinctively to defend themselves. The ogres thought that they posed a threat to their new found peace but the two seers prevented them from attacking Urim and Jetta.

'We apologise to you seer, we were unaware of your intentions to arrive in such a fashion.' Jericho, the new leader of the ogres since Amethyst's demise, acknowledged him with a slight bow.

'That is perfectly alright; my visit was one that I had not intended to make but circumstances have dictated that I take the two seers away from you. We have need of their skills back at Seers Tower. They shall return just as soon as we are able to spare them.'

Jericho bowed his head again to show that he accepted what Urim had said. 'Thank you seer, I accept that there must be a greater need for them than with us at the moment.' Turning to Eden and Elise he wished them well. 'I look forward to seeing you again upon your return and thank you for what you have done for us thus far. We shall continue to tend to the forest as you have directed and hope that you will not be parted from us for long.'

Eden gave some final instructions to Jericho and Jacob, along with the other foresters. She counselled with them on the healing that was being applied to the old forest of Ringwart so that it would eventually breathe new life as Hazelwood forest.

Elise approached Urim and asked in a hushed tone. 'What's the matter Urim? I understood that we were to remain here until the forest had been stabilised. Who is your companion?'

'This is Jetta and he is to join with us for a while. Terra had hoped that it would be the case that you remain here until such time as the ogres and the foresters could take over. Unfortunately events have taken a turn for the worse and we need to hold a council with all available seers present.'

'Does it have anything to do with what happened to Auger and Hamill when they left here?'

'Yes it does and we are all needed to be ready to defend against the last push from the wizards; they will very soon be at our doors.' Catching Eden's attention he indicated that they needed to go.

'Good-bye Jericho, Jacob; we hope to see you again before too long. Keep doing what we have discussed and all will be well.' She leaned forward and kissed them both on the cheek before stepping close to Urim and preparing to depart.

Before establishing the portal, Urim nodded towards Jacob and smiled. 'It does my heart good to see you again forester. May your sap never dry and your leaves never fail.' Urim gave the traditional greeting of friends between foresters and lifted his hand to wave farewell. Jacob returned the greeting and the gesture with a bewildered look on his face as he watched the seers ready themselves to depart. The three seers waved farewell and, along with Jetta, were encompassed by the bright light of the opening portal before they vanished from sight leaving the ogres alone.

Within the blink of an eye, they found themselves transported from across the other side of the land and into the council chamber at Seers Tower. They were welcomed back by Terra, Liam and Emerald but formal greetings were dismissed because of the urgency of the matter that needed to be discussed. Eden and Elise were impressed by the use of the portal and amazed at how quickly they were able to transport from one place to another. Their excitement about it had to be set aside for now and any discussion about it put off for another time because of the urgency to meet as a council.

Terra welcomed Jetta to Seers Tower and invited him to attend their meeting introducing him to Liam and Emerald. The bemused demon was speechless at the respect and friendship shown to him and simply nodded in response. He then fell to one knee in front of Terra to vow his allegiance to their cause and to use his powers to aid them in their battle against the wizards.

'We thank you, Jetta, for your allegiance and are happy that you have chosen to stand with us but you do so as an equal, not a slave. Stand and be counted as a friend amongst us.' Terra offered him his hand and raised him to his feet.

The seers were grateful for his presence and gladly accepted his offer of help; Terra stepped forward and embraced him. Jetta tentatively returned the show of friendship before smiling with his pearl white teeth at all the assembled seers. Only Hamill was missing from their number. A new Auger, of course, would have to be selected but this was not the right time to go about that process. Besides, the one who would most likely take the place of the lost seer was not yet at the Tower.

In their meeting, Terra informed Eden and Elise of the battle between them and three of the wizards, aided at the critical moment by Urim. He also told them that they had sealed the Tower off from the rest of the land. That was just as a precaution however and they had to find a more permanent solution to the ingress into their world by their nemesis the wizards.

Sitting in council together, the six seers discussed the best way forward. Liam and Emerald had tried, at Terra's insistence to see ahead in order to glean anything that would give them a clue as to the way they should go. As the two seers had expected, they were unable to discover anything that would be of assistance to them in their dealings with the wizards. The seers' efforts to maintain the balance of power between the world of Magog and their own would depend on the outcome of what they did here. As for Hamill and Jon, they had faced their challenge and been victorious.

Urim informed the council of what he had done before meeting with them. 'I have already intervened and ensured that Hamill was not able to reach Anram on his own and I have also returned Ebon to Magog where the wizards will undoubtedly have dealt with him. Jetta, as you can see, agreed to join us here at the Tower.' They all turned to look at the dark angel who bowed his head towards them as he stood ready to carry out any command that they might demand of him.

The seers held a brief silence in memory of their former brother-seer, Ebon, knowing that the wizards would not have spared him. Despite the fact that Ebon had betrayed them and sought to rule instead of them, they still felt sorrow for his demise. With Urim's assistance Ebon had been neutralised as a threat to them so all they had to do was to ensure that the wizards would never again terrorize their world. This was the task that lay before them and without the foresight that had always guided them via Liam's cards and Emerald's crystal; they were left guessing as to when the next attack would come and from where.

'Is there nothing that you can help us with here Urim?' Terra turned to him with an air of desperation.

'I am afraid not' I have no information as to what is going to transpire at this time. My knowledge is rather limited and I fear that I am unable to give you any counsel that would be of any use to you. However I do pledge to support you with all that I have that is within my power to give.'

'Thank you Urim, we are all indebted to you for your efforts and I am grateful for your involvement here. Indeed I am grateful to you all and I want you to know that I have absolute confidence in your support. This is what I propose we do...'

There was a buzz of expectation in the air and the Tower hummed like a beehive with all the activity of preparing for the anticipated attack upon them by the wizards. Some of the folk who served the Sight had been admitted back into the Tower temporarily in order to help with the arrangements. The thing that had caused the greatest sensation was the appearance of the dark demon that Urim had brought back with him from Magog. The reception that Jetta received was markedly different from that which he had been given from the captains of the guard and their legions in Ebon's army. There they had looked upon him as a fearsome angel of death whilst here at Seers Tower he had been welcomed as a valued addition to the seers and a friend and ally to their cause. He immediately felt warm inside making him feel different to how he had ever felt before. This was something that was totally alien to him. His life had been filled with cruelty and hardship; he had never been shown kindness and so had never known how to show it in return.

He was overwhelmed by the generosity and the openness of the folk he met. The seers were all so very different to what he had expected them to be. Ebon had portrayed them as vile despots who coveted their power and would not share it with anyone else; what he discovered was the opposite. They were kind and gentle and the elves were charming and the sprites beautiful.

The dwarf, Terra Standfast, had been a bit of a shock from what he had expected him to be, with his beaming smile and cheery greeting. Jetta could hardly believe that they were real and wondered whether the passage from one world to the other had unsettled his senses. He soon began to accept the evidence of his eyes and relished the forthcoming opportunity to help them in their fight against the wizards.

Chapter 30

Marsh-Mogs

None of the brave band of friends felt very comfortable with the prospect of a handful or more of the creatures surrounding them. Even the dwarves were nervous and Archer's eyes shifted to and fro trying to pierce the mist in search of a target to let fly at with an arrow.

Each one of them had heard the throaty growls from somewhere out in the mist but there was no sign of the creatures who inhabited this dank and desolate swampland. The sound of the guttural growls drifted on the breeze that stirred the haze surrounding the bank they stood on. The suspense was palpable and Jon felt his throat thicken; his palms began to sweat and he wiped them on his tunic. Drawing the knife that Hamill had given him from his waist band, he felt a bit more secure but realised that with the size of the marsh-mogs, it would probably do little good. The dwarves were all poised ready to defend themselves and each other; Braun had unsheathed his mighty broadsword and held it ready. The pale sunlight that filtered through to them reflected off its keen edges as he swung it one way and then another in practice strokes. There was quite an array of weaponry to be had amongst them, from simple knives to hatchets and double-edged axes as well as swords, not forgetting Archer's bow and Javelin's spear.

Jon recalled the time they were confronted by the Smarg and wolvets at Deadline Crack; they had survived that situation and there was no reason why they could not do the same here. Then he remembered that it was the appearance of the colossi that had saved them; he wondered whether Hamill could change into Holdhard again to save them from the marsh-mogs. He thought that Hamill was probably considering the same thing so kept quiet, not wanting to disturb the seer's thoughts at such a time.

Against any other foe Jon would have felt reasonably confident at their being able to give a good account of themselves, but the marsh-mogs were different. They were huge bear-like creatures with reptile heads and were surprisingly fleet-footed despite their appearance to the contrary. Jon remembered the first time that he saw them, when he had first met Urim and been rescued from certain death. He knew from that experience that they would all attack at the same time from every quarter so he whispered across to Javelin.

'I've seen them strike before, they will all charge forward at the same time after the leader has given the signal.'

'Thank you Jon; I too have had some experience with them.' The dwarf replied in a low whisper.

Jon felt awkward at having made the comment to the dwarf. He felt like crawling under a rock. 'Imagine me telling Javelin what to do; of course he knows what he's doing. I must try and not meddle in matters in the future.' He muttered, berating himself for interfering.

Archer was standing close to Jon and heard him chastising himself. 'Don't take it to heart young Jon. Javelin will no doubt have appreciated the warning. Never hold back on telling us anything that you think might be useful. It is better to feel a little foolish than to be dead.'

Archer's comforting words soothed the embarrassment he was feeling and he could see the compassion in Archer's expression. 'Thank you, I shall remember that.'

Hamill stood alone in the centre of the group at the top of the mound deep in thought. He seemed to sense Jon looking at him and he returned the gaze, nodding his head and smiling to reassure Jon that he was alright. Jon followed Archer's advice and told Hamill of his thoughts concerning the colossi at Deadline Crack and whether he ought to become a colossus.

'Yes I have considered that and it may be that I will have to do so. I can not wait here for them to attack; I shall have to take the initiative and go to them. My only concern is that the weight of a colossus in this wasteland could hinder my movements; I could easily go down in the soft soil or step into a sink-hole. I have, however been toying with something else but there are other dangers attached to that.'

The tension grew as they waited for the inevitable attack upon them and nerves were starting to get a little frayed. 'I wish they would just get on with it; I hate this part of confronting the unknown.' Trapper was, as always, eager to have a go at the opposition, whether they were gnomes or marsh-mogs, it made no difference to him.'

They were all looking out onto the flats trying to see anything move in the mist. Suddenly they were startled by the flapping of leathery wings behind them and a shrill shriek rent the air as a grist flew low over their heads and headed out over the marsh, gaining height with every beat of its powerful wings.

The appearance of the fearsome creature startled them all. They had been absorbed with concentrating on the impending attack from the marsh-mogs and had not considered anything such as the likes of a grist descending upon them. Jon spun around, Hamill had gone. The seer had transformed himself with the power of his staff and talisman into a grist. Was this the option that Hamill had been considering? It must have been and he had acted before anyone knew what was happening. Flying in circles above them, the grist/Hamill glided easily, sustaining its momentum with an occasional beat of its wings.

Jon's jaw dropped in amazement and awe at what Hamill was able to do. Such power and ability was not to be used idly. He was even more convinced that Hamill was the right choice to have replaced Ebon on the Council of the Sight. Jon thought that *he* would never be able to control the power that was contained in a seer's staff. For the first time he seriously doubted whether he was right to pursue a course towards being a seer himself one day. Yet Urim had told him that it was his destiny to become one and that they would meet again along the path that took him to Seers Tower. There was a lot he had to learn if he were to come close to being worthy of such a position.

All eyes were on the grist as it circled lazily above them; then it folded its wings over its back and plummeted to the ground, disappearing into the thick fog. A scream of pain rent the air and they feared that Hamill may have lost control and been injured as he hit the ground. The mist boiled at the point that he had crashed through and more cries of terror and pain reached them through the turbulence. The mist settled and they heard the beating of wings; the grist/Hamill rose steadily into the air, he was none the worse for his fall. They all assumed that there was one less marsh-mog for them to worry about.

The grist headed back to the mound and settled in their midst. It was a wonder to see and even more so when the creature began to melt away leaving Hamill standing there in its stead. He began to buckle at the knees but Braun was able to get to him before he hit the ground and gently lowered him down. Jon rushed to his side, concerned that he might be hurt but was relieved to see that Hamill was only suffering from the effects of his transformation. He was exhausted by the effort at not only maintaining the form of a grist but also of being involved in a fight with one of the marsh-mogs.

'Stand back everyone, give him room to breathe.' Digger stepped forward and took control of matters. His training in medical aid kicked in by instinct and he inspected the weary seer. He was not as proficient as an elf orderly or a physician but he was good at what he did.

Hamill smiled up at the dwarf as he received attention. 'It makes a change for me to be on the receiving end of treatment. I am grateful for your help Digger but I am fine really. I am just tired, that's all.'

'Then I recommend that you rest for a while, we'll keep watch for any signs of trouble.' Digger suggested rather than ordered. He deferred to Hamill's superior knowledge and experience.

'Thank you, I shall take your advice.' Hamill smiled at the dwarves concerns. 'You would make a good elf my friend.'

'Well, there's no need to insult me.' Digger teased him and they all laughed, easing the tension that they had been under. They returned their attention to watching and waiting for any sign of movement from the marsh-mogs. Apart from the occasional stirring of the mist, nothing happened and the marshland was quiet.

Javelin decided that it would be best for them to take turns at keeping watch; that way some could be resting instead of them all being on constant guard. 'I think that Hamill's foray against the creatures might just have been enough to scare them off but I believe that they will be back before too long so try to keep alert.' He instructed Digger and Mason who took the first watch.

It was coming time for them to change the watch when several low growls were heard out in the mist followed by a few coughing noises. The marsh-mogs were back. There was no need to wake the others, they had heard it as well and were immediately alert, standing ready to face whatever came at them. Javelin gave Hamill a sideways look, wondering whether he would again turn into the grist. He did not have time to finish the thought before the seer had once again made the transition from seer to beast and climbed into the air with huge beats of his wings. The dwarf stood in awe of Hamill's abilities and marvelled at how he was able to become anything that he thought of. Javelin tore his gaze away from the grist/Hamill and set his face in a stony glare, intent on giving a good account of himself in defending the others, especially Jon. He liked the lad and saw the potential in him to achieve great things. He believed that Urim had chosen wisely when he sought him out to accompany him on his quest to defeat Ebon.

The noise from the creatures escalated and the others began to grow concerned. It appeared there were more of them than there had been previously. Nervous eyes watched and waited for the grist to strike; moments later it dived into the haze. Screams again signalled that it had found its mark only this time it was accompanied by deep snarling and the sounds of a struggle drifted through the fog.

The dwarves desperately wanted to know what was happening and asked if Braun, with his greater height could see anything. He stood on tip-toe craning his neck in an effort to see into the mist from above but he was unable to discern anything. Yelps and screeches came in quick succession as the unseen battle continued. Concerned now that things were not well, they all stood nervously waiting for the grist to wing its way skyward. Then a bright green flash erupted from a little distance away, followed by silence and the mist settled into stillness. Moments passed with no sound or movement.

Jon began to fear for his friend and called out into the mist. 'Hamill, can you hear me, are you alright?'

'Jon, help me.' A weak whisper of a reply came back to them. Without thinking Jon dashed forward down the slope and into the mist in the direction that the voice came from.

'Jon, wait, it's too dangerous to go alone.' Javelin shouted after him but it was too late, he had disappeared from view leaving a wake behind him in the fog as he pressed forward concerned only for the welfare of his friend.

'Stay here whilst I go in after them.' Javelin commanded but Braun held him back.

'No, you are needed here. I will go after them; besides, you don't want to end up in a stagnant pond do you?' The reference to the metal-master's earlier mishap brought a smile to the old dwarf's lips. He conceded that Braun was probably the best candidate for this, relenting to the metal-master's suggestion.

'You speak wisely, my friend, go quickly but take Trapper with you.' Javelin nodded in Trapper's direction and the feisty dwarf hurried over, eager to be of help.

The two of them hurried after Jon trying to be careful with their footing and calling out to Jon for guidance as to where he was. They heard a splash just ahead of them and the sound of someone coughing up water. Within moments they came across Jon floundering in a pool just like Braun had landed in before. Reaching down, Braun hauled him out and set him on his feet berating him for rushing off.

'Now perhaps you'll listen before going off headlong into goodness knows what trouble.' Braun chastised but in a kindly manner. Jon stood there drenched to the skin covered in the foul smelling algae and thanked him for coming to his aid.

'Now that we have you safe, let's find that seer of yours.' Braun nodded to Trapper who took the initiative and led them carefully through the marsh in their effort to find Hamill.

Stopping briefly, Trapper spoke Hamill's name softly so as not to attract the attention of any marsh-mogs that might be lurking nearby. 'Where are you Hamill; give us a sign so that we can find you?'

They waited in silence for what seemed an age before Jon heard a muffled groan just off to their left. Creeping forward towards the place where the sound came from they saw shapes emerge from the gloom lying like boulders on the ground. They were the bodies of several marsh-mogs that had obviously been despatched by Hamill whilst in the form of the grist. Checking to see that they were dead, Trapper edged around them and found Hamill trapped beneath the carcase of another one. He looked to be in bad shape; blood trickled from a cut on his head and his cloak was bloodstained. They could not tell if it was his own or that of the marsh-mogs.

Braun tried to lift the dead beast off Hamill's legs but its huge bulk made it difficult even for him. After several attempts of pushing and shoving he removed his belt and looped it around one of the creature's limbs then dug his heels into the soft ground till he found something solid beneath the soil and pulled with all his might. The marsh-mog finally rolled over enough to free the seer from its dead weight and the other two dragged him clear. Braun then gently allowed the beast to roll back down and he retrieved his belt. Trapper and Jon gently cradled Hamill between them and lifted him from the ground. He was obviously hurt but how badly they did not know.

'Can you walk Hamill?' Jon asked his friend.

Hamill started forward shakily, still supported by them but stumbled forward. They stopped him from falling and Braun bent down to hold him then gently lifted him up and carefully cradled him in his arms. Trapper and Jon started back along the way they had come with Braun carrying the seer as gently as he could. They went past the dead marsh-mogs and around the pool where Jon had fallen in then heard Javelin call out to them through the mist, asking if they had found Hamill.

'Yes we have him but he is injured and needs attention, keep talking so that we can find you.' Jon replied.

Moments later the mound came into view and they could see the others standing on it, looking out for them. As soon as Digger saw Braun emerging from the fog carrying Hamill he rushed towards them and instructed him to carry the seer to the top of the rise where he started to examine him. Fortunately he had only sustained minor injuries; the blood on his cloak was that of the marsh-mogs.

'What happened to you?' Javelin asked, concerned for the seer.

'They had laid a trap for me and pounced as soon as I got hold on one of them; fortunately for me they were no match for a grist but even so I nearly went under. As it was, I only escaped being killed by reverting to myself and using my staff against the last one.'

'Well, that will be the last time you embark on another jaunt like that. They obviously have the intelligence to organise themselves so I don't want you risking your life anymore.' Javelin declared and everyone agreed with him.

'I'm not going to argue that one.' Hamill replied with a weak smile. Meanwhile Digger had bandaged his head and ensured that he had no other injuries that needed attention.

Javelin stood in front of Jon with his hands on his hips and feet planted firmly apart looking him up and down. 'Now then young Jon; I hope you've learned your lesson about rushing off without any thought for how you are going to accomplish anything. As it is you only managed to fall into a pond, but what if it had been a sink-hole? There would have been no one with you to help you get out. That is apart from not knowing whether there were any more marsh-mogs in your way. What would you have done then?'

Jon hung his head and acknowledged that the dwarf was telling him the truth. He had acted rashly; his only defence was that he had wanted to help his friend. Javelin realised that of course and softened his rebuke.

'Now I know that he is a particular friend of yours, but he is ours too and we care for his welfare as much as you do. Please remember in future that if anything needs to be done to aid one of our own, we will do it, but in the proper way. Do you understand?'

Jon nodded that he did and Javelin slapped him on the shoulder encouragingly then wiped his hand on the grass. 'Now for everyone's benefit get yourself cleaned up. You'd better stand over there until you have got rid of that foul smelling stuff or I might be forced to light up my pipe again.'

Chapter 31

Deliverance

Midday came and the cold of the mist penetrated into their bones causing them to shiver and stomp around to try and keep warm.

'Can't we light the fire again Javelin? I'm half frozen to death.' Jon complained; eager to feel the warmth of the fire but hoping that the mist would clear so that they could continue on their way.

'Whilst I would dearly love to oblige you and the rest of us; I'm afraid that we can't go anywhere all the time this fog covers the land and we may have to spend another night here. We will be in more urgent need of the warmth then and there is only enough wood to see us through another night.'

Jon recognised the wisdom of his words and nodded in acceptance of his decision but he still wished for a nice cosy fire. Hamill was better rested now and was able to sit up and take a sip of relk. He was accustomed to the kick it had by now, having tasted it on a couple of occasions, yet it still made him wince with its fire at the back of his throat. He coughed a few times then wiped the tears away from his streaming eyes.

'Thank you for helping me and for dressing my wound Digger but as for the medicine, I thought you were trying to make me feel better. That stuff is worse that chewing chilli peppers.'

Digger laughed and the other dwarves smiled at his reaction. Very few folk could develop a taste for the dwarves brew. It was made only in the western province of the dwarves' land, where the ground was ideally suited for the growing of its ingredients, and distributed from there.

Trapper told Hamill that he had visited the brewery some years ago when he had gone with a party of friends who had signed up for a trip there. Apparently dwarves visit the place on a regular basis to see how the process is carried out and are treated to a weekend of revelry. It is renowned across the land for one particular season in the year when the circus and funfair arrive and a festival is held.

'I haven't been to it yet but I hope to go when we get back. Perhaps you and Jon would like to come along.' Mason joined in their conversation.

Jon and Hamill looked at each other with an excited look in their eyes. Then Jon asked cautiously. 'Would we have to drink relk when we got there?'

'Goodness, no; there are many other kinds of ale and spirits available so you could pick and choose what you drink. The important thing is to enjoy the atmosphere and join in with the story telling. You'd both be very welcome as honoured guests; besides you have some amazing tales to tell yourselves. You'd be the toast of the town.'

Jon and Hamill were both keen to attend one of the dwarves' cultural events and agreed that they would love to go. 'Let's get out of this situation first though and return to Seers Tower, then we'll see about the arrangements.' Hamill suggested. Then as an afterthought he added. 'Has anyone got any food?'

'Not much, we only have a few biscuits and a little water in the flasks but that is running low.' Leader responded. He had been placed in charge of provisions.

Javelin tugged at his beard thoughtfully. 'It seems to me that we have no alternative than to try and find our way out of here. We don't know how long this mist is going to hang around for and I don't like the idea of spending another night here on this patch of ground.' He turned to Hamill and studied the seer for a few moments. Hamill; is it possible, do you think, that you could summon up the wind just long enough to get us out of here?'

Hamill thought about it then sighed. 'I can give it a try but Urim taught me that we seers could only exercise another seer's talisman for a few times before it stopped responding to our control. I can give it a go and see what happens but I don't hold out much hope; not after what happened before.'

'Nevertheless I believe that it might be our only hope of surviving this situation. Do what you can.'

Hamill got up and asked Mason for Auger's staff; he had been caring for it since they were deposited in the flats. Whilst they had been travelling, Hamill had not been able to hold it as well as his own and had charged the young dwarf with its care; something that he had willingly and excitedly agreed to do.

Standing in the centre of the mound, Hamill blew on the talisman. No noise was emitted but they all knew that if Hamill could call up the wind, it would be apparent soon enough. They waited in silence, listening for the tell tale sound of a whisper of breeze, scanning the horizon for any sight of a funnel of wind.

Long moments passed and nothing happened then Leader snapped his head up. 'I'm sure I felt a breeze on my face just then.'

'You probably did but it was a natural movement of the air, not the one we are looking for.' Hamill stated, recognising the difference between the two. Still nothing happened. 'I am afraid that it will not work for me any more. I thought it might not.'

'What if you tried using your own staff or perhaps change into Auger and try it then. If it works for the seer whose talisman it is, maybe you could use it then?' Jon suggested.

'I'm afraid that would not work either. The talisman knows who is using it and despite my change of appearance I would not be able to fool it into believing that I actually was Auger. As for using my own staff, again it would not work because it is the seer the talisman responds to not the staff. I used Auger's staff simply to help me control it better than I could with my own and we all saw the results of that.'

'Well, that's it then. We have to get out of here some other way. I believe that the marsh-mogs will be back before too long and if we are still here when they do, we will have to defend ourselves or die in the attempt.' Javelin was always the practical one and faced facts calmly. He was not afraid to die but he would rather live if there was an alternative, no matter how slim the chance might be.

Jon had been thinking and offered another suggestion. 'What if Hamill were to change into the grist again...'

'No, I don't want the seer to risk himself; not after what happened before. Besides, if he were to be lost there would be no chance for the rest of us' Javelin cut him short.

'No, hear me out. I was wondering that if Hamill were to change into the grist again; whether he could carry us out of the flats one by one, flying above the fog and taking us clear of any danger.'

They all looked at Jon in amazement.

'Now why didn't I think of that?' Hamill responded with a shake of his head. 'The only problem I can see is that the talons and claws of the grist are razor sharp and I might not be able to hold on to you without causing any harm. In fact, thinking about it, I would not be able to do it; you would all be cut to pieces.'

They all looked downhearted at having their hopes of being able to escape this predicament dashed before anything could be agreed upon.

'Is there anything else that you could become that might help us?' Javelin asked with only a little hope that the seer could think of something.

'Well, I could try being a Kite-folk but they are very slight beings and may not be able to take the weight. I could give it a try though. What do you think?'

'It's certainly worth a try but do you think that you could manage it seeing as there are six of us dwarves as well as Jon and Braun of course?' Javelin queried.

'I'm pretty certain that I could lift you dwarves without any difficulty and Jon shouldn't prove too much of a problem but I doubt that I could manage Braun.'

'That's alright Hamill; I'm not eager to be lifted into the sky anyway. I was not that keen on being in the wind and was glad when we landed; even though it was here in the marshes. You do what you can for the others; I'll be alright. These marsh-mogs will get a taste of my steel and wished they had never met me.' Braun spoke bravely but he betrayed his apprehension at the thought of facing a large number of the beasts alone.

'That will not be necessary Braun. If Hamill can't take you, he takes none of us. We all stick together in this and no-one is going to be left behind.' Javelin spoke commandingly and everyone nodded in agreement.

'So what do we do now?' Jon asked, lacking any further ideas himself and hoping that someone would come up with something.

No-one spoke and they all looked at their feet unable to come up with any thoughts that would mean their being delivered from this dilemma.

'As far as I see it we have two options; we either wait here to fight it out or we try to find our way through the fog and get to Seaview on our own efforts. I suggest that we put it to the vote. I'll save my vote as the deciding one in case of it being tied. Who's for staying here and making a fight of it?' Javelin counted the raised hands.' Four of the dwarves, Archer, Trapper, Digger and Mason all voted to fight. 'That means that you four are in favour of trying to get to Seaview; yes?'

Jon, Hamill, Braun and Leader nodded. 'That leaves it up to me and I have to admit that I am caught in two minds. If we stay here we will more than likely be overrun by the marsh-mogs but if we leave there is a good chance that we would become lost and disorientated in the mist or fall into a sink-hole. There is no guarantee that we won't run into a marsh-mog or two along the way; they may even be out there waiting for us to leave the mound so that they can catch us off guard.' Javelin was caught in indecision for the first time in his life; either option had its own degree of danger or merit. The dilemma he faced now was which one to choose.

His decision however was academic as without warning they heard the howl nearby in the fog that called the body of creatures to charge in on their quarry. Quickly taking up positions, standing in a circle around the top of the hillock, the group made ready to receive the attack.

They heard them before they saw them as a great whooping noise from scores of the creatures shattered the quiet of the day. The mound began to vibrate to the heavy thump of their feet as they stormed forward on the soft ground of the marshland; it was as if they were standing on a biscuit in the centre of a bowl of jelly. The mist stirred and then swirled as the creatures came towards them.

Moments before they broke through onto the mound Archer let fly with a couple of arrows, aiming at vague shadows in the fog. They found their mark and one of them went down but the other kept coming, maddened by the sting of the arrow in its chest. Archer had narrowly missed the heart on this occasion and he sent another into the beast as it reached the edge of the mound; it got no further. The others in the group had to wait for the marsh-mogs to come within striking distance but Archer accounted for another two before they did.

Javelin was the next to bring one down with a well aimed spear that went through the open mouth and into the brain of a beast that ran at him growling and whooping, its eyes fixed on its purpose. It went down with a thud but Javelin had no time to think about retrieving his spear as another beast was about to catch him in its rush forward.

Sidestepping and dropping to the ground the wily dwarf snatched his short sword from its sheath and slashed across the belly of the surprised beast and into its gut. Screaming in pain it went down holding its wound. Javelin finished it off by decapitating it with a single stroke before turning to face the next one.

The others were equally engaged in their own little battles either attacking their opponents or defending themselves from a creature as it aimed a deadly blow at them.

Braun swept his broadsword in huge arcs, slicing through the air at the creatures as they came within the reach of his cutting edges. He caught several of them leaving them with serious injuries; Digger and Mason then dashed in to deliver the finishing cut or blow and hurriedly retreated behind the big man and waited for the next ones to receive the punishing wounds that Braun's sword inflicted upon the beasts. Their union seemed to work well and soon the ground was littered with the dead creatures. All the dwarves accounted themselves well; they were all hardy veterans of hand to hand combat, even the younger ones, Digger and Mason.

Trapper and Leader had teamed up and were successfully defending the ground before them. They accounted for one between them and managed to avoid the grasp of two more that came charging at them, furious at the death of the others.

Dodging this way and that to avoid the lunges of the maddened creatures, the two dwarves cut and slashed at the beasts inflicting wounds in vital places, they finished them off with powerful thrusts of their swords. As the marsh-mogs went down, Leader was caught by one of them with a massive claw. The dying creature fell to the ground but it had inflicted a serious wound to the brave little dwarf. Blood ran freely from an open wound to Leader's shoulder. His tunic had been ripped through and a deep cut had sliced into the dwarf causing him to cry out in pain. His left arm fell to his side, the tendons severed by the strike. He was unable to move it and he could not defend himself properly against an oncoming creature that smelled his blood and rushed at him, intent on a kill.

Jon stood with Hamill in the midst of it all, he was not sure who was protecting whom but guessed that it was Hamill looking after him. Only one of the charging creatures made it past the outer perimeter of fighting and Hamill let it know that it was no match for a seer. He levelled his staff at the oncoming beast and sent a ball of green fire into its belly which stopped it in its tracks and the marsh-mog fell heavily on the ground a few steps in front of them.

It was at that moment that Jon saw Leader's predicament and ran, without thought for his own safety, to try and aid the wounded dwarf. Hamill shouted out for him to stop and levelled his staff at the creature but Jon got in the way and he had to withhold the blast that would have incinerated the beast. In the blink of an eye Hamill changed into Holdhard and ran down the slope of the mound. He pulled Jon back so hard that he fell onto his back from where he saw the colossus reach Leader and manage to prevent him from receiving a fatal blow. The marsh-mog was so surprised to see a colossus appear as if from nowhere that it took fright and backed away into the mist, whooping out a warning to the others.

The battle ended as quickly as it had started and the weary group stood to gather their wits and to catch their breath. More than twelve of the beasts lay dead around them; several others had retreated with wounds that ranged from serious cuts and gashes to minor scratches.

They had been reprieved but for how long?

The marsh-mogs could be heard growling and whimpering somewhere out in the mist, licking their wounds. There was no doubt that they would be back. Having been thwarted in their attempts to dislodge the band of friends from the hillock; they would be all the more determined to succeed the next time they charged. In the meanwhile Hamill, who had reverted to his natural self, tended to Leader's arm. Digger assisted him and between them they managed to stop the bleeding but could do nothing for the severed tendons other than to bind up the wound and place his arm in a sling.

The two of them checked the others to see if they had incurred any injury but apart from a slight nick on Braun's leg; they were in good shape. Jon thought that they had been fortunate to have had the dwarves and the metal-master here or things would have turned out differently. As it was, Leader would not be able to take part in any more fighting, much to his chagrin. The last thing any dwarf needs is for there to be a battle going on around him and he not being able to get involved; it was a matter of honour and pride.

Hardly having had time to recover from their exertions with their battle against the marsh-mogs, the noise of shrieks and howls rent the air and the fog began to boil just north of the mound. Javelin snatched his spear from out of a dead marsh-mog and ran to his position. 'Get ready my friends; I believe that they will be upon us at any moment.'

They all scrambled to ready themselves for the tidal flood of creatures and waited nervously for them to appear. Hamill whispered as an aside to Jon to stay close to him and not try any more heroics. His job was to protect Leader if any of them broke through. Jon nodded that he understood and gritted his teeth in determination to give a good account of himself. This was one time that he would not fail his friends. He held tightly to the knife that Hamill had given him, the one that Queen Ella had enhanced with her 'magic'. He knew that it would do more damage to any who opposed him than any sword or axe would do. He just had to keep out of the way of any blow that was aimed at him. He practiced in his mind what he would do in a given situation, preparing himself for the unexpected.

What he had not prepared himself for was what happened next. The heavy mist still hung over the marsh as they stood on the mound and they all peered into its swirling mass. They endeavoured to catch the first glimpse of movement that would signal the first wave of marsh-mogs.

A hushed silence descended over the mound; the marsh-mogs were strangely quiet and the mist had ceased to swirl. Then, from out of the gloom, shapes began to emerge; Archer readied to launch his first arrow but lowered his bow with a gasp of surprise. Out of the mist stepped a colossus, Bearer. Ten colossi in total appeared and stood at the edge of the mound, silent and unmoving; Jon recognised Holdhard immediately and then Amorphous. When the shock of their appearance faded, Hamill approached Bearer with a smile of relief on his face.

'Welcome Bearer; I don't know how you came to be in this area but your arrival could not have come at a better time.'

Bearer nodded in acknowledgement of the seer's words but turned to face Braun and bowed his head in a sign of respect. 'Master Braun, we were informed that you would have need of our assistance and we have come in response to that need.'

They all looked stunned at what Bearer had just said. How could the colossi have known that they would be in need of help? No message had been sent and Hamill's communication stone would not work properly. It was a miracle that the stone men had arrived to aid them just when it looked as if they were about to be overwhelmed.

'How did you know we would be here and that we were in trouble?' Jon asked, bewildered by what Bearer had said.

'The seer, Urim, informed us of your need many months ago and we set off at a time that was calculated for us to arrive before you met with any trouble.' Bearer looked around and saw that Leader had been injured. 'Unfortunately it would seem that we did not arrive soon enough. Please accept our apologies.'

Jon and Hamill looked at each other open mouthed; once again Urim had been aware of their needs and arranged for their safe deliverance. Hamill went forward and shook Bearer's hand vigorously. 'There is no need for an apology, Bearer; we are just grateful that you are here at all. What of the marsh-mogs? Have you scared them off?'

'Yes, they do not wish to challenge so many of us. They know that we are immune to their attempts to destroy us and have gone. Will you allow us to carry you all to safety?'

'I think that I would rather walk than for you to try and carry me.' Braun interjected. He did not imagine himself fitting comfortably in the arms of a colossus.

'As you wish metal-master; we assumed that would be the case. You may walk with me; the rest of you would be advised to let us take you so that we may more speedily remove you from this place.'

The dwarves all agreed; Jon and Hamill nodded their consent and so the colossi bent down and took them up, placing them in large slings that they had brought with them for that very purpose. Safely secured, Bearer nodded to his fellow colossi and they descended from the mound and out into the chill of the mist.

Chapter 32

Seaview

The fog enveloped them in its cold grip, chilling them to the core as the stone men set off for Seaview. The weary travellers huddled down into the makeshift hammocks that the colossi had slung around their strong necks. Each of the weary travellers curled into a ball, nestled in the protective arms of the stone giants, to keep any heat that was in their bodies from leeching away. The weariness from fighting and the steady rocking motion created as the colossi walked soon meant that they were asleep. Jon tried to fight it off so that he could witness the experience but he too eventually succumbed to the need for rest.

Braun had chosen to walk; it would have been somewhat more difficult for him to have been carried anyway. Bearer had guessed correctly about Braun preferring to walk and he strode alongside the leader of the colossi, keeping pace with his stride, as they carefully made their way through the fog that lay across the marshland.

The way through was difficult to make out and several times Bearer had to change direction in order to avoid stepping into a sink-hole or wander into a pool. The algae was so green that it looked as if it were solid ground, only the tell tale absence of any grasses growing in it gave them a clue about its dangers. Occasionally Braun heard the soft growl of a marsh-mog nearby but he did not see any and none dared to make any attempt to attack them. They could smell the presence of the colossi and they let them pass without hindrance.

Time passed and still they waded through the marsh, sometimes they walked on solid ground and at other times the colossi were up to their knees in water but they pressed on. The fog did eventually begin to thin and the ground became firmer until eventually they emerged into the warmth of the afternoon sunlight as it drifted towards evening. Ahead of them, only a few leagues away, Braun could see the coastal town of Seaview. They had made it safely through without any further danger to their lives. The colossi had saved them.

Setting everyone down on the ground, Bearer addressed Braun. 'Master Braun, we must leave you now and return to our home. We do not wish to draw attention either to ourselves or to you. I believe that you will be able to continue on your journey without any more difficulty; farewell and good fortune until we meet again.'

'Thank you Bearer and to you all, we are very grateful for your timely assistance; farewell.' Braun spoke for all of the group and they joined in with words of thanks for their deliverance from the marsh-mogs.

The colossi turned aside and marched away towards the east; striding along majestically they were a sight to behold. The group of friends were sad to see them go but understood their need for privacy and appreciated that there would be enough of a stir at their arrival in Seaview, without them being carried in by the stone giants.

Gathering themselves together they started off towards Seaview with Javelin at the head followed by Archer and Trapper. Digger and Mason walked either side of Leader in case he was in need of any assistance; behind the dwarves came Jon and Hamill with Braun at the rear. The dry road was a welcome relief from the wastelands of the Great Salt Flats and they made good headway, arriving in Seaview in time to locate a place to stay for the night before it grew dark. The first thing they arranged for was a physician to tend to Leader's wound. Although Hamill had all the skills, he lacked any of the equipment or medicines that would be needed if the wound were to be treated successfully. Within a turn of the hand of them settling in to their accommodation, an elf called to treat the dwarf. She was mightily surprised to find Hamill there and was initially rather nervous in his presence.

Hamill recognised the orderly as one of the newest apprentices at the Ward. 'Don't mind me, Sophie, you go right ahead and do what you know to be right. I will be here to assist you if there is any need.'

'Thank you Hamill; I must admit that I am a little awed at meeting you but I assure you that I am already quite accomplished, however your assistance would be most welcome.'

The two of them set to work in an effort to repair the damaged ligaments and tendons so that Leader would not be permanently disabled. The others all gathered in the saloon area of the guest house and waited with anticipation for the results of the operation. When the time came for the evening meal, Hamill and Sophie had still not emerged from the room where they were treating the dwarf. None of the others felt hungry enough to sit and eat so they ordered an assortment of foods to be set to the side in the saloon so that they could pick at it as and when they wanted to.

The time seemed to drag on interminably and they all sprang to their feet when the door opened expecting it to be Hamill with news of Leader. Instead it was the catering staff coming to see if they required anything else. They ordered some drinks before settling down again to wait. There was very little conversation, much like strangers would sit in a room whilst waiting to have their teeth examined. The night deepened and it was not until after midnight that the door opened and Hamill entered. He looked tired but he smiled and nodded that all was well.

'We have been able to apply a healing agent to the affected area and pinned the tendons back in place. It will be some time before he will be fit to travel and Sophie has agreed to stay with him for the next few days. He will need complete rest and then he should have some gentle exercise once the wound has healed. I propose to leave him in her capable hands whilst we carry on to Seers Tower. I have arranged for their board and keep so they will not have to worry about that. The promissory note of a seer is recognised as being as good as money in the till here at Seaview. Now then, is there anything to eat? I'm half starved.'

With much relief at the news that Leader was going to make a good recovery they all laughed at Hamill's request for food but now that he mentioned it, they all felt very hungry indeed. They helped themselves to the food that had hardly been touched and satisfied their hunger before making their way to their rooms and a much needed rest.

Soon they would be in Seers Tower and this journey would be at an end. There would then be no further need for them to stay together and they would be free to go their separate ways.

Jon was sad to think that after all this time they would part. He had made some wonderful new friends and he hoped that he could stay in contact with them in the future. Most of all he wished not to have to leave Hamill; but he was a seer now and needed to be about the work that a seer does. Maybe in the future Jon's dream of becoming a seer himself would be fulfilled. That was the desire that had been placed in him ever since meeting Urim last year. He did not know of any other seers who would be in need of taking on a novice at this stage, especially not a human one.

The only humans that were seers were Urim and Ebon but Ebon had been replaced by Hamill who was more elf than human. Maybe, Jon thought, that in order to redress the balance, he might be taken on as a novice to an elf. Now the only male elf on the Council of the Sight, according to what Hamill had told him, was Liam. He was quite old; perhaps he would be in need of a novice to train up. With these thought echoing through his mind, Jon fell asleep and found that he was in the garden with Anna.

Jon awoke with a smile on his face feeling much refreshed. The light filtered through the curtained window and he fairly bounced out of the cot and got ready for the day. He was very hungry, which was a bit of a surprise as he had eaten well last night, once they were told that the operation on Leader had been successful. He hurried downstairs wondering whether he would beat Hamill to the breakfast for once. There was no sign of him and the dining room was strangely empty; even the buffet had not been set out yet. He thought that perhaps he had beaten his friend after all and had awakened before anyone else. He approached the counter and asked when breakfast would be served. The attendant stopped and stared at him in amazement then cocked his head to one side and laughed before carrying on with his chores of stacking plates. Jon could not understand why the man had reacted as he had and was about to ask him what was wrong when Hamill entered the room.

'So, you've finally decided to surface have you?'

'What do you mean? What time is it?' Jon asked; confused at the behaviour of the attendant and at Hamill's remark.

'It's almost time for lunch, we all had breakfast hours ago and I have been arranging our transportation to Landfall. I came back to check on you and see if you had woken up. I see that you have.' Hamill said with a broad smile.

Jon stood dumbstruck, hardly believing what Hamill had said. 'Why didn't anyone wake me?'

'We tried, even Braun couldn't wake you. We tried shouting in your ear, pushing and prodding, all to no avail. I was called to examine you as the others thought that there was something wrong with you. I reassured them that you were just in so deep a sleep that we couldn't wake you. We decided to leave you to it. I trust that you feel better for the rest.'

'I certainly do but I'm amazed that I slept for so long. Where are the others?'

'I left them down at the seafront exploring the sights while I came back to check on you. If you're feeling up to coming with me we'll meet them there?'

'Well, I guess I'll have to wait until lunch before I get anything to eat here so I might as well; perhaps I can grab something on the way.' Jon was hopeful of getting a bread roll or some other snack to satisfy his hunger.

The two of them walked out of the guest house and into the sun of a beautiful spring morning. The sun shone brightly and the azure sky was dotted with fluffy white clouds that floated gracefully across the blue expanse. It was a welcome relief from the cold of the Flats and the sunshine rejuvenated Jon's spirits. There was a lot of activity in Seaview, being a busy port dealing with goods and folk from all parts of the land.

Nobody paid any particular attention to them and they dodged their way through the bustle of shoppers and traders. Seaview was renowned for its fishing fleet and it made up the majority of its trade. Passing the open fronted shops, Jon saw sea creatures on display that he thought existed only in stories but here they were for all to see.

The noise of the vendors selling their wares, encouraging folk to buy from them rather than the shop next door, filled the cobbled streets with a cacophony of sound. It was exciting to see and hear after the emptiness of the desert and the Flats. They continued on through the busy streets and Jon managed to find a snack bar where he was able to purchase a roll filled with crab meat. It was not what he really wanted but his stomach demanded to have something to fill it.

Reaching the dock, Jon saw that the port extended out into the sea. It was encompassed by two arms of rock wall that had been placed there to enlarge the already natural harbour. It nestled between chalk cliffs that rose above the town on either side. Towers stood on top of the cliffs; they were high up so that when the fires were lit at night they could be seen far out to sea and boats would be guided safely back inside the protective walls. The dock was a sight to see, filled with boats, their masts and rigging filling the sky. The waterfront was as busy as an anthill with dock workers loading and unloading goods by large cranes and jibs that held crates in strong nets dangling at the end of thick chains. Boxes and packages were being carried down the gangplanks of smaller boats and piled into stacks where they were being sorted and counted.

Jon had never seen anything like it and marvelled at the sight; it was as if he were in a different world. Seagulls circled overhead, squawking noisily and diving every now and again to pounce on a fish that had been dropped from one of the crates or any scrap that might constitute a free meal. There was much squabbling between them as to who would snatch the discarded item.

Hamill led Jon along the quayside, past the overhanging figureheads at the bows of the large wooden ships, each one different in its design and features. Some were representative of mythical sirens and mermaids whilst others were styled on the folk of the land; they all looked impressive and captivated him. He almost collided with one of the dock workers as he looked back over his shoulder at a particularly impressive figure; fortunately Hamill was able to pull him aside in time to avoid being knocked down.

'Here we are; I need to confirm travel arrangements for Auger's casket, it arrived here earlier.' Hamill led Jon through a doorway of a large wooden warehouse and into the office where they confirmed the name of the ship that Auger's crate would be transported on. Passage for Hamill, Jon, Braun and the five dwarves, Javelin, Archer, Trapper, Digger and Mason was arranged on the same ship which was to leave on the first tide in the morning. That would mean an early start so it was agreed that they would go on board this evening so as not to miss sailing at the right time.

Jon realised that it gave them enough time to explore the town and the rest of the day to relax, something that they had not been able to do since their stay at Foamesend.

'It seems rather strange, don't you think; knowing that we will soon be back at Seers Tower and this will all be over?' Jon said with a far away look in his eyes and a sad expression on his face. 'I shall not be sad that the challenges we've faced will be behind us, goodness knows we've had more than our share of those. It's just that after the last time I found it difficult to settle into any kind of routine. I hadn't told you this but I had planned on going to Ffridd-Uch-Ddu anyway. That is, after the rains had finished.'

'Is that so; well I'm glad that we were able to go there together, though it does seem an age since we were there. As for all this being over that is true but the work of a seer is never done and I suspect that you will discover that yourself some day.' Hamill replied with a wink of his eye.

'Do you really think so? I know that one should not aspire to such a thing but ever since I met Urim I've had this desire to be like him, to be a seer.' Jon hung his head and blushed. 'I never told you how I felt when I found out that you had been chosen to replace Ebon. I'm sorry to say that I was quite envious of you. Not that I'd deny you the position of course, I think that you were and still are the best choice. It's just that I wanted to go into Seers Tower so badly and Urim said that I couldn't, not then anyway. This time it will be different and I'm looking forward to be able to see inside.' Jon brightened with the prospect of finally being able to realise his long hoped for visit.

Hamill placed a comforting hand on his friend's shoulder. 'Even if there were to be no invite from any of the other seers; I am inviting you to join me when I go back. That alone will suffice if in no other way. I will not be parted so soon from you and I would hope that you would be allowed to stay to see the inauguration of the new Auger wind-rider.'

They were both excited at the prospect of it being one of the dwarves and they fell silent as they pondered on whom that might be.

'Wouldn't it be exciting if it were to be one of the dwarves we know? Who do you think it might be; Javelin, Archer; Trapper, or even one of the others?' They had both discussed this before and were still none the wiser; only time would tell. Thinking that thought brought memories of Urim back to Jon's mind and the first night they had met, when Urim asked whether Jon was ready for what lay ahead; he had said that time will tell.

The two of them walked along the sea front and found the others looking out to sea enjoying the onshore breeze. The clean fresh air seemed to blow all of their cares away and they all sat on benches that overlooked the harbour. They passed the time away watching the activity on the dock. They found a cafe on the waterfront where they had a fresh fish luncheon. Jon could not recall having tasted such a delicious meal. Their plates had been piled high with all kinds of sea fare, from cockles and other assortments of shell fish to a lovely sea bass in lemon and garlic sauce.

The group of friends took their leisure over the meal, not having anything urgent to do, and savoured the tranquillity of the afternoon. The quayside was quiet after the morning rush and they were able to enjoy the peace and tranquillity. Eventually they returned to the guesthouse for the evening meal before preparing their belongings. They were ready to go on board the ship they had tickets for; it was called the Fair Trader. Hamill considered it a good name and had enquired about its departure for Landfall when they had looked for passage earlier. He had ascertained that the ship was due to sail early tomorrow so it had suited their timescale perfectly.

Chapter 33

The Sea Voyage

Jon slept soundly that night, having enjoyed a good meal at the guesthouse in the evening before they all boarded the ship that would take them to Landfall. Hamill had asked the captain when he thought they would reach their destination.

'Well now, with the tide and the wind behind us, we should reach port by late afternoon; provided the weather holds.'

When asked if he expected it to, the captain informed them that at this time of the year it was not uncommon for the odd storm to break without warning. 'But don't you worry; this old ship of mine has come through many a tempest and delivered us safely home again.' His confidence in his ship was comforting but it did nothing to dispel the disquiet that Hamill felt about going on the water.

'Perhaps I could travel by coach and meet with you all at Seers Tower later.' He had said but the dwarves had all encouraged him to travel with them and he had reluctantly agreed.

'What if something was to happen to you or to us that needed the other's assistance and neither of us was there? No, we should all stick together, besides it's too late to change your mind now; Auger's casket is crated up and secured in the hold. You'd want to ensure that all was well wouldn't you?' Javelin's logic and encouragement won Hamill over and he was forced to concede that they should stick together and see the journey through to the end.

Hamill looked forward to the sea voyage being over and crossed his fingers in the hope that the weather would be good and that they would reach Landfall without having to sail through any storms. From there it would be only a few hours by coach to Seers Tower and their meeting with Urim and the other seers.

Jon could hardly wait, what with the excitement of not only being able to go inside the Tower but also to attend the inauguration of the new seer to succeed Auger. Ever since Hamill had been inaugurated he had wanted to see what took place when a new seer joins the Council of the Sight. Now that Hamill had invited him to be there when Auger's replacement was taken through the ceremony, he would have his wish fulfilled.

Jon was still trying to come to terms with the loss of the seer. He had not known him long, only for a few days, but his death had come as a shock to him and the others, especially Hamill who had taken it so personally. He still blamed himself for not saving the dwarf from drowning; it was such a stupid way for a seer to meet his end. It showed, however, that even the seers were subject to their own mortality, even though a change comes upon them when they become a seer, they are still susceptible to death.

Hamill had behaved strangely for some time after that and Jon had worried about him. When it was revealed that Ebon had been influencing them both, it explained a lot about the things that had happened. However, since Urim had taken Ebon away, there had been no further incidents to cause concern and they had both felt brighter. The fact that Ebon had used them both to further his own ends made him angry and he felt sick knowing that he had almost succeeded. If it had not been for Urim yet again coming to deliver them all from their fate Jon dreaded to think what might have happened. He still could not understand why he had not felt his presence. If any of them were to have been the one to have carried Ebon's essence it should have been Hamill; after all he used to hold the staff and talisman of the seer that Hamill now held.

The way Hamill had been behaving these past few weeks he could have believed it had been his friend that had been host to Ebon. To discover it was himself was a real shock. It did explain the dark dreams he had been having and Jon was relieved that they had stopped since

Ebon had gone. The headaches he had suffered and the moments when he could not recall what he had been doing were now explained.

He wondered what had become of the rebel seer and whether he would ever trouble them again. Jon was still quite surprised that Ebon had been able to do what he had; he had not thought that the former seer would have had enough power to achieve what he had but apparently he had. Somehow he must have had access to another source; perhaps Urim would be able to tell them what was behind it all. The thing that intrigued him most was the strange white staff Ebon had been holding when Urim had called him out of Jon's body, as well as the rebel seer's appearance; he had hardly recognised him. No matter how evil he had been Jon could not bring himself to feel anything but pity for him. He made a mental note to ask Urim about him when they met again in a couple of days.

It took a little getting used to, being on a ship whilst at sea and he found that he would totter from side to side as the ship rolled and pitched with the swell of the water's surface. The journey to the food area was quite an adventure as he hung on to the handrails for stability. When he entered the dining area he saw that the others were already there; they hadn't beaten him by long as they were just sitting down to their meal.

'Hello Jon; where's Hamill? Don't say that he's the last to arrive. I thought that the ribbing we gave him last time would be enough for him to never be late again.' Javelin jested as he nudged Archer who was sitting next to him.

'He did tell me that he did not like going on the water, perhaps he's not feeling well.' Jon replied.

Javelin stopped smiling and apologised. 'If Hamill's not well, then I am sorry for my remark and I'll go and see if he's going to join us or if he's in need of anything.' The dwarf was as good as his word and he made his way to Hamill's cabin and knocked on the door. There was a weak reply from within that sounded very much like Hamill had said for whoever it was to go away and leave him alone. Undeterred, Javelin opened the door and looked in on the seer. He was laying flat on his bunk groaning with every lurch and sway of the ship as it ploughed its way through the swell of the waves.

'Are you alright Hamill? Is there anything I can get you to eat?' Javelin offered kindly, thinking that a hot meal would do the seer the world of good.

Hamill seemed to turn a shade of green and he rolled over in his bunk and faced the wall. Javelin heard a muffled groan as Hamill covered his face with a large cloth signalling with a backward wave of his hand to leave him alone. Javelin could not help but chuckle silently at Hamill's discomfort but it was not malicious because he was not that way inclined. Leaving the seer to suffer in silence, the dwarf gently closed the door and went back to the others to have his breakfast.

'So is Hamill coming to join us?' Jon asked as Javelin entered the room without the seer.

'No, you were right Jon; he isn't feeling well; apparently he is suffering from the effects of the ship's movements.'

'Oh dear, I hope he feels better soon. Does he want any food taken to him?' Braun asked.

'I don't think that he would thank you for it, he seems to be off his food at the moment.' The dwarf replied with a shake of his head.

'Goodness he must be unwell; poor Hamill.' Braun sympathised with him because he knew how Hamill was feeling. He too was not very happy with being on the water but at least this ship was more substantial than the river boats and he could get up and move around, even though he did have to duck his head to avoid the beams.

They were all in a good frame of mind, now that they were returning to the Tower and Ebon had been vanquished. They raised their cups to a successful end to their journey and that the weather would hold so that Hamill would not suffer too greatly.

Jon was feeling quite hungry this morning and he had eaten a double portion of breakfast; he put it down to the sea air sharpening his appetite. The dwarves sat back in their chairs, relaxing after their meal. There was nothing for them to do on board so they decided to play cards and lit up their pipes. That was the cue for Jon and Braun to leave them in peace and they went up on deck.

The stiff breeze filled the sails and they appeared to be making good headway. The two fire-towers on the hills at Seaview could be seen in the distance behind them as they followed the coastline north. At this rate they probably would get to Landfall on time. They went to the bow where the spray from the movement of the ship through the water showered the foredeck. They did not go too near so as to avoid being soaked by the salty water but occasionally they would feel the droplets of water on their faces. Licking his lips Jon could taste the salt. The sky was clear, other than a few clouds on the horizon out to sea and Jon could understand why they called it the Great Salt Waters because that's exactly what it was.

'I've never been on the Waters before; it's exhilarating isn't it?' Jon shouted above the sound of the waves as the bow ploughed its way through and the sails billowed in the wind.

'Indeed it is young Jon. I too have never been on the Waters and I find it rather exciting; better than that small boat on Foam River.'

'Yes I agree with that; I feel a lot safer on this one.' The wind made Jon begin to feel cold so he said that he was going back inside to check on Hamill.

Braun nodded and said that he would stay on here a while longer. Jon made his way across the deck in stages; holding on to ropes and railings as he tried to compensate for the movement of the ship. Below deck he felt less vulnerable as he could hold onto the handrails in the corridor between the dining area and where the cabins were. He knocked on Hamill's door but received no response so he quietly opened the door and poked his head in. Hamill was fast asleep with his mouth wide open and gently snoring. Jon decided that if he was feeling ill, that was the best thing he could do and left him in peace.

He decided that he could do with a nap as well; obviously this sea air was affecting him. He went to the dining area where he found the dwarves under a great cloud of smoke still playing cards. 'I'm going to my cabin for a while if anyone wants to know where I am. I've looked in on Hamill and he's asleep so I left him to his dreams.'

'Yes; it's probably better that he stays where he is and sleeps away the journey. If you don't have sea legs, travelling in a ship can be rather a challenge to the stomach.' Digger commented.

Jon nodded and smiled then turned and found his way back to his cabin where he made himself comfortable and was rocked to sleep by the gentle rolling of the ship.

CRASH! Jon awoke with a start and he struggled to recall where he was. He fought to regain his senses and realised that the ship was heaving in all directions. The pottery jar containing water that had been placed in his cabin had fallen off the small table and smashed on the floor, spilling its contents. It took him a few moments to gather his thoughts as he had been in a deep sleep then realised that they must have hit bad weather. His immediate concern was for Hamill so putting on his boots he lurched along the corridor to his friend's cabin and went inside. Unbelievably Hamill was still asleep, despite all the swaying and bucking of the ship in these rough waters.

Satisfied that his friend was alright, Jon went forward to the dining room. Braun and the dwarves were there, though Braun sat at a different table as far away from the smoke as possible. He did not mind smoke normally, he was used to it from his forge, but the reek of the tobacco was too much for him. Indeed there were some other passengers sitting near Braun who had covered their faces with cloths to avoid breathing in the odious smell. In fact the dwarves had extinguished their pipes, seeing that other passengers were taking shelter below decks, but the smoke still hung in the air. Mason waved hello to Jon as he entered and the others all smiled and nodded their heads.

'Come and join us Jon, we're just about to have a light lunch.' Archer invited him, drawing up a chair.

'If you don't mind I'll sit with Braun; the smoke's still a bit too heavy for me in these conditions.'

The dwarves nodded amiably, understanding that not many folk could abide the smell of their pipes. Apart from the dwarves, who seemed to be able to cope with any situation, the rest of the passengers all showed signs of sickness, some more than others. Braun sat cradling his head in his hands and was braced against one of the ships timbers that stood next to the bench he was seated on. Jon joined him, walking unsteadily across the room as the floor pitched one way then another and sat alongside the big metal-master. Jon was not feeling too good either as his stomach lurched with each sway of the ship.

'How long has the storm been raging?' He asked Braun.

'Not long; it started when we drew level with Torport. I overheard some talk between the sailors of putting into the harbour to wait the storm out but the captain said that he had seen worse storms than this and that they would continue on their course to Landfall.'

Jon began to feel the effects of the pitch and roll of the ship and wished that the captain had gone to harbour. He would rather arrive in Landfall later than suffer the ill effects of this storm. It was just as well that Hamill still slept; he would not have enjoyed this one little bit.

They all jumped when one of the portholes crashed open letting what seemed to be half the ocean in before one of the crew members who were in attendance was able to close it again. Several of the sailors crossed their fingers and mumbled prayers saying that the captain must be mad to try and sail through such weather.

Their reaction to the storm did not garner much confidence among the passengers and a young child began to cry. His mother tried to distract his attention from the situation by holding a soft toy for the boy to play with but it only worked for a little while.

'Come, my dear, we will go back to our cabin; perhaps Jared will feel better there; we can let him lie down for a while and with any luck he will go to sleep.' The husband suggested so the three of them left, trying to keep on their feet as they went from one point to another, clinging on to whatever they could for safety.

The ship creaked and groaned under the stresses and strains placed upon it by the force of the wind and the waves. There was a rumbling sound every now and again from the hold below and soon afterwards several sailors rushed from the deck, down the stairway and into the hold. Something had come loose from its bindings and was moving around in the cargo area. Jon hoped that it wasn't Augers crate containing his casket. The ship seemed to change course and the swaying and rolling of the ship steadied a little; Jon supposed that it was to allow the crew to secure the loose item without having to tackle it whilst crashing from one place to another. A little while later they heard some shouting from below and a message was relayed to the captain that all was secure again. The sailors emerged from the hold and scrambled back on deck, ready to face the challenge of keeping the ship on course. No sooner had they disappeared up the stairway than the swaying and rolling began again. Jon assumed that they had altered course once more and were headed north again.

Jon looked around him at the other passengers; they were nearly all struggling with feelings of sickness; all that is apart from the dwarves. They were quite content to sit and continue playing cards. Jon decided that he wanted to take a peek at what was happening on deck; he was curious about being on a ship in a storm and he could not experience it properly from here in the dining area. He made his way to the stairs and grabbing a firm hold on the handrail, managed to climb up and onto the deck.

Great splashes of sea water crashed down and across the decking; the sails whipped in the wind with a sound very much like cracking-jacks set off at the year end celebrations. Holding desperately to the rails he clung on for fear of being swept away and he nearly lost his footing as a huge wave of water curled up over the bow and swept the length of the ship.

After that he realised that it was probably not a good idea to be up on deck; he took a last look at the mountainous waves and enjoyed the thrill of the wind as it whistled and howled its fury upon the vessel. Jon admired the tenacity of the captain and the skill of the crew as they battled the elements, steering the ship towards its destination and the safety there was to be found at the northern port of Landfall.

Somewhat reluctantly he descended the stairs to rejoin his comrades. He was soaked by the storm and regretted going up but then he thought what a shame it would have been not to have experienced it this once. He may never get the opportunity again. He went to his room to put on some dry clothing and fought the movement of the ship as he tried to dress. It was most difficult trying to put on dry socks but by leaning against the cupboard he managed it. He felt the ship steady and the rolling of the ship lessened and within moments the vessel was sailing calmly in a gentle swell; the storm was over.

Rushing back on deck, he saw the blue sky overhead and the bright sunshine dazzling as it reflected off the water. The storm had moved on and was speeding away from them into the east, taking with it the dark clouds and rain. The wind no longer whipped the waves up into great mountains but blew them forward with a more leisurely pace. He saw the sailors attending to the sails and rigging; they looked relieved to have come through without harm. The only incident that had occurred during the storm was when they had to secure the loose cargo in the hold. Other than that, they had made good headway; with the storm having blown from out of the south and east and along the coast, it had meant that they were further along their course than had been expected.

Jon understood now why the captain hadn't put into port when he had the opportunity to do so; he'd have missed the benefit of making the storm work for him. Now they would be in Landfall that much earlier he thought, excited at the prospect of arriving at Seers Tower sooner than intended.

Chapter 34

Landfall

'I'd go back inside for a while longer if I were you sir; the deck is rather slippery from the storm. You wouldn't want to fall overboard now, would you sir?' The captain advised him as he passed by to inspect the hold and its contents for any damage that may have been caused by the loose item.

Jon nodded and went to see if Hamill had awakened. He can't possibly have slept through it all. He had. When Jon opened the door he was amazed to find his friend still soundly asleep and snoring to his heart's content. 'Well now, would you believe it? Still I suppose it was better that you didn't wake. I don't think that you'd have enjoyed the experience.' Jon whispered and quietly closed the door then went in search of Braun and the dwarves.

They were still playing cards and Braun was looking much better than when Jon had last seen him. Everyone was breathing more easily now that the smoke had cleared from the room and they were clear of the bad weather. Folk were beginning to move around the lower deck and dining area again. Jon was actually quite surprised that being on the ship had not had any affect on himself. He'd never sailed on the Great Salt Waters and been in a storm like the one that had raged about them. He felt quite pleased about it and was almost disappointed that the adventure would be over so soon.

'Have you checked on Hamill recently?' Braun asked as he saw Jon enter the saloon.

'Yes, I've just been in to see him and he hasn't stirred from when I saw him last.'

'Probably just as well, for his sake. I don't think he'd have coped very well, what with the effects of the storm and all.' Braun sympathised with Hamill's dislike of the movement of the ship.

The dwarves continued with their game of cards and Jon sat to watch them. Intrigued as to what game they were playing.

'Fancy joining us for a round Jon?' Mason asked.

'No thanks; I'm not very good at playing cards, I always seem to lose; just like when I play sticks with Hamill. I'm happy to watch though. What is it you're playing anyway?'

'It's called Jackpot and you have to try and out bluff or outplay everyone else in the round to win what's been put into the stake. We all put our bet in at each turn and decide whether it's worth playing for or not; the last one in is the winner.'

'Oh yes; I've seen something similar back at Ashbrooke.'

Just then a crew member passed their table and Jon asked how long it would be before they reached Landfall?'

'Not long now sir; that storm helped us on our way quite a lot; we should be there in about two turns of the hand.'

'Are we nearly there yet?' Hamill stood clutching at the rail looking very pale and he wobbled on unsteady legs.

'Hamill; you're finally awake. How are you feeling?' They all asked; taken by surprise at his sudden appearance.

'I've felt better.' He replied. 'I dreamed that I was riding a grist in a great storm. I was glad to wake up and find that everything was normal.'

They all looked at him stunned then laughed. 'Well, you may not have ridden a grist but you certainly were in a storm.' Javelin answered with amusement. 'I'm glad to see you up and about anyhow; come and join us. Are you ready to eat yet?'

Hamill placed his hand on his stomach and nodded slowly. 'Do you know; I think I could eat something. This sailing lark isn't as bad as I thought it would be.'

Jon looked at him with amazement then helped his friend across the room to sit at the table. A waiter came in and they all ordered snacks to see them through to their evening meal at Landfall. Braun brought

Hamill up to date with what had happened; all Hamill could do was shake his head in disbelief.

The ship docked and the passengers disembarked eager to get back on to dry land. The dwarves thanked the captain for bringing them safely through the storm and for a pleasant journey.

'That's not what I would have called it.' Hamill said to Jon as they made their way down the ramp and onto the dockside. 'You all go to Voyage End, the guesthouse where we shall be staying, and get settled in. I need to make sure that the preparations are in place for Auger to be taken to the Tower. He'll be taken by freight wagon whilst we go on the coach first thing in the morning. I'll join you once I've taken care of everything.'

Jon went with Hamill whilst the others did as he had directed, ordering dinner for them all when they signed in at the desk. Trapper made sure that there was a supply of relk available for them to have with their meal; their own supply had been sadly depleted and needed replenishing. The owner of the establishment assured them that there would be several bottles placed on their table and that he would make certain that they had plenty to take with them when they left in the morning. All the dwarves smiled with satisfaction at the prospect of a good meal and a hearty drink to celebrate the final stage of their journey.

'I wonder what the mayor will say when we turn up at Ffridd-Uch-Ddu having disobeyed his order not to get involved.' Archer said.

'I don't really care what he says; it never carries any weight with me.' Trapper announced, puffing out his chest in defiance.

Javelin slapped him on the back with a bellow of laughter. 'Well he'd better watch out then; that's all I can say because none of us regret anything about the help we gave to the Seers and I'm sure Hamill will back us. I don't think that there will be any recriminations to worry about. He's all wind and bluster with no bite that new mayor. We'll be heroes and we will sing a mighty song about our exploits that will stir the blood of any who call themselves a dwarf.'

Trapper went silent for a moment and his head fell onto his chest as he remembered Gemon. Trapper had sought him out with a fervour that bordered on being obsessive and he had been filled with hatred towards him but all that had changed when he had shown his true allegiance.

The dwarf, who they had thought was a gnome at one point (having heard it spoken by a gnome who professed to be his brother due to his mixed ancestry) had proven beyond doubt, with the giving of his own life for Trapper's, that he was one of the most valiant of them all. Trapper had taken his death like a body blow; he had felt that he had lost his brother again. It had been a cruel turn of events because the two of them had just begun to understand and appreciate one another. Trapper had determined that he would return to Ffridd-Uch-Ddu and seek out Gemon's sick mother and care for her as if she were his own. It was the very least he could do towards repaying the dwarf for his selfless act.

They marched off to their allotted rooms; their arms around each other's necks and started to compose the song that they would share with their friends upon their return.

Braun smiled with pleasure at the dwarves; he would miss their company and that of Jon and Hamill but he wouldn't miss the adventures. He was ready to settle down and build a new forge back in Foundry Smelt. The colossi were more than capable of finishing the refurbishment of the mountain city. He missed the smell of the soot and the roar and heat of the furnace as he stoked the fires and made metal to glow white hot.

Their evening meal was a noisy one; all the tensions and fears of the past weeks and months were swept away with the roar of laughter and the singing of songs. The dwarves had started early on the drinking of relk; they had been in the saloon across the street, 'wetting their appetite' so they claimed. Jon suppressed a smile as Mason and Digger swaggered across the room, arm in arm, to join them, followed by the other three dwarves who were just as unsteady on their feet. As the dwarves greeted them, their breath testified to the fact that they must be very hungry indeed.

Jon was surprised that they were showing signs of being affected by the drink; usually they could handle it without the least difficulty. Then he realised that they had been drinking on empty stomachs which was probably why they were a little 'giddy'.

Hamill was feeling much better now and seemed none the worse for his earlier illness on board the ship. In fact he demolished more than he usually did from the loaded platters. He had second helpings of everything; Jon and Braun were not a whit behind him as they tucked into the rack of ribs and roasted potatoes with all the dressings. It felt like they were having a party and if truth were known, they were. They were celebrating the end of Ebon's attempts to subject them all to his will. They were celebrating their safe return from their encounter with Amethyst and the freedom of the ogres. In fact it got to the point where they were giving a toast to anything and everything, just for the sake of it.

The evening wore on and other diners watched in amazement at the antics of these strange travelling companions. No-one interfered with them or complained because in their midst was a seer and folk in the region held them in deep respect. Whatever they did was fine with them because the citizens knew that without them, the world would be a different place to the one they all knew. Little did they know that this particular party of revellers had been deeply involved in saving their world and preserving those things that the folk of the land took for granted each day of their lives.

The time came for them to get a good night's sleep. With the amount of relk that had been consumed (the manager had to bring extra bottles to keep up with the demand) the dwarves were assured of sleeping well; their snoring may keep others awake, but they would sleep soundly. Jon, Braun and Hamill had been more sensible with their drinking and only had enough ale to make them merry. There was a very important day coming up and they needed to be alert and steady for what was to transpire at Seers Tower.

They made their way to their rooms having dragged themselves away from the dwarves who had insisted that they stay for just one more little drink. Eventually they left them to it and wearily climbed the stairs and were asleep very quickly. The stresses and strains of the journey and all that had transpired during that time had worn them out. Now that they had relaxed and felt secure again; the fatigue had settled in to claim the long overdue need for rest.

Jon drifted off to sleep with the muffled sound beyond his door, from the dining area, of the dwarves finishing off the relk before stomping heavily up the stairs, singing away to their hearts' content. He heard the thud of boots being dropped on the floor in the room above his and the sag of a mattress as one of them sank into a cot followed by a loud belch, fuelled by the consumption of too much relk. The sound of them getting ready for sleep was followed very quickly by loud snoring. Jon did not know who it was that snored the loudest but the dwarves would very quickly have replied that it was Digger. Jon smiled as he imagined the look on Digger's face as his fellow dwarves levelled their accusation at him.

Jon tested his head when he awoke and gently raised himself from his cot. After drinking far more than he had intended to he expected to have a hangover but was surprised when all he felt was a little 'fuzzy'. Grateful for that, he dressed and went to join the others. Hamill had re-established his normal routine and had been the first to arise; he had been so quiet that Jon had not been disturbed by him when he had got up.

'Well, I couldn't have you teasing me again, not after the last time.' Hamill defended himself when queried about him being the first to breakfast again. The dwarves were yet to arrive but it would not be long before they came down; not if Jon knew them. Sure enough, moments later, they did and were none the worse for their drinking last night. Jon would never cease to be amazed at how they were able to drink so much of the most potent liquid in the land and yet still get up as fresh as day. All it would take for him to be rendered useless the next day would be to take two sips of their relk; maybe even one.

'Good morning everyone; I hope you slept well?' Javelin greeted them cheerfully.

'Yes I did thank you and I know you did, or one of you, because I heard you snoring.' Jon could not help but offer up a teasing rebuke.

'That must have been Digger. He's terrible for that.' Archer said and winked at the dwarf as he started to protest.

'I'll have you know...' He began but was pelted by three or four bread rolls that made him sit down with an undignified thump and a furrow on his brow before breaking out into a broad grin.

'I see that we are in good humour today. That's good and we can celebrate some more when we arrive at the Tower later this morning. Hamill announced. 'I have sent a message on ahead of us to arrange for our accommodation and I wouldn't be surprised if you were to be acclaimed as heroes of the land by Terra Standfast himself.'

That brought a cheer from the dwarves. It was something that they could sing songs about when they returned to their friends and family. To be honoured by virtue of their deeds in conflict, of whatever sort, was a great privilege and they puffed their chests out in pride. Never let it be said that a dwarf suffers from modesty. They know their abilities and are justifiably proud of them. Their culture is defined and strengthened by the heroics of their warriors. Now their deeds were to be immortalised in song to be sung through the generations yet to come.

They all clambered aboard the two coaches that had been contracted to take them this morning and were glad to be headed to Seers Tower at last. Within just a few short turns of the hand they would be in sight of its imposing walls and their journey would be at an end.

The roads were very good and there were no mishaps along the way. Braun sat atop with the driver as he could not be accommodated inside but that suited him very well as he could feel the breeze in his face and smell the fresh air. That was something that was in short supply in Foundry Smelt but Braun had become accustomed to this over the years and he was never happier than when at his forge.

Hamill had a faraway look in his eyes as the coach trundled across the countryside hitting the occasional rut or pothole in the road. Jon was too full with excitement at being allowed inside the Tower and meeting with Urim again. The seer had said that he would meet them there and, Jon supposed, would need to take part in the inauguration of the replacement seer. They would all soon know who that was to be and Jon could hardly wait.

He let his mind dwell on the dwarves; there were five of them accompanying them to the Tower. They must have realised that Auger's replacement would probably be one of them but he had never heard any one of them speaking about it. Surely they must feel some apprehension or nervousness with the forthcoming ritual? Perhaps they thought that

Terra would already have some other dwarf in mind for the role. Jon thought that it would come as a surprise to him if it wasn't one of his friends but which one would it be. Javelin was an obvious candidate because of his leadership abilities and determination.

Then there was Archer, a dwarf with a quiet strength that would sustain him and those around him through any situation. He and Javelin were close friends and they shared a common humour that lifted the mood in any time of difficulty.

Trapper had lost his twin brother, Tracker, the last time that they were here when Ebon had murdered him before being drawn through the energy barrier. They had all honoured the brave little dwarf and he lay in one of the tombs nearby; privileged to be where only the seers are interred. His sadness had been deepened by the loss of his new-found friend, Gemon and his commitment to care for the dwarf's sick mother was commendable.

Mason and Digger had been involved with their quest to defeat Ebon since before the rogue seer besieged Northill and had acquitted themselves well. Especially Digger, he had rescued his friend Mason from the underground river, after they had thought him dead. Then there was Leader, who was recovering from his operation in Seaview. He was a relative newcomer to their select band of brotherhood. He had joined them on the way to the Ward when Jon had been taken ill and been with them ever since, except when he had been captured by the ogres and sold into slavery at the Coven where Amethyst had met her end. Hamill had come across him there and released him so that he could aid them in the fight against the witch-queen.

It was going to be a difficult decision as to which of them would be chosen and Jon was glad he did not have to do it. Hamill would have an input of course as he would sit on the Council of the Sight to decide who the replacement would be. Whatever their decision, Jon knew it would be the right one.

Chapter 35

Poles Apart

Terra was confident that everything that could be done by them to prepare for the attack from the wizards had been completed. There was a risk of course, there always was in matters such as these but he was confident of success because Urim was with them. He had also brought a new and enigmatic addition to their ranks in the form of Jetta. They needed all the help they could get and having this new ally amongst them was welcome indeed. The outcome may not be certain as to who would survive this titanic clash between the two worlds. The energy beneath the Tower was strong and had served them well in their defences before. But it had never been tested against a power from another world that might be equally as strong.

He weighed up the things that were in their favour; there were six of the eight seers available to contend against five of the wizards. As far as he knew there would be no others involved but that was where his plans fell down. He could not be certain that it would only be the wizards that they would be fighting. If they were to bring to bear some other force or to have some ally that they knew nothing of then the outcome could be very different than that which he hoped. The unknown factor in this, from his perspective, was what Jetta would be able to achieve with his dark magic. Would it be enough to tip the balance in their favour? He crossed his fingers that they would emerge triumphant at the end.

A nervous air of anticipation fell over the Tower as those who served the seers were ferried across the lake to safety. This was the third time in a very short period of time that they had resorted to this course of action and Terra hoped it would be the last for a very long time.

Whenever a threat came to the security of the Tower all but the seers were to leave and return to their homes nearby. On this occasion the seers had a dark companion who joined them in their vigil against the anticipated attack from the wizards. Jetta remained in order to assist them in their efforts against the wizards. He had found a new and worthwhile purpose to his life; he would turn the dark magic inside him against those who would wrest the peace of this land out of the custodial hands of the seers.

Night came and the Tower stood as silent within as it was without. Three of the seers stood around the shaft in the courtyard; Terra, Liam and Emerald. If and when the wizards launched their attack it would be through the energy that connected the world of Magog with theirs. There was no other way that they could span the gulf that existed in space and time between them. Whether the wizards would choose to make a full attack aimed at them here in their Tower or not, neither Terra nor any of the other seers could tell. All they could do was to watch and wait.

Emrys and Maccus talked together in private, the leader of the wizards needed this time to clear the air between them before they committed themselves into the battle against the seers.

Emrys started the conversation. 'Maccus, I know that we have not always seen eye to eye on matters but I have always known that when it came to a battle between us wizards and any outside influence that I could rely upon your utmost support. I sense however that you are not entirely behind me in this our greatest moment when we shall be avenged upon the seers.'

'My brother; it is true that I have reservations about the purpose of this undertaking in what appears to me, and some of the others too, as a means to return to our old world. There are a number of us who feel we are no longer suited for that world and would be far better off remaining in this world. Ebon has failed us and our way back into their world has been made more difficult.'

'You are right in what you say about Ebon, Maccus, and as for my wanting to return to the old world, I cannot deny that it has been my desire to do so ever since we arrived here in Magog. If you and the other wizards do not wish to do so then I must bow to the will of the conclave and accept the majority decision to stay here. However, we have within our grasp the means to conquer these upstart seers once and for all and I would like to know that I can count on every member of our society to give of their all in this venture. I do not want to be watching my back whilst facing them as that would lessen our chances of succeeding. Do I have your assurance that you will support me in gaining our revenge upon the seers?'

'You may rest assured, Emrys that I too wish to strike out at them, as do we all, and we will give of our strength when the time comes.'

Emrys breathed a sigh of relief; he had feared that the coming conflict would give Maccus the opportunity he had been waiting for; to become the leader of the conclave. Emrys felt the truth of Maccus' words and knew that the wizards would act as one in this. That was all he wanted to know and was satisfied with the pledge that Maccus had given.

The two wizards went their separate ways and Maccus smiled knowing that what he had said was true, up to a point. They all wanted revenge on the seers but as for leaving this world in favour of that of the seers, that was a different matter. He knew that there would be enough support for him against Emrys when the time came for that decision to be made.

As a precautionary measure under Terra Standfast's plan, Urim, Eden and Elise, along with Jetta, stood ready against any incursion at the opposite source of power in Anram. If the wizards emerged through the keystone instead of though the shaft then Urim would bring the other seers from the Tower by means of the portal. Together they would then endeavour to repulse the invasion and seal the way forever. Urim kept the portal partly open so that if the wizards came directly at the others in Seers Tower, those who were at the keystone in Anram could quickly be transported to their aid.

At both places silence reigned as they waited for the first signs of the wizards. The night passed agonisingly slowly from one turn of the hand to the next and still there was no indication that the wizards were coming. Tiredness sapped their strength and they all struggled to stay alert; still nothing happened. The night chill settled upon those who were in the courtyard of the Tower, causing them to shiver against the cold. Their breath could be seen on the night air and they stomped their feet and hugged themselves in an effort to keep warm.

The temperature at Anram remained constant deep beneath the great pyramid and the air smelled a little stale. There had been no sight or sound from the Anramites; it was either because they were unaware of them being there or, more likely, they were sensing something that kept them at bay. Urim did not mind which it was, just so long as they were not a distraction to him.

Jetta glanced across at Urim who caught the subtle movement of the dark angel. The seer nodded and smiled gently reassuring him that all would be well. Jetta was not afraid; he believed that with his magic he would be equal to anything that was sent against him; it was the waiting that unnerved him.

Slowly the time unwound and still the silence prevailed. A subtle, soft swish of cloth that was almost undetectable pricked Eden's keen ears and her eyes opened wider at the sound. Drawing Urim's attention she signalled that she had heard the approach of something or someone; they all stiffened in response as the others heard it now. A cold draught swept through the chamber, causing the hair on their arms to stand on end. From out of one of the passageways, three hooded forms emerged and floated towards them. One of them held a sword before her.

'Do not defile our home by your presence, seers; leave us to our solitude or prepare to defend yourselves; either you shall leave this place in one piece or you remain here forever. If you value your lives, go and return to your Tower whilst you still may.' Erin challenged the seers.

Urim said nothing but simply nodded at Jetta and then tilted his head towards the ghost-wizards. Jetta needed no second telling, he was keen to act and Urim recognised this as an opportunity to allow their new ally to prove himself and give him confidence. If he needed any assistance the seers would help, Urim felt that these apparitions were no match for their combined powers. The three spectres advanced on the dark form that stood to oppose them, his eyes black and menacing with flashes of fire sparking across his body.

Cupping his hands in front of him he called up the magic within and sent a net of flashing black fire at them. Erin simply cut through it with the keen edge of her sword but before it dissipated a portion of it caught hold on Galan. He was wrapped in the net and could not escape its hold; the more he struggled the tighter he was held. Ignoring her companion's plight, Erin continued to advance with her sister wizard, Megan. This time they put some space between them so as to make it more difficult for them to be targeted and came towards Jetta.

'You are something we have not seen before. Why do you serve these monsters of deceit? We can free you from their tyranny. Join with us against them and we shall free you from your bonds.' Erin soothed with her false promises. Her voice the merest whisper in the air yet it sounded loud in his ears.

'I am already free from any compulsion to serve anyone madam and I have no need of any assistance from the likes of you.' He thrust his arms forward and unleashed a stream of crackling power at both of the ghost-wizards, catching them full on. They both screamed as the black magic wrapped them in its intensity.

Jetta had taken his eye off of Galan, who had managed to free himself from the magical bonds that had held him. He sent a surge of negative energy at Jetta that crashed into him before he could react against it. An explosion of colour lit up the chamber with a resounding clang like that of a huge bell being struck many times as it reverberated around the confined space. Jetta went sprawling across the floor giving time for Galan to aid his sisters and free them from the magic that had encompassed them.

Eden and Elise went to help him but Urim waved them away and shook his head. 'This must be his battle to win. We will aid him at the last if need be, but he must face them unaided if he is to stand amongst us and obtain that which he needs; our respect and confidence.'

Eden accepted what Urim had said and stepped back to her position around the keystone but Elise was not convinced and she stood ready to assist just as soon as she felt Jetta was in danger.

'Never fear Elise, he will not require our help; he must find his own way of dealing with this challenge. Besides, we must be vigilant against the arrival of the wizards should they decide to emerge from their world here instead of at the Tower.'

Reluctantly accepting the counsel of the seer they regarded with a high esteem she backed away and stood with Eden, watching the contest of wills unfold. Jetta had regained his feet and he smiled at the attempt to remove him from the conflict. Dusting himself down with the nonchalant air of supreme confidence he faced the spectres again and waited.

The three apparitions drew ranks and formed a triangle with Erin at the head, pointing her sword at him in defiance of his powers. Taking the initiative in the battle, Jetta slowly walked towards them until he was but a few paces away and the tip of Erin's sword was a hands breadth away from his chest. Eden and Elise grew nervous and stood ready for the word from Urim that would release them from their immobility and allow them to help Jetta. Still Urim said nothing and the two elf seers watched in awe as Jetta pressed his body against the sword allowing Erin to thrust it through him. The burning red eyes of the three spectres glowed brighter as they felt the power of the sword burn into the dark form that stood before them. Jetta did not flinch but continued to smile.

Placing his hands on the upper part of the blade that pierced him, he sent a blast of magic through it and into the astonished ghosts. This was not what they had expected and they felt the magic pass through them, binding them all together as it ran from Jetta, through the sword and into Erin, Galan and Megan. The three of them were thrown back in the surge of a blast of power that erupted from within Jetta. Slowly he drew the blade from his chest and held the sword in his hand. He had them at his mercy and he knew, as did they, that he could finish them off and destroy their remaining essence so that they would cease to exist. Instead he did something that amazed them; he returned the sword, hilt first to Erin.

'You know that I have the power to destroy you yet I choose not to do so. Instead I give you your lives, such as they are, and promise that you will soon be left in peace. Go now and find your rest, have no more hatred towards my friends the seers for they are noble of mind and mean you no harm.'

Erin and the other two ghost-wizards looked to Urim for confirmation of what Jetta had said and he nodded with a gentle smile. Lifting his arm in a gesture that indicated they were free to go.

'We never realised, we thought that you were evil and corrupt tyrants but we see now that we were mistaken. We give you our pledge that we will never again trouble you should you or any of your kind come here again; farewell.' They retreated into the darkness of the passages but not without first bowing to Jetta, acknowledging his act of mercy towards them.

Jetta turned to the seers with an air of triumph in his manner but it was not that of a prideful boasting; rather it was a quiet and serene air of having won a battle without shedding blood. It was true that he had won his first great victory in the battle with the wizards but it was more than that.

Urim placed a friendly hand on his shoulder and looked him in the eye. 'You have today proven yourself not to us as you had thought to do, but to yourself. You are now free in a way that you had not thought possible; you are free to make your own decisions and you are free from oppression.'

The other two seers looked at Urim with understanding now. That is what he was trying to do; to allow Jetta the opportunity to prove to himself that he was his own man, so to speak. Jetta was indeed free and he felt as if he could be content to be who he was now. He had found a place in his mind that he could be comfortable with himself. He had also found a place where he would feel of use; he would serve the Council of the Sight and fight alongside them to maintain the freedom of the land.

Eden and Elise stepped forward to congratulate Jetta on his victory over the ghost-wizards, patting him on the back and kissing his cheeks. Jetta had never known such camaraderie and flushed with such a show of friendship he stood speechless before them. He had found that which he had been searching for all of his life and he had found it where he had least expected it to be, in the company of the seers.

At Seers Tower, nothing was known of these events transpiring in Anram. Terra, Liam and Emerald maintained their watch at the shaft, waiting for the first sign that the wizards were returning. Their last confrontation had ended in them being repulsed, thanks to the intervention of Urim who had arrived at the very moment that all had seemed lost.

Morning was approaching and they had stood guard all night, not daring to rest from their vigil in case they were taken by surprise. Terra looked up into the sky as it lightened with the advent of the new day and the stars began to fade.

'What would the day bring?' He asked silently. They could not be expected to keep up with this waiting day and night. Something would have to be organised in order that they could rest and be fully able to face the wizards. He did not understand why they had not come. He had been certain that they would have launched their attack on them during the night. It would be most unlikely that they would try it during the day because it did not suit the purposes of the wizards who preferred the darkness. Their power, which was based on the negative energy, was most effective at night and he had been sure that Emrys would have played things to his advantage. 'Perhaps he had thought to wear us down by playing these delaying tactics.'

Terra thought on this and realised that it was a sound approach to the battle and if he were in Emrys' place, he would do the same. If that were true then he would succeed in catching Terra and the other seers when they were at their weakest, having kept watch the whole night and they were tired from their lack of sleep.

'If they do not come within the next turn of the hand then I believe that they will not come at all today. He will wait until we have sapped our energies by standing another night in wakefulness, then he will strike.' Terra was convinced that in order for the seers to be successful against the wizards, they must remain vigilant but also try to maintain their strength. Whatever happened, this would decide, once and for all, who ruled in this land. He knew that they must not fail but he could not guarantee that they would come out of this either triumphant or unscathed.

When the wizards had been banished by the first seers there had been casualties on both sides. The wizards had lost three of their number, Erin, Emrys' wife and Maccus' sister, as well as Galan and Megan; all had fallen in the conflict with the seers. This had made very powerful enemies of the two wizards against the seers, especially Terra Standfast and Urim Tome-keeper. These two seers, the first of their kind, had despatched the three wizards and helped seal the fate of the others.

One of the original seers, Emerald, had been their only casualty in the confrontation as she had died defending the thing she held most dear, freedom. The seers had needed to find a replacement for her and had approached the sprite queen to select another from the sprite realm. With the sprites, selection of who was to follow after the death of the one who served was done by the sprite queen and not the Council of the Sight. On each occasion the choices had been absolutely right and the sprite-seers were always of the highest calibre. It was just such a quality that would see them through these most difficult of circumstances.

Terra's thoughts were not permitted to continue as like a lightning strike that comes without warning, a great boom of sound erupted from the shaft and sent out a shockwave that caught the seers by surprise.

Chapter 36

The Worlds at War

Fire shot high into the air as it accompanied the deafening sound, blinding them momentarily so that they were unable to see the wizards at first when they emerged from the shaft. It was not altogether unexpected that they would choose to strike here instead of through the keystone at Anram. It was where the seers would be gathered and a powerful attack against them here stood the greatest chance of success. Also by entering the seers' world here the wizards hoped that it would enable them to destroy their opponents quickly rather than having to work their way through the land, giving the seers a chance to rally their defences. Terra Standfast had opted to prepare for either eventuality and was not going to allow the wizards to triumph. The wise old dwarf had planned for just such a development.

When their vision cleared, the three seers saw the wizards staring down at them with their blazing red eyes, intensified by their pure hatred and rage. 'This was not going to be an easy task by any means.' Terra thought; silently wishing for it to be all over and the wizards defeated. The five wizards stood in a circle of fire looking out at their bitter enemies; longing to tear them apart and utterly rid themselves of their nemesis.

'Terra Standfast; you know me.' Emrys spoke with a voice of thunder. 'Your predecessor showed me to you, when you took up the mantle of becoming the leading seer. Although you are not the one who fought against us all those millennia ago; you represent them and must therefore take responsibility for their actions against us. We have returned to claim that which has been denied us and to have our vengeance upon you.'

'I know who you are.' Terra said boldly. 'You are mistaken to believe that you were wronged by the first to be called seers. They simply defended themselves against your tyranny, as we do now. If you will return to your world of Magog; we will not seek to destroy you as you do us but you will be left in peace.'

'Ha! Lies; I have heard it all before. The orchestra is different but the music is still the same. We will never be at peace until you and the rest of the seers, along with all those who have aided you, have been eradicated from the face of this world.'

'I don't know by what power you have been able to get through the barrier but we shall shortly be sending you back from whence you came.' Terra stamped his staff on the flagstone courtyard with a resounding clap of thunder.

'Huh! I am not concerned by your threats; if you wish to know how we were able to get here I shall tell you. Tell me what you see.' Emrys held forth a white rod, shaped like a bone. It *was* a bone and Terra guessed whose it was.

'So you have killed Ebon; that was not unexpected; in fact it was predictable which was why Urim delivered him to you. We could not punish him for his deeds but we knew that you would. It pains me to know that he is gone but it had become necessary, for the peace of our land.'

'It matters not to us; what you wanted to know was how we managed to break the binding that you, or rather your predecessors, set up to keep us prisoners in a strange world. Well, I shall tell you. It is by the power that is in this rod. When Ebon came through to Magog he established a rift in the energy barrier; we simply enlarged it enough to allow us to use it as a conduit through which we could escape. However, Ebon betrayed our trust so we had to make use of him in some other way. You see, his presence in our world was the link between the two; he has gone now but still the link remains in this, the Rod of Retribution and you shall feel its sting.'

Urim felt the emergence of the wizards through the shaft and into the Tower courtyard by means of the portal that he held partly open. The force with which they came through snatched his attention away from the praises that were being given to Jetta.

'Eden, Elise, we must aid our fellow seers; Emrys and the other wizards have broken through and are at this moment gathering their strength to throw against them. We must hurry before it is too late. Jetta, I want you to remain here as a safeguard against any intrusion; I believe that you may yet save us from oblivion. Trust me and have faith in yourself; do as I ask and we may yet prevail.'

Urim steadied Jetta by placing a firm hand on his shoulder and looking earnestly into his black eyes. Jetta wanted to go with them; he felt that he should be fighting alongside of them as opposed to standing idly by at the other side of the land. Once Urim and the others departed, the portal would close and there would be no way of him being able to help them at the Tower. Nevertheless, in his brief time with Urim, he felt that he could trust him and so reluctantly agreed to wait; to guard the keystone and ensure that it was not used by the wizards or any who aided them.

Terra, Liam and Emerald stood their ground, defying the wizards to overcome them. Emrys saw that there were only three of them and he could not resist a taunt.

'So you believe that we are of so little significance that just three of you face us. Well we shall see about that.' Bringing the rod in front of him he sent a great beam of dark light that sliced through the air at Terra. He was prepared for the strike because it hit his protective shield and withstood the torrent of negative energy that tore at it in an effort to destroy him.

The other wizards were not a whit behind their leader and they too sent their own attacks against Liam and Emerald. They had a tougher time maintaining their shields as they were targeted by two wizards each but again the power beneath the Tower was strong enough to fend off the deadly forces unleashed by the dark figures.

Emrys laughed as he toyed with Terra, leaving his fellow wizards to deal with the other two seers. 'Ha! You have underestimated me I think. This will be a pleasure I have looked forward to for a very long time.'

Gathering his negative power in an effort to smite Terra and eradicate him from the face of the land, Emrys felt the build up of energy he was tapped into through the conduit back to his prison world of Magog. He held back from releasing the strike, increasing the intensity of the power he held at his command.

He was distracted from his intent at the crucial moment when he was to have let the raw energy rip across the courtyard at Terra. A bright light flashed at the corner of his vision and he saw Urim with two more seers step out of thin air. Emrys released the pent up energy but it lacked precision because of the distraction so Terra was able to defend against it and quickly sent a bolt of red energy at the wizard. Emrys had to move fast so he brought the Rod up in front of him for protection and it absorbed the impact of Terra's strike.

Liam and Emerald were trying to defend themselves from a constant barrage, first from one and then another of the wizards giving them no chance to level a blow at them in return. The wizards would have succeeded before too long in cutting through their defences had not the others arrived when they did.

The tide had turned in their favour now. Six seers against five wizards meant that they could challenge them more effectively. Working as a team they combined their powers to enable four of them to defend from the blasts sent against them whilst Terra and Urim were able to direct stabbing and probing assaults against one or another of the wizards.

Emrys rallied the others into merging their strikes into one, controlling and throwing each blast at the seers by the Rod that he wielded. The contest was one of a battle of wills more than one of power. The Rod gave the wizards some advantage over the seers but having one extra person than the wizards, the seers were a match for anyone. Were they strong enough to defeat the wizards? That would become apparent soon enough.

The smell of discharged energy filled the courtyard as blasts and surges of power were sent cracking and ripping between the duelling wizards and seers. From outside the Tower, anyone watching would have seen a brilliant display of coloured lights flashing and dancing up into the air, only for them to fizzle out and disappear into the early morning sky.

The battle was at it's fiercest as both sides attempted to dislodge the other from their world. Terra and Urim targeted one of the wizards and kept a constant barrage of bolts, blasts and blows hammering against her until she was so enraged at being singled out by them that she dropped her defensive role among the wizards and concentrated her maddened mind on hitting back at them.

It was the break that the seers had been waiting for. Before the wizard could send any form of attack against her protagonists, Urim had unleashed a peculiar white globe of light that smashed into the wizard, cutting through the defences as if they did not exist. The light extinguished and the wizard had gone. There were only four of them now to face the seers but Emrys would not be swayed by this change in events. He was determined that this was the time that they would finally rid themselves of the ones he held accountable for their woes.

Urim had been instructed by Terra before the battle commenced that if the opportunity presented itself; he was to use the portal to send one or more of them back to Magog. Urim had seized his chance and successfully managed to open the portal enough to use it against the wizards.

Far from being discouraged by the loss of one of their number, it only seemed to intensify the rage and ferocity of the attacks against the seers. Recovering from their setback they changed their way of working together and intensified their defensive shield so that the seers were unable to penetrate it with the portal again. Urim tried but was unable to have any effect against the newly increased defences. A new strategy had to be developed by the seers if they were achieve any further hits against the wizards, not only in defending themselves but in being able to penetrate the force that surrounded them.

For some time neither side scored any amount of success and it appeared that a stalemate had been reached. Emrys saw that the seers were unable to dislodge them and he knew that he and the other wizards could not achieve what he wanted against them. It called for a better approach to the battle and he knew just what to do about it. He allowed the shield around them to weaken, just enough to give the seers a belief that they were at last beginning to get through.

The tactics being employed by Terra and Urim seemed to be wearing the wizards down as they would score a hit every now and then against one or other of the wizards. It was not all going their way however as a sudden attack upon them by Emrys sent a blinding bolt of power at them. Liam was hit and burned by the flash of power that had mostly been dissipated by their defences. A residue of the blast had managed to filter through and had caught the old elf on his shoulder causing him to cry out in pain and falter momentarily. Terra saw the danger as their shield began to buckle from the intensity of the wizards' continuous lashing whips of raw energy. He changed from his attacking role in order to assist the other seers and to assess Liam's injury, leaving Urim to fling bolts of blue power at Emrys. Liam had been burned and was in pain but he nodded to Terra that he was still able to fight and resumed his part in the affray.

Emerald, disturbed and angered by the hurt inflicted upon the old elf, remembered the gift that Queen Ella had given her. She produced the silver bell from her robe and shook it. No sound was emitted. The scene went quiet as the noise of the battle subsided into silence, as if a great blanket had been thrown over them.

Moments later a lone sprite appeared and stood in a halo of light beyond the darkness of the wizards. The bell had rung and summoned Emerald, original sprite-seer to bear that title, from beyond the barrier between life and death. She smiled and nodded in greeting towards Emerald. She raised her hands, weaving them in an intricate pattern before her, and unleashed a pulse of energy that struck the wizards from behind catching them unawares. The forces that the wizards were summoning through their dark portal shuddered and faltered in their intensity as the other worldly energy was disrupted in its flow.

Seeing the advantage that it had given them and angered by the hurt inflicted on his oldest friend, Terra gritted his teeth and gripped his staff with a new determination. 'Urim, touch your staff to mine.' Without stopping to ask why, Urim did as he was asked by the leader of the Council and the two staves seemed to become as one. A huge surge of red and blue power ripped through the air and sliced through the defence shield catching two of the wizards full on. They screamed in agony as the positive energy that came from beneath the Tower slammed into them.

They were unable to participate any further in this battle. Emrys knew that they were beaten and raised the Rod of Retribution high above his head. With a shout filled with anger and despair three of the wizards disappeared, Emrys had sent them back to Magog to lick their wounds and count the cost of their defeat.

For millennia Emrys had harboured his hatred of the seers; he had come so close to achieving his revenge but he knew now that he would not prevail. With the appearance of the sprite behind them and the combined efforts of the seers, Emrys knew that he would not prevail.

'You have beaten us this time Terra but there will be an accounting between you and I and it will be sooner rather than later.' Bringing the Rod down with a sweeping movement he was wrapped in a black cloud and disappeared from sight.

The seers sank to the floor exhausted by the encounter, thankful that it was now all over, they had beaten off the wizards for the second time in just a few weeks. This time they hoped that it would be much longer before they saw them again. They were grateful for the timely assistance from the spirit of the first Emerald Crystal-gazer, who had responded to the call of Emerald's bell. When the Wizards had gone she waved farewell and disappeared from sight.

Something troubled Urim and he chewed his lip with concern, worried that he was missing something important. Leaping to his feet and making the others jump, he shouted. 'Emrys; he didn't go back to Magog; he's still here.'

'What do you mean Urim?' Terra queried the trusted seer.

'When the others went there was no cloud, they simply vanished, much as one would with the portal, but when Emrys disappeared he did so in a cloud. He did not go back; he is still in our world. I must go to Anram.' Without saying any more and before Terra could insist that he go with him, Urim had used the portal and been transported away.

Jetta was engaged in a fight for his survival. Urim had guessed right in that Emrys had not gone back to Magog but had used the connection between the keystone at Anram and the shaft at Seers Tower. What Emrys hoped to gain he did not know but he was glad that he had left Jetta guarding the way.

The air was already filled with the smell of burning from spent energy bursts as the two combatants wrestled to gain control over the other. It looked to Urim as if Jetta had been acquitting himself well against the leader of the wizards as Emrys had been burned by the fire of Jetta's magic. Obviously it had come as a surprise to him that anyone should be waiting here to guard against just such an eventuality.

Urim waited, trying to judge if Jetta needed his assistance or not. He did not wish to interfere and take the reward of victory away from him but neither did he want to have Jetta come to any harm.

The contest appeared to be pretty evenly matched as Jetta's dark magic must have been quite a shock to the already battle weary wizard. What Urim did observe though was that Jetta seemed to be unable to gain any further advantage over Emrys. The wizard was using the Rod in such a way that he was gaining control over Jetta, just as Ebon had ruled the dark angel through the rod, so Emrys was exerting all his will into Jetta's domination. Soon he would succeed and then, no doubt, Emrys would turn his new slave against the seer and Urim would then have to enter a battle with the dark magic that Jetta would be forced, unwillingly, to level against the seer.

For Jetta to be subverted in such a way was unthinkable and could not be allowed to happen; as much for his own sake as for that of the seers, Urim had to intervene. He had to prevent Jetta from falling under the control of the Rod. There was nothing for it but to prevent that from happening. Acting almost with instinct Urim leaped into the affray, using his staff as a cudgel he brought it down hard on the forearm of the wizard. He had not expected this physical attack and he yelled in pain, dropping the Rod to the ground. Seizing the initiative, Jetta lunged forward and caught the wizard in a grip of iron, holding his arms pinned to his sides. Jetta looked at Urim and smiled. 'Thank you Urim for showing me who I am. I am content to have been of service to the seers but I fear that I must leave you now; good-bye.'

Closing his eyes a net of dark magic spun around the two of them as Jetta held tightly to Emrys who shouted out in fear. 'No, no, stop him; don't let him do this to me.'

With the sound of the rushing of air, the net collapsed and they were gone. All that remained was a circular black mark that covered the keystone; it seemed to be alive somehow as flashes of power could be seen moving within its pool like surface. Urim stood alone in the silence of the chamber; he guessed that Jetta had taken Emrys back to Magog, which was Jetta's home world.

The pool of dark liquid that covered the keystone intrigued him and he wondered whether Jetta was now free of the dark magic which had controlled him. He hoped not because Emrys and the other wizards would show him no mercy; without the protection of the magic to save him he would be made to suffer horribly.

Chapter 37

Seers Tower

The approach to Seers Tower is always one that is filled with awed anticipation for anyone who has not seen it before. How one feels about it is dependent on the purpose of that visit. If it is with good intentions in your hearts then there is only happiness and joy at the sight of it. If, however, there is a shadow within, trying to deceive, then the experience will be an unhappy one.

Jon recalled seeing it for the very first time from the coach window with Anna last year; there had been a thrill inside that exceeded his expectations. Anna had seen the Tower before he did as they peered out of the coach window and through the trees. They had both looked at it with wide eyes and open mouths; Jon recalled that he felt the hairs on the back of his neck stiffen when he laid eyes on it.

The Tower sat upon a stub of rock, surrounded by the cold, black water of the lake and was guarded by the Hammerhead Heights. It was an impressive sight as it soared into the sky, topped by pinnacles on each of its eight towers. Jon felt the tingle of anticipation now as he had then and as it came into view, that same thrill ran through him as he looked at it from the window of his coach.

'Not long now, Jon before your wish is fulfilled and you see inside.' Hamill smiled as he watched his friend's excitement play across his face.

'I will never tire of seeing it, Hamill; it is such a beautiful building.'

'Yes it is, to those of a good heart who wish to see it but there are others that would feel only dread and foreboding.'

Jon thought on his friend's words for a moment, he chewed at his lip then he shrugged his shoulders and let out a sigh in sorrow. 'I suppose that may be the case with someone like Ebon who had rejected it, or Amethyst who knew the threat that it was to her ambition to rule. I think that it's sad that they should feel that way about it but I think I can see why they might.'

The coaches halted at the end of the track where there was a turning point for the coaches. It was but a short walk to the landing stage where the flat wooden ferry was tethered and Jon jumped onto the grassy meadow with eagerness and anticipation. He was brought up short in his enthusiasm as he realised that this is where the tragic story of Tracker's death had unfolded. It was with mixed emotions then that he surveyed the scene before him as shadows from the past flittered across his mind.

Bringing his vision back to the present Jon noticed that Hamill too looked as if he was reliving those moments and their eyes met. A moment of silence descended on the two of them that was broken when Jon smiled at his friend and they clasped hands in a token of understanding for each others thoughts. Standing there alongside his friend he was overcome with a strong feeling of coming home.

There was little to hold his interest back in Ashbrooke since Anna had gone. He could see her and be with her in his dreams no matter where he was but for him to return home again after all he had been through would be a hard thing for him to do. A bond had developed between him and Hamill that he did not want to end and he feared that time was drawing in on him. So it was that his feelings were a mixture of both joy and dread.

They were all grateful to be able to stretch their aching bodies from the cramps that always accompanied a coach journey of any duration. Jon remembered the last coach trip here, that had lasted for three days and he was glad that this one had only been for a few hours. Braun climbed down from the driver's seat and ran his fingers through his hair in an effort to put it back into some semblance of order; the problem was that it never had been neat in the first place. It was a bush of red curls that had frayed and his beard matched it perfectly. Jon could not imagine him looking anything other than he did; it would just not be the Braun he had come to respect and appreciate.

The dwarves all clambered out of the second coach, taking care as they jumped down onto the ground, there smaller legs having difficulty with the gaps in-between the treads of the steps. They too were impressed by the Tower, especially Digger and Mason who had not seen it before. They stood there pointing across the water at the Tower that sat on the rock in the middle of the lake. A standard was raised on the flagpole and the sound of a horn reverberated across the stillness of the meadow they stood in.

'They honour you my friends and welcome you to Seers Tower.' Hamill explained, grinning with pleasure. 'Come; let us cross the lake and meet with the rest of the seers; no doubt they will all be here by now and eager to see you.'

They filed down to the ferry platform and it wobbled as they walked onto it; Hamill steadied himself and Jon held on to him as much to support himself as to help his friend. Braun took hold of the chain that ran through the metal eyes attached to the ferry's posts waiting for them all to stand on the platform and for the signal to begin pulling. Pulleys fixed to the tethering posts on opposite sides of the lake enabled the work of hauling the ferry across to be easier. At Hamill's signal the metal-master pulled and the chain clanked noisily through the guides. The platform began to ease across the dark water and they lurched backwards, steadying themselves against the sudden movement towards the Tower and whatever awaited them there.

'I must remember to suggest that we install handrails for folk to hold on to.' Hamill commented quietly, holding his head as if it were swimming.

'Are you alright Hamill?' Jon asked, seeing how his friend reacted to the unstable craft.

'I will be fine once we have reached the other side; it's the movement across the water; it always unsettles my stomach.'

'Oh!' Jon said; understanding Hamill's discomfort after seeing how he had suffered on board the ship.

Two seers stood at the other side of the lake on the landing stage beneath the imposing walls and defences of the Tower waiting to greet them. Jon recognised Urim straight away and he had to restrain himself from waving excitedly; instead he simply put up a hand in welcome. Urim smiled and did the same in response. The other seer also signalled a greeting to them all. Jon supposed that, as the seer was a dwarf, that it was Terra Standfast who had come in person to see them safely onto the rock of The Tower.

Hamill alighted first and Terra hugged him tightly, there was a tear in his eye and he held him between his outstretched arms. 'Welcome back dear Hamill; I cannot tell you how grateful I am to have you safely with us once again. We will talk about your experiences later.' Turning to Jon the dwarf reached towards him with an outstretched hand in welcome. 'You must be Jon; I have heard so much about you and I'm glad to meet you at last.'

Glancing between Jon and Urim as if comparing them, he nodded and smiled. 'Yes, I can see the link between you, it is unmistakable. Please, all of you come with us and we will show you our home. I hope that you are hungry because we have prepared a meal for you.'

Terra led them up the slope and through the defensive gates, across the double drawbridge and into the courtyard. Urim stepped alongside Jon and placed a reassuring hand on his shoulder. Jon could see the joy within Urim's eyes, that he was glad to have him here. 'I can not express how pleased I am that you will at last be able to tread where we seers do and to join with them in one of the most sacred procedures; induction into the Council of Seers.'

Jon gulped his emotions down past a lump in his throat. I too am more than happy to be allowed to be here and to see you again, Urim.' Jon thought it odd that Urim had called the ceremony for the new Auger an induction; he had thought it was called an inauguration where the newcomer actually becomes the seer and not just a novice.

His mind didn't dwell on it for long as he was too wrapped with taking in the sights of the Tower. He could hardly breathe as his heart leaped and pounded the blood through his ears. He walked automatically and missed seeing the shaft in the courtyard; he only remembered crossing the threshold of the dining room having been in a kind of mental fog until then. He was asked if he wanted something to eat but he could not tell who it was that had asked; he just nodded his head dumbly as he smiled awkwardly.

They were all seated at a large table in the food hall that had been decorated especially to mark their safe return. The catering staff tended to all of their needs and supplied them with choices of different foods that they could select from the platters that were offered. The sounds of voices gradually impinged upon his senses and took shape; the fog that had enveloped him for the past few moments began to dissipate. The excitement of actually being here in Seers Tower had robbed him of any sense of reality and he was uncertain as to whether he was hungry or not.

Everyone was in a buoyant mood as their drinking vessels were drained and refilled almost instantly by the ever attendant staff. Jon saw that his friends were tucking into a rich choice of foods and he decided that he was hungry after all so he piled his plate up with the things he liked most.

Hamill had, as expected, helped himself to the most and was halfway through his first plateful and looking eagerly at what to have next. Jon thought that it was a wonder that he was so slim considering his appetite. The others were also making the most of the fare that was placed before them and a great party atmosphere permeated the room.

Terra Standfast stood with a cup raised and called for silence. It took a few moments for the noise to subside as the dwarves were behaving like a gaggle of schoolboys but they eventually controlled their joviality for Terra's sake.

'Thank you all for enabling us to honour you in a small way for the gallant work you have done in overcoming not just Amethyst the witch-queen, but Ebon as well. We understand that Urim was much involved throughout and we are all indebted to his influence. Without him we seers would all still be held captive behind Ebon's energy barrier and the land would be a far bleaker place. I therefore wish to raise a toast to you all but in particular, to Urim.'

They all stood and raised their tankards, taking a deep draft before settling down to resume their feasting.

'There is one dampener to our celebrations and that is the loss of my dear friend Auger Wind-rider; so I would like to make a final toast in remembrance of his name. I know that it will live on when his replacement is inaugurated tomorrow.'

They all stood and sombrely drank to his name.

'There is one final thing that I must say to you before I take my seat in the council chamber and allow you to continue with your meal. I am afraid that the drinking will have to be curtailed as we must begin the process of choosing the one to take the place of our dear friend, Auger. I therefore call upon all the seers to convene in the central chamber in a full turn of the hand. My secretary will invite each dwarf to attend us there in order to assess which of you will be staying here at the Tower, not as a guest but as the new Auger wind-rider.'

Silence descended on them as the impact of what Terra had said settled upon them, especially the dwarves who eyed each other nervously. The seers left the room to prepare for their meeting leaving the band of friends alone, quietened by the import of what was to take place later. Terra put his arm around Hamill as they walked. 'I understand that another of the dwarves is still in Seaview and is expected to take some time to heal from his wounds?'

'Yes; that's right. I left Leader in the capable hands of one of the elf physicians.'

'Well, what I propose is that we bring him here by means of the wind. If you would give me Auger's talisman, I will need to pass it on to his replacement. In the meantime I have asked Urim to bring Leader here by means of his new staff so that he too can see what happens here. I am sure that he would want to be with his fellow dwarves and be a part of it.'

Hamill smiled and nodded as he handing Auger's talisman to Terra. It was of no use to him now anyway as it had ceased to work for him. Once the new Auger had been installed and used it, the talisman would once again be open for limited use by the other seers. Mason had already passed Auger's staff over to Terra and he was glad to be relieved of the responsibility though a little sad to see it go, not that he could or would have used it.

When the seers had all left the room Archer leaned across and caught Javelin's attention. 'I suppose that it would be a little premature to offer my congratulations to you, Javelin.' He gave his friend a quick dig in the ribs with his elbow.

'I think that it is indeed, especially as I believe that Trapper will be the one to be chosen.'

'What? I happen to agree with Archer; I think that you will be chosen.' Trapper threw the speculation back into the air.

'Yes, we agree, Javelin is the obvious choice to be the one.' The other dwarves spoke up in support of the unofficial nomination.'

Braun entered the debate as he changed the direction of the conjecture to centre on the injured dwarf they had left behind in Seaview. 'But it could just as easily be one of you, or even Leader. I overheard Terra talking with Hamill when they left and Urim is going to bring Leader here by means of his staff.'

The dwarves fell silent and Javelin ended the debate by saying. 'There is no point in us throwing names into a hat so to speak; we shall just have to wait and see who the seers choose. Whoever it is I don't envy them one little bit.'

All the other dwarves nodded their heads in agreement with Javelin and sat in silence for a while.

Jon had to say something; his heart was full of emotion as he had come to love these amazing dwarves like brothers. 'Well, I wouldn't want to be the one to choose who it would be; I think you all have merit and each and every one of you has shown yourselves to be valiant and courageous. Without you, none of us would be here today; you have saved our lives on more than one occasion and I for one feel privileged to know you and to call you friends.'

'Here, here.' Braun applauded the comment.

Javelin sat forward in his seat, his hands clasped firmly in front of him on the table. 'Brothers; it would appear that one of us is to be chosen as a seer and will no longer walk with us when we leave this place. I suggest that we sit around the fire together and light our pipes for one last time before the next Auger Wind-rider is chosen.'

They all nodded in silence and moved across to the fireplace on the other side of the hall. They sat in a semi-circle, toasting their feet in front of the flames as their pipes began to emit the foul smelling smoke that hung heavily around them. Jon and Braun did not join them, not because of the smoke from their pipes; it was more as a respect for their need to be together for one last time. Realising that this was a solemn moment, they decided that they would ask where their rooms were so that they could clean up after their journey to the Tower. Jon bathed and lay on the cot in his room, wrapped in a towel cloak. He felt well fed and the cot had the softest mattress he had ever come across and within a blink of an eye, he was asleep.

In the council chamber, Hamill sat in discussion with the other seers trying to determine who would be the best choice from the six dwarves to stand in Auger's stead. Urim had returned with Leader who had been made as comfortable as possible.

Terra turned to the keeper of the golden tome for the name that they needed. 'Your input would be invaluable Urim if you would tell us who the new Auger is to be.'

'Unfortunately, I am unable to give you his name; the decision must come from the united voice of the Council of the Sight. Hamill and I have had a close association with these dwarves but Hamill's input particularly would be of assistance to you because he has walked with them more than I have.'

'Very well then, we shall do this by the time honoured means of selection. Ask Javelin to come in will you Eldrid.' Terra signalled to his secretary who exited the chamber and came back momentarily with the courageous dwarf. It must be noted that Javelin, who was by far the most battle seasoned of the dwarves, would rather have faced the Smarg at Deadline Crack single handed than to have been subjected to the nerves he felt at this moment in time.

He sat in a chair that had been brought in and was suited for his size. Nervously tugging at his beard, he looked into the eyes of the seers as if they were about to tie him up and offer him as a sacrifice. Hamill smiled at him and Urim nodded in encouragement but he still sat frozen with fear.

The other dwarves, who were seated outside in the antechamber waiting their turn to be assessed, were fraught with uncertainty and fear. Fear of being chosen to become something that none of them felt worthy or ready to become. Who would have thought before they set out on this journey that one of them would end up becoming a seer? Certainly none of them; their thoughts skipped between thinking of Auger and his unexpected loss and the huge responsibility that one of them would shoulder before the day was done.

A half turn of the hand passed and the doors to the chamber opened; Javelin came out wiping the sweat from his brow and he smiled at his companions in relief that it was over. He did not know whether or not he would be selected but he rather hoped that he would not. The thought of not fighting the gnomes with his comrades and of not being free to return to his beloved home at Ffridd-Uch-Ddu saddened him; besides the others were far more suited to the task. He was a warrior, not a diplomat.

Javelin collapsed into a chair with the other dwarves as they sat in the antechamber waiting their turn. One by one they all went through the same questions that Javelin had done and by mid afternoon all of the dwarves had been in to be examined by the seers. They had tried to make the assessments as pleasant as possible but as the dwarves all knew the importance of the meeting it had been a challenge that none of them had enjoyed.

They were glad, in a strange kind of way, to have experienced it; there are very few who get to sit in front of the Council of the Sight on such an important issue. Despite their reservations and nerves, they all agreed that it would be worthy of a song and it would conclude with the name of the one that would be chosen.

Braun had been treated to a tour of the Tower's workshops whilst the process was taking place and he was amazed and pleasantly surprised at the number and size of the forges. He would never have believed that it was possible to have had all that he saw within the walls of the Tower. He saw it through new eyes and he was impressed.

Chapter 38

The Council of the Sight

The Council deliberated for some time before deciding that it would be advisable to hear more about the dwarves. Following the advice of both Urim and Hamill, Terra instructed Eldrid to invite Jon to join with them; he would be able to provide some important insights into their characters and abilities. They had to make a choice and they had eliminated four of the dwarves from their selection list. Not that they were unsuitable, rather it was only because there were two they had decided would be best suited for the role. The decision had not been easy as every aspect had to be taken into account; hence the reason for inviting Jon to join them. He may have information that might appear to be insignificant to him but could sway their decision one way or another.

Jon entered the chamber and was taken aback by the spectacular wooden carvings of the ornate panels. The chamber was a magnificent place; his eyes were drawn upwards to the roof that was supported by eight stone columns with eight beams that stretched towards the centre of the room. From them more beams curved upwards and over in huge arcs meeting in the centre where an octagonal lantern shaped tower allowed light to enter, casting streams of light down onto the great octagonal table. The seers were all seated on large, carved wooden thrones at their designated places; their names were carved into the backs of each throne. Jon noticed that Hamill's chair had a new nameplate inserted. That would have been because Ebon's name would have needed replacing due to the change in name for his position. Terra sat upon a throne with a canopy overhead and Jon supposed that it was to denote his leadership of the council.

'Welcome Jon of Ashbrooke, we are pleased to welcome you to our council.' Terra smiled and spoke kindly to him, indicating for him to sit on the vacant seat that would soon be filled by one of the dwarves.

Jon nervously looked at Urim, who stood next to Terra Standfast and he gave Jon a nod and smile of encouragement. Jon felt very awkward sitting at the seers table; all of them were in attendance, having returned from their assignments. To the left of Terra sat Liam, then on his left was Emerald who was on Jon's right. Next to Jon sat Hamill, then Elise, Eden and finally Urim who stood behind his chair.

Jon had to swallow to moisten his dry throat; he felt so small and insignificant amongst these great folk who held the destiny of the land in their hands. For him to be here in such a company was truly a privilege and he would remember this day for the rest of his life.

Urim must have noticed that he was thirsty because he offered him a drink of water.

'Yes please; that would be nice; I am feeling a little thirsty.'

Eldrid placed a glass of cold, clear, refreshing spring water in front of him which he lifted in shaking hands to quench his thirst. Having done so, and leaving half of it for later, he looked sheepishly at Terra, waiting for the questions to be asked that he knew would help them decide which of the dwarves would be chosen to follow in Auger's footsteps. All six dwarves flashed through his mind and he was glad that he did not have to choose who it would be.

Terra clasped his hands in front of him and smiled. 'Thank you again for being here to help us in our deliberations as to who we should choose to become the new Auger Wind-rider. I hasten to add that you will not have to make any decisions. All we require is your input on what you know of each of them. Your knowledge could be of significance to us in our decision. So if you are happy with that we would like to ask you some questions about each one of them; I believe that you have all grown close over the time you have been together?'

'Oh yes indeed; I value their friendship and camaraderie. Many times they have saved our lives, often at great risk to themselves. I am certain that we would have failed in our efforts had they not been with us.'

'Who would you say stands out from them all?' Liam asked.

'That's a very difficult thing to say. Each one of them has had times when our safety has depended upon their actions. From the very first time we met at Foundry Smelt, Javelin has guided us throughout with his experience and determination. He and Archer have such a good rapport and work well together. Archer has a steady hand and a modest nature; his sense of humour has kept us amused when things were going against us. Trapper has developed an understanding of folk. Losing Tracker last year and then having to deal with Gemon's loss was difficult for him but he has shown himself to be resilient in the face of danger.'

'Ah yes, we heard a little about Gemon. What can you tell us about that situation?' Eden asked.

Jon went on to tell the seers about the dwarf and how he had been born of mixed parenthood; of the fears they had had about him. Jon told of Trapper's determination to apprehend him followed by the reversal of his feelings and the bond that had existed between them at the end. Other things Jon related to the council about each of the dwarves; of Digger's bravery and gallantry in rescuing Mason from the underground river caves; of Leader's courage in fighting against Amethyst and of Mason's faithfulness.

Throughout all of his revelations the seers sat and nodded wisely, sometimes raising an eyebrow at something he disclosed and at other times smiling at the antics of the dwarves. What did come across to them all was the deep friendship that had developed between them all and of the bond that would last throughout their lives.

The questions ceased and they all sat looking studious. Their eyes turned towards Terra and they nodded at him when he caught their attention. All had, it seemed, reached a decision about who was to be the next Auger.

'Now then Jon; you have told us a great deal about the dwarves and Hamill has informed us of the stalwart efforts of the metal-master. Is there anything else that you can think of to say about your experiences that would merit our attention?' Terra cocked an eyebrow and smiled warmly.

Jon did have something to say and that was to inform them of the promise Auger had made to a young lad named Cameron and his friend Elliot. That he would bring them to Seers Tower for a visit. Jon explained briefly that the lad had been extremely helpful to them. What Jon omitted to say was the reason why Auger had made that promise. He wanted to spare Hamill's blushes.

'Thank you Jon, we will ensure that the matter is dealt with and the promise fulfilled by the new Auger. Is there anything else you think might be worthy of mention?'

Jon sat chewing his lip for a moment before a light flooded his expression and he looked mischievously at Hamill then leaned forward. 'Yes there is. I daresay that Hamill has omitted to tell you of his part in all of this; so I would like to tell you of the struggles and the successes he has achieved since the time I have known him.'

'That would be most enlightening, thank you Jon.' Terra nodded with satisfaction and settled back in his chair to listen to what Jon had to say.

Hamill started to protest saying that none of this had any relevance to what was being discussed at present. Terra overruled him and the other seers agreed that what Jon had to say was very relevant to what they needed to discuss further.

With a gleam in his eye and a grin on his face, Jon glanced at Hamill who was sitting with his arms crossed over his chest and a scowl on his face. He drilled a look into Jon that spoke volumes. Hamill did not like himself being the centre of attention; besides, he felt awkward about all the mistakes he had made along the way.

Jon began to unfold to the council all that he had observed of Hamill's progression, starting from when they had met at the Spotted Cow Tavern in Foundry Smelt. Jon told them of his increasing abilities and strength, of the way in which he had led them against Amethyst right up to the way in which he had dealt with the ghost-wizards in Anram and his protective nature when there was trouble around them. The only thing he did not talk about was Sylvia; he thought that too personal and not significant to the discussion.

Having put before them the account of their journeys, Jon sat back and took a large gulp of water. The room was silent for a while as they digested the information. Then Terra stood and the rest of them followed suit. He looked straight at Hamill and began to applaud him. One by one the others joined in and Jon beamed with delight as he too applauded his friend. Hamill looked rather abashed and wriggled uncomfortably in his seat, inspecting his shoes and wiping at his face with his sleeve.

Terra sat and waited for the applause to stop before saying to Jon. 'We are indebted to you for your report and are pleased to know that our young seer acquitted himself well in the face of such determined efforts to disrupt the stability of the land. We can see that without his faithfulness and diligence, we would not be here today and the Council of the Sight would perhaps no longer exist. We are all grateful to have you as a brother seer Hamill. Now seeing as Jon has embarrassed you in recounting to us tales of your achievements; would you like to tell us about his?'

Hamill grinned and looking at Jon said that nothing would give him greater pleasure. Jon's face dropped and a look of panic filled his expression. He, like Hamill had done, started to protest but Terra held up a hand to quash his appeals and encouraged Hamill to commence. Looking to Urim for moral support, the seer simply shrugged his shoulders and smiled.

Hamill grinned then looked at Jon and winked. Jon realised that Hamill was finally going to get his revenge on him for the time he had laughed at Hamill's embarrassment when Jon had introduced Sylvia to him back at the Ward. Hamill relished the moment and took great pleasure in expounding the qualities of his friend. Jon wondered at times whether he was actually talking about him with all the praise he was heaping on him but Hamill only told the truth. Jon just did not recognise it as being so. All of their travels and experiences together were retold, leaving nothing out except the things that Jon had thought but never shared with anyone else.

The seers sat listening intently to what Hamill had to say; occasionally an eyebrow would twitch or a smile would spread across their faces but all Jon wanted to do was to curl up under his chair and only come out when everyone had gone. Eventually Hamill concluded his remarks and Jon was treated to a round of applause just as Hamill had done. Urim held his hand across his eyes as he looked at his feet; it appeared that the telling of Jon's exploits had affected him deeply.

Terra stayed standing when the others had taken their seats again. 'Well, Jon; it would appear that you have been faithful in all of your actions.' Terra looked at Urim briefly then back to Jon. Urim has informed me that we owe you a debt of gratitude but I had not realised just how much. I fear that he underplayed your importance in these events so I am grateful to Hamill for telling us these things. Now if you would excuse us, we must decide on who is to replace Auger.'

Jon stood up and whilst turning to leave, gave Hamill a scowl; Hamill just continued to grin. When the door closed behind Jon as he exited the chamber, Terra added. 'My fellow seers, there is also the matter of what to do concerning our brother-seer and dear friend Urim; I suggest that we consider what we have heard as we make our final preparations.'

Jon met up with Braun who had just returned from his tour of the Tower. He was deep in thought and had clearly been impressed by what he had seen. The two of them did not have very long to exchange news of their experiences of the afternoon as Eldrid emerged from the chamber and sought out Braun.

'Metal-master; the seers would be grateful if you could accompany me to the chamber. They wish to speak with you on a matter of some importance.'

Bewildered as to why the seers would want to see him; Braun followed the elderly secretary into the chamber and a meeting with destiny.

Braun stood dumbfounded, unable to speak because he was so shocked at what he had heard.

'You are offering me a place here at the Tower, to work in the forges as the overseer? I hardly know what to say.'

'Yes, would be the answer we would all like to hear but the decision is of course up to you. We realise that you must miss your home in Foundry Smelt and acknowledge the work you have done in building the channels of communication between the colossi and the rest of the land. In particular we are grateful for the way in which you have offered your services in the successful completion of the tasks that were undertaken by Urim and Hamill. Without your strength and skills, we would have failed in our attempts to secure peace in the land. You are much appreciated and we wish for you to join us here at the Tower in our battle to maintain peace and harmony in the land. You are, of course, free to visit with the colossi or your home at any time and for however long you wish, but we offer you a permanent place here.'

Braun stood open mouthed but managed to gather his wits to respond. 'I would love to accept your kind invitation. There is nowhere I would rather be than here and to continue my association with Hamill and whichever dwarf you will choose as the next Auger. I accept your offer gladly.'

Terra smiled; he had feared that the big metal-master would not agree to stay, so Braun's acceptance was a visible relief to him. Looking at the other seers with a questioning look, he asked for their permission to share with Braun the results of their deliberations and to tell him the outcome. They all agreed and invited Braun to stay whilst they issued the call to one of the dwarves to become a seer and to sit in council with them as the new Auger Wind-rider.

The dwarves all stood nervously in front of the Council of the Sight; their discussions were over and it was time to reveal their decision. Braun stood to the side with his hands behind his back as though he was concealing something, smiling at the dwarves he had come to appreciate and respect. Jon had also been invited in to witness the call being issued to the dwarves; he was almost as nervous as they were.

Terra Standfast, as leader of the seers, approached the line of dwarves with outstretched arms and shook hands with them all. 'My fellow dwarves; whilst the occasion is a momentous one in the life of the one we have chosen it is also a sad one for us because of the loss of a dear friend. However we do not wish to dwell on that because you who are to join with us as his replacement will also become as dear a friend as he was. Our decision has been a rather difficult one due to the fact that there is merit in all of you and any one amongst you would have made an excellent choice as Auger's replacement. Finally, however, we are all in agreement. Having heard testimonials and weighed all the facts before us the one we invite to join with us as the latest in a long line of dwarves who have taken the mantle of the seers known as Auger, is Trapper. Will you accept?'

The other dwarves all crowded round the surprised dwarf and congratulated him; slapping him on the back and jostling him with excitement. Trapper was shocked and bewildered but when the recognition of what he had heard sunk in he smiled and his eyes misted. Quietly and nobly he nodded, unable to speak for the emotion that he felt. A cheer went up from the dwarves and from Jon and Braun. Trapper was swept off his feet and carried around the chamber on the shoulders of his friends as the others looked on and laughed, applauding the shocked dwarf.

Urim came forward to be the first of the seers to congratulate him; he had to wipe away a tear of joy in seeing Trapper accept the position.

When order had finally been restored, Terra cleared his throat to signify that he was to say something. The voices stilled and Terra announced that the inauguration would take place the very next day. Another cheer erupted from the band of friends and everyone in the room smiled. Terra signalled for silence again as he had not yet finished. 'You now know who is to replace Auger; what most of you do not know is that Braun has agreed to stay here with us and oversee the forges at the Tower.' There was a brief silence as what Terra had said filtered into their understanding before another great cheer was echoed around the room and it was Braun's turn to receive the attention of his friends.

'There is one final thing that remains to be announced. Urim would you like to make it?' Urim shook his head and signalled for Terra to continue. 'Very well then; what none of you know is that we are in need of creating a new novice to one of our seers.' Terra stopped momentarily and swallowed; his head bowed and he paused momentarily. Gathering himself together he continued. 'As I have said, we need to appoint a new novice to one of our seers and it has been agreed that Jon is to be that novice seer.'

Jon heard the announcement and recognised the name but did not associate it with himself. He did not quite register the words and when the others all whooped and cheered he did so as well, not realising what he was doing it for. When he became aware that his friends were congratulating *him* it finally struck home what Terra had said.

The room wobbled as his head went into a spin; he could feel the blood drain from his face as the shock hit him and his knees buckled. Had it not been for the dwarves lifting him up and carrying him around the chamber as they had Trapper, he would have collapsed onto the floor.

Finally when all the excitement had died down, Liam shook his hand and welcomed him to the Tower as the latest novice. 'I promise to help train you in all the arts that you will need to know in order to fulfil your role. I will not be alone in this however; the other seers, Terra included, will school you in the ways you are to follow.

Finally Urim managed to get to him and embraced him. 'I was right in what I said when we first met; that time will tell if you are ready, and it has. You are now ready to take on the role of a seer. The road you will travel will prepare the way ahead in achieving that which is ordained to be.

Chapter 39

Induction

Jon had not slept; he was too excited for that and had spent the night reflecting on the past year of his life. They had been the most enthralling and wonderful months that he could remember. True they had been filled with adventure and even danger but he would not have changed his experiences. They had forged him into the person he was today. The only thing he would change, if he were able to do so, would be to have Anna with him still. He treasured the rare moments that they had together and the conversations that they were able to have now that she could talk but it was not the same as having her with him.

He had hoped that she would have come to him last night but she had not. Their moments together were becoming less frequent and there were times, he had to admit, that he would gladly have stayed with her and not been awoken to his own world. Where she was reminded him of the sprite world as it was so beautiful and peaceful. As far as he knew there were never any rogue seers or witch-queens to trouble their quiet serenity. It was almost an exact opposite of where Ebon had been imprisoned. Jon had learned that the place where Ebon was held was called Magog; a world that was ruled by the wizards through fierce warlords who dealt out swift and merciless justice to all who dwelt there.

It made the times when he was with Anna that much more precious and he was grateful that she was happy where she was. He had asked her if she would come back with him, to the world she had known, if she had the choice and she had replied without hesitation that she would.

However she was unable to do so; she had been informed that something about where she was had altered her and she could only survive for a short period of time out of her world. Therefore she had to accept her condition and was content to remain there in her paradisiacal world.

Jon would have loved to have seen her more often and had tried on a few occasions, unsuccessfully, to contact her. It was almost as if being with her was like trying to get into the sprite realm; the more one tried, the harder it was to obtain. Perhaps it was meant to be this way because if Anna had not been taken by the energy barrier, he would have stayed with her. He would not have accepted the call to serve as a member of the Council of the Sight.

Jon wondered how it had been with Urim; if he really was his father, but he could not understand this one thing; if he had truly loved his mother, why had he not returned to be with her instead of becoming a seer. It had caused Jon some difficulty in the way he viewed Urim and he had struggled to come to terms with the way things were. Jon believed that if he had been faced with the same decision, he would have abandoned any idea of becoming a seer if it meant that he could have been with the girl he loved.

It still seemed surreal. Who would have possibly thought that he, Jon, would have become a seer? If someone had said to him a year ago, that he would be getting himself ready for his induction as a novice; he would have laughed in their face. Yet here he was, standing in a guest room at Seers Tower, preparing to do just that. He looked long and hard at his reflection and asked some searching questions of himself.

'Are you ready for this? Do you believe that you can be entrusted with the staff and talisman of a seer? Do you, Jon of Ashbrooke, really believe that you are capable of being like Liam, Urim and the others?'

He took a long hard look at himself and raised an eyebrow before straightening his shoulders and sighing. 'Well, you're here aren't you?'

He shook his head in disbelief as he turned his body this way and that so that he could view the robes of a seer that he was required to wear. He looked at his face. It had become thinner and his eyes had developed a dark intensity. It struck him just how much like Urim he was. The family resemblance was very pronounced now that he wore the mantle of a seer. True he would not become a real seer until he had completed his training and education but he would be one of them just the same. He would have all the powers that his office would demand and develop the ability to use them as needed.

Today was the day when he would discover who he was to be tutored by and who he was to replace. He had a pretty good idea. He reviewed in his mind the different members of the Council of the Sight. Terra Standfast; dwarf and acknowledged leader of the seers. It would not be him. It certainly won't be Hamill's office; he had only just taken over from Ebon. Neither would it be Eden Yield-keeper or Elise Saranya nor Emerald Crystal-gazer for they were all female seers. He knew that Auger would be replaced by Trapper and was to be the new Auger Wind-rider. That position was always held by a dwarf and it was usual for the replacement seer to be from the same background as the outgoing one so it had to be one of the dwarves.

That left Liam Card-reader, but he was an elf. Jon recalled his earlier thoughts about it, that Ebon had been a man but had been replaced by Hamill who was more elf than man. Maybe it would balance things out if Jon were to take over from an elf. The more he considered it the more convinced he was that he was right; he was to be apprenticed to Liam. Nothing else made sense. He felt surprisingly comfortable with the idea. He had not had anything to do with Liam as yet, other than to meet him when he had been presented to the Council of the Sight.

Jon had expected to have been inaugurated there and then just as they had with Hamill but Urim had explained that it had been a special case. Ebon had been removed from this world and there was a need to have his position filled quickly, whereas Jon was to take the place of an existing seer. That meant that he would pass through an initial induction ceremony and be admitted as a novice. He would not have the full powers and authority of the one he was to replace until he was inaugurated but he would have access to those abilities in order that he might learn how to control them. Urim had encouraged him to learn quickly.

Jon studied his reflection in the looking glass again and caught himself chewing nervously at his lower lip. He laughed and wondered whether it was a habit that would ever change. He guessed not because it was a nervous habit that Urim did from time to time. 'A family trait, no doubt,' he mused. Sighing heavily he disrobed and placed the mantle carefully on the special hanger. He would be ceremoniously robed at the time of his induction. It was strange but he felt naked and exposed without it, almost as if it were a part of him already. He felt as if he had always been meant to wear it.

A breeze wafted in from the open window and brought him out of his reverie. The sky was lightening and dawn was approaching; he could hear the birds as they began their dawn chorus, marking their boundaries with their songs. Soon he would be called upon to stand once more in front of the assembled seers, only this time it would be for the last time as an outsider. This was the last morning that would greet him as plain old Jon of Ashbrooke. Following the ceremony he would be an apprentice seer. His stomach knotted and he began to feel sick but he was not sure whether he was ill or just hungry. He decided that it was a little of hunger but mostly of nerves. He decided to go to the kitchen area and see if there was anything he could eat; if nothing else it would help to pass the time.

There was a comforting silence as he left his rooms, the warmth that pervaded the place settled his nerves and raised his awareness of his surroundings. The Tower was coming to life as the folk who tended to the running of the day to day affairs began to emerge from their quarters. It was as if he were becoming as one with the place. Gradually, as he descended from the upper levels, he heard the sounds of activity. He passed folk in the corridors laden with baskets of food for the kitchen or clothes that were probably being taken to the laundry.

The level of activity increased and soon there was a buzz about the place. When he met with others they would bow or curtsy and acknowledge him with a smile and a chirpy greeting. He would respond in a similar manner, feeling rather awkward and almost embarrassed at the attention he was receiving. He bumped into Hamill who was on his way to Jon's room.

'Good morning Jon. I was just on my way to see you. I thought that you might not be able to sleep in this morning so I thought we might have an early breakfast together. What do you say to that?'

'I'd say that sounds like a great idea. You're right about me not sleeping in; I haven't slept at all. It's been a very thought provoking night and what with the excitement of the ceremony today; I haven't felt the need for it.'

'I know exactly how you feel. I remember when I was given the responsibility of becoming a seer. I didn't sleep either but then I didn't have to wait until the next day. Urim had told me to wait outside of the chamber whilst he spoke with the Council and I had been there for what seemed ages as they debated my inauguration. It was all a bit of a blur as I remember. I was presented to the Council and I recall seeing them seated around the central table dressed in their ceremonial robes. It was quite a daunting experience.'

'Isn't it wonderful that Trapper is to be inaugurated to replace Auger? I think that I'm as excited about that as I am with my own induction.' Jon said, filled with excitement at the prospect of being in attendance at the ceremony.

'I was really pleased for him; now he can fight against oppression in a far greater way than if he was to remain a dwarf. Of course he will always be a dwarf but his existence will be enhanced after he officially becomes a seer.' Hamill added.

Jon thought on what Hamill had just said. 'What happens to you when you become a seer?' He asked, his curiosity getting the better of him.

'There is nothing that can describe it adequately; you don't feel any different at all but I have noticed an increased ability to carry out ordinary tasks. We are supposed to live a lot longer; barring accidents of course.' They both recalled how Auger had died and continued walking in silence.

Entering the kitchen area, the smell of the food confirmed to Jon that he was hungry. They stood at the counter where the two of them helped themselves to the various components that were to make up their breakfast meal. As was customary Hamill was the first in the queue, not that there was one yet.

'Good morning Hamill. My but you're even earlier today than usual. Were you unable to sleep?' The chef in charge of the breakfast preparations addressed Hamill with ease and affability. He had obviously got to know Hamill well since becoming a seer.

'Yes, I mean no, I slept fine but my friend here hasn't had a moment's shuteye all night and we were both feeling rather hungry. He's being inducted as a novice this morning you know.'

'Yes indeed I do. Welcome young master. Will you be accompanying your friend to breakfast every morning? It would be a shame if someone were to beat him to the head of the queue.' He added his last statement with a smile and a slap on the back for Hamill who gave him a look of feigned indignation before smiling broadly and sheepishly moving on to the next section of the serving counter.

They headed for a nearby table in the dinning area where they sat and happily consumed the lot, washing it all down with fresh fruit juice. Jon could not remember when he had enjoyed a breakfast as much. It was even better than the one Hamill had prepared for him back at his home in Ashbrooke. With his hunger satisfied, he was feeling a little more relaxed thanks to Hamill's easy banter.

Jon felt as if he had come home. The challenges of the last few months had definitely changed him and he believed that he was as ready as he could be to put on the robes of a seer. He knew that it was going to be a long hard road until he could become anything like Liam and the others but with their help he believed that he could achieve what was required. Urim had said to him when they first met that Jon needed to be ready and time would tell if he were. It was the one statement that Jon remembered most of all about Urim and the seer used the term a lot.

Well, time will tell if Jon had done the right thing in seeking to become a seer himself. It seemed to be his destiny. Queen Ella of the sprites had said that he should follow his heart and that as Urim was, he could become. At the time he had not realised just how true that was but now he was here, in Seers Tower, about to become one himself.

Since he had arrived at the Tower Jon had not seen much of the seer, his initial reaction those many months ago in realising the truth about Urim had been mixed. He had wanted, more than anything, to believe that the man who had introduced himself as his uncle was in fact his father. When his yearning had been realised and Urim had told him that he was his father, in more ways than one; he had felt a different emotion. Joy in finally knowing what became of the man his mother had loved was followed by anger as well as resentment and it had seared through his wounded heart.

His anger was for having abandoned his mother and resentment for not being there when Jon had needed him. That had passed with time as he realised that perhaps Urim had not known that he had been born. Had he been, then things may have been different. What mattered now, he had convinced himself, was that he was here now and he would see his son become a seer; to follow in his footsteps and join the Council of the Sight. It did not pay to dwell on the past; it cannot be altered and carried too many painful memories. Only the future can be changed and that was determined by what we did now, today, this very minute.

Preparations were beginning to get under way in the central council chamber as an army of workers cleaned the place from top to bottom. They laid out fresh flowers and draped the banners that represented each of the seers' background races from the hangers behind their chairs, dwarf; elf; sprite and man. Two chairs remained untouched, of which Jon would take one to be his own.

Following his induction into the council he would continue to be known as Jon. He would maintain his name until it was time for his inauguration. That only occurred when the present holder of the title died or, as in Ebon's case, had vacated their office. Had Ebon not been taken into the other world, he would have been removed and his rights to serve on the Council been revoked.

When a seer becomes aware that their time to serve is drawing to a close, a debate is held as to who might be a worthy replacement. That individual would have to be tried and tested over a period of time and if found wanting, a new search would take place to find a suitable candidate. It had never been known for the selected individual to fail to come up to requirements. Jon hoped that he would not be the first to do so.

Once all the necessary testing, tutoring and proving had been completed, the candidate would receive approval by his mentor. When the incumbent seer died the seers would reconvene and declare the novice a seer in their own right. They would then be inaugurated into the Council of the Sight and take up the position that had just been vacated. Then; and only then, would they become a seer not just in name but also in power and ability. Until that time, it had been explained to him, Jon would learn the skills and duties that would befall him as a novice. Then he would be endowed with the title name of the outgoing seer and be truly one of the Council of the Sight.

At his inauguration, Hamill had taken the name of Ebon but after some deliberation, that name had been rescinded and the Council agreed that Hamill should be the first of his line. The name Ebon carried too many bad feelings and memories for the folk of the land for it to be wise to continue with its usage. Hamill had earned the right for himself to keep his own name and all others who would follow after him would take the name of Hamill Lodestone. It had been a portentous moment in the history of the Council of the Sight. These names had been the designated titles for the individual seers for countless generations, so to have had a change such as that was truly significant. Jon wished that he had been there to see it.

They did not see any of the other seers whilst they ate their breakfast. Hamill said that they had either eaten earlier or would have something later. It was more likely that they would eat later; very rarely did someone beat Hamill down to breakfast. Emerald entered the dining area and joined them at the table. She had chosen a healthy selection of fruits and juice with a dairy derivative in a pot. Jon had never liked it, saying that it was revolting thinking about what it was that she was eating.

'Have you ever tried it Jon?' Emerald asked him.

'Well, no I haven't but I just can't bring myself to eat it.'

Emerald smiled and laughed softly, her gentleness wafting over them like a breath of fresh air. 'Then you are the one who is missing the benefits of it. You really should try it some day.'

Jon wrinkled his nose and pulled a face to demonstrate his distaste for it. That made both seers laugh and Hamill slapped him on the back.

'For all you know you've eaten worse. Remember that meal we had in the desert shelter, when we had that spiced meat stew? Did you ever find out what it was made from?'

Jon shook his head and held up a hand as if to fend off any further comment from his friend. 'Whatever it was I don't want to know. I've just had breakfast Hamill and my stomach's feeling twitchy as it is without you telling me horror stories about what I may or may not have eaten. Have pity on me, I'm nervous enough about today without you adding to my concerns.'

Hamill raised his hands in a submissive gesture and sat back in his chair. A broad grin stretched across his face and his eyes twinkled with mischief as he laughingly said. 'Alright my friend, but one of these days I will tell you what was in it.'

A Word of Caution

Before you continue reading the next chapter you should be warned that you will gain information concerning the identity of the seer, Urim Tome-keeper.

This information has been and should remain a closely guarded secret. It should be obvious why this information could be of interest to those who harbour ill-will against the guardians of the land, especially Urim, because of their unique abilities.

Anyone discovering the truth behind the enigma of the seer and not holding that secret inviolate could bring about the downfall of the Council of the Sight. You are therefore required to enter into a seers promise, to hold this information secret.

Continue only if you are willing to enter into this binding promise.

Chapter 40

The Ninth Seer

The two of them returned to Jon's room where they waited for the escorts to arrive who would take Jon down for his ceremonial induction. The time soon came for Jon to meet with the assembled Council of the Sight. He thought that he had been nervous enough with the build up to this moment but now he knew that the butterflies he had felt in his stomach earlier, were just a preliminary to the nerves he felt now. He levelled his hands out in front of him palm down and looked at them; they were shaking and his knees felt weak.

Hamill smiled encouragingly. 'Jon, I cannot even begin to say how pleased I am that you are to join us and become one of the Council. I couldn't have wished for a better thing to happen for you. We shall be able to share the experiences of the future together as brothers, you and I. Good luck with the ceremony; I believe that it is quite a short one. Do you remember the speech that the mayor of Ffridd-Uch-Ddu gave when we arrived in the dwarves' capital?'

Jon did and they both laughed at the memory of how they had tried to drink the toast but he kept adding things in to say.

'Well, you needn't worry about that happening here. Terra believes in being short and to the point. It will be over before you know it and you shall be a seer. True you'll have to wait until your inauguration to become a fully fledged one like me; that would mean the passing of one of the other seers so it may be some time before that happens.'

They fell silent for a while, both of them reflecting on the past and especially of those who were no longer with them to share in this moment, most sadly of all, Auger Wind-rider.

Hamill broke the silence. 'Well, I must join the others in the chamber to participate in Trapper's inauguration; I wish you luck my friend. I shall see you in a little while. Don't be nervous, we are all happy for you. Incidentally, Liam told me that he is looking forward to teaching you.' Hamill added with a knowing wink then left the room. Just as he was leaving the two attendants arrived who were to help Jon get ready for his ceremony.

They were workers at the Tower and lived in a nearby village although whilst serving in the Tower they had accommodation here. They both greeted him in a warm friendly manner and helped adjust his clothing so that he would appear at his best and be ready to receive the robes of a seer. The clothes he had tried on earlier had been removed from his room and placed in the central chamber awaiting his induction.

The time had come to attend the meeting in the great central chamber. He did not feel anywhere near ready but he was eager to go through with the procedure and to begin his training. He wondered what would be the first thing that Liam instructed him in, hoping that it would not be something too menial. He was keen to make a good impression but realised as he held reign on his enthusiasm that he should not try to rush into his training. He had learned from mistakes that he had made in the past that being hasty did not create a good platform upon which to build.

Standing outside, waiting for the doors to open and be invited in was probably the most nerve-racking experience of his life. He had not been this nervous when he had been summoned to appear before his headmaster at school after failing to do his homework.

The doors were opened and Jon was ushered into the chamber. His two guides bowed as he entered then directed him to a spot that was marked on the floor. They bowed again and left, closing the doors after them. Each of the seers were dressed in their finest robes and sat in their appointed places with Terra Standfast at the head; denoted by the crest on the top of his canopy.

Jon searched for a familiar face and saw Hamill grinning like a cat. He nodded in the direction of his left and he saw Trapper, wearing the ceremonial robes of a seer. Jon was filled with pride and excitement for him and could hardly contain his feelings.

The staves belonging to each of the seers were laid upon the table with the tip pointing inwards to the centre. Only Urim remained standing, next to Terra; he held the Staff of the Portal firmly in his left hand with it planted on the floor in front of him. One place remained empty and behind it there was a clothes stand that had the robes of a seer placed upon it. The staff of the seer lay on the table with the head pointing outwards. Jon guessed that he was to be the recipient.

Terra Standfast stood and spread his arms wide. 'Welcome Jon of Ashbrooke. I have looked forward to this time when you would come amongst us. You have passed through some challenging times and done well. But now it has come time for us to commence the ceremony of your induction to prepare you for the time when you will replace one of us.'

Jon shot a glance at Liam who grinned and nodded to recognise him. Urim remained impassive but his eyes were bright and he held his head high.

The dwarf continued. 'Jon of Ashbrooke, are you willing to forsake the life into which you were born and to follow the code of the Sight?'

Jon knew that he was supposed to say yes but he felt his tongue shrivel and dry. His mouth felt like the sands in the desert of Anram. Looking to Urim for help that he knew he could not give and then to Hamill who smiled encouragingly. He finally found enough saliva to swallow and say what he knew he had wanted to say ever since he had met Urim in the Redwood forest all those months ago.

'Yes, I am.'

There was no going back now. He had committed himself to the life of a seer. He crossed his fingers as he held his hands rigidly at his sides hoping that he would prove worthy. Terra nodded to Liam who stood and took the robes from the stand behind the empty chair and approached him with a broad smile. His elfin features demonstrating his joy and delight at welcoming Jon to the council. He placed the robe upon him and helped Jon tie the belt and straighten the folds. Stepping back he bowed slightly and formally acknowledged him as a seer.

'You join us as one from another world. The door is open now to enter a new realm. Step forward and be one with us.'

Liam took Jon by the hand and helped him advance one step towards the empty chair.

Each of the seers stood in turn, starting with Trapper, who had now taken the name of Auger; he spoke the same words that Liam had said and advanced Jon one more step. Jon could feel Trapper's nerves as he took his arm to help him make the next step. Then Hamill came forward to embrace him and welcome him as a brother seer. They all repeated the same welcome and helped him step towards the chair that would be his one pace at a time. When it came time for Terra to greet him he had made the last step and stood ready to be seated. Only Urim remained but he still maintained his stance at the side of Terra's chair nodding in approval and with a shine to his eyes.

Jon was curious as to why Urim had not taken part in the ceremony thus far but supposed that it was because of his being his father that he could not participate.

The seers had returned to their places and stood applauding Jon. He felt rather self-conscious but grinned back at them and winked at Hamill who was applauding the loudest and with the biggest grin he had ever seen. For the first time since he could remember, Jon felt at peace and he had to wipe a tear from his eye.

The applause subsided as Terra raised his hands to signal that he wanted to say something. They all sat down and Terra invited Jon to do the same; he did so and looked around the table and then at Urim. He felt strangely odd sitting at the table with the seers but something was wrong. This did not feel right and he began to question himself as to his readiness to become a seer. Recalling all that he had been through and Urim's counsel to him about the role of a seer; he decided that he was as ready as he would ever be.

'So if that's not what the problem is; what is it that seems wrong?' He asked silently. He could not put his finger on what was amiss. Then it dawned on him; Urim was still standing. Why was Urim not in his chair? Glancing to his right, he wondered why it was that Liam sat beside him. Surely it should be Liam that was standing and not Urim.

Doubts and a dark fear slowly crept into Jon's mind and he failed to hear what Terra said as he saw a shadow fall over the whole room. All he could see was Urim; all he could think of was the seer who had introduced him to this new life. Then it began to dawn on him; he was to replace Urim.

'NO.'

The voice echoed around and around in his head and he felt as if the whole room swayed. He felt faint and sick and wanted to collapse. This cannot be right. Urim must not die; it was not fair. He had only just found him and now he was to be parted from him.

'NO.'

Again he fought against the inevitable conclusion that he was to be the next Urim. He would refuse. He would rescind his covenant to be a seer. This must not happen; shock drained his face of all colour and he mouthed the words; 'Urim; father.'

His voice was merely a whisper but it stilled the room into silence. The others came back into view and the darkness that had pressed in around him dissipated. The seers sat with bowed heads and an uneasy feeling had developed. Hamill looked around at the others in bafflement and stared at Jon in disbelief. He too had realised that it was Urim whom Jon had been called to replace and not Liam.

Terra Standfast signalled to the gathered seers and slowly they stood and withdrew from the chamber, each taking their staff from the table.

'No, not you two, Hamill and Trapper, sorry, I should say Auger. You will want to know what is to transpire here.'

Terra invited them to sit and they sank back into their chairs, each with a look of shock and bewilderment on their faces.

'We owe you an explanation Jon, and to you, Hamill and Trapper; forgive me, Auger.' Terra smiled and winked at the new holder of the talisman that controlled the wind. 'Until now it has been impossible to do so but now that you have taken your vow it is time for the truth to be known. I knew that you thought it was Liam that you would be replacing and I am sorry to say that I encouraged that thought, but it was necessary. You will no doubt be wondering why it was that Urim did not join us in our ceremony? That is because he is not a part of our council. He is from outside of our time; a time that is yet to come.'

Jon heard the words but they did not register. He did not understand what Terra was trying to tell him. Hamill too looked puzzled and the two friends looked at each other in confusion.

'If you would permit me Terra; I believe that it is my responsibility to inform them of my position here at this time and I should not shirk it. Thank you for your consideration for my feelings but I would like to take up the narrative from now on.'

Jon sat open mouthed and felt like he was having a bad dream. He shook his head as if to clear it of the nightmare that was unravelling around him. 'I don't understand. What do you mean that Urim is from a time yet to come?'

Urim smiled wearily, stepped forward and laid his staff, the staff of the portal, on the table. There were four other staves that lay there; Terra Standfast's, Hamill's, Auger's and one in front of Jon. 'What I have to tell you is a hard thing for me to do. I recall my feelings when *I* heard it myself but you must trust me Jon when I say that you will be a better man for it.

Do you recall when we first met that I told you I was your uncle? Of course you do, how stupid of me. You then believed that I was your father and I encouraged that belief or at least I did not discourage it. You see if you knew the truth then of what I am about to tell you, it could have had devastating consequences on your development. You are now at the stage where you must know everything that there is to know. When we first met I promised you that one day you would have the answers to all your questions; that day has come.'

He sat in the chair next to Terra and leaned forward resting his forearms on the table as he clasped his fingers together. Terra sat back in his chair and tugged at his beard, listening to what Urim had to say, nodding in agreement.

Urim continued. 'You must not blame Terra or the other seers; they all knew the importance of keeping this from you and once you have been told it must be kept a closely guarded secret. Do I have your word that you will do so?'

They all nodded, intrigued as to what Urim had to say.

'It is difficult to know where to begin. Perhaps I should start by saying that I am neither your uncle nor your father.' He paused in his explanation and struggled to phrase the words. Looking Jon in the eye he held his gaze then delivered the bombshell. 'You and I are the same. Your mother was my mother. Your father was my father but I am not your brother. I am you.'

He waited for the impact of what he had said to register and smiled with satisfaction at the reaction his news generated. The new Auger did not know who to look at first, Jon and Hamill both looked at each other in disbelief, hardly knowing what to say. It was Hamill who spoke first.

'So you're telling us that you, Urim, are really Jon, but from the future.'

'Yes, that's exactly what I am saying.'

Jon finally found his voice and stuttered in his response. 'But that can't be possible. I can't be in two places at the same time, so how can I be twice in the same place at the same time. Does what I just said make any sense?'

Urim smiled again and bowed his head before replying. 'It makes very good sense of what is a fact. *You* can be in the same place twice, as is proved by your being here as well as I. You are finding this very difficult to accept; I know because I remember the experience myself, almost twenty years ago now. Let me try to show you that what you are hearing is true. You have a pouch that you bought at the market in Ashbrooke. Compare it to mine.'

Urim placed his time worn leather satchel on the table; Jon did the same. They were identical other than that Urim's one was well used.

'That doesn't prove anything at all. I bought it because it reminded me of the one you have.'

'Yes, that is true and it has been with me ever since. 'Very well, I concede that it is not a very good proof but you also have a knife. It was given to you by Hamill in Amethyst's coven and you used it to rescue Hamill from her collection. Do you have it with you still?'

'Yes, he said I could keep it.' Jon replied defensively, the shock of what Urim had disclosed beginning to settle.

'I know. Hamill was also told that I would be there to rescue him when he got into trouble.'

'But you didn't come. We thought that you would but it was Jon that rescued me, not you.' Hamill's voice trailed off into a whisper as the enormity of what he was saying becoming clear to him.

Again Urim smiled and spread his hands before him, leaning back in his seat as if his point had been proven. 'Would you agree with me that there could only be one knife like that one?'

The two friends nodded in unison and held their breath as Urim drew forth his knife and placed it on the table. The two friends looked at each other again in shocked silence. It was identical to the one Hamill had given to Jon.

There was stunned silence before Urim continued. 'You are aware of the things that we have in common; the similarity of our looks, the same nervous chewing of the lip, the same superstition of crossing our fingers when wishing for good luck. We are one and the same, you and I. Jon, it is the right time for you to join with the Council of the Sight; you need to become what I am today in my time. You see, that which Terra told you is correct; I am not a part of this council. I belong to a future council, one that was approached by the Urim of this time, your time, to help deliver the seers from the grip of the energy barrier that Ebon had imprisoned them in.'

Urim paused in his telling of these events and allowed Terra to take up the story again.

'What Ebon did not count on was the ingenuity of the council and the determination of one in particular, Urim; our Urim. He had not trusted Ebon and had concealed his staff and Talisman here in the chamber before Ebon rebelled. Knowing that if Ebon were to turn against the Council, which of course he did, he would try to usurp the power of the other seers by taking their talismans and staves. Urim replaced his with copies that were useless to the rogue seer but by the time he realised, it was too late. He had already sealed us inside the Tower and himself outside.

Ebon had used his powers to meld our staves into the wood of the table you see before you so that we would not have the ability to use them. Without them we were powerless to stop him. He also took our talismans from our rooms after locking us in here by means of the energy beneath the Tower. Without the ingenuity of our Urim, we would have remained here and Ebon would have succeeded in his attempts to rule the land.

By using the staff that he retrieved from its hiding place, Urim was able to release ours from the table but we were locked in the chamber and there was no retrieving our talismans; they had gone with Ebon. All that is but for Urim's which is a miniature representation of the Golden Tome that contains the history of our land. Not only is it a history of our land and the events that make up that history but it is also a means of travelling to those times. There was only one problem, he had never tried to travel into the unknown; the future. We decided that it had to be attempted and we gathered to combine our staves with the energy beneath the Tower to send him to a time when we would again be free.

Not knowing when that would be we agreed to try for a time many years from now. He succeeded but at a terrible cost to himself.' Terra allowed what he had said to register and take effect.

Hamill leaned forward and tried to clarify what he had heard. 'So Urim sitting here now is not your Urim but he is really Jon from a future time.'

'Yes, that is what we are saying.'

Trapper/Auger sat back with an understanding look and nodded in agreement. He accepted the truth of what Urim and Terra had been telling them with a silent chuckle. However Jon and Hamill were both having difficulty in understanding this and needed to get things clear.

'I can hardly believe what I am hearing. It…It is just so difficult to take it in. But if Urim is from the future; where is your Urim, the one that belongs to today?'

'He returned here to our time after successfully making contact with the future council of which Urim here was a member. His influence here in our day has been a tremendous help to us. Without his intervention and I must say the assistance of you three in no small way, we would still be held prisoners within the Tower. Urim, or should I say you, Jon; had to be careful however in what he did; too much knowledge of events before they happen could influence what one does. Any misuse of that knowledge could have as disastrous an effect on things as us allowing Ebon to succeed would have had.'

Jon interjected. 'I'm sorry to interrupt you but I do not pretend to understand all of this at the present, if you will excuse the pun. No doubt it shall all make sense later but I would still like to know what happened to the Urim you sent to the future.'

'As I have said, he is here but he is dying. The journey through time to the future against the barrier that Ebon had installed was not a smooth one. He returned to us in great distress and pain. He had suffered a wrenching of his internal body parts that had meant he was literally turned around inside. He has been cared for by our workers since then but he will not survive. Once the barrier had been removed we called upon the expertise of the physicians from the Ward in secret through Janine Tanner, the co-ordinator at the Ward whom you all know of course. She sent her most trusted physicians and they have been in attendance since then but they are unable to heal him. Even the sprites with their weird magic could not undo what had occurred.

Our Urim had managed to get the message through however and we knew that help would be forthcoming. With Ebon on the loose and us powerless to stop him, the only way to succeed was to have a seer on the outside of the barrier. What we had hoped for was for a future member of the Council of the Sight, Urim to be exact, to travel back in time from their perspective and to release us so that we could deal with Ebon. Urim here was initially unable to release us from the barrier and so began the story with which you are familiar. As to what happened when our Urim made contact with the seers of the future I shall leave for Urim to explain.'

Urim again began to unfold the details of what transpired when the Urim of the present was sent into the future. 'In my time, we were gathered in the chamber discussing a matter that was of concern to us when a portal opened up above the table and the Urim of today appeared. He was caught in a struggle with the elements of the portal and was clearly in a distressed condition but he was determined to deliver his message and was able to outline the situation to us. It was an occasion that we all knew would occur but what we did not know was when. In order for the past, from my perspective, to unfold as it should, I had to wait for the Urim of today, your present time but my past, to appear before the Council. Until that happened, I dared not return for fear of altering the past.

I immediately knew what had to be done and promised him that I would return to assist them. You see Hamill and I had lived through that day, as had Auger. We had already experienced this conversation, the one we are having now, and we knew that I had to travel back here to when I was a young man. I had to be your Urim, Jon. I had to do what you saw your Urim do so that Ebon could be stopped and the seers freed.

Having completed my preparations I used my talisman and the power within my staff, the one you see before you on the table, to make the journey here, I tried to release the seers on my own but failed. That is how Ebon became aware of my presence and with the aid of the crystal talisman that he had stolen from Emerald he was able to see the truth of my reality. That is why he formulated his plan to capture you, Jon. He thought that if he could kill me when I was still a young man and before I had become a seer; then I would not be able to stop him and he could continue in his efforts without fear of failing. Unfortunately what I failed to realise was that by coming back so far in time, I would lose a lot of my memories. That is why I knew some things but not others. I had to second guess on occasion.

What I did remember was that Hamill became a seer after we had defeated Ebon. I knew that I, or rather you, had to become a seer, Urim to be exact and so I became your instructor. I have taught you and encouraged you just as I remember Urim did for me. Only it wasn't Urim, it was me, or should I say, you. That is why I said that I was a father to you in more ways than one. In a way I was your father because I put you on the course to become a seer. To become what you are today and now my task is done and I must return again to my own time. I have done all that I needed to do, you may have need to see me again after this but remember Jon, that some time in the future you will need to return to help a young man become what he is destined to become. Urim Tome-keeper, seer of the Council of the Sight.'

Epilogue

Urim, the Seer

Jon had finally accepted what Urim and Terra had related to him as being the truth, though he still found it difficult to take in. He had spent some time with Urim to receive some last minute instructions before Urim had to leave. It was necessary for him to return to his own time; his work here and now had been completed. This seer from the future had succeeded in rescuing them all, bringing Ebon to justice and setting Jon on the road to becoming a fully fledged seer. Now it was up to Jon to walk in his own footsteps as it were; travelling a loop in time that would be repeated over and over again. The thought became confusing and he decided not to try and understand it; a paradox existed that could not be explained. Whatever lay ahead of him, Jon would try to remember the events of this last year so that he could act for the better when it was time for him to make the journey back, as it were.

The words of Queen Ella returned to him in clarity now that he understood who he really was. 'Remember your past and it will serve you well.' It was the counsel she had given him when he and Hamill had departed from the sprite realm. At the time he had been confused by what she had said but now it made perfect sense and he would honour her advice and be true to the charge.

Urim squared his jaw to the task of returning to his fellow seers; his task was over, for now. He had to take up his place in his own time on the

Council of the Sight and in his position of Keeper of the Golden Tome. It was his task to record the events of these past months for future eyes so that they may learn from the things that had occurred. It was his task to keep the things of the past alive in the land. To have the present day events recorded that others, at some future time, might gain wisdom from the struggles of those who had gone before.

Urim was troubled by what he had said to Jon. Had he made the right decision in telling him who he was? From the time of their very first meeting in the forest he hadn't liked misleading Jon and he felt equally uncomfortable with what he had just told him now but he knew deep inside that it had been necessary for him to know the truth. He had taught him of the ways of the seer and given him the insight he needed to start his own quest. It was up to him from now on and he knew that he would succeed. He was living proof of it.

It was strange to experience things from his perspective, as Urim the seer. He mused as he strode along, his staff thumping out a regular rhythm with every placement of it on the road that would take him back to his place in time. He hoped that he hadn't said too much, and as he searched through his thoughts and memories he had of this time from his youth; he believed that all was well.

Of all the experiences he had witnessed in his turbulent life, this had been the strangest, the most challenging, the most troubling and the most dangerous of all. Yet without them working together as Urim and Jon and even the loss of his beloved Anna, they would not have succeeded. He had tried to save her but knew that it was fated to happen; Ebon had also had his part to play in these events turning out the way they had. It was only poetic justice really that it was Ebon who had created the barrier around the tower, and it was Ebon who had removed it. There perhaps had been no other way for it to have been disconnected; had they not succeeded then, the story would have had a different ending to record in the Golden Tome and he, Urim, would not have been the one to have recorded it.

He wavered momentarily, stopping to consider his options and resting his hands upon his new staff, the Staff of the Portal. Terra had insisted that Urim keep it, they would manage without it; besides, if there came a time when it was needed, they knew where to look for it.

He wanted to turn back; to tell Jon the way to go but he knew he could not. He must find his own way; it would be difficult, it would be painful, the Creator knows how he, Urim, had tried to cheat time and to change what had happened in his past, but it was not to be. Things are as they are and must continue to be, no matter what changes he made, no matter what influence he had on things, it all turned out exactly as it was intended to be; as it had been before.

A little knowledge is indeed a dangerous thing in the wrong hands; it can also be equally dangerous in the right hands. Often more damage is done by acting with good intentions than through any other means. He had tried to change the past and gone against the code by trying to save Anna. He of all the seers should have known better; you can't cheat time.

Still the urge was great to return to Jon, to tell him what he should do and what to avoid, to tell him.....his thoughts took him to a time when years earlier, as a young man, he had stood in a churchyard by his mother's grave and watched tearfully as the seer, Urim, had departed. Events had come full around and more.

He remembered the pain he had felt at that initial parting back there in the village, standing at his mother's grave. He knew only too well how Jon had felt because they were his feelings too and he experienced them all over again, this time it had been as the seer Urim.

Time; what a paradox it could be and what a dangerous element to play with; Not without good reason are the seers chosen carefully who guard the Golden Tome, they alone hold the keys to the past, the present and the future.

Second only to the dwarf Terra Standfast in responsibility for the land and its inhabitants; Urim was entrusted with the very fabric of their existence. Only rarely did the council exercise the power vested in them to send one of them on the slide through time. Only in the most critical of circumstances does the Sight unite to send the seer who is Urim, back in time and only once has it happened that they sent him to the future. That was when the Council were held captive in the Tower, betrayed by one of their own.

The Urim at the time of Jon's youth, an older man who was nearing the end of his time as a Seer, had been sent into the future by the Sight.

They had found a way to penetrate the energy field by sending him ahead; to a time when Seers Tower was once again free from its confinement and others held the mantles of the Seers.

The Urim from the past delivered the message to the Sight of the future that they needed help. Only a seer could help them; and only from the outside. One of the council of Seers, the Urim of the future, could break them free. Time was short for the Urim of Jon's day; the slide into the future was temporary and costly to their limited resources; he had been drawn back to his time line before matters were resolved.

The council of the future met and discussed the unusual circumstances that they had been presented with. Urim recalled that period of time in his life when he had been a young man and what had transpired. They consulted the Golden Tome and scanned its leaves, seeking for knowledge of the past so that Urim might act in accordance with history. The pages were blank, as if wiped clean at the appearance of the Urim of the past. No guidance was available from that source; it was as if the history was waiting to be written. He, the Urim of the future, declared his intention of returning to the past; he knew what needed to be done and he would have to act his part based on his memories of that time.

The council had changed somewhat from the time when Jon was inducted. Liam, friend to Terra Standfast, had trained up a novice, an elf from the Ward, to act in his place and had passed on. He was now laid in the tomb where those who had borne the name of Liam before him rested. Emerald, Eden and Elise still served; as did Hamill and Auger. Terra Standfast, resolute and true to his name, remained as the leader of the Council of the sight, though he was nearing the time when he would select another to take his place.

When Jon had been inducted into the Sight many years earlier, he had learned that the seer Urim he had met as a young man was not the Urim of his time, but the Urim of the future. He would have to travel back through time some day to act out the role of Urim the Seer to himself as a young man, Jon.

It was his encounter with Urim when he was a lad that led him to the council and his place in that line of seers named Urim. If he failed to return, history would be rewritten and their very existence now would be in jeopardy. He had been faced with little choice but to go.

Urim had left the Tower with a warning from Terra not to interfere with time, or the energy of the Tower would become destabilised and it would be worse for them all than if he had never gone back.

There was a code that all seers named Urim were to uphold, which was, not to interfere, they could intervene, but never interfere. They were not permitted to bring back the dead and they could only return once to a given period in time. Having gone there and returned, the doorway closed; therefore Urim was to exercise extreme caution, for any mistakes would be irrevocable.

Each person had their time to etch in the Tome, some for good, some for evil. The code maintained that even evil has its place and that good will overcome. He knew that now. He had come back in time to what was his past but Jon's present and seen how evil had corrupted the seer Ebon of this time. Urim had tried to remove the barrier on his own by using the power within his seers' staff but to no avail. Ebon had discovered him there and they had fought one another. Ebon was successful against the seer from the future, using his army of marsh-mogs who had rushed at Urim causing him to flee, narrowly escaping the clutches of the rebel seer.

Ebon had been intrigued as to who this other seer was whom he had caught trying to remove the barrier that had been placed around the Tower. Ebon had used the power of his staff to see into the crystal that he had stolen from Emerald. It held the ability to gaze into the future and the past. He had poured a lot of power into the stone, forcing it to reveal who this stranger was and it showed Ebon that Urim was a seer from the future; that his name in this present time was Jon and that he would become this Urim of the future. He had learned that Jon lived in Ashbrooke, a small town bordering the plains of Uniah. The same town that Ebon had come from when he became a seer. Ebon conceived a plan to kill Jon now and prevent him from becoming the Urim from the future.

Urim knew from his own memories, from the time when he was the lad Jon; that Ebon would seek to destroy him and had set off to warn his younger self. How strange it had all been; to have sought oneself in order to prevent one's own death. He had obviously succeeded otherwise he would not be here now. Unfortunately, a great deal of his recollection of this time had been lost when he had been sent back here from his future;

he had only fragmentary knowledge and would have to trust to instinct and gut feelings to try and keep his shadow over the past as small as possible; not an easy task considering the difficulties that had lain ahead of him then and now.

He remembered that, after the battle with Ebon at the Tower, Anna had come to him in his canvas shelter. That night, when she had first appeared following her fall through the barrier with Ebon, she had spoken for the first time. Urim had sat outside the shelter so that he could relive the moment again. He had been desperate to hear her voice and this was one time when he knew that she would appear, because it had already happened for him in his past and he was reliving it again but from a different perspective. It had pained him greatly and he had cried for a long time sitting there outside the shelter, just as he had cried the first time as Jon on the inside.

Urim had learned much from his experience here in the past, it was always a strange feeling walking amongst those who had lived before; to walk and talk with the great people of his time when they were still young and unaware of what lay ahead. In his wanderings amongst them he had been responsible for the nudge that directed them onto the course that would lead them to their destiny.

He had done that for Jon; for himself. His memory was complete now; having relived what was his past. Had he changed what had gone before? He did not know. He had tried to change things to prevent Anna's passing into the other world, but it seems, her passage there was inevitable. He had taken a very great risk by trying to save her, all to no avail. He knew from his own recollections what lay ahead of him as Jon. He could only guess at what lay ahead of him as Urim of the Council of the Sight, Keeper of the Golden Tome.

He approached the outcrop of rock that was in the meadow outside of Seers Tower, the one that Bearer and Petros had seemingly come alive from when they had defeated Ebon. It was the nearest sure place that Urim knew would remain the same throughout time that was outside of the energy barrier that Ebon had installed. Through this rock he could tap into the earth power, by means of his staff, and use his talisman to return to his own time. He sat facing the Tower and sighed heavily, satisfied that his task had been completed. Holding the talisman before him in an open palm, he summoned the power that would take him home.

The scene remained the same but his head spun as if he were on a merry-go-round. The seasons came and went, passing before him in a whirl until he returned to his own time; the time just after he had departed for the past.

His old and trusted friend was there to greet him; Hamill; older now than when he had seen him mere moments ago but just as he should be in the time that Urim undertook the journey back.

'Hello my friend. Did you do it, you were only gone a few seconds?' Hamill grinned in relief at seeing him.

'Yes; I have done what I had to do.'

Reflecting on what had transpired over the last few months that he had experienced yet in reality only seconds that he had been away from his own time, he smiled with satisfaction.

'There is one more task that I must complete before everything is done. I must go to the colossi in their exile and convince them to return in enough time to help defeat Ebon at Northill. First I need to rest, there is time enough for that I believe.

Walking back to the Tower alongside his friend, he was certain that he had made the right choices throughout his life. An echo of his own voice drifted through his thoughts; he remembered something a wise and mysterious stranger had once told him. He had met him one night whilst alone in the forest as a young lad many years ago; he had said....

'Time will tell.'

A Rare Gem

So began a new era under the watchful eyes of the Council of the Sight with the aptly named Terra Standfast at the helm. Not only was there a new seer on the Council of the Sight but also a new novice who had joined the ranks of the seers and begun to adapt to the rigours of the office to which he had been called. Jon of Ashbrooke, as has been stated, would continue to be known as that until such time as the incumbent seer, Urim, passed on to his final resting place.

As you have seen, it came as a surprise to Jon that he was to become novice to Urim but not the Urim he had known. What was more of a surprise was that the Urim he had thought was his father was in fact himself from a future time. Jon had resisted the urge to ask what lay ahead of him as he had realised that too much information about the future could adversely affect what he did. He realised that he had learned that Urim was right in being frugal with the truth. Although Jon had found it frustrating that Urim had been so closed to any questions about things, it was the right course to follow.

Jon laughed as he realised that it was he who, in the future, or should he say the past, would be the one to be economical with his information. The whole concept of being two people yet one was far beyond his understanding at the moment and it made his head ache just thinking about it. He still found it hard to believe that Urim was actually himself from the future, yet Terra confirmed what Urim had said and he would not lie about this. It actually made sense in a strange sort of way but he decided not to delve too deeply into its mysteries for danger of it becoming an unfathomable enigma.

When you first discovered the record of the Chronicles of the Sight, written in the Golden Tome, you may have thought that this particular episode was about two individuals; Urim and Jon. You now know that they are in fact one and the same person. Consider then what you were told before you studied the history of this pivotal moment in the lives of the folk who lived in the land of the seers.

Do you recall the concept of the gem, a priceless gem? That although it has many facets and it can be admired, even coveted, from many different angles yet it is still the same stone. No matter how you look at it and it can be viewed from many different ways; the fact remains that it is one and the same. Pure, simple, clear and undefiled it represents something different to all who see it.

Pressure has been applied to the raw material that was the young man, Jon. He has been honed and moulded, disciplined and taught until now he has become like that stone. He has been able to gain depth of character, maturity and determination to overcome whatever challenges lie ahead.

He has become what he was destined to become and you shall see how he makes the transition from novice to seer. The history is there for you to read but that is for another time.

Seers promise

Now, I wish you to enter into a seer's promise; that you will not reveal what you have learned to the uninitiated. For one to know the true identity of the young man, Jon, before the proper time would prove his undoing.

You may, if you wish, discuss these things with others like yourself who know the truth and have entered into this promise, you may even want to return to the beginning; to Time Will Tell; and discover the things that, to those who know, clearly identify the connection between Jon and Urim. As you do so, it will become apparent what brought a simple country lad to the attention of one Ebon Lodestone, formerly of the Sight.

For a signed photograph of the author and to register for your Seer's Certificate upon completion of the first three sections of 'The Chronicles of the Sight from the Golden Tome'; apply to:-
seerstowerlibrary@msn.com

Lightning Source UK Ltd.
Milton Keynes UK
UKOW050805260313

208196UK00001B/110/P